history, made extraordinary by chance and circumstance, offers a vision of a past that isn't dusty, archaic and over, but vivid, engaging, alive."

Wendy James, author of the award-winning
Out of the Silence, The Steele Diaries
and The Mistake.

"With skilful attention to detail, Sophie Masson weaves a compelling tale of a nation caught up in a madness fuelled by a reckless and unrealistic idealism, and the four friends who, wittingly or not, were its victims. Set against this chilling account of the collective madness that led to the murderous rampages and bloodthirsty executions of the French Revolution is the story of Jacques' love for Flora – a love that will test everything he believes and holds dear. A great read for lovers of historical fiction with a dash of romance."

Felicity Pulman, author of
A Ring Through Time.

Black Wings

A novel of the French Revolution

Black Wings

A novel of the French Revolution

SOPHIE MASSON

The Greystones Press

First published in Great Britain in 2018 by

The Greystones Press Ltd
Greystones
37 Lawton Avenue
Carterton
Oxfordshire OX18 3JY

A CIP catalogue record for this book is available
from the British Library

ISBN 978-1-911122-19-7

1 3 5 7 9 10 8 6 4 2

Designed and typeset by Nigel Hazle

Printed and bound in Great Britain by Clays Ltd, Elcograf S.p.A

Contents

Bliss was it in that dawn to be alive,
But to be young was very heaven!

*(from 'The Prelude' by William Wordsworth, written
in 1805, inspired by a sojourn in France in 1790)*

———————

At the banquet of life I've only just started
A moment only have my lips pressed against
The rim of the cup still full to the brim.

*(from 'The young captive', written by French poet André
Chénier in prison while awaiting execution, 1794)*

For my father, Georges Masson

Prologue

3pm, 30 April 1854, Paris

The old man was dying. When I climbed the stairs that led to his room, I wasn't sure what I would find, though I had been told he still had his wits about him. The servants had red eyes and frightened faces; many of them had been in the great man's employ for so long that they couldn't imagine the world without him.

I was ushered into his room. It was a beautiful place: full of the sunlight he loved, and smelling of the spring. On the bedside table was a book, and in a vase, one of his beloved early roses. The Baron was sitting up in bed, propped up on his pillows. He had become very thin, very old, the bones showing painfully under his papery skin. Only the famous blue eyes were still youthful.

I greeted him. He responded rather absently. I knew his moods, so I sat by his bedside, and waited. It was then I noticed how his hands trembled, how they gripped nervously at the edge of the covers. That did surprise me. The Baron had never been known to lack courage.

Suddenly he spoke. 'Maître Dumas, do you believe in ghosts?'

It startled me. The Baron had never been one for such things. I stammered, 'Er . . . I . . . I'm not sure. But I think there are things that defy explanation . . .'

He cut me off. 'Go to my desk. Open it.'

This was more what I had expected. When I'd received his summons, I'd thought he must want me to change his Will. People often did. On their deathbeds they frequently changed their minds on who should inherit. In the Baron's case, his heir was his great-nephew Maurice—a dissipated and rather unpleasant youth, but the old man's only living relative. Perhaps he wanted to cut Maurice out and leave his fortune to charity instead. People had strange ideas, when they lay dying.

Obediently, I went over to the desk. I opened it.

'There is a drawer in the right-hand corner,' he said. 'Open it.'

I did so.

'You have small hands, Master Dumas. Long fingers. I've often observed it.' He gave a wheezing, unamused laugh. 'So this will be no trouble to you. Slide your hand into the drawer—at one side there is a small depression—press it and you will hear a click.'

I did as I was told and the whole bottom of the drawer slid across, revealing a secret space, in which lay a piece of thick paper.

The Baron said, 'Take it out. Look at it.'

I slid it out gently. It wasn't a document, as I'd expected, but a small sketch, of a young man's face. Just a few lines, on a piece of paper, but so skilfully done that it was almost as if the portrait were alive. An unusual face stared up at me—unfashionably long, tangled hair framing strong features, a thin, sharp nose, a hard mouth, and black eyes—such eyes! They are hard to describe, but it was both as if the man were blind, and as if he could see right into me. The expression in those sketched eyes was like nothing I'd seen before, and yet it held a curious familiarity. Unaccountably, I shivered.

I looked up, and got a rude shock. The expression in the Baron's eyes was one of naked fear, and a kind of eagerness. 'You see,' he whispered.

'I . . . I'm sorry, sir,' I said, after a little time, 'I'm not sure that I do.'

'That man is the Devil himself . . . He swore he would get me, even if Death itself barred the way.' He spoke so wildly, so strangely, that I grew frightened in my turn, and quickly crossed myself. He gave a sharp, bitter laugh. 'I've told everything to my Father Confessor, do you see, Dumas, but it's still not enough. There are . . . things I must do. Things only you can help me with. Practical, real things. Reparation, in this world, if I am not to be damned in the next.'

I was silent with astonishment and a strange fear. I could not help looking down at that vivid, terrible sketch. The eyes seemed to burn into me. I said, 'I don't understand.'

'Go to the desk again, Dumas,' said the Baron, wearily. 'In the last drawer on the left, you will find a notebook. Take it out, and go. When you get back to your office, read it. Read all night, if need be, but right to the finish. And come back first thing in the morning, with your idea of what I should do to satisfy that hungry ghost.'

'But, sir!' I protested. 'I can hardly attempt to—'

'Don't argue, Dumas. Haven't I always been loyal to your firm? Haven't you benefited from my patronage?'

'Yes, sir, of course, but . . .'

'I'm at my wits' end, Dumas,' he broke in, sharply. The skin was drawn tight over his face, making him look like a death's head. 'You cannot begin to understand the torment . . .' He broke off, then went on, more strongly. 'If you come up with the right idea, I will reward you greatly, Dumas.' He paused. 'I was thinking of changing my Will, do you see—and leaving half my fortune to you. After all, you've done more for me than that scoundrel of a Maurice ever has. You're a good man. You have a fine family. You could do with a little money.'

I could scarcely believe my ears. This was hardly a

proposition to make to a respectable notary. And yet—I wouldn't be human if I wasn't tempted. Sorely tempted. 'Sir,' I said, 'surely a friend, or . . .'

'You're the closest thing to a friend I have in this world, Dumas,' he said. 'Oh, don't look so surprised—yes, I have any number of hangers-on, toadies, acquaintances. I move in the best circles. I'm praised by all the right people. I'm famous. I'm honoured. But I have no friends. No *real* friends.' He paused. 'But that is of no consequence. Will you or will you not do this for me, Master Dumas?'

I looked at his thin, haunted face. I looked down at the face of the young man in the sketch. I don't know what possessed me then—I still don't understand it—but I ignored all the cautious instincts of a lifetime, and said, slowly, 'Very well. I will do it, Baron.'

He gave a great sigh, and lay back on his pillows. 'Thank you,' he whispered. 'Now, get the notebook, and go.'

'The sketch . . .' I began, already moving to the desk.

'Put it away, where you found it. He'll know. He'll give me time, now.'

I didn't say anything, though a part of me—the sane, respectable part—thought that the old man was definitely mad. I replaced the sketch—with a great deal of thankfulness—and opened the last drawer on the left. In there, as he'd said, was a notebook. A fat notebook, bound in water-damaged black leather, with a clasp to hold it tight. I picked it up. 'I have it, Baron,' I said.

He didn't answer. He had closed his eyes, and appeared to be sleeping, though I was sure he couldn't be. I bowed, farewelled him, and went out of the sunny room, clutching the notebook.

I told my secretary that I was not to be disturbed, and locked my door. I sat down at the desk and opened the notebook. The clasp was a bit rusty, and flakes of dull red, like old blood, spread on the first page as I began to read, the hair rising on the back of my neck.

6 May 1794, Saint-Lazare Prison, Paris

My name is Jacques Verdun and these are my last days on this earth.

Yesterday I learned that my case is going to trial in four weeks' time. The trial will be swift, so much swifter than the waiting for it. The outcome is in no doubt. No one is innocent. Everyone is guilty. Madame la Guillotine awaits.

Am I afraid? Not of death itself, I believe. But the moment of dying . . . that is a different thing. My life has not been long. I am only twenty. But I have seen so many terrible things that my heart is sick with them, and I am old before my time. For the black wings of Azrael, Angel of Death, shadow my poor bleeding country from east to west, north to south.

Many times over these long, numb months, waiting for my fate, I have taken up the quill to tell my story. Only to put it down again, consumed by anger, by hatred, by despair, by profound and blinding grief, unable to put into words the things that brought me here, to this stinking place.

But last night—the night I learned of my fate—I had a dream. Not the nightmares that have plagued me for so long, but a real dream. A sweet one. I dreamed I was at the old place again. Flora was there. And Edmond. And Pierre . . .

We were fifteen years old. It was autumn. I could see the elm trees along the Bellegarde Manor avenue so vividly; flaming bright yellow, like torches. I saw us together, the four of us, as we used to be. I was back in the old world, at the very moment it began to change.

When I awoke this morning, I knew it was a sign from Heaven. I must begin writing. I have only four weeks to set it all down. It may seem a small thing and a poor and weak one, too, to set against the dark madness of the reign of terror where there are no friends, no memories, no gentler feelings, only fear and hate and betrayal and a desperate need to forget the past. Yet I know I must do it, now. And so I take out my papers, I sharpen my quill, and I begin.

One

The elm trees lining the avenue are yellow as flaming torches the day of Richard de Bellegarde's memorial Mass. Flora and her mother, still in deep mourning, stand at the door of the Bellegarde parish church, flanked by the elderly priest, Father Jantot, and Edmond with his father Charles. Pierre and I stand behind them while our families and a large crowd of well-wishers, from the village and beyond, line up to give their condolences.

Richard de Bellegarde had died a month before, and though his death had been expected—he'd been ill for two or three years—it had still come as a shock to many of us. His funeral had been enormous—his memorial Mass was almost as big. He'd been a popular man, liked by his peers and his tenants alike. He was a sad loss to the family, and the village.

It's one of those glorious golden early autumn days,

8

full of birdsong. Yet something grips at my heart, and it isn't just the solemn sadness of the occasion. It is a sense of something chill lying just under that golden stillness, something more than just the threat of approaching winter. I shiver; and in that instant, turning my head slightly, I catch Pierre's eye. He has what I can only describe as his 'other face' on. It's as if he's blind, and yet as if he can see right into you. It's the face he wears when he sees his visions—when the Sight comes on him. For half a moment, his 'other face' stares right into mine, and I am seized with a terror I can barely explain. Then suddenly, he smiles, very slightly, and the 'other face' melts away, leaving his normal impassive expression behind.

Later, everyone—friends, family, villagers—goes back to the house for a glass of cider and a piece of cake. The Bellegarde manor-house isn't very big, and so it's very noisy, and very crowded, and soon I've had enough. I escape to the back garden, and find Pierre and Edmond already there.

Edmond and I begin discussing the day's events, but Pierre doesn't speak. He seems lost in thought. At last, Edmond says, with a teasing look, 'What are you plotting, Pierre Bardon? You look as though you're about to lay an egg!'

Pierre flushes. 'I was thinking of Mademoiselle.' That's what he calls Flora, these days, though he's known her since they were both babies, just as he's known us.

Nobody has asked him to distance himself from her in this way—it is of his own choosing. But he still calls Edmond and me by our Christian names.

Edmond's eyebrows lift. 'Really, Pierre?' Flora is Edmond's cousin, but as close to him as the sister he'd never had.

Pierre flushes even darker, but he persists. 'I've been thinking this now for some time. Mademoiselle has no father to protect her now, and no brother.'

'She has her uncle. And her cousin,' puts in Edmond lightly, but Pierre ignores that.

'I was thinking that the four of us, we were all born in the same year,' he continues. 'We grew up together. We are good friends, already. But now it needs to be something more. We need to swear a vow.'

There is a small silence as we stare at him, nonplussed, then—'Heavens, man!' says Edmond, languidly. 'Do we swear in blood, like the Indians?'

'No,' says Pierre, frowning. He is not one for jokes. 'We swear by Our Lady.' He looks straight into Edmond's eyes. 'We swear to always protect Mademoiselle and Madame, her mother. We swear that because dark times are coming. I've seen them.'

Edmond snorts. His father, Richard de Bellegarde's younger brother Charles, has brought him up in an atmosphere of rationality and enlightenment. Well-known philosophers come to their smart house in Paris to discuss the most pressing issues of the day, to dispute on diverse plans to remake the world and to debate how to improve human nature. Visions and premonitions are not a part of this new world, and certainly not for bright, ambitious, modern Edmond.

He raises his eyebrows. 'Oh no. He's been looking in his crystal ball again.'

Pierre's black eyes flash. 'Mock me if you like. But I've seen what I've seen.'

Edmond explodes. 'Oh, for God's sake! Visions! Forebodings! What kind of barbarous nonsense is this, Pierre? You aren't just a peasant boy. You can read and write. Father Jantot says you are one of the brightest boys he has ever taught. Man is a creature of light, Pierre, not darkness. Throw off these superstitious blinkers, they stop you from seeing clearly!'

'For heaven's sake, Edmond,' I say, hastily, as I see Pierre's face darkening, 'can't you ever stop being the philosophy lecturer?' Then I break off, because Flora has come into the garden.

Mourning becomes her. The dull black brings out the fine gold of her hair and the soft blue of her eyes and the creamy tones of her skin. Since her father died, she's become a bit quieter, but she is just as beautiful as ever. My heart flips over, as it does every time I see her— every time since last year, when I realised I was deeply, hopelessly in love with my childhood friend.

Flora looks at the three of us. She senses the charged atmosphere. But all she says is, 'Your father's looking for you, Edmond. The carriage is waiting.'

'The coachman can wait a bit longer!' says Edmond, casually. 'He's used to it.' He pats the stone bench beside him. 'Come and sit with me, Flora, sweet cousin. We're about to swear a vow. It's about you,' he goes on, linking his arm with Flora's, ignoring the embarrassed look on my face, and Pierre's stony glare.

She smiles a bit sadly up at him. 'About me? Are you boys to have secrets from me? Am I no longer to be friends with you, now we've all passed our fifteenth birthdays?'

Pierre swallows. I can see his Adam's apple bob convulsively. But he doesn't say anything. It's Edmond who says, lightly, 'We were about to swear a vow to protect you, dearest cousin, now that Uncle's gone. It's Pierre's idea. He has looked into his crystal ball again and says dark times are coming. Whatever that means.'

Flora gently disengages herself from Edmond. She looks up at Pierre. 'I think a vow is a fine idea. But I do not think it should be just to protect *me*, but one another. Let us swear, the four of us, to be friends for ever.'

Edmond laughs. 'Well played, Flora! Pierre will be even more your devoted slave, Jacques will write poems about how noble you are, and I will have to paint a beautiful portrait of you, depicting you as our Goddess of Friendship.'

Flora's face darkens. 'Don't be silly, Edmond. This is serious. Isn't it, Pierre?'

Pierre says, softly, 'Yes, Mademoiselle. The black wings are almost over us. Brother will turn against brother, son against father, husband against wife, friend against friend. The fields will run with blood, and wolves inherit the land.' He speaks quite calmly, as if reciting a list, and his black eyes, staring into ours, are without expression. But a thrill of pure, cold terror ripples over me, and Flora's eyes widen in fear.

But Edmond is furious. 'This is nonsense. Absolute benighted medieval arrant nonsense. You are to stop this nonsense at once, Pierre! Do you understand? Or I will—' He breaks off as he sees the expression on Flora's face.

'Don't you dare speak to Pierre like that,' she hisses. 'You have absolutely no right, Cousin. You cannot threaten anyone on my land.'

How splendid she looks, with her head held high like that, her eyes flashing! She holds Edmond's gaze for an instant; then he shrugs. 'Have it your own way, Cousin. But I don't think you should encourage such things. It is foolish, and dangerous.'

She ignores him. She turns back to Pierre, who during this whole exchange has been standing as still as stone, looking at the ground. 'Don't listen to him, Pierre. Tell *me*. Was it a dream? Or a waking vision?'

He flushes. 'It was not a dream,' he says, reluctantly.

Flora has always been the only one who speaks to him willingly of his *thing*, his peculiarity, his second sight. Edmond mocks it, and I am made uneasy by it. It must have been a very powerful vision for him to speak of it in front of us.

Flora puts a hand fleetingly on his arm. 'Shall we swear, then? Shall we swear on Our Lady's head?'

'On Our Lady's head,' agrees Pierre. He lifts his head and stares almost vacantly into her face. In that moment he looks half-witted, I think. I feel a sneaking sympathy for Edmond's point of view. Flora really shouldn't encourage this. I steal a look at Edmond. He has a little sardonic smile on his face. But thank God, he says nothing.

And that was how we came to make our vow. Four hands on top of one another, four childhood friends united for the last time. Pierre said the words, very simply, and we repeated them: 'Our Lady Mary, Mother of God, help us in our vow. We swear eternal friendship with one another, and promise to come to one another's aid whenever we need it, and protect one another. Amen.'

It is a solemn moment, and though I can't help noticing the sardonic smile still faintly curled at Edmond's lip, he says the words along with everyone else. As to me, I feel so moved I can barely stammer the words. But Pierre and Flora speak quite clearly, and unselfconsciously, and look at each other in what appears suddenly to my jealous mind like perfect understanding, as if every difference—the huge, the insurmountable differences between them—makes absolutely *no* difference at all.

Two

Early in the spring of 1789, Edmond was sent by his father to Rome, to further his art studies. He sent frequent letters back to Bellegarde, which Flora and I read together. His letters were sharp, funny, embellished by charcoal sketches of places he had visited, and people he had seen in the street.

I was thrilled by his letters but also very envious. I was writing a good deal of poetry, and I would have liked to be allowed to pursue a literary career—but my lawyer father would not hear of it. Writing, he said sternly, was a career best suited to the sons of the minor nobility, and to those who had an independent income, or to those madmen whom one saw trying to hawk poems and songs at street corners, with famished looks and desperate entreaties. I was not either of the first two types, he said, and he was damned if he was going to let me turn into the third. Besides, France always needed lawyers, and especially now. After a century of tyranny and stagnation, exciting political change was in the air. The King himself was full of reformist ideas, and the newly reopened parliament offered a new start for the nation.

As a prominent local man, my father was involved in compiling the *cahiers de doléances*, the regional complaints books which were to be sent to the new parliament, to form the backbone of reform efforts. The King actually wanted to know the state of his country, and the views of his people! It was unheard of, exciting. Father toured the district with other worthies, collecting evidence and anecdotes and requests from the peasants, the artisans, the merchants and the country nobility. At home, he was full of talk of tax reform, and changes to landlords' rights, and inheritance laws, and game and forest laws, and apprenticeships, and properly organised road-works, and reform of military service, and the possibility of civil constitutions: things which I can't say fascinated me much, though I tried to look interested, for my father's sake. I wanted change, all right; didn't most of France? Everyone knew things couldn't stay the same, everyone knew we had a historic opportunity to begin afresh.

But the change that lay closest to my heart was the one I didn't dare mention to anyone else at all, least of all my parents. I dreamed of one day asking Flora to marry me. But the way things were, it was impossible. Her family was not rich, and not powerful either, except in the small world of Bellegarde. But they were nevertheless aristocrats, of an ancient family that could be traced back to the Crusades. My family, though decent, respectable, well-educated and fairly well-off, didn't have a drop of noble blood in it. We could be friends but never spouses.

Once, the four of us—Flora, Edmond, Pierre and I—had been inseparable, especially during the long summer holidays when we all gathered in the village. Flora and Pierre had been closest of all, as they spent all their time in Bellegarde, unlike Edmond and me. But over the last year or two, things had begun to change between us. And now life intervened to separate us more permanently. Childhood was over.

Edmond was in Rome. I was destined for the dusty precincts of a lawyer's office in our local town, Tarny. And Flora was bound for Court. Through the good offices of her Uncle Charles, Edmond's father—now a reformist deputy in the parliament, and a man of some consequence in Paris—she was to be presented at Court this very summer. And she would pass out of my life for ever. As to Pierre, his life was also transformed. The winter of 78–79 had been a particularly harsh and bitter one, with crops failing all over the country, rivers freezing over in October, and wolves, driven by hunger, coming into villages. Desperate beggars roamed the roads, food was scarce. But not at Pierre's house. With the old flintlock rifle left to him by his late father, he had spent much of the winter hunting. Pierre was a great shot. Not only did he get rabbits and birds for the family pot, he also bagged a large number of wolves, and sold their skins to a tannery in the nearby town, for quite a good sum of money.

The Bardon family—Pierre, his widowed mother and his sickly younger sister Marie—had no land, apart from their little kitchen garden. They chiefly lived off the charity of the other villagers, the herbal potions Pierre's mother concocted for the locals, the contract work Pierre did for several of the farmers, and the bit of smuggling that he sometimes engaged in to supplement family income. Last year, he'd smuggled salt—at the time it was taxed very heavily, and so there was a brisk black market trade in it—but his mother was worried about him getting shot by customs officers, and so he'd had to give it up.

Now spring was here, the resourceful Pierre had decided on another way to keep bread on the table. This one was perfectly legal. In those days, single men between eighteen and forty were drafted into the militia, their names drawn out of a hat. The chosen ones then had to go for compulsory military training several times a year, leaving their fields and businesses behind.

The enlistment lasted for six years. The militia didn't just do military exercises; they were also drafted to repair roads, construct public buildings, all kinds of necessary but backbreaking work. People hated it. Enlistment caused havoc with farm work and with town businesses. It was one of the strongest complaints against the government in the countryside, and the thing most people hoped would be changed.

But even then there was a loophole. If you could find someone willing to take your place for money, a 'volunteer' over the age of thirteen, which was the legal age for bearing arms, then you could avoid conscription yourself. Pierre had decided he would be one of these 'volunteers', and he had quickly found someone—the only son of a prosperous farmer—more than willing to pay Pierre handsomely to take his place. So Pierre was to leave in July for army training in Brittany, and his family would get the money.

Since that day when we had vowed eternal friendship, Pierre had not mentioned any more premonitions of disaster. In fact, he seemed remarkably cheerful. Perhaps it was because he had, for the first time, been able to treat his family to one or two extra things—some fabric, some ribbons—as well as put food on the table.

But perhaps it was also because of Edmond's absence. Away from our friend's sophistication and mockery, Pierre was a more relaxed, less wary creature. We snatched pleasant moments together, the three of us, that spring, when, freed momentarily from our various chores and plans for our future, we could pretend we were children again. We rowed up and down the stream, and fished, and played at hide and seek.

If you have never seen our countryside, you will not

know that much of it is like a natural fort, hidden behind high hedges and heather scrubland and deep green woods, with sunken paths and streams and little hills taking the place of moats and walls and towers. Children can devise grand games in that country; and none more so than Pierre, whose hunting experience had taught him to remain perfectly still and quiet until the last moment. We had picnics, too, and listened as Flora played tunes she'd made up on her little flute, and talked not of the future but of the past. We laughed a lot, and I tried to forget the shadow that hung over us, the shadow of separation. For I would soon be the only one of the four left in the district. Left with my dry law books and my vain dreams. The thought was too much to bear, and so I tried hard not to think of it, and just enjoy these few last weeks of freedom.

One very fine June day in 1789, we were sitting by the side of a stream, Pierre and I finishing off the cold chicken Flora's cook had packed for us, and listening to Flora playing when all at once she laid aside her flute and said, 'This morning, Mother received a message from Paris. Uncle Charles is remarrying.'

We both stared at her, stunned. Edmond's beautiful, delicate mother Juliette had died giving birth to her son. Her heartbroken widower had sworn never to remarry. Edmond didn't remember his mother, of course, but he'd been brought up on the story of his parents' perfect love. It was dear to his heart.

'Edmond doesn't know yet,' said Flora. 'Uncle Charles can't face telling him. He wants Mother to break the news to him when he comes here on holiday. '

I said, carefully, 'Who is the lady?'

'Béatrice de Darmant. She's the daughter of another deputy. It's a very good alliance for Uncle Charles, in many ways. The family is very well-connected.'

'What sort of woman is she?' I asked. 'In her person?'

Flora shrugged. 'I don't even know if she's pretty, or what age she is. All I know is what I've told you.'

'We must try and find out more,' I said. 'I will ask Father if he knows anything of her, and her family. Perhaps the more we can tell Edmond about her, the happier he'll be.'

Pierre had said nothing in all this. Now he spoke. 'And what if she is a wicked woman?'

'Don't be silly, Pierre,' Flora scoffed. 'Of course she won't be.'

'In Edmond's eyes, she will be,' said Pierre, 'whatever anyone else says.'

'Well, he must be made to see reason,' said Flora impatiently. 'He is grown up now; his father can hardly be faulted for wanting to end his long solitude. Jacques, let's find out more about her. You ask your father; I'll ask Mother.'

Between us, we soon had more details. The Darmants were nobles, but not 'nobles of the sword', descendants of medieval knights and feudal lords, like the Bellegardes, but what was known then as 'nobles of the robe': judges, lawyers, administrators, even accountants, who had acquired nobility not through deeds of arms, but services to the Crown. The family was known to be bright, ambitious, wealthy, and ruthless. Born politicians.

They had served three kings, but were also on friendly terms with many of the reformers. Béatrice de Darmant herself was said to be intelligent, handsome, and possessed of a good dowry. At twenty-two, she was also twenty years younger than her prospective husband, and only six years older than Edmond. How would he take it all?

Three

Edmond had changed, physically and otherwise, in those months in Rome. He affected the romantic look; his hair had grown and he wore it loose, unpowdered, in great dark waves over his shoulders. He wore a wide-brimmed soft hat, pushed far back on his head, a loosely tied cravat, and crumpled linen and velvet—of the best quality, of course. His diamond self-assurance had become even harder, more polished; his tongue sharper. His art had changed, too. No more pretty paintings of landscapes and shepherdesses, and soft portraits, but big, blustering canvases based on Roman myth and history. He was full of the things he'd seen, the places he'd been to, the people he'd met.

But he said nothing about his father's impending marriage. Flora told us what happened, that morning her mother finally decided she must tell him.

'He turned quite white,' she said, 'and he stared at Mother as if he had been turned to stone. He didn't ask any questions. It was eerie. Mother said something to him about the date of the marriage, and I said that we had found out a little about the lady his father was to marry, and that she seemed well enough. He looked at us then—I will never forget that look—and he said, very quietly and perfectly calmly, that we were not to mention the subject ever again. Then he smiled, and asked Mother if she had seen his painting of the Colosseum, and had she noticed the detail of the stonework?'

She broke off, biting her lip. 'I do not understand it. I was ready for everything, but not this. It is so unlike him.'

I said, 'Don't worry. He's had a shock. He will get over it.'

Pierre shook his head. 'You do not think so, do you, Mademoiselle?'

She looked at him. 'No. Edmond admired his father so. That Uncle Charles should not only marry again, despite his vows—but also get someone else to break the news to him—that, I think, he cannot forgive.'

'But, surely,' I said, 'he must accept this, he has no choice. And she may not be all that—'

'Ssh,' said Flora, 'here he comes.'

'Well?' said Edmond, flinging himself on the grass beside us. 'What secret are you plotting, with those transparently guilty faces?'

Flora said, demurely, 'We were just deciding whether we should throw you in the stream, Edmond, right now, or later.'

He laughed. 'I'd like to see you try!' He rolled up the sleeve of his linen shirt, and flexed his biceps. 'Look! I have been working on my muscles, in Rome—when you see all those Herculean statues, you feel rather puny.' He grinned at Pierre. 'Now—well I may not be Hercules, but I have the feeling I would beat even you in a fair fight, Pierre Bardon!'

Pierre grinned back, unperturbed. Tall and broad, he had always been strong and imposing, physically. 'Any time you wish, Monsieur Edmond.'

'What else did the Romans teach you, Edmond,' I said hastily, 'beside the necessity of physical exercise? I have heard it said that they are very fond of words and disputations. Have they improved your eloquence?'

Edmond shrugged. 'Eloquence! The Romans are strutting peacocks, fond of meaningless phrases. But at the French club in the city, I met an extraordinary speaker, visiting from the Jacobin Club in Paris. Jean Casgrain is his name. And he's a revolutionary—the real thing—not some dull reformer who can't see further than the end of his nose! He said the time was coming when France would lead the way to the new world, that her light would shine bright amongst all the nations, and that tyranny and oppression would everywhere be forcibly swept away, and replaced by the pure rule of reason and liberty.' His face was aglow. 'Oh, I tell you, it was splendid! I wished I were back in France, instead of in Rome, surrounded by ruins and chattering Italians.'

'You're not thinking of giving up your studies, are you?' scolded Flora.

'I haven't decided,' he said lightly

'But, Edmond, your father . . .'

'My father has nothing to say on the matter.'

Before Flora could respond, he turned to Pierre. 'What is this I hear about you joining the militia?'

'I'm going next month,' said Pierre stolidly. 'To Brittany, for training.'

'Brittany! Can't think what they'll teach you, there, except their barbarous tongue—but then, the ways of the King's Army are a dark secret to all, including the generals themselves. Tell me, did Goudon pay well for your services?'

Goudon was the name of the well-to-do farmer who'd paid Pierre to take his place.

Pierre nodded warily. Edmond laughed. 'Well done. Well, now I'll have a lawyer friend, and a soldier friend—I expect to see you captain soon, Pierre—and soon I'll have a cousin at Court. What more could a poor struggling artist want, if it wasn't for some fat comfortable cleric or a corrupt politician with deep pockets?'

His tone made me uneasy. There was an undertone of anger and contempt in it that seemed quite out of place. I said, clumsily changing the subject, 'I was very interested to see your painting of Hercules fighting the Hydra—it was very lifelike, and quite unusual.'

'I am glad you like it,' he said. His face was aglow again. 'It is my own favourite. Do you know, I gave the face of that marvellous Jacobin speaker to Hercules?'

I remembered the painted face: narrow, gaunt, with a sharp, thin nose, and glittering eyes in hollow sockets, it was hardly the kind you'd have imagined for the strongest man in the world.

'That must be what made it so unusual,' I said, carefully.

'It's all allegorical, do you see,' said Edmond. 'The Jacobin Hercules smiting off one by one the monstrous heads of tyranny and oppression.'

'Just as long as it isn't real heads,' Flora joked.

Edmond laughed. 'Whatever happens, it won't be your pretty little head, my darling cousin, anyway!' And he went on talking gaily of Rome, and what he'd seen and done there. But not one word of his father, or the prospect of a new stepmother.

The whole of his stay, he stayed quiet about it. He was taking it badly. How badly, we didn't suspect yet. But there was nothing any of us could do.

Before he went back to Rome, he left me with a great gift. He suggested to my father that I might be reconciled to the law if I was sent abroad to study for a spell, perhaps to London where my father had a friend, John

Wills, a lawyer like himself, and a member of the Inns of Court.

When Edmond chose to, he could charm the birds from the trees; very soon he had my father believing that this idea was his own, and insisting that of course I must go there. I had some tolerable English, and Mr Wills spoke French well, apparently, for his wife came from France (he had met her in Paris, where he'd also met my father, who'd been doing his studies there). Mr Wills would be delighted to host me, Father said; he had a son only a couple of years older than me, and it would do me good to see something different. He would write immediately to Mr Wills, and set everything in train right away.

Edmond wouldn't hear of my thanking him for the idea. 'Bah! To think of you being the only one stuck in our native mud, it quite turned my stomach on your behalf, my poor Jacques,' he said lightly. 'I in Rome, and Flora in Paris, and even Pierre in Brittany—no, it just wouldn't do to have you here on your own. Besides, it's selfish, you know; I will be expecting letters, and entertaining ones, from London. Promise you'll write, won't you?'

Of course I promised. I was warmed by his thoughtfulness and by his renewed friendship. Besides, he had the knack of making you feel that such things were of the greatest importance to him, just as Flora did, even when you suspected they'd be thinking of something else the very next instant.

Mr Wills replied in a most friendly fashion to my father's letter, urging him to send me immediately. During the legal terms, I could stay with him and his son Jonathan, who was also training for the law, in chambers in London and for the breaks go home with them to the family's Kent property. I could stay till the following summer, if that was agreeable to my father, and then perhaps Jonathan might come back with me, for a while, to France?

All this was indeed most agreeable to my parents, who I am sure were secretly relieved at the thought of not having a morose son moping around the house, missing his friends. As to Flora and Pierre, they were delighted. Flora said that she would try and persuade her mother that they must come and visit me in London; they also had distant cousins in England, it appeared. Pierre laughed then and said *he* wouldn't go there, as he had no notion how he would talk to those heathen English over the water. But he would think of me, especially if he was training by the sea.

We were all full of a wild, silly excitement in those days: sad at the thought of being separated, but also sure we would all meet again soon, and happily. There was an atmosphere in the whole country, of hope and a happy sense of new beginnings, of possibility. For the four of us, it seemed personal. Each of us was going to something new, fine, exciting; and we would all meet again. We would all meet again and, in my heart of hearts, I thought maybe the world would have changed, and a marriage between a Verdun and a Bellegarde would not be out of the question any more.

Flora left first, on the last day of June. I will never forget that last sight of her as, unmindful of our adult dignity, Pierre and I ran after the carriage down the avenue, shouting and waving. She had her blonde head out of the window and was waving back, her eyes full of tears and laughter mixed. Pierre and I ran and ran till we could run no more, till our sides ached, till the carriage had long turned the corner and bumped off down the road that led to the town.

At last we stopped, and threw ourselves on the grass by the side of the road. I felt suddenly very heavy then, but could not express it. I shot a glance at Pierre and saw that there were tears in his eyes. I'd never seen him cry before, and it made me feel even odder. But I said nothing, and we lay there on our backs in the grass, trying to master ourselves, trying not to say the thing I imagine we each had in our hearts. At last Pierre sat up, brushed the grass off himself, ran a big hand through his tangled black pony-tailed hair, clapped his shabby hat back on his head, and said, 'I must go. There are traps I need to check.'

I sat up, too. 'And I suppose I'd better be back to my English studies, or I'll be like a landed fish on English shores, opening my mouth and no sound coming out.' We walked along together, quite companionably, but not talking. When we reached the gates of Bellegarde Manor again, I looked down the avenue, green-shaded now with the elms in summer leaf, and a sudden terror assailed me, for what reason I do not know. And it made me say to Pierre, quite suddenly, 'You remember that time last autumn, after Flora's father died and we made our vow?'

'Of course,' he said quietly.

'Have you had any more of those visions?' I trailed off at the sight of Pierre's expression. His black eyes were fixed on me with a curious intensity.

'You feel it too, don't you, Jacques?' he said softly.

'I don't know what you're talking about.'

He shrugged, and gave a strange, sad little smile. 'Never mind, Jacques, I won't tell anyone you're a sensitive too. I see things; but you *feel* them. But they are the *same* things.'

A ripple of cold stiffened my neck. I tried to speak, but couldn't. Pierre looked at me, and shook his head. 'It doesn't do any good, Monsieur Jacques,' he said, rather formally. 'We can try to warn people, but we don't often know ourselves what it is we are warning them about. We see—or feel, or hear—snatches of things, but not enough to be quite sure.' He paused. 'I have seen that thing you refer to twice, twice only. Once last autumn. Once, just after Christmas, when I was hunting. I hope and pray I do not see it a third time. I have prayed for that; prayed that it is but a nightmare, sent by the Devil to make me despair and fear. And so it may yet be. But you must understand that what you feel is real.' He looked down at the ground. 'You must pray, too, Jacques. Pray for us all.'

'I don't need you to play the priest with me,' I said, angrily. 'I can look after my own soul, thank you very much. Besides, I think we are both imagining things. There is nothing to be afraid of. Things are going well. Father has told me. The King has understood the demands of the people; the parliament is moving to address the abuses and to strike down the privileges which weigh too heavily on the people. We are in an age of reform.'

'Not everyone will be satisfied with that,' he said quietly. 'Not everyone actually wants that. Do you think Hercules will be satisfied if the Hydra is merely tamed? Do you not think the raging blood in him will not be satisfied if he cannot use his sword? Again and again and again?'

I started. I had never heard Pierre talk like this before. He smiled again, rather wearily. 'But it doesn't matter. Whatever we do, there is *nothing* we can do. What will be, will be.'

I took my leave of him soon after that. We parted on

good terms, good friends as we were. But his words had left a chill on that summer's afternoon that even now, in my prison cell, my last home on this earth, still makes me shiver.

Four

After a long and arduous journey, I arrived exhausted and feverish in London, and spent the first few days of my English stay sick in bed in the Willses' Middle Temple chambers. Mr Wills and Jonathan were kindness itself, and their housekeeper, Mrs Bradley, looked after me as if I were her own son. After a few days, I had recovered enough to take short walks around the Middle Temple gardens with Jonathan, who seemed glad to have someone his own age to show around.

It was an unusual place, Middle Temple, and indeed all the Inns of Court—a kind of lawyer's city. I had never been in such a place before, though I suppose there are such areas in Paris too.

Jonathan spoke quite good French, for which I was most grateful, in those early days. I knew I must learn English well, and soon, but in my weakened state, it was a comfort to be able to converse in my native tongue.

In looks, Jonathan took after his father, Mr Wills. Two years older than me, he was tall and thin, with a head of mousy brown hair, which he wore tied back neatly with a black ribbon. He had a rather pale face, mild hazel eyes, and was soft-spoken, and controlled. But his calm looks were deceptive, as I came to realise.

When I had fully recovered, he took me out of the legal city and into the bigger metropolis. He had walked everywhere, it seemed, and knew most places of interest.

He was fearless; we even went into places which most young men of his age and class would not have dreamed of entering—the haunts of drunks, of prostitutes, of criminals of all stripes. Strangely, though he was not at all strong-looking, or imposing, we were never challenged. Once or twice, I saw sly eyes sliding towards us, resting thoughtfully on his thin face, and then turning away.

There was something about him, some unseen atmosphere that emanated from him, which warned the dangerous and the sly to keep away. Some people have that. It's a gift, like any other, and cannot be analysed exactly. I know that I don't possess it; that without him, I would no more have dreamed of going to these sorts of places than I would have thought of flying to the moon on a broomstick. But as it was, it certainly was an education; an education in the other side of the law, as it were. That's what Jonathan called it. He said if we were to be lawyers, we must not just understand the paper version; we must see where the papers didn't penetrate, where the outlaw reigned. We must know about the criminal world, not just the legal one.

Two weeks after I arrived in England, the London newspapers were full of thrilling news: the taking of the Bastille in Paris on July 14. The crowd had marched on this hated prison, and had soon overcome the feeble resistance of the few guards. They had freed the prisoners and killed the prison governor and several guards. But then they had hacked off their heads, and paraded them on pikes through the streets, rioting as they went, looting shops, beating up passers-by, burning houses . . .

Exciting though it was to hear about the Bastille's fall, the rioting and savage murders frightened me. But it was Paris. Everyone knew the mob was bloodthirsty in Paris. They'd always been that way. It wasn't at all like our region.

Nevertheless, I wrote to my parents immediately, and soon received a reassuring reply from my mother. I wasn't to worry, she said. Paris was seething, but the rest of the country was peaceful, though isolated rioting and looting had broken out here and there. Our own region was quite calm. She hoped I was happy in England. She had heard news of Flora and Pierre. Flora had been presented to the King, and was now attending parties and balls, while Pierre was doing well in his regiment in Brittany. She had not heard from Edmond or his father, but she presumed all was well. She finished by saying my father hoped I was learning a great deal about English law, and that they were considering coming to visit me in the autumn.

A few days afterwards, I left London with Mr Wills and Jonathan, to travel to their Kent home. Willesdene Hall, it was called. It was a smallish estate, but quite productive, with working orchards and hop fields. The house itself was of Tudor origin, and though a little shabby, quite pleasant and comfortable, just like its owner.

Mrs Wills proved to be a small, pretty woman with prematurely grey hair and a distracted, vague air. She had now been in England for twenty-five years or more, and considered it her home, though she still spoke with a French accent, and still had an interest in certain French things, principally the stage, and fashions, of which she was most fond, in a dreamy sort of way—for a less fashionable lady it would have been hard to find. Besides Jonathan, she and Mr Wills had three other children, all girls, one older than Jonathan, the other two younger. Emily, the oldest at nineteen, was engaged to be married; the other two girls, Jane and Charlotte, were thirteen and eight respectively. Emily was a pale, gentle, quiet girl who bore a marked resemblance to her mother, though in her the prettiness had become real beauty; Jane was a talkative and rather pert girl who loved romantic novels, and who took after her father and brother in looks, while Charlotte was a dark-haired little tomboy who was allowed to run wild all over the estate. The younger girls had a governess, a Miss Fanshawe, who appeared to be perpetually looking for her rebellious charges all over the estate—an undertaking not helped by the amiable vagueness of their mother.

Jonathan and his sisters got on extremely well. I felt a little shy, at first, thrust into this warm and even overwhelming family atmosphere, but the younger girls didn't allow me to hang back or mope.

'We love having visitors,' Jane told me, 'it is so very dull living here in the country and never seeing any of Jonathan's smart London friends. Have you brought any of the new novels from Paris?' She went on, without drawing breath, 'Maman says they are not for my age, but I am really remarkably mature for my age, Miss Fanshawe says so.'

'I do not think it is a compliment on her part, Jane,' said Jonathan, grinning. 'And don't try and worm your way past Maman's rules, you put poor Jacques in an impossible position.'

'In any case, I haven't any new novels,' I said, honestly, flushing a little. 'I must confess I do not read very much these days except law books.'

'And those would most definitely cure even a bookworm like our Jane of reading,' said Jonathan, laughing.

The days went on happily at Willesdene, and soon I was so sunk into the warm and friendly atmosphere of the family that I forgot about what might be going on in

France. Mr Wills went occasionally in his carriage to the nearby town, but if he bought the newspaper, or heard news from over the water, he did not tell me, and I did not think to ask. Mrs Wills was not one for politics or news, either, unless it was local news of births, deaths and marriages, and so the long summer days passed unclouded and untroubled.

We went back to London in the third week of September 1789. There was a letter waiting for me there; Mrs Bradley said it had only arrived in the last few days. It was from Edmond, who had given up his studies in Rome and returned to Paris.

It seemed like the wrong thing to be doing, the wrong place to be, dear Jacques, he wrote. *There is a new dawn in our country, and Paris is the only place to be. I am lodging not with my father, for I cannot bear his recriminations and that woman's false interest—but with a friend. You remember Jean Casgrain, that orator I was telling you about, whom I painted as Hercules? Well, it is with him, and his twin sister Athénaïs, where I am lodging. They are marvellous people. And through them I have met some of the greatest revolutionary leaders, the men from the Jacobin Club—Desmoulins, and Robespierre, and Saint-Just, and Danton and, oh, many others. Oh, they are such men! The official press and the corrupt politicians like my father call them extremists, Jacques, but that is a badge of honour for them! They care not for the timid and the craven and the opportunistic; they have a chance to remake the world, and they'd rather die trying than accept anything less. It is such a privilege, Jacques, just to be on the edges of their society, of their conversation! Oh, Jacques! Life has really begun for me, do you see! I am sorry for you, stuck in rainy, cold England. Such passive, dull people they are, so satisfied with small things, I imagine they must be very envious of our boldness and daring.*

I looked up from my letter and saw Jonathan watching me. My feelings must have shown in my face, for he said, quietly, 'Trouble?'

'Yes,' I answered. I explained a little about Edmond. When I'd finished, Jonathan said, rather wistfully, 'I can understand his feelings. He must feel really alive, in that fiery atmosphere. It has an air of danger. The stakes are high. All your senses tingle.' I thought of him in those sailors' haunts and the low criminal dives he'd taken me to, and I thought then, that's what really attracts him to them, not a high-flown ideal to see all the ramifications of the law, but danger itself. Risk.

'You're right,' I said. 'It *is* what attracts Edmond. But if he should find himself in prison—or worse—because of his association with these rabble-rousers, then what?'

'Then he will no doubt ask his father to bail him out,' said Jonathan sardonically.

'But he doesn't get on with his father. I can't help thinking he's associating with these people just to spite him. Oh!'

41

I had turned over the letter and seen the scrawled postscript. *By the way, Flora's no longer in Paris; she's gone back to Bellegarde with her mother. My aunt thinks Paris has become too unsettled and dangerous. Flora did not appear to think very highly of the prospective suitors that were presented to her while she was there—but my aunt has told me that a certain rich and dashing baron is hoping to change her mind.*

I felt my heart constrict. Flora might not like this baron—whom already I hated, with all my heart—but she was a dutiful daughter who would no doubt do as her mother wanted. And if Madame de Bellegarde liked this baron then the die was already cast. And my hopes were permanently dashed.

Five

In late November my parents arrived. We all left for Kent, where we spent a pleasant couple of weeks. My father and Mr Wills seemed to renew their friendship very easily; my mother and Mrs Wills struck up a happy relationship too.

I asked Mother about Flora—subtly, I thought, hiding my wretchedness—and she looked at me, smiled, and said gently, 'Flora is just the same as ever. Nothing's changed with her.'

'I heard that a baron was going to ask . . .'

She shrugged. 'As far as I know, none has. She lives a quiet life with her mother. Jacques, why don't you write to her? I'm sure she would be very glad to hear from you.'

I spent days over that letter. It started as a wild, flowery declaration, was ripped into shreds, rewritten, rewritten again, and then again, and ended up very plain and brief.

Dear Flora,
I trust you are well, and that Madame de Bellegarde
is well, and that all goes well in Bellegarde. England

43

fares tolerably well, though wet at present, and I
have made fast friends with the Wills family, chiefly
Jonathan. Have you heard from Edmond? Is Pierre
back yet? Do write soon.

I remain your most faithful and affectionate friend,
Jacques Verdun.

Would she guess how much I had invested in that
'affectionate' and 'faithful', humble and cool words which
were all that remained of my first wild declaration?
Would she guess how much my heart had fluttered as I
had written her dear name? Unlikely. Why should she?

Still, I sent the letter to the post with clammy hands
and a racing pulse, and tried hard not to be too impatient
about a reply.

After two weeks, Mr Wills, Father, Jonathan and I
went up to London for a few days. We'd spoken very little
of the situation in France while we were in Kent. But on
the way up to London in the coach, my father and Mr
Wills began to discuss it in depth. Father said things were
very tense in Paris. The Bastille riots had provoked a new
rash of laws against the gathering of crowds, as well as a
tightening of curfew. But they hadn't stopped trouble, by
a long way. There had been more riots, robberies, rapes,
house-burnings, assaults and murders.

There was also real trouble in the army—ordinary
soldiers were refusing to obey their officers, navy ships

had been taken over by their crews. A new volunteer army, the National Guard, had been created. Its officers were to be elected by the men. Each region would raise National Guard units, composed of ordinary citizens. The idea was that the army was both overstretched and unreliable; this way, anarchy could be kept at bay not only in Paris but in the regions.

Meanwhile, revolutionary journals and pamphlets proliferated and the political clubs were full of wild orators, but the most extreme agitators were being hunted down by the police, so it was hoped things might settle down.

More worrying, said Father, were the attacks on the Church. Church land was to be seized and sold off. And parliament also intended to close down monasteries, abbeys and convents. These were often the only refuge for the poor, the homeless, orphans and the sick. Monks and nuns and priests also ran schools in just about every village. The government appeared to have no plans to take over the charitable works of the monks and nuns. What would happen to all those people who depended on them?

'The politicians have gone mad,' said Father. 'The parliament's full of people all shouting at once, all sure they're right. Meanwhile, the King dithers. Poor man—it would need a real genius to cope with all the demands—not to speak of the fact there are those for whom no reform would be enough. Those who block his ideas at every turn, who constantly speak of him as though he were a bloodthirsty tyrant instead of a weak and confused man trying to reform a flawed system.'

'But Father,' I burst out, 'yes, these attacks on the Church are stupid—but all too often, the bishops forget Jesus's words. They too often take the side of the powerful. And surely you must agree that change had to come in France! '

'And how will it help the powerless if the religious houses are closed down?' said my father. 'Do you forget they are often the only refuge for the poor? I don't hear of any politician wishing to sink his money into charity! Besides, I'm afraid that the reforms we all wanted are being transformed into something else by ruthless fanatics.' He was silent a moment, then went on, 'I am afraid your friend Edmond is keeping company with some of the most dangerous radicals of all. I cannot think that his father is pleased at Edmond's associations, but he has done nothing about it. After all, there are a great many noblemen's sons in the radical parties. Perhaps Charles thinks it might be useful one day. In any case, he continues to send him money.'

Mr Wills raised an eyebrow. 'Goodness me! If Jonathan joined the Revolution Society here, I think I'd have something to say!'

'You need have no fear on that score, Father. I have no interest in a group of pasty-faced chamber revolutionaries shouting blood and thunder at each other, when I know they'd faint at the mere sight of blood,' said Jonathan languidly. 'Give me a good brawling sailor or a back-streets criminal any day. At least they're honest in their violence, and don't send others to perform it for them.'

'How about Pierre?' I asked, wondering what he was feeling in this uncertain new France.

'He is still in Brittany. I heard he has impressed his superiors with his marksmanship and his hunting skills, but that he has a little problem with discipline.'

I smiled inwardly. That was typical of Pierre. He might have been a peasant's son, born in a mean cottage in the meanest part of the village, but he was his own man, always.

Six

My parents went back to France. Weeks and months passed. 1789 turned into 1790, winter turned into spring, then into summer and autumn. Despite missing Flora, I was enjoying England. Here, I could avoid my father's expectations more easily. Mr Wills was much more sympathetic to my literary ambitions than my father, and it was accepted that sometimes I would take a break from law and go to the British Museum. There I would sit and write. By this time, I had decided on a novel kind of literary idea. I would write a history of our time, in verse.

It was proving quite difficult, but it was exciting work. Meanwhile, I also wrote some little odes and sonnets, mainly about nature, and about yearnings for love, poetry I dedicated firmly in my mind to Flora, far away.

She had replied to my letter with a very friendly epistle of her own. She was well and happy, and helping her mother to run the estate. All was well in the village; none of the disturbances of the cities had penetrated our sleepy and peaceful countryside, and they'd had no visitors, either. The big news, Flora wrote, was about Pierre. Sadly, his mother had died a few months ago, carried away by a summer cold. But he would not be alone to look after his little sister, for he was getting married, to a girl from Nantes, called Anne. Flora wasn't at all sure she was good enough for Pierre, but there was no doubt she was pretty, and she had a bit of land of her own which her father had given her as a dowry. And how were things in England? Had I met any interesting people there? I must make sure to tell her all about it. She signed off, 'your humbly affectionate friend, Flora', and I don't know how often I kissed that dear signature, that symbol of her charming, insouciant self, thrilled beyond saying that she was still free, that the baron had not made an advance.

I wrote back post-haste, of course, trying to be as entertaining and interesting as possible, and through the months kept up a regular, eagerly awaited (at least on my side!) correspondence with her. I started to send her poetry—though just the odes I wrote about nature; I was too shy yet to send her anything more intimate. Yet as the months passed, I imagined her letters were becoming more affectionate—and thought that maybe, maybe, she was allowing herself to be wooed, ever so gently.

As to Edmond, I heard from him infrequently. When he did write, it was all about how he was contributing to revolutionary papers, painting portraits of revolutionary deputies, and going to revolutionary philosophy discussions. In obedience to the spirit of the new age, he announced he was dropping his *particule*, the *de* which indicated his noble blood. So I was now to write to him as 'Edmond Bellegarde' or 'Citizen Bellegarde' if I wished. Several of the radicals with noble blood, such as Robespierre and Saint-Just, had done this already. I must admit I thought it too ridiculous for words; but I was also troubled, knowing it was a complete rejection of his father and all he stood for—though no doubt Edmond was still accepting Charles de Bellegarde's money. He would have seen it as his due; as guilt money.

But I was also saddened because Edmond's new enthusiasms played havoc with the quality of his letters. No more gaiety, irony, or amusing asides. No more quick sketches or cartoons, either. Now he went in for page after page of pompous polemic and philosophy which I only half-understood. I certainly had no idea what was happening to him as a person. Did he meet any girls? Was he enjoying life? There was no clue.

And when I wrote to him, he hardly bothered to reply to my jaunty descriptions of English life and manners, other than with an airily dismissive commiseration about how I must be bored with ordinary life and ordinary people in a dull country that had no understanding of revolution. I began to think that maybe I would not like this new Edmond any more, and that our friendship was only a relic of the past.

Seven

December 1790 brought me very good news. Two of my nature poems had been accepted for publication by two different magazines, and duly appeared, one in *The Gentleman's Magazine*, the other in *The Annual Register*. The Wills family was delighted. Jonathan joked that now I was a fully fledged Englishman of letters I must start making political speeches and statements as so many other writers were doing, arguing over the turbulent events in France. But even if I'd wanted to do so, I had no idea what I really thought about the situation. I changed my mind about it practically every week.

Sometimes I read the daily reports of riots, disturbances and killings with a sinking heart. What if the doomsayers were right, and bloody catastrophe was about to descend on France? But then you couldn't trust all you read, especially something about France in an English newspaper! Many people here hated the Revolution and what it stood for. Many hated France herself as well. Maybe they were exaggerating things, on purpose.

Besides, how could you be young and *not* be inspired by the hope of change, by the glorious adventure of it? How could you want to keep the old world, with its many injustices and abuses, where what you were born to decided your fate? 'Man is born free and equal and everywhere he is in chains.' How could you not be thrilled by the prospect of freedom? I was a bit worried by some of what Edmond and his friends said, but I understood them, nevertheless. There was no good reason at all for things to stay as they were.

So I was not convinced by the pessimism of Mr Wills, who was dead against the Revolution and who said that 'the agitators must get you young, before you really know deep within what you'd really die for—for in impulsive youth they can *tell* you what you should die for, they can make you take life itself, God's greatest gift, as a thing lightly to be tossed aside.'

But that, I told myself, came from a very personal source: for rather to my surprise, and Mr Wills' intense disapproval, Jonathan had begun frequenting political meetings, such as those of the Constitutional Society, and the Revolution Society. He was neglecting his studies to do so, and quarrelling with his father.

That was a frequent occurrence in those days, in both France and England; young men defying their fathers politically and socially. The printing presses churned out pamphlets by the dozen, for and against what was openly spoken about now as a real revolution, across the Channel. A new spring for Europe, they proclaimed, loudly. A new dawn for man!

There was a tense atmosphere even in London, and rumours the government would crack down severely on all this talk of treason and sedition and support of foreign revolutions. There was talk of secret documents being passed back and forth across the Channel, and armies of spies from both countries watching and listening, both to their own people and to foreign agents. Dark conspiracy theories abounded. Some people saw the meddling hand of foreign governments in the troubles in France; some émigré French nobles in Austria even claimed that the radicals were in the pay of England herself, cooking up mischief for her old enemy! This seemed ludicrous to me, given the anxious atmosphere in England.

Jonathan was right. Every author under the sun thought they should rush into print about the biggest issue of our times. Some went further than words. The American Revolution fighter and firebrand, Thomas Paine, spent most of his time shuttling back and forth between England and France, loudly rebuking those, like the eloquent Irish lawyer Edmund Burke, who saw nothing but bloodshed and catastrophe looming for France. Anything could happen. Anything! It was exciting, in its own strange way. It was exciting, to be living in the middle of such important times. But still, I didn't feel inclined to go back to France. Not yet. Truth to tell, I was hoping to make a little money and a name for myself in England—and then maybe I'd feel as if I could hope that in the future, I could ask for Flora's hand. For she was still unattached, living quietly with her mother, apparently uninterested in any suitors. I had begun to hope that perhaps it might be for my sake.

Then, just before Christmas, I got a disturbing letter from my mother, which changed everything. I had sent her and Father a copy of the magazines in which my poetry had appeared. She wrote thanking me and praising my work, telling me how my father had showed the poems to everyone he knew, even those who did not have a word of English.

You know, none better, my dear son, your father's views on literary men. But Monsieur Wills has greatly reassured him as to your application to your legal studies as well. And this is what we wish to tell you—we would have no objection if you chose to stay in England, and perhaps be called to the Bar there. He says that he could arrange for you to become an English subject in time; and that he would help to open doors for you. Your father and I think this may be a good idea, in view of the perilous circumstances in our country. He sends word to you that if he were younger, he would do the self-same thing. But he must stay, as

must I—there are two things in our lives that are most
important, at our time of life: the safety and future of
our child, and the familiar love we have for our home.
Neither of these will we sacrifice. Everything else is
unimportant.

Your affectionate Mother.

Burning with annoyance, I took the letter to Mr Wills.

'Yes,' he said gently, when he'd read it, 'I have indeed advised your parents that in my view you should stay here. It is plain to me that France is on a course of destruction. Able and sensitive young men such as yourself—'

'Sir,' I interrupted, 'I am more than grateful for your family's kindness and hospitality. But though I like England very much, I am French, you understand!'

'I do understand,' said Mr Wills, 'but I believe that you have found a life here which may be very well-suited both to your temperament and inclinations. Better than your native country, at least for the moment.'

'I do not know that yet,' I said, trying to control my temper. 'I do not even know what is really going on in France, only what's been reported in the newspapers and journals. And everyone says different things. I cannot believe things are as bad as Mr Burke paints them, nor as good as Mr Paine does. But sir, you must understand—I cannot just abandon my parents and my

55

country, because of apprehensions about some imagined future.'

Mr Wills looked at me, smiling a little sadly. 'You are a decent young man, Jacques,' he said. 'And you have the courage of youth. But I am old enough not to be ashamed that I am afraid. I fear a civil war can be the only result of events in your country.'

'Oh sir, but—'

'Listen to me, Jacques,' he said urgently, 'you know we had a revolution here ourselves, a hundred years ago. King Charles was more of a tyrant than your Louis, and he had abused power but it went too far. It always does. We got a terrible civil war. And then we got Cromwell and his Puritans, instead of the King. We got *good* men—men determined to make us perfect. They knew what was best for us. They alone knew God's will. So they took away the old pleasures, the old beliefs, the old things. They strove to make us into new men. But when Cromwell died, do you know what people did? They danced on his grave. They rejected the Puritans and everything they'd stood for. And they welcomed back the monarchy.' He looked at me. 'You see, we never wanted the tyranny of the King—but equally we did not want the tyranny of Heaven's republic.' He sighed. 'I can see you think this is of no relevance to France, and perhaps it isn't. These men who are bent on the destruction of the old order, they speak like idealistic revolutionaries, but it is my belief it is *power* they want, absolute power. They speak of the General Will, the way the Puritans spoke of God's will, but it is *their* will which must dominate. Take care, Jacques—if you follow Paine's teachings and throw out all the lessons of history, you'll find yourself repeating every costly mistake of the past, while adding more of your own.'

'*I* don't follow Paine,' I said, a little crossly. 'I don't follow any of them. That's Jonathan's way—not mine.'

'Ah yes,' he said, sighing heavily, 'you are quite right to reproach me with my son, Jacques.'

I coloured. 'I wasn't trying to reproach you, sir.'

'I know you don't think so,' said Mr Wills, 'and I am perhaps only showing my own self-reproach. But you must know my son is a man who lives on the edge of life, and he is running to danger as a wolf runs to his prey. You are different, Jacques. He will thrive in the midst of blood and danger and plots but you will not. Oh, don't look like that; you're as brave as he, but you do not court risk for its own sake. I love my son dearly, believe me. Yet I can only put it like this: though I would trust you with my daughter's happiness, I would not trust my son with that of my friend's daughter.'

I was astonished. 'But sir, Jonathan would never insult a woman's virtue.'

'It is not that,' he said impatiently. 'Virtue, vice—what does it matter to Jonathan? He is after much bigger game. He does not see the effect he has on a woman, or indeed on anyone else, because he is living in a different world to most people, most decent, ordinary people. Perhaps he is a man for this time; his peculiar talents will suit this new world. But he is not like you, Jacques. Not like you at all.'

I was stung. Decent and ordinary indeed! If he'd thought I'd take that as a compliment, he was wrong. 'Sir, my mind is made up. I will finish my year's study and return to France as soon as practicable. I do not know what I think of this new world yet, but I know only that I cannot abandon the ones I love.'

Mr Wills smiled that sad smile again. 'Very well, Jacques. You must do as you see fit. And I admire you for it. However, I urge you to think carefully about your future. Regarding your parents, despite your mother's words, I believe we may well be able to persuade them to come here. I know my wife would be very happy to have more of your mother's company, and I think your father's long experience in the French legal system may well be of interest here. There are already, as you know, people emigrating to this country from yours.'

That was true. It was common now to see French people in London, exiles from the troubles. There had even sprung up businesses to cater for them. There was an inn or two which some of the émigrés frequented, to complain and reminisce and plan mad schemes to halt the revolution in its tracks. I couldn't see my quiet, modest parents in such frantic company. They would hate all the wild talk. They would pine for their own home, their surroundings, friends, work. I knew exile wasn't a fate I could wish on them.

But I didn't want to antagonise Mr Wills any further, for he had been so kind to me. 'I certainly do not mean to give the impression I don't want to come back, sir. I just need to go and see what things are like, for myself. If things are as bad as you fear, then I shall try and persuade my parents to come here with me.' I hesitated. 'Do you understand, sir, that I must do this?'

'Of course I do,' said Mr Wills gently. 'Whatever happens, you will always be welcome among us, Jacques, should you choose to return.'

Eight

Bad weather delayed my departure for a while but, eventually, in late January 1791 I made my way back across the water and into my own country. I arrived in Boulogne on a very cold but sunny afternoon, and took a bed at an inn while I waited for the coach that would take me south the next day.

Over dinner, I fell into conversation with a middle-aged doctor, on his way to England with his wife and daughter. The women were not at table; the doctor told me that his daughter was near collapse after a terrible riot in their home town, near Paris, which saw several people killed, including his sixteen-year-old assistant Etienne. 'A Jacobin orator turned up and incited a mob, who went looking for victims. Unfortunately, they found poor Etienne, among others. A witness told me he had the imprudence to laugh when they asked him to identify himself, and ask by what authority they were doing this. That sealed his death warrant. They killed him and hacked off his head, and paraded it along the streets, with those of the others they'd murdered. My daughter saw it from a window.' He paused, and wiped his forehead with a handkerchief. 'Later, I went to the municipal authorities to try and get some justice. Not against the mob, because that is pointless—but against the man who stirred them up. A man called Casgrain.'

I stared at him. 'Casgrain? Jean Casgrain?'

'Yes. Do you know him?'

'I do not know him. I have heard of him.' I faltered.

'Then you will know he is a devil,' said the doctor, and his eyes blazed. 'I demanded they have the police arrest this man, but they said it was impossible. He had committed no crime and was not responsible for the mob's actions. They said Etienne's death was very sad, but implied he had brought it on himself by his rash actions. In short, they refused not only to prosecute, but to investigate.' There were tears in his eyes. 'He was his parents' only child. They are modest people. Their dreams were all for their son. Their lives are shattered. Their hearts broken.'

There was nothing I could say to comfort him. I took my leave of him very soon after, oppressed by his story, afraid of its implications. Edmond was staying in the house of a man who incited mobs to murder. What was my old friend doing, allying himself with such men? I must speak to him, I thought. I must try and speak to him, make him see sense. Edmond might have revolutionary fire in his blood, but he had never been an apologist for murderers. Surely he hadn't changed so much as to be comfortable with such things?

At last, I fell into a fitful and restless sleep, and straight into a ghastly nightmare. I was a helpless observer at the edge of a crowd. It was a crowd swarming like jackals around a bloodied, broken figure. I heard howls of inhuman glee, I saw hands red with blood hacking at the man's head, and holding it aloft. And with a cry of horror that woke me up, I saw that the mutilated face looking back at me was my own.

Nine

The terror of that nightmare was still with me when I boarded the coach that would take me home. But the long, slow journey somewhat calmed my fears, especially as my fellow passengers seemed quite relaxed, normal and cheery, and from what I could see outside, little had changed in the provinces since I had left. Gradually, as I sat in the corner of the coach and listened to the others' conversations, the horror of the nightmare, and the doctor's story, faded from my mind.

People seemed the same as ever. They grumbled about the new laws and taxes just the same way they had grumbled about the old ones. They spoke of their families, of their business dealings, of plans for the future. As the hours passed, I lost interest in all this ordinary talk, and fell asleep, and this time there was no nightmare waiting to ambush me.

Finally, I was home. Mother welcomed me with kisses and exclamations, and Father shook my hand and told me he'd want to discuss the finer points of English common law with me one of these days now I was such an expert. They seemed quite calm and composed; it was only after a good meal, and a sleep, that I realised they both looked older, anxious, the grey hairs sprouting thickly now through Father's black hair, the lines of worry at Mother's mouth.

Over breakfast that first morning, Father talked politics. The municipal assemblies, of whom so much had been hoped, were useless. Talking shops with no power. Bureaucracy was horrendous; complaints got lost in mounds of paper. Worse still, the National Guard was called out often by nervous municipalities against un-armed protesters. They'd fired on angry crowds, causing many deaths.

The attacks on the Church were being stepped up. All clergy were to become civil servants, paid for by the State and not the parishes. Bishops would no longer be appointed by the Pope. And all clergy would have to take a formal oath of allegiance to the French State.

Some clergymen supported the changes, but most did not. There had been petitions sent to the National Assembly to protest the new laws, to no avail. Priests who signed these petitions had their pay docked or withdrawn. In Paris, many clergymen had already been thrown into prison. Freedom of conscience and religion was supposed to be guaranteed by the new Rights of Man charter, but it was being completely ignored by the very same politicians who had written it.

That was all Father talked about—but when he had left on his rounds, I learned from my mother that it certainly wasn't just political concerns that were besetting my parents. There were much more personal worries. Several of Father's clients, fleeing to England, had defaulted on money they owed him. We had lost a great deal. The financial situation of our family was becoming increasingly serious, and debts were mounting. It was likely we'd have to sell our town house. We'd still have the village house, and we would have to retire there, with only one or two servants.

My parents had not sacked anyone yet, as they knew work was very difficult to find nowadays, with so many employers fleeing abroad. But the time would come when hard decisions would have to be made.

I realised now, rather guiltily, that my upkeep in England had been eating into their finances. I knew I would have to really grow up and get to work. My literary ambitions would have to wait.

Two days after I came back, I went to visit Flora. She seemed very pleased to see me, and though she didn't greet me as a blushing lover but as a welcome friend, I was still hopeful. My heart swelled with every warm word, every friendly glance, every glad smile. We were friends, old friends. So be it. But we could be much more. She hadn't married. She wasn't engaged or even seemingly interested in anyone else. I had a chance. I still had a chance.

Then, at the lunch table, Flora said, 'Oh, Jacques! I almost forgot to tell you—Edmond's coming down next week for a visit. Won't it be wonderful? Just like old times.'

'Mmm,' I said, thinking dismally of how I'd have to tackle Edmond about what I'd heard, and not feeling in the least that I wanted to.

But Flora had not noticed my reticence. 'It will be wonderful, all of us together again. We can go and have a meal with Pierre.'

'Flora, my darling,' her mother broke in gently, 'I do not think that would be a good idea. It would put a burden on Pierre and his family; they do not have enough to go round as it is, with Anne so ravenous in her pregnancy. Yes, didn't you know, Jacques? They are expecting a baby in a few months' time. She is already so big; the midwife says that most likely she is carrying twins!'

Flora's face darkened. 'Very well, then, Pierre can come here. Without Anne, if it tires her so.' There was a sullen undertone to her words I didn't understand.

'He has his own life now, Flora,' said her mother sharply. 'You cannot expect things to stay as they were.'

'She is making him miserable,' Flora said. 'She is not a good woman.'

'She is his wife. His choice. And it is not up to you to pronounce on it,' said Madame de Bellegarde tartly.

Flora tossed her head. 'Oh, very well. I don't care.' She turned to me. 'Come on, Jacques, I want to show you what I've been doing with my little experiments in the greenhouse. I've become quite the accomplished gardener, you know. I intend to restore the Bellegarde family fortunes by breeding an entirely new kind of rose! Isn't that a grand ambition, my friend?'

So, her arm linked in mine, she led me away, chattering about her rose-breeding experiments, and so happy was I at being with her, so close, that my anxieties about Edmond and the company he was keeping melted like snow in the sun. In Flora's company, the turmoil in France felt like an unreal nightmare, easily dispelled in the zestful brightness of the morning.

I called in at Pierre's cottage myself, late that afternoon. His young wife, Anne, was, as Madame de Bellegarde had said, big with child. I can't say I took to her very well, either. She was a pretty little thing, but with hard, suspicious eyes and a discontented expression. And I thought that Marie, Pierre's little sister, didn't look happy. Not at all.

Pierre himself had changed, too. He looked harder. There was a blankness in his face I didn't like. It wasn't because of money worries. He told me he was making a good living at the moment, selling pelts to the tannery in town, and trapping game. And the garden was going well. I thought he was probably smuggling a little again, as well, but of course I didn't pry. Instead, I asked after the army, and he said he had enjoyed it, and had saved a good deal of his pay.

To my embarrassment, Anne then said sharply that he shouldn't even think of going back, that everyone knew the government was running out of money, that the regular army wasn't paying well, and that he should join the National Guard instead. He replied quite calmly but with an implacable look in his black eyes that he could never fight in those units, who were responsible for firing on their own people, for the arrest of priests and the sacking of churches.

She shrugged and said then that he was a fool and that the whole world would pass him by and he'd still be a poor man. I didn't know where to look, especially as he said nothing, nothing at all, to her tirade.

I told him of Flora's invitation only when he had come outside to bid me farewell as I mounted my horse. I didn't want to mention it in front of Anne, who I was suddenly sure would try and stop him. He looked at me and asked quietly if it was really Mademoiselle's wish, and I said yes. So he nodded, and said he'd come, and that it would be a pleasure also to see Monsieur Edmond again, he had seen nothing of him for so long.

'I think we have to assume Edmond's changed a lot, Pierre,' I said, rather hesitantly. 'The people he's been with in Paris, they . . .'

'Yes?' said Pierre, rather absently. I had been about to say something about Casgrain, but thought better of it at that moment. Pierre was busy with his own concerns. Why should I burden him with this?

'I had best be leaving, then,' I said. 'Madame de Bellegarde expects me for supper.'

'*You* haven't changed, Monsieur Jacques,' said Pierre.

'None of this *monsieur* with me, Pierre,' I said lightly. 'This is the age of equality, when all might hope for the best in all of us.'

'Is it, now?' he said, very low. He scuffed with one clog at the ground. 'Are you certain of that?' And he looked at me full in the face then and I saw something in his eyes that I didn't understand. Or perhaps didn't *want* to understand. I'd always thought of Pierre as strong, the rock of ages, granite-hard in his being. But in those eyes I read a kind of bleak unhappiness which made me very uneasy. Just for a moment; then his expression changed, and he said, quietly, 'Will you tell me something? Your father told us a letter had been sent to Paris, about the signing of the oath of allegiance for priests. Has any news come back?'

'I'm not sure,' I said, 'but I believe there is no change.'

Pierre nodded. I said, 'You know Father Jantot won't take the oath. What do you think, Pierre?'

He smiled faintly. 'Does it matter what I think?'

'You know the village better than any of us. What do you think people in general feel about it?'

He shrugged. 'Surely you don't need to ask that. We love and respect Father Jantot. We will support him in whatever he does.'

'Yes. I admire his courage, but might it be perhaps wise to—'

'What? To swear an insulting oath? The government never questioned his patriotism before. What is wrong with these people in Paris, that they should so question the motives of their own countrymen? Or is it that they seek empire over our souls as well as our bodies?'

I stared at him. There was a wild glitter in his eye that troubled me. I said, rather feebly, 'Surely that isn't what they want? They only seek to simplify things.'

He shook his head. 'You don't believe that. I *know* you don't.' He looked hard at me. 'The reformers are mostly fools and windbags, but in the shadows lurk evil men who will visit disaster on all of us.'

'For goodness' sake, Pierre,' I interrupted, exasperated, my heart beating fast. 'Don't start on that. There's no indication of it. The reformers want change. Some are more noisy about it than others. That's all.'

'They seek empire over our souls,' said Pierre quietly,

his eyes burning into mine. 'They mean to destroy the image of God in us and to replace it with one of their own creation. This is *our* God, Jacques. He is *ours*—not theirs, to tinker with as they will. Don't you understand, Jacques, they want control of everything, they want to see into your soul and mould every thought, every feeling, every belief?'

'If that is what Father Jantot's been telling you, then I can only say he is imagining things,' I said, rather crossly, to cover my deepening unease. 'No one can do what you fear. It's not possible. People would not stand for it. We aren't puppets or bits of clay to be moulded by other men.'

'It's not what Father Jantot says,' said Pierre. 'It's what *I* say. Father Jantot says that we must be patient, and that good sense will prevail and the evil men will be defeated.'

'Well, then,' I said lightly, 'you should listen to your priest, Pierre. He has more experience of the world—and of evil—than you do.'

Pierre smiled faintly. 'Yes, *Monsieur*,' he said sardonically, and he turned and went striding back to his cottage without another word, while I stood there irresolute and shaken.

What would happen when Edmond and Pierre met each other again? They were separated now by much more than class or money. They were separated by a fundamental difference in their way of seeing the world. They were at extremes to each other now.

It could lead to terrible unpleasantness. Flora must be protected from it. I must not let either Edmond or Pierre spout their rubbish in front of her. We must keep things on a light footing, have fun together as old friends. We must not talk politics or religion or anything likely to cause what I was sure now would be an irreconcilable falling-out.

I was glad I had not spoken of Casgrain to Pierre. He would have been sure to think that Edmond was tainted with the same evil. And I certainly could not mention it in front of Flora, either. She must be kept innocent of such things. She, alone of anyone else I knew, was untouched by the violent emotions sweeping France, her charm and serenity unaffected. It would be a crime to change that in any way. No, I would speak about it to Edmond on his own.

Ten

Edmond came with gifts from the capital: a beautiful shawl for Flora, jewellery for her mother, and for me, a new volume of poems which he said were the latest craze in Paris. Relieved that he hadn't burdened us with political pamphlets instead, thankful he hadn't become the humourless fanatic I had feared, I put off tackling him about Casgrain. I didn't even feel resentful about the fact that Flora and Madame de Bellegarde asked him far more questions about Paris and his life there than they had seen fit to ask me about England. That was normal; he was family, I was only a friend, and not one from their social class at that.

The meeting with Pierre went well, at least superficially. But after he left, Edmond sighed gustily and said, 'I do believe Pierre looks more vacant than ever these days. What a benighted life these peasants lead! I do not think it much higher than that of animals, truly.'

Flora looked at him, astonished. 'Whatever do you mean, Edmond? You speak as though you don't know

Pierre. He is a good man and, moreover, he is very intelligent.'

'My dear little cousin,' said Edmond, kissing her lightly on the cheek, 'you do not need to spring to your faithful dog's defence quite so quickly. If you do not mind having such relics around you, then why should I?'

'I think you are making a big mistake, underestimating Pierre,' I said, trying to speak lightly, for I was dismayed by his attitude, too. 'He is an extraordinary person. And in this new age of equality, his personal qualities should count for more than his class, shouldn't it, Edmond?'

He shrugged, but before he could reply, Flora put in, 'He's very brave, too. Did you know he fought a huge wolf single-handed last winter? With his bare hands?'

Edmond threw back his head and laughed. 'Pierre the Wolf-Slayer! That would impress a superstitious medieval audience, surely, but not a modern one. We are living in the age of reason, my friends.'

'Is that the age when men do not fight wolves but seek to *become* wolves instead?' I snapped. 'An age when words are used to turn human souls into ravening beasts?'

Edmond looked at me, as did Flora. I regretted my rash words when she said, uncertainly, 'Whatever do you mean, Jacques?'

'Yes, Jacques, whatever *do* you mean?' echoed Edmond. There was a new look in his eyes—a mixture of anger and challenge and contempt. It made my stomach churn and my hackles rise. I longed to throw it back in his face, but I was mindful of Flora. 'Nothing, really,' I mumbled.

'You've been listening to calumny and lies,' said Edmond, unrelenting. 'Being in England has poisoned your mind against our Revolution.'

I flushed. But before I could answer, Flora intervened. 'Please, Edmond, no politics,' she said, linking her arm in his. 'You're not here for long. Don't let's quarrel.' She looked at me, her eyes pleading. 'Please, Jacques—for me.'

'Of course,' I said, my throat painful with unsaid words. Edmond raised an eyebrow. 'Very well, Flora, dear,' he drawled, 'we will do just as you say. How can we not offer all our homage to your beauty and gentleness?'

'Edmond, you are being silly,' said Flora, and I saw the dismay still in her eyes, a bewilderment that caught at my heart-strings. I longed to banish any pain from her gaze. I longed to shelter her, put things right. And so I squared my shoulders and forced the gaiety back into my voice and my manner.

Edmond did not let me get away with it quite so easily. He cornered me a few hours later, when Flora had gone to bed, and we were alone.

'You haven't told me much about what you did in England, Jacques,' he said, stretching out his legs in front of the fire, and throwing back a glass of the excellent claret Madame de Bellegarde kept in her cellar.

'I don't suppose much of it would be of interest to you,' I said, taking a sip from my own glass. 'It was all fairly ordinary. I studied a great deal. I wrote poems—I even had some published. I walked around London with Jonathan, and I went to the country to the Wills family place.' As I spoke, I had a sudden, wrenching memory of the peace and beauty of Willesdene. In retrospect, it seemed like a dream—a peaceful dream; out of time, out of place.

Startling me, Edmond said, with a sideways glance, 'So you didn't go to any political meetings? I heard London is quite mad for it at the moment, and the clubs are full of revolutionary ideas.'

'I wouldn't know about that,' I said. 'You'd have to ask my friend Jonathan. He frequents such places. I didn't. I had no interest in doing so.'

Edmond sighed. 'What is the matter with you, Jacques? Can you really not be interested in the fate of your country, and the great things that are being tried here? Why, man, we're a beacon of light for the generations! It is to us that all the eyes of Europe are turning! Can't you see we are making history?'

'The Black Death also made history,' I said, the words slipping out before I'd actually thought about them. Edmond went scarlet.

'Take care what you say, Jacques,' he said, between clenched teeth. 'You are my friend and I should not like us to quarrel. But by God, you will retract those words!'

'Forgive me,' I said hastily. 'That was wrong of me. I did not mean it, not really. But, Edmond, you must surely see—the tide of history could turn for the good or the bad. I am afraid that some of your new friends—these dreamers, these radicals—they might mean well, but they do not understand that they might unleash some frightful things upon the world.'

He shrugged. 'That is timid talk, for women and Englishmen, Jacques! And I thought you were all for reform. You know the old system was rotten.'

'Not rotten,' I said, 'just sick. Sickness can be cured—rottenness cannot be reversed or reformed. All you can do with a rotten tree is chop it down and plant a new one.'

He smiled. 'Exactly. Trust a poet to find the right analogy.'

'Don't be absurd, Edmond! I think this project to replace everything is wrong-headed, crazy. How can you possibly do it? People will fight you.'

'So they will,' he said, still smiling. 'So?'

'So it will probably mean civil war, Edmond!'

'It hasn't so far,' he said.

'What do you call all these riots and demonstrations? Not all of them are in favour of your new world.'

'Of course there'll always be those opposed to change,'

he said. 'Fools and knaves—people either happy to live in a rotten system because they profit from it, or those too stupid to see it *is* a rotten system. Do you think that the King and his cronies would have agreed to *any* changes, if they didn't feel a little threatened by what might happen if they didn't? Do you think they'd compromise on anything at all?'

'That's nonsense,' I said angrily. 'You know the King wants reform! It was the King who re-convened the parliament.'

'Only because he felt obliged to,' said Edmond, lazily twirling his glass, and smiling a secret kind of smile, as if he knew something I didn't. It drove me wild.

'You and your friends are going too far,' I said. 'I heard your friend Casgrain incited a bloody riot near Paris which resulted in several innocent deaths.'

Edmond looked at me. He raised an eyebrow. 'Who told you that?'

'A man on his way to England, fleeing from—'

'A traitor to his country,' broke in Edmond. 'A man running like a rat!'

'It wasn't he who was hurt,' I said angrily, 'but his sixteen-year-old assistant, who was killed.' I told him the story, hotly, urgently.

Edmond waited till I'd finished, then he shrugged. 'You're out of your depth, friend Jacques. You are prepared to trust the word of a renegade—a man prepared to leave his country behind—over mine. How do you know it wasn't a lie?'

'Why would he bother lying to me? You haven't said anything worth taking into account, and you've just insulted a stranger whom you've never even met!'

'So have you,' said Edmond, refilling his glass, and leaning back in his chair with every appearance of enjoyment. 'You don't know Jean Casgrain at all, Edmond. Yet you presume to judge him. You say he "incited" people to riot. But that is not so. Jean speaks—and the people are awakened to the truth. The truth of their oppression, of the injustices around them.'

'That boy didn't oppress them. He did nothing to them. He was innocent. Just in the wrong place at the wrong time. That was his only sin.'

'Well, I don't know. Even if what you say is true— well, sometimes people do react violently. In an ideal world they shouldn't. But we don't live in an ideal world. We are only trying to make one come about.' He leaned towards me. 'Look, Jacques, when I go back to Paris, why don't you come with me? I'll pay for you—I know your family's short of money. Let me do it, Jacques! I can introduce you to Jean. Make up your own mind about him, and all of us. See if you think we're really monsters, or just misunderstood. Will you do it, Jacques—for the sake of our friendship?'

We stared at each other. I was the first to drop my

gaze. 'Very well,' I said, rather grudgingly. Edmond laughed. 'Good man,' he said. 'Now, how about finishing the last drop of this wine? And tell me—what are English girls like?'

Time is pressing. Nine days have passed since I started this recital. I have less than three weeks left on this earth. Yet while I am writing I hardly see the damp prison walls any more, or hear the thud of the guards' boots, and the rumble of the carts outside as they start on their way to the scaffold, and the howling of the mob outside as they bay for fresh blood. Some of my fellow prisoners are praying every minute of every day, saying their rosaries over and over again; others lie on the floor and stare at the walls, eyes dull with despair, still others fight like cornered rats, thieving bread off each other, fighting over nothing. It is a sad and terrible place.

Yet some of us have also made friends. Strangely, we can speak more freely here than outside the prison walls. Even the guards do not treat us too harshly, because they know we are dead men and women walking. We are a strange kind of society of the condemned, thrown together haphazardly. Some of us are here for armed rebellion; some for being in the wrong faction at the wrong time; some for crossing a person of influence; some for being royalists; some for being moderate Republicans, or extremists, or indifferent, even; some for wearing fine clothes and some for being vagrants; some for being atheists and some for being believers; some for an unwise word or even glance.

One poor old woman, who sings and rocks herself all day and all night, was arrested for 'looking sarcastic' when some wretched busybody in her neighbourhood was ranting about revolutionary virtue. In vain did she protest she wasn't even listening to what he'd said; that admission was enough to damn her, for revolutionary virtue is what everyone must think of, day and night, in thoughts and dreams as well as speech and actions . . .

So it is for them, too, for my fellow prisoners, that I write this, that I bend obsessively over my writing. They beg me to tell them over what I labour; so at night, now, I have taken to reading aloud the bits I have written that day, and they beg me to write more, and faster, and faster, as if, somehow, this story of mine, pushing against our fate, racing against time, is going to save us or at the very least, make sense of it all. Yet it is so huge; it is so inexplicable. I do not know even now how we got from there, to here.

And then I think of Casgrain, standing in that cold room, in Paris, in late February 1791.

Eleven

He was smaller than I'd thought he'd be, having only seen him in Edmond's painting of Hercules fighting the Hydra, and then imagining him as a bloodthirsty orator. Small, yes, with a thin, narrow face, but not slight—he had a wiry strength, a strong handshake, a surprisingly soldierly bearing.

He was about twenty-five or so, plainly dressed, though in good-quality clothing. He wore a neat wig over his cropped dark hair, and his skin was that of a youth; soft and creamy and beardless. The eyes in the hollow sockets were not dark, glittering points, as I'd imagined, but of a clear, untroubled blue.

He smiled as he held out a hand to me. His voice was rich and deep. 'Jacques Verdun, how very pleased I am to meet you. Edmond has told me much about you.'

I murmured polite greetings back. I'll have to admit I was disconcerted. I had expected a wild-eyed fanatic, spouting shrill, murderous nonsense. Instead, here was this courteous, deep-voiced young man.

Edmond caught my eye. 'I think Jacques was afraid he'd find himself in the midst of killers and thieves!'

Casgrain smiled. 'Well, he's been in England. There's a lot of propaganda against us there. And he's from the provinces, where anything new is bound to be suspect.'

'Jacques told me he'd heard an evil story about you, Jean,' said Edmond, to my dismay. 'Some story about a boy getting his head cut off because of your words.'

Casgrain looked at me. He said, 'You mean the riot in—' He mentioned the name of the town the doctor had told me about. 'Ah yes, it was a terrible thing. I was on a lecture tour of several towns. I made a stop in that town. But the riot did not happen on the day I was there; it only occurred days later and was sparked by something quite other. But I heard our enemies were blaming me for it.' He sighed. 'I am afraid that often happens.'

'I told you, Jacques!' said Edmond, beaming.

What was I to say? That I didn't believe him? But perhaps it was true. Perhaps in his grief, the doctor had conflated two separate events. So I said nothing.

Casgrain smiled. 'I hope what you see here will not only change your mind about us, but convert you to our cause. We have a beautiful dream, Jacques—to install the reign of virtue on Earth, and to banish vice for ever. We can always do with more good and honest men to help us in our endeavour—and I trust Edmond's assessment of you as one such man.'

Edmond looked pleased at this praise, but I was panicked.

'I think you misunderstand, Monsieur Casgrain . . .'

'Jean,' he said, waving an impatient hand. 'Or Citizen Casgrain, if you like.'

'Er, Jean, I am only here for a few days. My family need me at home. And besides, I am not really a lover of causes, sir. I do not think that we can change human nature. I do not know what I could possibly do.'

'Oh, don't worry,' said Casgrain, though his gaze had hardened. 'We do not force anyone. And I think you are wrong about human nature—quite wrong. Man in his original element is good. Evil only came with a corrupt system. With proper instruction and legislation, we can not only encourage but *compel* virtue.'

'Surely that cannot be so,' I cried. 'Good cannot be compelled. It is the grace of God that . . .'

'Nonsense,' said Casgrain. 'Of course you can compel it. Or why have laws at all?'

'Because man is *not* born wholly good—because we don't always do what is right, naturally,' I persisted, though I could see Edmond looking crossly at me. He didn't like me arguing with his hero.

Casgrain smiled coldly. 'I can see Edmond is right about you, Jacques Verdun. You argue like a Jesuit. It is most stimulating—but I fear it will bring neither of us light. Still, no matter. You may not be ready to join us—

though I hope you may change your mind. But perhaps you could tell us a little about England—what you saw and heard there, what people think of our cause, what the clubs are saying?'

'I do not think I know all that, Jean,' I stammered. 'I did not really frequent the clubs.'

At that moment, to my intense relief, Casgrain's twin sister, Athénaïs, came in. Edmond had told me on the way to Paris that he and Athénaïs were lovers, and it was easy to see why. She was a strikingly pretty girl, with her brother's dark hair and blue eyes but a lovely figure to match, and mischief rather than intensity in that azure gaze. Edmond had proclaimed to me that his affair with Athénaïs was part of the new order of things: that free and honest love between men and women was all part of the new social contract, and that the old oppressive and humiliating ways of the marriage market would be done away with. He had said this with a great deal of force.

I knew that his father and stepmother, utterly estranged though they now were from him—and in all the time I was in Paris, I did not see them once at Edmond's house, or hear of Edmond going to theirs—still expected him to marry someone from the *right* sort of family. They held the threat of cutting him out of the will, of withdrawing title and estate from him, but Edmond ignored that. Though his stepmother had had a baby, it was a girl, and she could not inherit. Any court of law would back up his claim. There was little they could do. Myself, I thought secretly that it was all very well. He thumbed his nose at them, but he was happy enough to take their money. He slept with Athénaïs, but I doubted that he'd marry her. He was simply doing what young men of his kind and class had always done, sowing his wild oats.

But now I set eyes on Athénaïs, I wasn't quite so sure. She was a woman of spirit and intelligence as well as beauty. You could see that at once. This was no casual affair.

Edmond said, 'Athénaïs, this is my friend Jacques Verdun. You remember, my childhood friend, the argumentative one I told you about?'

I flushed, but the other three laughed. 'Oh, I am so glad to meet you, Monsieur Verdun,' said Athénaïs. 'Edmond told me you are not only most argumentative, but that you are a poet. A real published poet, with an international reputation!'

I coloured. 'Well . . .'

'I hold a little literary salon sometimes, you know, Monsieur Verdun. Just for a few friends and neighbours. I would be honoured if you might be a guest at the next one.'

'Why, thank you, Mademoiselle, it is very kind of you. But I'm not sure if I—'

'And perhaps I can introduce you to people who could publish your work here,' she interrupted. 'Our little journal isn't really suitable, but perhaps Camille and Lucile Desmoulins might help to place it. Our people really try to support artists and writers. Isn't that right, Edmond?'

'Oh yes,' said Edmond, smiling happily at her. 'I've had several works commissioned by wealthy sympathisers of our cause. I'm doing quite well, you know, Jacques.'

She smiled. 'It is very important to have the artists with us, if we are to inspire the people of France.' She led me over to a chair in the corner of the room. 'Now, come, sit down, tell me—how did London look to you? Jean and I visited there a few years ago, but I'm told there have been some changes.'

Jean and Athénaïs Casgrain, orphans but with a small income from their parents' estate, rented an eight-room apartment in the district known as the Cordeliers. It was a modest but lively district, situated near the national theatre house. Here lived actors, playwrights, artists, poets, journalists, printers, typesetters, students, philosophers, young lawyers and radical politicians. As well as a lively social life, the Cordeliers boasted excellent cafes and cheap lodgings. Independent, proud and radical, it had long had running battles with the police. But in these days of reform and freedom of speech, it was left well alone, and the police rarely dared to go in any more.

The Cordeliers was a mini-state that ruled itself. Here the Casgrains had set up their own news-sheet, called

Cri de Paris, which competed with a myriad other fervent little news-sheets in the city. Jean Casgrain himself was closely associated with both Maximilien Robespierre and Georges Danton, two of the most able of the Jacobin leaders, and his star was rising with theirs. As to Athénaïs, as well as being an occasional journalist and a consummate hostess, she also dabbled in painting. It was that which had brought her and Edmond together.

I was glad to know that in his revolutionary fervour, Edmond had not given up on his art. Quite the opposite— as he'd said, he was doing rather well. Not as well as the lion of the revolutionary artists, Jacques-Louis David, but then David was quite a bit older than him, and well-established.

Edmond had his own studio in the Casgrains' lodgings, and he showed me some of the paintings he was working on—large-scale canvases inspired by Roman myth and history. One of them he'd even sold to a man in the household of the King's radical cousin, the Duke of Orléans, who freely gave out money to revolutionary artists and writers. The radicals were great ones for the history of Rome, particularly its Republican era. They saw themselves as living in a corrupt imperial age, the reign of a weak and venal Claudius, and longed to return to the great days of Republican Rome, before Julius Caesar betrayed it.

Like Jacques-Louis David, Edmond had painted

several of the Jacobin leaders in Roman guise. These included a brilliant portrait of Casgrain's mentor, Robespierre, as Brutus—not the Brutus who assassinated Caesar, but his ancestor, the legendary founder of the Roman Republic. There was also a sketchbook full of images from the tumult in Paris—including one he clearly didn't intend my seeing, and which I only got a glimpse of: a horribly vivid sketch of severed heads on pikes, dating from the taking of the Bastille. I could see he was uncomfortable about that sketch, and I couldn't bring myself to say anything. Then he showed me a few sketches he had done while in the village—among which was an arresting charcoal sketch of Pierre, caught, somehow, in that instant when he wore his 'other face'. I thought it was brilliant, and said so. Edmond shrugged and said that he was planning to use all these sketches to devise a whole new set of paintings, an allegory depicting the great events of our time. I thought it was unlikely Pierre's likeness would play a flattering part but, after all, the young peasant wouldn't see it, and it wouldn't matter to him even if he did.

He and Edmond now lived in completely different worlds, and were strangers to each other, I thought. It was true they hadn't had much real sympathy for each other for a long time. It was only their mutual attachment to Flora that kept them civil, as well as the fading memory of friendship. But whereas Edmond frankly looked down on Pierre and thought him and his 'benighted' kind as of little consequence in the great experiment now unfolding, Pierre knew Edmond and *his* kind mattered. He took him seriously. Heaven alone knew what he'd decided, in that stubborn mind of his.

I said nothing of this to Edmond, of course. He would not have understood. For him, as for the Casgrains, and most of those who came and went so freely in the Cordeliers district, people like Pierre hardly existed, and certainly not as human beings like themselves, capable of thinking, and judging, and coming to their own conclusions. They would have laughed at the very idea that such unimportant people might seriously think of thwarting their grand designs for France.

Athénaïs' salon was a glittering and noisy occasion. There were artists, and actors, and poets, and journalists, and most of the prominent radical politicians. They were a varied and amazing lot. There was snobbish, ambitious Manon Rolland and her dull, pedantic husband; there was effervescent Jacques-Pierre Brissot, and elegant Condorcet, once a Marquis. There was handsome, influential journalist Camille Desmoulins and his passionate wife Lucile; neat, fussy little Jacques Hébert, whose dainty manner belied the filthy language of his popular newspaper, *Le Père Duchesne*. There was the lion of them all, big, untidy, hot-blooded Georges Danton and his gentle wife, Gabrielle; and then there was Maximilien

Robespierre, who, in his impeccably cut green frock coat, freshly powdered and dressed hair, shining buckled shoes and snooty dislike of noise and vulgarity, seemed quite out of place in that colourful, disordered, chattering, romantic crowd.

I cannot say I ever imagined that the fastidious Robespierre would become the feared dictator of all France that he is today. The young lawyer from Arras didn't look or behave like a fire-breathing radical. He was tall and slim, with unblinking, almond-shaped green eyes, a little nose and thin mouth set in a narrow, pale, catlike face. Sometimes he wore green-lensed glasses which accentuated the colour of his eyes. He spoke softly—though at great length—and his manner was prim and cold and rather pompous.

With him at all times was his closest friend and disciple, the beautiful young dandy Louis-Antoine Saint-Just, who dressed in the height of extreme fashion, with very high cravats, long curly hair, long, manicured nails, and great golden hoop earrings. That elegant, languid, moody exterior hid a ferocious tiger's heart; later, because of his fanatical enthusiasm for the spilling of blood, the young man became known as the 'Angel of Death'.

I did not meet the famous Jean-Paul Marat that night—the jerky, shambling, smelly, half-crazy extremist doctor and journalist beloved of the Paris underworld, who trailed a sulphurous, terrifying reputation behind him. Everyone courted him, but everyone was afraid of him, for he controlled the mob. At that moment, he was on the run from Lafayette's police again, because of yet another bloodthirsty article in his newspaper, *L'Ami du Peuple*. In any case, though Marat had many associates here, a literary salon was not his element at all.

These then were the men who were to change France for ever, though I didn't know it that night, of course. Yet even then I felt in the presence of an elemental force to be reckoned with. Revolution wouldn't easily be pushed back while such men and women existed. I watched them all night; how they laughed and talked and joked and planned, and watched each other. They were supposed to be friends, but I soon felt that the friendship masked a deeper rivalry.

Typically, it was with Danton I had the most interesting conversation—about Shakespeare, of all things. Danton had lived in England whilst on the run from the police and he was very well-read in English literature.

In fact, Danton was the one I most took to out of all of them. He adored his Gabrielle and his children and was warm, genial and amusing. His dreams of revolution seemed to be more about extending his own pleasures—a good pot of chicken soup, a few acres of arable land, a cheerful family life and a library full of good books—to everyone in France than high-flown notions of Roman virtue or worship of some abstract 'General Will of the People'. His idea of revolution was one I could easily have shared. But Danton wasn't interested in me any more than the others were. Like all of them, he was preoccupied with the great chess game of power, and nowhere did an obscure and uncertain stranger like me feature in it, even as a pawn.

I felt like a dull-witted ghost beside them all. I could well understand Edmond's fascination with them, and his disconnection from his earlier life. For a painter, here was Life, in all its mythological, history-making grandeur, here were dramatic heroes to capture on the canvas. He was one of them, *with* them.

Not I. In my essential being, I shrank from them, their hot words, their dramatic gestures, their restless eyes. But there was also a strange regret that I could not be like them. It must be wonderful to live in the midst of such searing certainties, to know yourself for a hero who would change the world for ever!

But because Robespierre, his closest ally, had praised my 'admirable restraint' to Casgrain, Edmond's friends now quite accepted me as one of their own. Edmond was happy, too, because he thought he'd won me over to his beloved cause.

I went with him and Casgrain to discussions and meetings at the Jacobin Club, and in the gardens of the Palais-Royal, Philippe of Orléans' domain. Such talk there was, in those meetings! More talk than I'd ever heard; more plans than I'd ever dreamed possible, more daring dreams and bold schemes than I'd ever dared to imagine. I had very little to contribute, for though under their influence I tried to imagine such schemes for myself, always my mind kept coming back to Bellegarde, and Flora, and her roses, and my family, and my poetry. They were so much more real to me than any of this talk, though I was beginning to feel ashamed that this was so, to think I was dull-witted and chicken-hearted.

Then one night, I went with Casgrain and Edmond to meet with Marat in his beloved underworld of Paris—the world of the mob, of the *sans-culottes*, of the poorest of the poor, and the criminals.

Marat—dirty, unshaven, smelly, wild-eyed—took no notice of me, raving instead about conspiracies left, right and centre—but Casgrain observed my instinctive reactions to what I saw and on the way home taxed me about them. And I had to admit that what I saw there, in those dirty streets, in those wretched hovels—the misery, the degradation, the violence and suffering—certainly shook me. I had seen nothing like it in our town, or in the village, though Heaven knows there was struggle and poverty enough.

This vicious underbelly revolted me. Human beings— fellow children of God—shouldn't live in such conditions. Shouldn't behave so to each other. There seemed no love here, no softer feelings, nothing. I could see now how that awful, senseless murder of the doctor's assistant had happened. These people were like an alien race. How could they get like this? Could it be true that it was, as Casgrain had said, the system itself that had produced such ugliness and pain? Or was it as the priests had taught us—that the fault lay with human beings? Jesus had said the Kingdom of God was within us—but then, so was the Devil's kingdom.

Casgrain said that I was missing the point. Human beings were born both good and free. And everywhere we groaned under the yoke of evil, everywhere we were in chains. All we needed to do was break those chains; then free, virtuous Man would stand proudly under the sky. He spoke persuasively; but I still wasn't convinced. I thought of the mob killing the doctor's assistant; I thought of Marat's followers—brutes whose sole understanding of revolution was the joy of cutting throats and spilling blood. Nothing to do with virtue there, nothing to do with making things better, just a terrifying lust for destruction and death which was all the more frightening because it could be harnessed to a high-minded cause. To a *good* cause.

It wasn't that I'd never imagined such creatures before—I'd seen some of the same kind in London, whilst following Jonathan on his prowls into the underworld of that city. Yet it was perfectly plain to

95

me that while Jonathan and his kind sought merely the thrill of rubbing shoulders with the damned, the radicals were quite willing to make use of these beasts in human form.

Casgrain saw my revulsion, and argued with me all the way home about how a true revolutionary must swallow his disgust, how such unpleasant people were necessary to the revolution, if the reign of virtue was ever to come. 'Maximilien says that without terror, virtue is powerless,' he said cheerfully. 'Virtue must be able to impose her will. But once her reign begins, there will be no more need for terror. Even those whom you fear now will be transformed by proper instruction.'

'Why not transform then *now*?' I said hotly. 'Perhaps by example the whole world would be transformed, without bloodshed or cruelty or turmoil.'

Before Casgrain could answer, Edmond snapped, 'You ask the impossible, Jacques. You do not live in the real world if you think that is possible.'

'And you *do* live in the real world, I suppose,' I snapped back, 'believing in stupid fairy tales about transforming the damned, who'd cut your throat as soon as look at you. The mob is a fickle creature, and the criminal an unstable friend of virtue, I would have thought.'

Edmond laughed. 'You really were frightened in there, weren't you, dear Jacques? Don't worry—we are well known in all these dens of vice—they'd not hurt us. Not only do they love Marat, but they really admire Maximilien, you know. They know we're his followers.'

'Fortunate Maximilien,' I said, 'to have his virtue admired by these vicious men.'

'The truest compliment, surely,' said Casgrain, with a faint smile. I couldn't argue any further. They had an answer for everything. Besides, unlike them, I was not at all sure of my ground. It wasn't just the viciousness I'd seen that had revolted me—it was the suffering. It made my blood boil. It also made me feel hopeless—all these centuries of Christian teaching, had they achieved nothing? Man was still a wolf to man, just as in Roman times.

Twelve

I don't know what would have happened if I'd stayed longer. Perhaps I'd have joined Danton's faction. Perhaps not. But Fate took a decisive hand. Two days after our excursion into Marat's underworld, in early March I received an urgent summons to return home. Father had had a stroke.

Paris and Jacobins and political turmoil and philosophical discussions fled completely from my mind as I raced back home to find him in such a bad way that he could not speak, and my poor mother in terrible distress. I set myself to the task of attempting to do Father's work for him, to keep our family afloat, and to try and banish the desperate fear from my mother's eyes. For months, I was unable to lift my head above water. I spent my seventeenth birthday buried in paper. As Father slowly recovered his faculties, I sat at his elbow for hours on end, trying to understand the full extent of the business, getting to know the clients through his eyes.

It was during this time that I learned just what

an extraordinary man my father was; and how much he was respected by other people in the district. As to my mother, I was in awe of her strength and courage during those months, despite her mortal fears about our predicament.

It was at this time too that Flora and her mother really showed their friendship for us. Madame de Bellegarde spoke to her friends and agitated for me to be given extra work, mostly clerical, but all very useful, bringing us extra money at a time when we really needed it.

But at the beginning of summer, we finally had to sell the townhouse, and move to the village permanently. We didn't get as high a price for the house as we'd hoped; there had been bloody riots recently just over the Loire River, in Brittany, and disturbances in our own town, and people weren't really looking to spend their money on property but hoard it in case of worse to come. Still, at least we had a little money set aside now—all the rest of our savings had quite disappeared. And though we did not have much land, there was enough to grow vegetables and fruit and keep chickens and pigs and a cow. We'd survive. Quite well, too, if we were careful.

Unfortunately, we had to dismiss most of our servants and employees. Only our faithful cook/housekeeper remained. We employed a couple of village men casually for the farm work but, with no clerks left, I did all the work of the business, from the merest clerical detail to the painstaking preparation of writs and briefs, with my father's constant guidance.

Then in the middle of this unrelenting work, in late June 1791 came startling, frightening news: the King and his family, panicking at the mounting tension in France, had tried to flee the country, and had been arrested in Varennes! They had then been brought back to the Tuileries Palace in Paris, and put under house arrest.

Rumours ran wild. Some said the King had planned to go to Austria, Queen Marie Antoinette's homeland, and raise an army against France. Some said he was plotting to assassinate the radical deputies. His supporters cried that he had been put in an impossible position, that he was afraid for the safety of his family, that radicals had intended assassinating him, that the mob had invaded the palace, and so forth. There was no way of knowing what the truth was. What was perfectly clear was that Louis had lost his nerve and had played right into the radicals' hands. They could paint him as a traitor now, as well as a tyrant.

Mother and I didn't tell Father for a few days. We were afraid he might have a relapse if he knew. But I allowed myself to discuss it a little with Mother—not too much, as I knew she loved the King and would not want to hear too much against him. But even she was dismayed at his lack of judgement. She was inclined to blame the Queen. Even fervent royalists were rather cool on the subject of 'the Austrian woman', poor, doomed Marie Antoinette.

The whole village was buzzing with the news. Everybody discussed it, even Flora and her mother, who were inclined to say that things would blow over. At least, that's what they *said*; but I saw the anxiety in Madame de Bellegarde's eyes, as she attempted to speak lightly about it in front of Flora. My dearest girl did not appear to show fear, though. She was preoccupied with progress on her Bellegarde rose.

The other person who showed surprising equanimity was Pierre. Partly, it was bone-tiredness—his twins had been born not long before, and they were noisy, fretful infants who woke up every hour all night long. Anne, exhausted by the birth, was ailing and kept to her bed, and so it was up to him to look after the three of them. But partly, it was a lack of surprise. His vision had told him to expect the worst. He knew apocalypse was coming, and it held no fear for him. He would be ready for it.

In the midst of all this turmoil, a letter arrived from England. It was from Jonathan, saying he would be in Paris in the autumn, and would then come and visit us.

It was odd, getting that letter, like a missive from another world. My English sojourn had almost passed from my mind, as though it had been a dream. But I was pleased, still. I had liked Jonathan. I would be glad to see him.

So I told him that of course he must come and stay with us, we would look forward to it. As an aside, I mentioned Edmond and his revolutionary friends, whom he might like to meet, and gave him Edmond's address.

Thirteen

For a while after the King's forced return, there was violent unrest. Mostly in Paris, of course, but in the provinces as well. The National Guard was called out more than once in our district, to deal with angry crowds, some pro-King, some anti. Of course, they still fired at the crowds in the name of the King, but everyone knew the King could no more command troops now than he could make his own decisions on anything.

The Assembly held practically all the power these days and its radical factions, especially the Jacobins, were getting stronger and stronger, setting up networks of agitators and sympathisers in every city and town. Meanwhile, the moderates attempted to calm things down by cobbling together plans for a hotchpotch Constitution which aimed at turning the government into a constitutional monarchy like Britain's, but at the same time incorporating many radical ideas. Eventually, it was to be passed in September 1791—but the new regime would last barely a year. The radicals had smelled blood—the end game was in sight. To make matters worse, the Austrians were making threatening noises; war with them seemed imminent.

It seemed Heaven itself was disturbed by the turbulence. All over the Vendée and Brittany, miracles happened that summer. Our Lady appeared to visionaries, with messages of both hope and warning, and thousands and thousands of people flocked to the places where she had been seen.

Quite a few people from our village had gone on pilgrimage to the sites of the apparitions, including Pierre. The authorities had panicked at the size of these large gatherings and called in the National Guard, who fired on crowds, destroyed shrines and arrested visionaries. Many people were flung into prison. Those from our village had all avoided any trouble, fortunately, and returned home. But since then Bellegarde was seething with tension. And, one morning, that tension came to a head.

Very early, we awoke to the sound of shouting and rushed out into the street to find a municipal officer from the town, a tricolore cockade in his hat, cowering in a menacing circle of villagers at the door of the church. The poor man—he was a rather pudgy, comfortable-looking fellow, whom my father knew slightly from his days in the assembly—was absolutely terrified. Father insisted on dressing immediately and coming out into the street, leaning on my arm. There, he addressed the villagers and asked them what the meaning of the commotion was, and what did they think they were doing, harassing an official who was only doing his duty? Many of them mumbled, and shuffled their feet, and several began to drift away. But a few stood their ground, amongst them Pierre. He had his 'other face' on, and his eyes looked directly through me and Father as we walked rather unsteadily through the crowd to rescue the official. And there we saw he'd nailed a proclamation to the door. Father looked at the proclamation. His eyebrows raised. He said, very politely, to the official, 'Why does our government pick these fights?'

The official's mouth opened and closed. His face still looked pale, his hat was crooked, his wig askew. I looked past him at the proclamation. It said that any priest who still refused to take the oath of allegiance would be subject to instant dismissal. Churches occupied by rebel priests would be resumed and given to other, loyal priests.

The official regained his speech. 'I thought if I came early, there wouldn't be any disturbance,' he said quietly. 'I am grateful to you, Monsieur Verdun.'

'You couldn't come early enough,' said my father, a little sharply. 'Not for this kind of thing.'

The official flushed. 'It's a shame people don't respect law and order any more. Don't they understand they must obey the government? Don't they have respect for the representatives of that government?'

Father looked at him. 'I don't believe they do,' he said gently. 'But then, Monsieur, is that so surprising? Liberty means we are free to choose the path we want; equality that no office, whether it be that of the King or that of a municipal officer, commands automatic respect; fraternity that we defend what we feel to be our own brotherhood.'

'That is sheer anarchy,' said the official, flushing even more.

'Perhaps it is,' said Father. 'But some would say that is what the age demands of us. I deplore it, but it is a fact.'

'A most deplorable fact!' said the official, drawing himself up with dignity.

'Indeed,' said Father. 'Would you like to come and have a restorative glass with us, Monsieur?'

'Thank you. I wouldn't say no,' said the man gratefully. 'I don't mind telling you, Monsieur Verdun, that I feel rather shaken.'

Murmuring comfort, my father led the man away, ignoring the bland yet watchful gazes of the villagers who remained. I turned to Pierre. 'Where's Father Jantot?' I said.

'He's not awake yet,' said Pierre. 'But this vile document will break his heart.' Deliberately, looking into my eyes, he tore the proclamation from the door.

'That won't help,' I said, though secretly I was rather impressed by the gesture. Pierre shrugged, and crumpled the document in one large hand.

'They'll be back,' I went on.

Pierre shrugged again. 'Let them.'

'With National Guards this time!'

'Good,' said Pierre, and smiled—an odd, wolfish smile that sent a little shiver up my back. He really *did* think it would be good, I thought. He really did want to fight them! He longed for it.

'Father will send a letter,' I began.

Pierre interrupted. 'For the love of God, Jacques, don't you see? The time is long past for such things.'

'You *want* it to be,' I said. The breath was hot and painful in my chest. 'You want the civil war to start—the real thing.'

He shook his head sorrowfully. 'No, I don't, Monsieur Jacques,' he said, very quietly. 'I have a wife and children. I want my children to grow up—to grow up in *our* home, in *our* own ways, believing in *our* God, faithful to *our* King, and *our* honour. We never asked for anything else. Why should we let strangers change all that for us, destroy it all on their whim?' He paused. 'I hope there is to be no war. But if it is to come—I will know what it is about. Will you, Monsieur Jacques?' And with these words, he turned on his heel and walked away, and I was left standing staring after him.

But the repercussions we had feared didn't happen straight away. It wasn't just Father's intervention that saved the day—Father told me that the official, after a glass or two of the fragrant herb-flavoured liqueur our cook was famous for, relaxed enough to tell him that in fact he was rather dubious about the whole thing. 'After all, why wake sleeping dogs?' he complained. 'I'm not a lover of the Church, Monsieur Verdun, but I know how dearly our country-people love their priests. It seems a little foolish to me to pick a fight you can't win.'

'Just so, just so,' Father soothed.

'I do my duty,' the official went on, 'and I'm a supporter of reform—I have no love for these puffed up *aristos* and their privileges. But, you understand, Monsieur Verdun, I do not think it is wise to keep picking fights. Change has to come slowly. Too many people are in too much of a hurry.'

'I heartily agree,' said Father, pouring him one more glass for the road. By the time the official finally, unsteadily remounted his horse, Father not only knew that the man would not report the incident but that, if they played their cards right, Father Jantot might be safe from immediate persecution. Bellegarde was not an important place. The authorities wouldn't bother too much with it.

Father Jantot celebrated a special Mass that evening, re-dedicating the village to the protection of Our Lady and Her Son. The entire village was there, all of us, united in a common relief at having been spared, and a common mixture of hope and fear for the future.

Fourteen

August went by without incident, then September. Things calmed down. The Constitution was duly signed by the King, who was released from house arrest. The National Assembly kept debating more laws and more bills. The Austrians toned down their sabre-rattling, but nobody breathed easily. All of Europe was watching us, and not kindly, either.

Meanwhile, the National Guard shot protesters dead in several towns and villages in our region and in Brittany, but nobody, thank God, came to disturb the tranquillity of Bellegarde. People said the Virgin and her child were protecting us, holding us close. Her shrine at the entrance to the village was filled with flowers and votive candles and other offerings, so many that the statue was almost in danger of disappearing under the weight of it all.

It was a beautiful early autumn, full of golden light, and, strangely, one of the best periods of my life. I spent my mornings working with Father, and many of my afternoons with Flora. We walked by the stream, and took tea, and I listened to her playing the flute or reading me the fairy tales of Perrault or Madame d'Aulnoy. Sometimes I read her some of the poems I'd written—the safe ones, on nature. We talked a lot about the Bellegarde rose and the possibility of its success—Flora had written to a rose expert in Paris, who had expressed an interest in being sent a specimen next summer. Sometimes I sat with Flora and her mother in the conservatory and listened to them gossiping, with a great sense of contentment.

Flora had always been my friend, but that autumn, her mother subtly changed her attitude to me—she became warmer, more friendly and open. She also started inviting my mother to come with me, and spent more than a little time in our house. I thought she was frightened and lonely. Most of her grander friends and relations had already left the country. She must have thought of doing so herself. But she was too deeply attached to her home to seriously consider leaving it; and not only her home, but also the graves of her husband and her infant son, who had died when he was just two years old. She did not speak of her worries, or of the situation in the country at all but, at times, I caught a look in her eye that was anything but serene.

As to Flora, she showed no sign of fear. I thought she felt the village was sufficiently far away from the furnace of politics, and her family sufficiently modest, not to attract any unpleasant attention. They were just two women, and their relations with their few tenant farmers had always been good. They had never thrown their weight about. There were several local merchants who were far wealthier than they were. And they had never been politically active, despite being related to Deputy Bellegarde, far away in Paris. So Flora must have felt quite safe. Who would bother her and her mother? Who could possibly profit by their persecution?

Alas, I have to say I was in a fool's paradise too. All I could think of was being in Flora's presence, feeling the warm touch of her fingers on my arm, the laughing glance of her blue eyes, the sweetness of her breath. I felt—I hoped—that she was changing towards me too that autumn, subtly, gently falling in love with me.

There was a new tenderness in the looks she gave me, her face lit up when she would see me coming in at the door, and her fingers would linger more on my arm. One afternoon, she even kissed me; softly, on the cheek, a kiss light as a butterfly, the kiss of a good friend, no more, but which I hoped promised a great deal.

I went home with sunlight in my heart and stars in my eyes, and Mother said I looked as though I'd seen a vision of Paradise. Which I had. That night, in my dreams, the vision grew stronger, more golden, more urgent, and I woke the next morning in a fever of joyous anticipation which fizzed in my veins like the very best champagne. I sat right down and wrote a poem, one of the first I'd written in months. 'The Bellegarde Rose', it was called. It was about Flora, of course, though the image was of her flower, tended with such loving care. It started like this:

Rose of our summer, waking like love
In the secret warm folds of the morning . . .

I showed it to her, the next day, and she read it, and smiled, and said she'd write a tune for it, and then we could both sing it, together. She was as good as her word; two days later, she played me a lilting, sweet tune on her flute which she said was the voice of the rose, answering . . . How happy I was! I could have died, in that moment, and been perfectly content!

I saw very little of Pierre during this enchanted time. Anne had recovered and was on her feet again, but rumour in the village had it that husband and wife were not on the best of terms.

I knew that Madame de Bellegarde had visited them during Anne's illness and had helped them out with several things, but that Flora hadn't gone with her. There was something strained between her and Anne— something that seemed finally to have broken that deep bond of hers with Pierre—for she never talked of him these days, or suggested we visit him or invite him to visit. I have to say I myself had felt a little distant from Pierre after the incident at the church door. It troubled me to think of the violent thoughts going on behind that impassive face. I knew my friend was unhappy, but there was nothing I could do. Life had made its choices, for both of us.

So October came creeping in, and with it came news of Jonathan. I could not spare the time—or the money—to go to Paris, but Edmond had happily offered to meet him, and guide him around the capital. They would both come down to the village later in the month, he said. Sometimes, as I thought of Jonathan and Edmond and Casgrain visiting the *sans-culottes* haunts, I thought I'd like to be a fly on the wall, hearing their discussions. But only sometimes. Mostly, I was very glad I was not in their company, but rather here, in the company of Flora, her mother, and my parents.

My relations with my parents had changed, too, because of Father's illness. I was much closer to both of them, and no longer resentful of Father's desire that I should be a lawyer. I saw them both much more as people now, people who had always tried to do the very best for me, their only son; fine people.

I learned some surprising things about their past. Mother, who was the daughter of a doctor, had been engaged to a well-born gentleman when she met Father, and her cold, ambitious, snobbish mother—who had died before I was born—had not spoken to her again, after her daughter broke off that advantageous union to be with a man who, though a lawyer, was merely the son of a brewer. 'I'd never met a man like your father,' she said, 'so very bright, and vivid, and interesting. It was as if the sun had come into a grey room.'

I learned too that Father had himself nursed literary ambitions when he was a young man, though as a philosopher rather than a poet. He said, laughingly, that he was glad these had come to nothing, and that the world was much better off without yet another turgid tome of self-important reflections on existence. But I was sorry. I thought I would have liked to know him as a young man; and if not, then a book would have been a good thing to know that young man by.

Hesitatingly at first, I began to show him a little of my poetry and, to my surprise, he seemed not only to like it, but to be capable of assessing it, in a fair, informed manner that was like music to my ears. Once, he said to me that he was sorry he had been so harshly against my pursuing a literary career, that he had been wrong, and that I would most likely have made a mark in it. It touched me more than I can say. 'There's still time, Father,' I said brightly, 'I'm not an ancient yet, only a few months past my seventeenth birthday.'

'But you're bowed down with grey worries already,' he said. 'You are growing old before your time. Oh, Jacques. I'm very glad you're here—you have been a great comfort to us—but I wish you were still in England.'

'I don't,' I said quietly. 'I only wish to be here, with you.'

He gave me a sharp look. 'And with others, perhaps?' he said. I didn't trust myself to answer.

'It's a strange time,' he said at last. 'The best of times, the worst of times. I am glad that you—that perhaps these times may bring you a great happiness you could not have dared hope for before—but I am afraid. More afraid than I can say.'

'France may yet ride the storm,' I said, understanding what he meant about Flora, relieved that he had not said it straight out. I was almost superstitiously afraid to talk of it, in case my hopes should vanish in a puff of smoke. 'There is the Constitution now. It is all legal—all parties will have to abide by it.'

'Only if they feel anything for it,' he said, sighing. 'But what party really respects it? Is it more than paper? A law must be held in people's hearts to really work. And I am afraid these dreamers and schemers in Paris take no account of the hearts of their own countrymen. They do not understand their own country.'

'Some of them must, I'm sure,' I said, a little absently because Flora's image kept coming to my mind and I felt warm and benevolent even towards 'dreamers and schemers'.

'No,' he said, 'the times are for the hard and ruthless, not the others. They are not for the lukewarm or the reasonable or the peaceful or ordinary or gentle. Our poor King, for instance—he would have made a good peacetime monarch. But he is not what we need in this furnace of change. Oh, Jacques! I know we cannot choose the times we live in. But I wish to God we could.'

Jonathan and Edmond arrived in the village on a blustery, cold afternoon. They'd had a shocking adventure on the way down. Halted at an inn in a town some way out of Paris, they'd got caught up in an anti-monarchy riot. They narrowly escaped being killed by the mob—because they did not wear a red-white-and-blue cockade in their hats and were taken for royalists.

They'd had to beat off their attackers with the flat of their swords and run for their horses tethered nearby. Edmond was obviously more disturbed than he cared to admit. 'Fools,' he said vehemently. 'They are so ignorant that they imagine putting a coloured ribbon on your hat is a sure pointer to the state of a man's heart! Spies and hypocrites can sport them just as well as patriots.'

'They didn't know you're Robespierre's disciple,' I remarked, 'you should carry a letter of approval from him wherever you go. For how are those brave patriots to know if you harbour the right feelings, otherwise? You look a bit too much like a haughty *aristo*, my friend.'

Edmond frowned. 'Don't be facetious,' he snarled.

Meanwhile, Jonathan was looking more and more

amused. He drawled, 'I see you haven't changed, Jacques Verdun—still just as fond of putting the cat among the pigeons.'

I stared at him. Whatever did he mean? 'I think you mistake me for my friend Edmond,' I said lightly, and took them into the house.

Jonathan stayed with us, while Edmond went to the Bellegardes'. But we spent a great deal of time together, myself, Jonathan, Edmond and Flora. It was like old times, four friends—though with Jonathan replacing Pierre. It was a more comfortable arrangement, I'd have to say, than any including Pierre these days, though once or twice I thought about that autumn three years ago, when we had pledged eternal friendship. But times changed; old vows no longer held. Besides, Pierre was a family man, albeit an unhappy one; these days he had other, much more pressing concerns.

It was a new band of four, and one that seemed happy enough. We talked and laughed together; Edmond and Jonathan vied for who would be the most amusing, the most charming, and told us sometimes hair-raising, sometimes funny stories of their adventures together in Paris. There was some interesting news: Casgrain had joined the National Guard and had been elected an officer. According to Edmond, he was a popular one. *Sans-culottes* and respectable citizens alike had flocked to his unit. He hardly mentioned Athénaïs, though, and I took this to mean he had fallen out of love with her. I didn't ask. You didn't ask Edmond that kind of question.

Jonathan had changed, too, subtly. He carried himself differently; his eyes were both watchful and laughing. He spoke rather like Tom Paine these days. Paine's own frequent visits to France, where he had many admirers, had, so he said, inspired Jonathan to come and see this Revolution for himself—as well as come and see me, of course, he added, laughing.

I asked Jonathan about his family, and he told me that everyone was well, that his eldest sister was expecting her first baby and that he would be an uncle by the time he returned to England. He said that Jane had taken to painting watercolours, very well indeed, and that Mrs Wills had had a little fall in the summer but had recovered from it. He did not mention his father very much and from that I deduced there must be some coolness between them. Hardly surprising, in view of the fact Jonathan seemed to have adopted the ideas Mr Wills most hated.

Edmond returned to Paris after a week. He had a valuable commission he must finish, for an important client. But Jonathan stayed on for a few more days. He seemed to enjoy chatting with my parents, visiting Flora, and walking in the woods with me. When we were alone, he spoke of a girl called Jenny with whom he'd fallen in love, of his sisters, of literature, or of his plans for the future, but very little of his politics, which was his greatest topic of conversation when Edmond was there. I wasn't surprised by that, at the time, I knew that he thought me uninterested in such things, even perhaps naïve in my opinions.

One afternoon, we were heading down one of the sunken woodland paths, talking softly of a thousand things. We came across Pierre. He was sitting under a tree, eating something out of a small bag, his rifle by his side. It was clear he'd been hunting. He looked peaceful, at rest: his long legs were thrust out in front of him, his thick black hair was loose, his wide-brimmed hat pushed back on his head. His sun-brown, handsome, hard face broke into a slow smile as he saw us approaching.

'Why, good afternoon, Monsieur Jacques.'

I felt wrong-footed at once. 'Pierre—please, you know I don't like to be called *monsieur*. This is my friend, Jonathan Wills. Jonathan, this is my friend Pierre Bardon.'

'The Englishman,' said Pierre, as they shook hands.

'Why yes,' drawled Jonathan. 'I hope that does not present a problem?'

'Why should it?' said Pierre impassively.

'Our government doesn't like yours,' said Jonathan.

'Doesn't it?' shrugged Pierre.

A little silence fell. I said, desperately, 'Jonathan's been staying in Paris with Edmond, Pierre.'

'I heard,' said Pierre.

But I thought I heard a note of reproach in his voice and said, 'I'm sorry I haven't introduced Jonathan before. But we've been—'

'Very busy, I know. As have I,' said Pierre coolly. 'I am glad to meet you today, Monsieur.'

'And I you,' said Jonathan. 'Jacques has told me a great deal about you,' he added.

Pierre's great black eyes rested on me for an instant. 'Is that so?' he said.

'You are a man of many talents, it seems,' Jonathan persisted. I found this inquisition embarrassing, to say the least. Couldn't Jonathan see Pierre was waiting for us to be gone so he could finish his meal in peace?

'Monsieur Jacques is too kind. I do what I can,' replied Pierre.

Jonathan nodded at the bag of game. 'Had a good day?'

Pierre looked wary. 'Perhaps,' he allowed.

'You're a good shot?'

Into the black eyes came a flash of temper. 'Some say I am.'

I was beginning to feel distinctly uneasy. I knew my old friend did not take kindly to such curiosity. I said, 'I suppose we'd better start heading back, Jonathan. Mother and Father will be waiting for us.'

Jonathan gave me an odd little smile. 'I suppose they will. Well, Pierre, I am very glad to have met you. Perhaps we shall meet again.'

'Perhaps,' said Pierre again, and I could feel his gaze on us as we farewelled him and turned back down the path again.

'A man of few words,' said Jonathan, when we were out of earshot. 'An unusual man.'

'Why, because he doesn't speak much?' I said, with my own flash of temper. 'That's not so unusual, you know, except among us lawyers!'

Jonathan laughed. 'You are quite right, my dear friend! No, he is unusual because he is a man out of time—a man cast in the heroic mould. It's not just that handsome physique of his—though Heaven knows that's impressive enough—he must flutter the local ladies' hearts a good deal.'

'He's married,' I said, taken aback by this unexpected vision of Pierre as a ladies' man. 'And he's the faithful sort. I'm sure he never . . .'

'I am sure of it too,' said Jonathan, unflustered, 'and it's not just that, as I said. It's something more. He is like a hero of olden times.'

'An Ancient Roman, you mean?' I said.

Jonathan laughed again. 'Like our friends in Paris? No. There are many Ancient Romans these days. It's quite the fashion. No, not an Ancient Roman, with their cities and their ideas of stern Republican virtue, but an Ancient Gaul, perhaps. A Druid, maybe? Or Vercingetorix the warrior? They possess more than strength and courage—they have the force of the land behind them.'

'Pierre's a good Christian,' I said lightly, to mask my surprise at his words. 'He'd hardly thank you to compare him to a pagan warrior, worse still, a pagan priest!'

Jonathan shrugged. 'I'm not speaking to Pierre, but to *you*, Jacques. You know just what I mean. Well! If I was those Ancient Romans, I'd watch out.'

I stared at him. 'You speak as though . . .'

'As though I wasn't one of them? Oh, Jacques. I'm no hero, Roman or Gaul. I'm a watcher. An observer. Tacitus, perhaps, eh? Or Suetonius?'

'Not you,' I said. 'You'd never *just* observe. You'd want to be part of it. What is it you are doing in France, Jonathan?'

'I told you. I wanted to visit you. And I was inspired by friend Paine's writings. I wanted to take a look for myself.'

I stopped, and looked him full in the eye. 'Are you a spy, Jonathan?'

For the first time since I'd known him, he looked disconcerted. Only for an instant, then he shrugged. 'I don't know what you mean.'

I thought of the subtle changes about him, about what his father had said about him liking risk and danger. There was more than one way to court those. I said, angrily, 'For God's sake, Jonathan, how can you do this to Edmond, who trusts you?'

'Do what?' he said, eyebrows raised.

'Come here to report on him and his friends,' I snapped.

'You forget. It was *you* who suggested I should visit him.'

'You know what I mean,' I said hotly. 'You're working for the English government, for Mr Pitt, aren't you? You pretended revolutionary sentiments so you could come into France and infiltrate the radical groups.'

He smiled bitterly. 'Just how important do you think I am? Why should anyone care what I think?'

'It's not you, personally—everyone knows there are lots of English spies here. Maybe even Paine himself is one.'

This time, Jonathan laughed properly. 'I'd give anything to see our staunch friend of the people hear you say that! He might die of apoplexy on the spot. Anyway, Jacques, there are many French spies in England, trying to stir up trouble, too.'

'*Too?*' I pounced. 'So you admit it.'

'I admit nothing. I am here principally to see you, but also to see at first hand this Revolution they're all talking about.'

'It is not a thing I like or trust,' I said, honestly, 'but it is *our* concern, not that of England.'

He shook his head. 'You're wrong. The radicals think their mission is to remake the entire world, not just France. That is only the first stage. After that, the Revolution is to be exported to all of Europe. Jacobin agitators are everywhere in London and other cities already. And they have their English sympathisers perfectly happy to stir things up. Casgrain gives a rousing speech on the matter. You know he is now an officer in the National Guard. He will have guns to back his master Robespierre with now, not just words.'

'I don't like Casgrain much,' I said. 'I distrust him, and all those radicals. But Edmond is one of my oldest friends.'

He put his hand on my shoulder. 'I understand. And I will *always* be your friend, Jacques. Yours, and your parents', and Flora's and her mother's. Never forget that. There may come a day when you need to remember.'

'Heavens,' I said, startled both by the sudden gravity of his tone, and the strange way in which he had echoed that promise we'd made, all those years ago. He seemed to be waiting for more, so I said, a little lamely, 'It's very kind of you, but even should we need to, you're far away in England.'

'There is someone I know in Nantes,' he said, holding my gaze. 'His name is Henri le Goff, he's at rue Sainte-Croix. Don't forget his name. Promise.'

'I promise,' I said, struck by his uncustomary seriousness. Then I added, 'But if it does come to the worst—which I devoutly hope it won't—I am sure we can rely on ourselves—and on our Ancient Gauls.'

'I am sure you can,' he said, without smiling. 'But just remember.'

I was silent a moment, then said, 'You haven't asked me not to tell anyone.'

He looked at me. 'I *know* I can trust you,' he said. 'You're the best man I know.'

I flushed. 'Don't be silly. Does your father know?'

'Oh, he has a suspicion, I think. At first he thought I was turning into a revolutionary, but it puzzled him. He knows I've never been one for abstract ideas. You must understand, Jacques, I am neither a follower of Paine, nor of Burke; neither of your King, nor of your Robespierre, or any of the others. I reserve my judgement on your Revolution. I'm not interested in making a mark in politics or in thrusting myself forward in any way. I'm interested in people, Jacques, and in secrets. I like to live in a world of shadows and to hear things I shouldn't. I like to live on my wits.'

I thought it sounded like hell. 'What about your Jenny?'

'She doesn't ask. And I don't volunteer.' He smiled. 'Speaking of love—did you know, by the way, that Athénaïs has transferred her attentions to someone else? A young deputy by the name of Rousselin.'

'I guessed something like that was in the air! But I thought it was Edmond who had taken farewell of her.'

Jonathan laughed. 'You mistake the balance of power

there, my friend! Athénaïs likes your friend well enough, but she is an ambitious woman and he is just a minor artist, of little consequence. He doesn't have what it takes to be a politician. Rousselin is an ex-actor, but a rising young deputy. He's moving in powerful circles—he's close to Danton. He also has a somewhat unsavoury reputation with women—but that may be part of the attraction. Women love to think they can tame tigers.'

I winced. 'Well, Edmond's better off without her, in that case. And what does Casgrain himself have to say?'

'Nothing much. He's had to keep it hidden from Robespierre, that's all. Our prudish Incorruptible doesn't look kindly on human frailty, especially in the fairer sex.'

'It all sounds very tangled and unpleasant,' I said, as we trudged on. 'I am glad I do not have to live in the midst of it.'

Jonathan looked sideways at me. 'No, I can see Bellegarde holds a lot more attraction for you,' he said, and smiled at my confusion.

The next morning he left at dawn. I was sorry he was going, but also relieved. I thought of him handing in his report to whoever he worked for, back in London, and it didn't make me feel angry any more, just sad. I thought of what Mr Wills had said, about his son wanting to be on the edge of things, running like a wolf towards prey. I thought of Edmond and his friends, in Paris, agitating and making history; I thought of Pierre with his rifle by his side and his 'Ancient Gaul' look, as Jonathan had dubbed it. Alone of all of them, I was uncertain, borne along on a tide of events I could not even see clearly, swept along by a crowd of strong wills I could not even begin to resist. It was I who was out of time: irrelevant, helpless and irredeemably ordinary and lukewarm.

But my self-pity didn't last long. How could it, when I had my Flora, my beautiful Rose of Bellegarde, to be with, and think about?

Fifteen

Something terrible happened in our parish on All Souls'
Day that year of 1791, which destroyed the golden feeling
of peace we'd lingered in for months. A young woman,
daughter of a man from an outlying farm, was found
murdered. She'd been visiting a friend some distance
away, and had failed to come home. Her distraught father
had called in his neighbours to help him in the search;
Pierre was one of the men from Bellegarde who combed
the woods and hedges for her.

Two days after she disappeared, her mutilated body
was discovered. She hadn't been buried, just covered
with leaves; wild animals had already found her. It was
a gruesome sight, Pierre said, when I met him coming
home from the search, his face white and streaked with
mud. His black eyes were bleak. 'Not all wolves go on
four feet these days, Jacques,' he said, quietly, before
shouldering his rifle and trudging off home.

Requiem masses were said for the soul of poor
Mathilde Pernet, and the village men talked excitedly

about the need to track down her murderer and kill him. In the village, there was talk of a pedlar known as Gros Jean who had called, with ribbons and other trinkets for sale, at Mathilde's friend's house, the day she disappeared. Apparently, in recent weeks, there had been three or four similar, unexplained murders of young women in far-flung corners of the district, in a roundabout route which might be explained by a pedlar's wanderings.

Many people in the village were already convinced of Gros Jean's guilt, especially since he had vanished. The village women were terrified that this bloodthirsty Cain might be waiting to ambush them one dark night; the village men, Pierre among them, spoke of forming a patrol to protect them. Gros Jean, who in life was a fat, unremarkable individual with an obsequious manner, assumed now, in many people's minds, the face and features of the Devil, complete with burning eyes and sulphurous breath.

For a while, women went about with a protective male escort. Every able-bodied village man equipped himself with a weapon of some sort, whether that was a gun, a knife, or merely a sharpened scythe or stick whittled to an eye-gouging point. We were not immune from the general panic either, and kept our guns well-oiled and ready. For quite a while, I kept a kind of unofficial patrol on the Bellegarde house as well as ours, with Pierre and several other young village men.

But weeks went by, and Gros Jean was not seen again. Rumour said he had fled far away, or even that he had died—perhaps drowned in one of the floods that swelled the Loire River that winter, or perhaps set upon by wild beasts in the woods.

By Christmas, things had almost gone back to normal in the village, though there was still tension in the air. The murder wound like a bloody thread through the peaceful tapestry of village life, and there were many who felt it was a sign of the evil times, and spoke about the pit of Hell opening, and the Devil stalking openly in France. Like the other villagers, I was taken with a fear that had as much to do with the supernatural as fear of violent, cruel men, but I tried my hardest not to show it to Flora who, after the first day, never spoke of the murder or its consequences, but, instead, more and more, of her rose and her dreams and plans for it.

New Year's Day 1792 came and went. It was a very hard winter, again. Heavy snow, which cut us off completely from the outside world for a couple of weeks, combined with sickness to afflict our village. Several villagers died. Father Jantot was laid up in bed; his frail frame looked even thinner by the time he was finally able to leave his sickbed. Madame de Bellegarde caught a chill and was dangerously ill for a few days. Poor Flora was terribly anxious; she sat by her mother's bedside night after night, her eyes red with exhaustion. She would not let me help her; she said I must not get ill, too, and that it was her duty to care for her mother. I had a few desperate days of worry—but, fortunately, Madame de Bellegarde recovered fully, and Flora never caught her mother's sickness at all. Meanwhile, in our house, everyone, by the grace of God, stayed healthy enough. Then just as everyone thought things were getting better, and as the thaw was beginning, tragedy struck Pierre's house. First his sister Marie fell ill, and though we tried desperately to save her, she succumbed within a few days. Then his twins became desperately ill; and though, by the grace of God, they survived, their mother, who had nursed them devotedly, fell victim to it in her turn. And she did not survive.

No one in the village had much liked her. But there was no gainsaying the fact Anne had been both brave and selfless in her care first of her sister-in-law and then her children. At her funeral, the whole village turned out, sad beyond telling.

It was the most terrible thing, too, to see how grief had ravaged poor Pierre. He was like a living ghost in those first few days, and the village women took it in turns to help him with the children, the cottage, the cooking. Madame de Bellegarde visited him too, and Flora, and slowly, very slowly, he began to recover, though for months he never smiled and hardly even spoke a word.

The snow finally cleared. The horrendous winter was at an end. Spring was in the air. But nothing would ever be the same again in Bellegarde.

A few weeks into spring, I received a letter from Jonathan. He did not mention the last conversation we'd had, but spoke brightly of how he and his Jenny had been married. They were now peacefully settled in lodgings in London, coming down frequently to the country. They'd had a wonderful family Christmas, at Willesdene. There'd been roast goose, and ham, and plum pudding, and port and claret, and Jenny's father had revealed an unexpected talent for singing comic songs, which had kept them all in stitches.

Reading the letter was strangely soothing. On an impulse, I took it to Flora's house when I went to see her one afternoon and, translating it, read it aloud to her. It was the right thing to do. She'd liked Jonathan; she didn't know anything of his double life and, when I'd finished, she asked me to describe Willesdene again to her, and the family, and what one might do there. I talked and talked, embroidering a little here and there. When I stopped, at last, out of breath, she said, softly, 'I love your stories, Jacques. They are like fairy tales, only real.'

'Would you like me to tell you more?' I asked, clasping her hand.

She smiled. She took her hand gently away. 'Yes, I would,' she said, and sat back in her chair, her eyes closed, as I began to tell her a vastly inventive account of my adventures in London with Jonathan, leaving out anything horrid and turning it all into a picturesque adventure. By the end of it, her eyes were open again and she was laughing. The sparkle was back in the eyes that had grown altogether too solemn and fearful in recent times.

Blustery April arrived and, with it, unexpectedly, Flora's Uncle Charles, from Paris. He had news: his wife Béatrice, their infant daughter Solange, and Béatrice's parents and brother had already left France and fled to Austrian territory in Belgium, where Béatrice's mother had close relatives.

The Darmants, already nervous at the growing power of the radicals, had heard a rumour that anyone who had Austrian connections would be arrested, for war was imminent. They sold up all their property and fled. Charles de Bellegarde wanted Flora and her mother to join his family. But Flora's mother refused. She had no Austrian connections, she told her brother-in-law. She was a good Frenchwoman, with not a drop of foreign blood in her veins. Why should she be panicked into leaving? Besides, if she and Flora emigrated, their property would be seized. It was family property—they couldn't just abandon it, and neither would they sell it.

Charles de Bellegarde told her such things could be

easily arranged; she just had to appoint a trusted lawyer. He then haughtily informed her that as the oldest male in the family, he was responsible for his womenfolk's protection, and that he felt it his duty to warn her of the danger in which she might stand. Flora's mother told him tartly that so far she and Flora had coped perfectly well with the dangers of our time, and would continue to do so in the future. Everyone in the district knew who they were, and they were on civil terms with everyone. When her exasperated brother-in-law told her she was being a blind fool, that loyalties changed quickly, that people could turn on her in a trice, she retorted that politicians must mix with some very unpleasant people, and judged the whole world according to their lights.

Flora, who told me all this, smiled with unfeigned delight at the memory of the baffled fury on her uncle's face then: 'He's always been a bully,' she confessed, 'and I've always been a little afraid of him. It was splendid to see Mother standing up to him!'

So Charles had to leave Bellegarde without Flora and her mother. Short of kidnap, he could not have changed Madame de Bellegarde's mind. I was very happy, of course, that they hadn't gone; but I was also uneasy. Charles de Bellegarde was a consummate politician, a go-between for many different factions. He had many connections throughout Parliament, and the administration. He knew a great many secrets. He probably knew much more than he had told. His survival instincts were sharp. If he thought the women were in danger, perhaps they were indeed.

I decided to write to Edmond. His father, so Flora said, had not even mentioned him—the estrangement between them seemed to be profound. And if Edmond's father was now going to leave France and join his family, the break would be permanent.

I think, in the back of my mind, there was also an idea that if the worst came to the worst, and the radicals did take over, then Edmond's connection to the Jacobins would protect his cousin and aunt. I thought that if I hinted at this in my letter, Edmond would understand and would take whatever measures were necessary.

He wrote back harshly, passionately, shockingly. The letter's contents were burnt into my mind.

My father is a fool as well as a traitor. By fleeing to Austrian territory with his family, he has shown where his real sympathies lay, like so many of those around the King and his cronies. Of course Jean Casgrain and my other friends know where my heart is, with the patriots and the Revolution, but it is nevertheless painful to know that a small doubt as to my soundness might have been implanted in their minds, because of my father's foolish actions. Mind you, I blame that woman Béatrice especially. She always was a harpy. It is her fault. But from this day forward, I have no father. I recognise no one from that family, no one. I have cut off all ties with them. I will refuse any further communication from them. In any case, I do not need my father's money any longer. Not only am I selling my paintings, but I have joined Casgrain's National Guard unit. I am being paid a soldier's wages, Jacques. It won't make me rich, but it will pay for my keep. And I will be doing my patriotic duty.

As to Flora and my aunt, I'll thank you not to teach me my duty towards them. You are to tell them this: if there is trouble in the countryside, they must come to Paris. I will look after them here. They will be safe with me and my friends. They are in no danger from them. Why should they be? It is only tyrants and traitors like my father who should tremble.
Liberty, equality, fraternity—or death!

Yours,
Edmond Bellegarde

I can hardly describe the swirl of emotions I felt when I read that letter. Shock, yes, at the violence of the sentiments; but a wild anger, too, at its dismissive and haughty tone. He wrote to me as though I were a nobody to be reproved. I was his oldest friend, but it seemed his new friends deserved more consideration! Underneath it all was sadness—a sadness too deep and too bitter to be just a nostalgic yearning for the peaceful past.

Edmond a soldier! I couldn't see it—he might know how to strike an attitude, and he certainly did not lack courage, but how could he put up with the discipline of army life? He always thought he knew best. Taking orders, surely, would not be much to his liking. Still, in this new kind of army, perhaps that would not be so much of a handicap. And if his new best friend was the commanding officer, anyway, he would be safe enough from any problems.

I gave an edited version of what he'd said to Flora— just about how he was permanently estranged from his father and stepmother, how he'd joined the Guard, and how he'd said Flora and her mother should come to Paris. To my dismay, Flora looked pleased. Of course, she shared Edmond's dislike of his father and was perhaps secretly proud of her cousin for throwing his father's money back in his face. But what did really surprise me was her reaction to the idea of going to Paris. Her eyes shone, her cheeks flushed, and she began chattering about how she wanted to take a slip of her rose there. She said she'd dedicated the rose to Our Lady, that it was to be called the Lady of Bellegarde, that it was important and beautiful, and so on. I listened to her, unable to believe my ears, my heart sinking. For the first time, I considered the notion there was something wrong with my beloved girl—something really wrong. How could she possibly think of *roses* at a time like this?

But her mother soon put a stop to any nonsense about Paris. 'That boy is as big a fool as his father. As if I would go anywhere near those terrible men who are making the unhappiness of France! I will write and tell him that I do not like the company he keeps any more than I like the company his father keeps, and that I have no intention of leaving my home. It is here we will be safest, surrounded by our own people, not among devious, two-faced strangers in Austria or in Paris!'

I thought that Edmond would not take kindly to this reproof, but nevertheless I was glad. He deserved it. And I was glad to see, too, that Flora, after a small protest, seemed to accept her mother's verdict, and stopped talking of going to Paris.

Sixteen

My quill grows eager, my hand races over the paper. I cannot stop, to eat or sleep or even to think. In my disordered memory, it seems to me that the flight of Edmond's father and his family mark an evil omen, a point at which events, in the country, and for us in Bellegarde, began to move so fast, so violently, that all the anxious and uncertain time before seemed in contrast like a long, slow, golden dream. The wheels were unstoppable; bloody-handed History was upon us in her scything chariot, crushing all in her path, reaching for our throats. The Angel of Death had begun his final descent towards us, his black wings blotting out the sun.

In April of 1792, the thing Flora's father had warned of came to pass. The parliament, which had become dominated by the radical party known as the Girondins, allies of the Jacobins, declared war on Austria and Prussia, against the King's wishes. His scruples were not appreciated by the Paris mob. They tried to storm the Tuileries Palace, baying for the Queen's head.

She was influencing the King! they screamed. That wicked foreigner was making him weak towards the Austrians! She would make him commit treachery towards France! They'd always hated the poor Queen—the pamphlets and speeches against her had been foul from the beginning, much worse than what was said about the King. She was too pretty, too flighty, too meddling. Too foreign, especially.

The mob was only repelled with great difficulty. But after that, anyone who had Austrian connections was indeed in great danger, and many people left very hurriedly. The parliament was full of yelling, shouting deputies, many of them openly calling now for the violent overthrow of the King and the immediate setting up of a republic.

There were pitched battles in the streets—not only in Paris; all the cities and towns were overtaken by a kind of madness. In many places, business came to a standstill. Employees refused to work, preferring to run to meetings and demonstrations and street battles. There was looting and general disorder everywhere. Though the National Guard was supposed to quell the rioting, many of its members openly supported the overthrow of the monarchy, and did little to quell those disturbances. I was sure the unit Edmond was in, responsible for the radical municipality of Paris, would most definitely be one of those. They'd probably happily join in those street battles themselves, encouraged by the fiery speeches of their Citizen Officer Casgrain!

In the midst of this chaos, war broke out. The Austrians and Prussians, who in the past had been enemies, were now united in their hatred of the French revolutionaries, and determined to destroy them. Our army's first attacks, surging over the border, were quickly parried. The soldiers were neither well-prepared nor well-disciplined, and over the next few months they kept losing battles, the enemy pushing the army back, back, poised on the frontiers, and in some cases pushing over them. It had become a fight to the death—and one we were by no means certain of winning.

There was panic in the whole country. Everyone, even in Bellegarde, which was far away from the field of battle, was sure the foreigners were going to overrun us. Martial law was introduced in many districts, there were food shortages everywhere, and fear in every heart, whether royalist or revolutionary, as well as all those who had no politics at all. The ships headed for England were full to bursting with exiles.

Then came news which could only inflame the situation further: all priests who hadn't yet signed the oath were to be regarded as traitors, arrested, and deported. Riots and demonstrations broke out anew, as nonconformist priests were dragged out of their churches, beaten and imprisoned, with other priests, who had sworn the oath, being installed in their places.

One fine morning in June, the National Guard turned up at last in Bellegarde to arrest Father Jantot. They were too late. The priest had vanished.

What had happened was this: a week before the 'Blues', as the villagers called them, had come marching into our village, Pierre and three other men, including two of Father Jantot's nephews, Raoul and Robert, had set off with the old priest deep into the woods. Before he left, Father Jantot celebrated a last Mass for us all. The church was packed to the rafters. With tears in his eyes, he told us that every Sunday at midday, wherever he was, without fail, he would say Mass. 'I will be here, in this church, in spirit,' he said. 'Come here at that time every Sunday, and a Mass will be said for you all.'

He begged our forgiveness for leaving us, but said that he had decided that staying would only mean his immediate arrest and inability to minister to his flock at all. He hoped he would only have to hide for a little while. He was a loyal Frenchman. He hoped the government would come to its senses.

There was a forester's hut, deep in the woods, where he would live. Pierre and the other men would take it in turns to guard him. They all had rifles, and they were all skilled woodsmen. They would make sure our priest had everything he needed; would shoot game for him, and bring food from the village. He would sit it out, and wait. There was nothing else that could be done.

When the National Guard came that Friday afternoon, Pierre was away. It was his turn to be with Father Jantot. The soldiers brought with them a priest who had sworn the oath, and who was supposed to be our priest's replacement. I wouldn't have liked to be in his shoes as he walked down the long twisting lane to the church, the silent crowd gathered around, saying nothing, doing nothing, just staring. But then, he was not the kind of man who seemed affected by the palpable hostility, at least not at first. He was a small, round, bustling, fair-haired man with bright button eyes and a firm mouth, and he wore a tricolore cockade in his hat. By his accent, he was from somewhere in the north of France. He addressed the sullenly silent crowd, telling us he was Father Martin, that he was a good patriot, that he was glad to be serving the Church and the people, and that he hoped we would come to look on him with friendship. 'The time for superstition is over, my good people,' he said. 'True religion is not in danger, however. We are merely returning to the primitive beauty, dignity and decency of the Church, such as it should be. We must imitate the virtue of the apostles and the divine saviour of the world. I hope you will join me in this sacred task of restoring virtue.'

Nobody said anything. The priest didn't look discouraged. He just smiled a little smile, as if he had expected this sullenness, and went on, 'Tonight and tomorrow, I will be receiving confessions. Mass will be at ten o'clock on Sunday. I want the bell to be rung to call the faithful. Who is the bell-ringer here?'

Nobody spoke. Father Martin raised his voice. 'Who is the bell-ringer?'

The Guard captain said, roughly, when still no one spoke, 'Answer him! He is an elected official of the State, and you are bound to answer him!'

A ripple spread through the crowd. Someone laughed nervously. But still no one spoke, or stepped forward. I was at the back of the crowd; the priest's eyes, for some reason, fell on me. He said, 'You, my son, will you tell me?' There was a pleading look in his eyes that suddenly made me feel sorry for him, despite everything.

I said, uncomfortably, blushing furiously, because I could feel the eyes of everyone on me, 'I don't know, sir. People take it in turns.'

'I see,' he said. 'Thank you. Well, if that's the case, I will have to find out whose turn it is, won't I?' He smiled again, and turned to the soldiers. 'Escort me to my quarters. It will be all right. These good people won't do anything against me.'

'We're staying here, Citizen, till you've settled in,' said the captain. He waved a hand at the crowd. 'Go. Go home, all of you, right now. I want to see you all at Mass tomorrow morning.' His distrustful gaze roamed over the crowd, which began to disperse. Unlike the priest, he was a local—or at least from the town. He must have been aware of the depth of hostility here. He must have been aware too that our own priest must be still somewhere in the vicinity. I was sure he'd start looking for him. Rebel priests couldn't be allowed to thumb their noses at the law.

'You, Citizen,' he said, now, startling me. 'You are to come with us. There are questions we want you to answer.'

I wished I'd kept my mouth shut, earlier. I said, 'Please, Captain . . .'

'Citizen Captain,' he said, without a smile.

'Citizen Captain, my father is ill.'

'What in the Devil's name do you think we're going to do to you, boy? We just want you to answer a few questions,' he said, not unkindly. 'Come with me.' It was an order, and I knew it. I fell into step behind them, aware as I did so that village eyes were watching me from every corner, village eyes judging me from behind shutters.

'What is your name, my son?' said Father Martin, as I walked miserably along.

I said, unwillingly, 'Jacques Verdun, sir.'

'You have always lived here, Jacques?'

'We have always had our house here, sir. Before,

though, we lived mostly in the town. My father—he's a well-known lawyer in these parts.'

'Ah,' he said. 'You have fallen on hard times?'

'Not so hard, sir. Not so hard as those many other people have had to endure.' Because he looked kindly enough, I dared to say, 'Including our poor priest, Monsieur Jantot.'

'Ah,' he said, without anger. 'Yes. It is a shame. Believe me, Son, I do not like having to take another priest's living away from him.'

'It's not his living that is of concern, sir,' I said, before I could stop myself. 'It's the fact he's been treated like a traitor, like an unclean thing! He has always been with us, sir—he is a good, gentle old man, full of that virtue you spoke of to us. Why should he be persecuted? He is only following his conscience. And conscience is a sacred thing!'

'Ah, my boy! Conscience itself is only the moral sentiment of good and evil! Does your priest's conscience put me amongst the evil ones, because I have sworn what is only my duty—to uphold the sacred Nation, the holy Constitution? Why, the King himself has accepted it—has accepted all the changes! How then can it be bad? Do such men as your Father Jantot have a sixth sense not given to other men, including other priests, that they persist in their foolish opposition?'

There was passion in his voice now, and colour had mounted in his cheerful round face.

I faltered. 'I'm sorry, sir—I meant no disrespect to you. I am only trying to explain. In the past, priests were not compelled to take any oath of this kind. It was not imagined that they might betray their country. He does not . . . *we* do not understand why what was good enough for our forefathers might not still be good enough for us. We still have the same number of eyes, legs, arms, noses, mouths, as our ancestors—we live, die, marry, laugh and cry just as they did.'

'My poor child,' said the priest sadly, 'I see you are stuck in the same mud as all too many Frenchmen and -women still are. Do you not see that we live in a new age, or at least the dawning of a new age? Do you not thrill to the notion that we might all learn to be wholly good, to cast evil away from us for ever, to live without stain, without sin, like angels? For such is the holy project of the age—a project that can surely only find favour in the eyes of God!' His eyes shone with a fanatic brightness that for a moment seemed to me to be out of this world.

At that moment, the Captain spoke. 'Citizen,' he said to me, 'if you know where this rebel priest is, you will have to tell us. It is an offence to harbour rebels against the State.'

I gulped, an icy feeling tightening on my scalp. Father Martin and I had been speaking softly. I had not thought the Captain had heard us. But before I could answer, the priest said, 'Citizen Captain, I will not have you threatening a member of my flock before I am even settled here! What sort of impression do you think this would make? We want the villagers to accept me, not to make martyrs!'

The Captain grunted. 'Impression be damned! You've got a lot to learn, Citizen, if you think these iron-headed bumpkins can be persuaded and cajoled into good behaviour . . .'

'Nevertheless,' said the priest firmly, 'I must insist. Virtue is to be taught by example, not fear.'

I thought suddenly of Casgrain's words, about virtue needing terror to be enforced, and shivered. How glad I was to hear Father Martin saying the opposite! He went on, 'Now, Jacques, if you might help me to persuade the people I mean them no harm, I would be most grateful. I do not expect you to reveal anything about your previous priest.'

'I do,' growled the Captain.

'Give him time,' said the priest, soothingly. 'Citizen Captain, remember I am, as you reminded the crowd, an elected officer of the State too. Let the boy be, today. Don't ask any more questions. Let him be.'

The Captain looked as though he'd like to say something rude then, but all he said was, 'Very well. I'll wait a little.' He shot me a hard look. I knew he wouldn't forget, or let up on me. I was trapped. And I was terrified. I had no idea what I was going to do. Of course I could not, *would* not betray Father Jantot, but what would the Captain do to me if I held out? Oh, why had I been out in the street at all that afternoon? Why hadn't I stayed with my books inside, instead of going to see what the commotion was? And why, oh why, hadn't I kept my cursed mouth shut?

Seventeen

Mother and Father had been on a visit to friends in town for the last couple of days. They were due back late that afternoon. As soon as they returned, I told them what had happened. Mother looked frightened, Father grave. 'We must remain calm,' he said at last. 'The Captain has no authority, on his own, to do anything against you. But we must act at once. We will return to town immediately. As you know, my friend is in the municipal assembly. He will be able to help us.'

So the coach was turned around and we drove the many leagues through the gathering dusk into town, arriving as night had already fallen. My father's friend, Monsieur Rochas, understood our position at once. In the morning, he said, we would go and see the Mayor. I should not worry, he said, genially. I had done nothing wrong. Everything would be smoothed over. The Mayor would, he was sure, provide a letter to give to the Captain, that I should not be molested. Reassured, I went to bed in one of their guest bedrooms and slept the sleep of the just.

In the morning, we went to see the Mayor at his house. Alas, it wasn't as our friend had hoped. The Mayor was not in a good temper. He was a large, florid man, who had a drapery shop in town, and he was having trouble with some of his staff, whom he claimed were lazy and insolent. He regaled us with details of the iniquities of these people, and only seemed to listen with half an ear to what my father and I had to say. When we'd finished, the Mayor frowned and said, 'I don't understand, citizens. I am an elected official. I have taken the oath. Why shouldn't this priest?'

'But, sir,' said my father, shooting a wry glance at me, 'that is not what we came to speak of.'

'Disobedience, that's the flavour of this age,' said the Mayor fretfully. 'No one will do as they're told. They are headstrong. They only follow their own whims and notions.'

'Yes, sir,' said my father carefully, 'but will you please see that my son . . .'

'Your son won't die from answering a few questions,' broke in the Mayor, crossly. 'I know the Captain. He's a good man. A soldier. He won't hurt your son. Now, go away. I have other things to think about.'

Poor Monsieur Rochas had gone almost purple by this time. Now he burst out with, 'Really, Gilles, this is no way to speak to a respected notary like Monsieur Verdun! He is one of this town's leading citizens.'

'Not any more, he isn't,' said the Mayor, with a sideways glance at us. I saw that there was a nasty little gleam in his eye. 'He has retired to the country, hasn't he? He lives in peace and serenity on his land, now. Perhaps he fancies himself a cut above us now that his son pays court to a nobleman's daughter?'

I started. He smiled unpleasantly. 'Word gets around, my boy,' he said. 'Fancy—the idea of a Verdun paying court to a Bellegarde! Truly, wonders will never cease, in this new democratic age of ours.'

My father jumped up. 'Come, Jacques,' he said. 'There is nothing more to be said here.' And he marched out, slamming the door with a terrific bang. Uneasily, I followed him.

'Father, what will happen to us?'

'Nothing,' snapped my father. 'That man's a fool, a jumped-up pompous bullfrog. He always was. Give some men a tiny bit of power and they think they're the King.'

Monsieur Rochas came puffing after us. He was mortified. 'I can't think what's got into Gilles,' he said as we drove away.

'I can,' said my father quietly.

'I'm so sorry,' said my father's friend. 'But it's not the end of it. We can easily go to—'

'No,' said my father. 'Thank you, my dear friend. Do not worry. We will think of something.'

In the coach, rattling along the road on the way home, though, he said, 'There's only one thing to be done, Jacques. You have to leave.'

I stared at him. 'No, Father, I'll never do that! I won't leave you and Mother.'

'We will go with you,' he said. 'I know now that we should have done this long ago. Mr Wills sent me a letter. He says that the émigrés in London might well need a lawyer like me. There would be plenty of work—much more work than we've had here. You know it's been drying up.'

That was true. It had been yet another source of anxiety for us; the dwindling numbers of our clients.

'I've been thinking of it for a few months now,' said Father. 'I know I've been against leaving before; but now I'm sure we're headed for total destruction. I cannot leave your mother any more in such anxious circumstances. And you have to have a future; you have to get out of France.'

'But . . .' I began. My father understood without being told.

'We will ask the Bellegarde women to come with us,' he said. 'I will make arrangements so that their property will be safe. There are legal ways of doing so. We are not at war with England. They may be persuaded to come. You must persuade them, Jacques. You *must* make them understand.'

'I'll try,' I sighed but, inwardly, a kind of happiness was slowly stealing over me. Imagine if Flora and I could be together in England, in that safe, peaceful little country, far away from the constant tumult and uncertainty! She could take the slip of her rose, and grow it there—English people were very fond of gardens, and especially of roses. Perhaps we could even grow it in the greenhouse at Willesdene? Then she could market her new rose strain and I would resume my interrupted poetry career, as well as work with my father.

Such dreams . . . such beautiful, rosy dreams I had, all the way home. I couldn't wait to get back to the village, to go and see Flora and her mother, and to persuade them to come with us.

Alas! When I arrived at their home, hot and sweaty from having run all the way from our house, the servant who opened the door told me, in a frightened voice, that Mademoiselle Flora was not there. She had gone away—gone with her cousin, who had arrived at dawn that morning. Madame was still there, though. The blood rushed to my head as I heard her words. I pushed her roughly aside, and went shouting through the house, calling for Flora's mother. I found her in the conservatory, watering her plants with a trembling hand. Her eyes were swollen, red with weeping. Her face was crumpled. She looked as though she'd aged ten years. But her voice was controlled as she said, coolly, 'Ah. I thought you'd gone away. What is the meaning of this invasion, Jacques?'

'Flora,' I gasped.

'She's gone. Edmond came and took her away this morning. To Paris.'

'I don't understand . . . I thought you didn't want her to go to Paris! I thought you said that Edmond . . .'

Her head was turned away from me. 'Jacques, do you love my daughter?'

I swallowed, coloured. She turned her head and looked at me. She repeated, rather more sternly, 'Do you love my daughter?'

'Yes,' I whispered. 'I love her with all my heart. I would like to ask her to marry me.'

'Ah.' She was silent for so long that I grew afraid, and with it, angry and rude. 'Is that why she left? Did you get her out of the way, for that reason? Because I'm not good enough? Because I'm not a nobleman's son?'

She went deathly white. Her eyes stared straight into mine. Then, very quietly, she said, 'Perhaps what you say is just, Jacques. Perhaps, in the past, I didn't see . . .' She swallowed, then went on, very low, 'But now, in this turmoil of our country, which I fear will never end, I have learned certain things. I have learned to recognise—to understand that a true heart is worth more than anything. I would be very happy to have you in our family. You are a dear, sweet young man. You love my poor, darling daughter. I can see it in every glance, every gesture. I know she would be safe with you, protected, happy. I do not know if she loves you. But her safety and happiness is the dearest wish of my heart. And so I hoped . . .'

My throat was thick with unshed tears, my heart gripped by wild emotions. 'Then what . . .'

'We hadn't realised just *how much* she wanted to go to Paris, Jacques.'

'I don't understand. Why would she so want to go there?' I hesitated. 'Is it Edmond she loves?'

She shook her head. 'No. Or at least not like that. I'm not sure Flora knows how to love like that, not really, not yet, anyway. She's like a child, still. She hasn't quite grown up. But Edmond might well have feelings like that for her. I remember, once . . .' She broke off, seeing my expression.

Hatred for Edmond, and fear for Flora, rose up in me in a black wave. How dare he even think of it! Of course, I knew it was certainly not uncommon for cousins to fall in love with each other, but there'd been nothing like that between them, before. But now, he'd be alone with her, without any brake or restraint, in his crazy, dangerous new world. He'd been humiliated by Athénaïs. Who knew what might happen? He gave himself every right in the world already—wasn't he a man of the new age? Who knew what he might consider right for an uncommon man such as himself—even the seduction of his vulnerable cousin?

'But why would she want to go to Paris so much, if she doesn't love him?' I persisted.

'Oh, Jacques!' She turned and began pacing around the room. 'Did you ever think, Jacques, that there is something wrong with my darling girl?'

I stared at her. I swallowed. I could not speak.

'I see by your face that you have. Oh, I know she does not show it, outwardly, but she is tormented by the fear that has gripped our country. Since poor Mathilde's murder, since the deaths in the village—poor Marie Bardon, and Anne, and the others—it's become something that never leaves her. She loves her rose. It is the only thing—forgive me—the *only* thing that brings her real peace. When she's with it, when she thinks of it, she's not afraid. You know she dedicated it to Our Lady?'

'Yes,' I said.

'And so I think she thinks that if only she can bring her rose to all of France then it will help to heal our country, as she believes it healed me. She put dried petals from it on my bed, you know, and said that was what rescued me from the brink of death. It has become an obsession for her, Jacques. She sees it as her mission, from Our Lady Herself.' She bit her lip. 'I fear she is not in her right mind.' She paused. 'That is why she wants to go to Paris. And Edmond encouraged her. He told her he knew scientists, experts, top gardeners. That he could introduce her to the chief gardener of the Duke of Orléans. That he could help her.'

I said, stupidly, 'But he's never been interested in roses! And he wouldn't approve of a mission from Our Lady— he'd think it was stupid superstition.'

'He wants her to come to Paris,' she said simply. 'He thinks she'd be better off there. He thinks this *benighted place*, as he put it, is driving her mad.' She paused. 'He wanted me to come, too. He's convinced it's his duty to look after us.'

I winced, thinking of his letter, hating myself for having written to him in the first place. 'But you didn't go.'

'No. I said I would never go. I forbade her to go. But she ignored me. Terrible . . . terrible words were spoken between us. And Edmond was quite against me. He said that as the only male member of the family left in France, he had the right and the duty to do as he saw fit and proper.'

'Just like his father, then,' I said.

'Yes, just like his father. I could have dealt with him in the same way as I did his father but my daughter refused to obey me. She's always been such a gentle girl. But she was violent, Jacques! Oh, so violent. She even said I would be damned if I stopped her! What could I do? I couldn't strike her. I couldn't hold her and Edmond just bundled her off, and away . . .' She trailed off, looking at her hands.

'I wish I'd been there,' I whispered. I was filled with unbearable grief and fear. How could I not have seen what was happening to Flora? What kind of a lover was I, that I did not see it? How could I have been so blind?

Flora's mother said, heavily, 'But you weren't there. I sent a messenger to your house, as soon as Edmond arrived. But the servants said you'd left for the town. I'd heard about the commotion this morning. I heard about the Captain's threats. I thought perhaps you were gone for good. What could I do? While you were here, I knew Flora would always be safe. But without you I decided in the end that perhaps she would indeed be safer in Paris, with her cousin. He knows she's not well. He'll look after her.'

'I'll go to Paris,' I said heatedly. 'I'll bring her back. I can't let her go. And neither can you, Madame!'

She looked at me. She shook her head. 'She won't come back here. Perhaps Edmond is right. It is this place which is driving her mad. I should have seen it. I should have taken her away when I had the chance. Oh, I am so tired, Jacques, my dear. I cannot fight any longer.'

My voice trembled as I said, 'Madame, I do not know if I am the right companion for her, but you must know Edmond most certainly is not! You know he is selfish, dangerous and arrogant. You know he *won't* look after her! He just wants control of her. He wants to mould her according to his ideas. You can't let this happen!'

An icy determination was taking hold of me now. Flora might never love me, but I was not going to let her get lost in Edmond's dark and violent world.

'I will go to Paris, Madame,' I said, when she didn't answer me. 'My parents and I were planning to go to England. I will try and persuade Flora to come with us. There, in that peaceful country, she will recover. She can even grow her rose. The English love their gardens.'

She nodded, and said, dully, 'As you wish.'

'Will you not come with us, Madame?'

'No.'

'But if she agrees to come to England?'

'If she does, then I will be very happy,' she said, picking up her watering-can again. Her voice was quite steady. 'Bad things passed between us, when she left. I can't unsay them, just yet. Maybe later, when time has passed, I will come to England, and see her.' She looked down at her hands. 'Oh, Jacques! We live in evil times indeed, when daughter turns against mother, and nephew against aunt, and friend against friend.'

Eighteen

How can I describe my feelings as I walked away from that house? I don't even know how I got back home. I don't remember the words with which I informed my parents of what had happened. I listened to their anxious words blankly, and to the various plans they discussed: they would come with me to look for Flora and we would all leave France together; no, Mother would set sail from Brittany and go straight to England, and only Father would come with me; no, what was Father thinking of? Flora needed a woman too, and what about poor Madame de Bellegarde, surely she must be persuaded?

It all washed over me. All I could think of was Flora, and how I had failed her. I thought of the hectic shine in her eyes and her cheek when she spoke about dedicating the rose to Our Lady and how it was important she go to the capital, and I groaned inside at my criminal stupidity and infinite blindness. My darling's mind was going to pieces before my very eyes, and I had not even noticed it. Sunk in my own fears, I had imagined Flora to be immune to those same fears, to be innocent as a lamb, or an angel. Worshipping her, I had forgotten she was human.

By nightfall, my parents had decided on a course of action. They would both come with me to Paris. As soon as we had found Flora, Mother would take her to England. Father and I would come back here, put our affairs in order, sell the house, pay the servants, and try and persuade Flora's mother to come with us. Then we'd all go to England. We would sit it out there, until true order was restored. Father said General Lafayette, who everyone thought of as a genuine national hero, was ready to make a move against the radicals. Things would get better. The Constitution would be enshrined, and the King regain respect. I need hardly say that I paid practically no attention to these wistful theories. Truth to tell, just then I didn't care a fig for the King or the parliament or the revolutionaries or the whole useless, pointless, stupid, violent charade. All I cared about was Flora.

But I fell in with my parents' plans. I couldn't think of anything better myself. I went to bed that night with a headache that felt as though it would split my entire being open, like an egg, but I welcomed the pain fiercely. It seemed to me it was the very least punishment I could receive.

I was lying sleepless in bed when I heard a rattle of pebbles at my bedroom window. Immediately, I sprang up, a mad thought flashing through my head that Edmond had changed his mind, that he'd brought Flora back.

It was a bright moonlit night. Pierre stood outside, grey as a ghost, all colour except for his soot-black hair and eyes leached by the unearthly light. For an instant, staring at his tall figure, I was taken with a shiver deeper than reason, deeper than thought. He looked—I can't explain it—he looked as if he was a being out of this world. Then he smiled and gestured at me to come down, miming urgency. I pulled on my boots—I hadn't undressed—and came down at once.

'Mademoiselle's gone,' he said flatly. 'And you're going after her.'

'How did you know?'

'I saw it,' he said. 'And when I came back from seeing to Father Jantot, I spoke to Madame. She told me he had taken her.'

'You saw it? What do you mean? Were you there when Edmond . . .'

'No. I saw it,' he repeated stubbornly, and I knew he meant he'd seen it in a vision. It made me furious, suddenly.

'If you saw it, why didn't you come earlier, stopped him from taking her away?' I cried.

'I could not get back in time. Besides, he is doing the right thing, for once. She had to leave this place. But you must go to her. You must give her this.' He took something from his pocket. I saw it was a little cross, made of hazel twigs lashed together. He said, 'Last year, I took this on pilgrimage with us. It was blessed with holy water from the fountain where Our Lady appeared. It will protect Mademoiselle. It will soothe her bruised soul, and bring her peace. Tell her to always carry it with her.'

I said, gently, more touched than I could express, 'I will do that, Pierre.'

'Remember our vow,' he said. 'We are all in this together again, you, me, even *him*. For Mademoiselle.'

'Of course,' I said, 'of course.'

His eyes were fixed on me, black as a moonless night, yet with a curious shine and intensity to them that scared me a little. I murmured, 'But you know what this means, Pierre? That she might never come back here.'

A spasm crossed his face. 'I know what it means, Jacques,' he said, quietly. 'Give it to her.'

I took the cross. I said, 'Will I tell her that it comes from you?' There was a strange beat in my throat as I said this, something unsaid that troubled me, that reawakened my old jealousy about their closeness.

But he shrugged. 'As you wish.'

I could not hide the relief in my voice. 'Very well. What will you . . .'

He smiled faintly. 'What will we do? Oh, we will fight, Jacques. Don't look so grim. Not with guns—or not yet. We will fight with our souls and our spirits. We will not go to that intruder's Masses. We will refuse to be confessed by him. They can send the Blues in after us, but it won't do them any good. They may take away the liberty of the body, but not that of the soul. We will resist them to the end.'

How can I describe how splendid he looked, saying these fighting words? How can I say how much I was stirred, how much I envied his certainty and his courage? But I was glad, too—glad to leave him behind, glad to leave the whole thing behind me, concentrating only on saving my beloved from the madness that threatened to engulf her. Tears suddenly started to my eyes. I laid a hand on his arm.

'Pierre, my dear friend,' I said, 'please take care.'

He smiled. It was a genuine, warm smile, sweetening the hard planes of his face. 'Of course I will,' he said, grasping my hand lightly, then, just as lightly, letting go. 'I have no intention of being reckless. You know me, Jacques.' He paused. 'And you must not worry about Madame de Bellegarde. I will make sure no harm ever comes to her, till you can return to take her away to safety as well.'

'You are a true friend,' I said, with great emotion, 'and I am glad of your friendship.'

'As I am of yours,' he said gently. He was silent a moment, then said, 'You will take her to the house of your friend? The Englishman?'

I was startled. I said, 'Yes, I think so. Well, at least, Jonathan's parents. They are good people.'

He nodded. 'I am glad to hear it. And now I must return to my post,' he said. 'Goodbye, Jacques.'

'This cannot be goodbye,' I said, stupidly, 'only farewell.'

The expression that came into Pierre's eyes then made me feel as though I were a child, and he an adult far beyond my years. 'Farewell, then, if you wish,' was all he said, and then he turned and strode rapidly away, his black hair flapping like ragged wings. In an instant, he had disappeared.

I stood there for a moment, staring after him, the hazel cross clutched tightly in my hand. I had a sudden feeling I would never see Pierre again, not in this world. I went back up to my room and lay on the bed, the cross under my pillow. Whether it was its miraculous properties, or my own tiredness, I don't know, but I was asleep within minutes, sunk into a deep, refreshing slumber.

Nineteen

We had decided to leave separately the next day, to avoid the National Guard. I left at dawn, on my old horse, Jolie. My parents would leave later, in the carriage. We were to meet over the Loire in Brittany, near a village where my parents had a farmer friend who would look after Jolie, who was too old and tired to go as far as Paris.

When I galloped through the village, first light was only starting to glimmer on the horizon. I passed the church, and the presbytery, where our new priest and his bodyguard were bivouacked, without incident. I passed the forge, the bakery, the shrine to Our Lady, and then the avenue that led up to the Bellegarde manor.

I nearly drew rein there, thinking that I should make my farewells to Flora's mother; but thought better of it, and galloped on. Past the last village houses, past the outlying farms; and came to the woods. The path I wanted skirted the edge of the woods. It was fairly well-protected from the main road that led to the town.

Jolie seemed cheerful and sprightly; I did not have

to urge her on too much. Towards midday, I stopped by a stream, drank, and ate the bread and cheese Mother had packed for me. I resumed my journey very soon afterwards. I met very few people along the way.

By nightfall, I was still a little way from my destination. I arrived in a village and put in at a rather miserable inn. By chance, I heard a conversation the innkeeper was having with a customer. It was about a big, violent demonstration that had taken place only a few days ago, when the 'Blues' had attempted to impose a new priest on the community. The man who was talking about it kept mentioning a word: *Chouan*. It soon became apparent that he was talking about a person called Jean Chouan and his brother François, who were among the ringleaders of the demonstration. It was the first time I—and France—would hear the name 'Chouan', but certainly not the last.

At first light, I left. I soon covered the last few leagues that led to our meeting-place, met my father's Breton friend, Thomas le Braz, and devoured a good breakfast at his farmhouse table as we waited for my parents. We spoke a bit of the situation, and le Braz said that Brittany, which was traditionally proud and independent and had often fought against the French central government, was on the brink of open war. It was only a hesitation to go against the King—who even if he could control nothing in reality, was at least still a figurehead to whom loyalty was owed—which prevented the Bretons from launching into immediate outright hostilities.

I told him of what I'd heard at the inn last night. He nodded. 'Oh yes, that's the Cottereau family,' he said. 'They're known as Chouan, because their grandfather was a gloomy old bird, who used the hooting cry of the tawny owl, the *chat-huant*, as a rallying cry in the woods—he was a notorious smuggler, you know, and his grandson Jean's carried on the tradition. Both the boys and girls in that family are fiercely independent and quarrelsome. I shouldn't be surprised that if it comes to a real fight with the Blues around here, the Chouan family will be in the advance guard.'

My parents arrived in the early afternoon. They were tired and a little anxious, because they'd been stopped by the National Guard on the road, interrogated and searched. They said they were looking for 'brigands' who had attacked a National Guard unit only a few hours before, and had wounded a couple of soldiers. Le Braz's glance met mine, and I remembered what he'd said about the Chouan family. I wondered how long it would be before the same thing happened in Bellegarde.

Father told me that the Captain had not come looking for me. It seemed that Father Martin must have persuaded him to wait a little longer. I spared a kindly thought for that well-meaning man, and went back to trying to think through what we would do once we were in Paris. It was of far more moment to me than even the thought I might be targeted by the National Guard as a friend of rebels.

We left Le Braz's farmhouse, and Jolie, a couple of hours later. On fresh horses, we headed for Le Mans, where we spent the night. The next morning, with the horses rested, we were on the road to Paris. We got there in two days.

As we approached the capital, the crowds on the roads grew greater. Soldiers, townspeople, beggars, rascals of all kinds, walking; horsemen; the more fortunate in carriages, farmers with carts—all sorts. There was a restless air to all this activity; at an inn where we stopped for an hour's rest, we heard it being said the Prussians had breached the frontier and were on their way to Paris. There would be many such alarms in those fearful months but this was the first time we'd heard it, and we were as uneasy as the others. We made the coachman push the horses as hard as he could, so that we arrived in the great city just after dark. We found reasonable lodgings, and then Father and I, leaving Mother to rest from the bruising, uncomfortable ride, went straight around to Edmond's lodgings.

Casgrain's manservant opened the door. He heard our request in silence. Then he said, 'Citizen Bellegarde is not here. He left for the provinces days ago. He has not returned.'

Father and I looked at each other. 'Could we . . . could we speak to Monsieur—I mean, Citizen—Casgrain?' I said. My heart was performing painful leaps and flops inside my chest; a feeling of doom was icing my veins.

'Citizen Casgrain is at Citizen Robespierre's house,' said the manservant frostily. 'He will not be back till tomorrow.'

'Are you expecting Citizen Bellegarde back soon?' Father said.

The servant shrugged. 'I have not been told.'

'Mademoiselle, Citizeness, I mean, Casgrain.' I faltered. 'Where is she?'

'She does not live here any more,' said the man, pursing his lips disapprovingly.

He made as if to shut the door, but I said, 'Please tell Edmond if you see him, when he returns, to come and see us immediately at . . .' I gave him the address of our lodgings, and he nodded.

'I will tell him, Citizen.' With that, he shut the door.

'We must return here in the morning,' said Father, but I shook my head.

'We must go to Robespierre's house. I know where he lives. I've been there before. We must speak to Casgrain. He's an intimate friend of Edmond, he will know what he was planning to do.'

'Perhaps he has merely stopped along the way,' suggested my father, as we walked rapidly through the streets. 'He was only a day ahead of us; he may have stopped for a rest in some town along the way.'

I wanted to believe that. But I was afraid. I thought it quite possible that the pair of them might have been attacked and be lying dead in a wood somewhere. Or, more likely, that Edmond had taken it into his head to make Flora disappear so we should never find her.

Robespierre lodged with a family called Duplay. One of the Duplay daughters came to the door. I had met her once. She remembered me, or at least pretended to. But it was no good. Casgrain was no longer there; he'd gone out with Robespierre and Saint-Just. She had no idea where they had gone.

We had to admit defeat, and slowly retraced our steps back to our own lodgings, heavy of heart. I felt my failure keenly. For some reason, I hadn't even considered that we wouldn't find Flora at Edmond's lodgings. I had just assumed it, all my energies focussed on getting to Paris. But what if he never intended to bring her here at all?

I spent a terrible night, despite the comfortable feather bed. In the morning, after breakfast, I went out alone, back to Casgrain's house. Edmond still wasn't there, but Casgrain was. He was dressed in his military uniform: he was on his way to the barracks, he said. He greeted me politely, and listened to my story, though I left out a great deal, not wanting to reveal Flora's inner torments.

He said that Edmond had not informed him as to

when he'd be returning to Paris. Edmond had said he had been summoned to help his cousin, who was in some sort of trouble; by his comments, Casgrain had obviously assumed Flora was pregnant, or some such thing. When I begged him to tell me what Edmond had said he might do, he looked sharply at me. 'This cousin of his is obviously of importance to *you*, Jacques. Your muse, perhaps?'

I coloured. 'I love her,' I said simply.

Casgrain nodded. 'I *see*. And Edmond doesn't approve.'

'Edmond doesn't know.'

He laughed. 'I wouldn't be so sure. This trouble of hers—it could be *you*, in his eyes.'

'He believes in equality,' I said coldly. I was half-afraid Casgrain might be right, but I didn't want to discuss my childhood friend with this man, nevertheless.

'Equality for others, perhaps,' said Casgrain, his eyes fixed on my face.' It's different when it comes to his own flesh and blood. Especially as you are neither *aristo* nor patriot, but an ordinary man.'

I flushed angrily. But before I could reply, he said, 'Don't be insulted. You are what you are. You should not be afraid of the truth.'

'What makes you think you know the truth, and I don't?' I snapped. 'You're all the same—all of you! A plague on your houses. I care nothing for any of your truths. I just want to know where Flora is. She is worth a thousand of me, of Edmond, of you. And I have failed her. I have left her defenceless before the wolves.'

He laughed. 'How very dramatic you are, Jacques! I am sure our mutual friend is no wolf to his own cousin.' He turned away from me, then seemed to relent. 'There is a little cottage in the country, near the forest of Ermenonville. Edmond goes there sometimes to paint. It is a peaceful, beautiful spot, and it inspires him to be near the place where our great Rousseau wrote his last works. You might try there.'

He gave me directions. I thanked him, confused. He waved a deprecating hand. 'Tell Edmond he should be back here soon. His sentiment should not overwhelm his duty towards our cause.' Then he walked away, with a military firmness of step, and I was left to find my own way out.

Twenty

The great woods and gardens of Ermenonville, north of Paris, are set around its castle, which at the time was still owned by Count Girardin. He had been the philosopher Rousseau's last patron and protector. It was decided I would go there alone, on a fast horse. There was no guarantee Edmond and Flora would be there, anyway.

I set off before lunch and arrived in late afternoon. It took me a little while to find the cottage Casgrain had described, down the end of a muddy path. Smoke was coming out of the cottage chimney as I approached, leading my horse, my heart pounding madly. I knocked on the door. Edmond opened it at once, as if he'd been waiting.

'Doctor, I . . .' he began. Then he saw it was me. His eyes widened. 'What are you doing here? How did you know I was here?'

I pushed past him. 'Your friend Casgrain told me.' I could see, in the corner of the room, a screened-off alcove. She must be there.

'Casgrain! By what right?'

'Shut up, Edmond,' I said wearily, pulling aside the curtain.

'She's ill,' he said, behind me. 'Very ill. I've sent for the doctor.'

Flora was lying on a rough sort of bed, her eyes closed, pale as death. Her breath rattled a little. I touched her cheek, very gently. 'She's burning!'

'I told you, she's very ill. A fever. She's been like this since yesterday—fell into a faint on the way here.'

'You damned fool,' I said tightly. 'You damned, damned fool.' I took out Pierre's little cross. I touched her forehead gently with it, murmured a little prayer, then put the hazel cross on the pillow, next to her head. Edmond made a movement towards me, then stopped.

He said, 'She'll be all right. You'll see. She couldn't stay in Bellegarde. You know that.'

'I know nothing of the kind,' I said harshly, 'and neither do you. How could you, filling her head with nonsense?'

He gave a short laugh. 'Hark who's talking, with your superstitious talisman! Did that benighted peasant give it to you? Ah, I thought so!' He was going to say more but, suddenly furious, I punched him, hard. He gave a surprised squawk and fell back, his nose streaming with blood; then he recovered, sprang up, and hit out viciously at me. I lunged back and, in an instant, we were fighting in earnest; punching, kicking, scratching, an undignified, clumsy, painful fight such as we hadn't had since we were very small boys. His breath was sobbing in his chest, as was mine. I think I was yelling, some of the time.

'What in the name of God is happening here!'

The astonished voice made us spring apart. A grey-haired man in sober black, carrying a bag, stood in the doorway. Edmond got to his feet. He dabbed ineffectually at his nose with a lace handkerchief. He said, 'Good afternoon, Doctor. Forgive us. We are old friends.'

'So I see,' said the doctor, but made no further comment. He went over to the curtained alcove and sat on the bed. He looked at Flora, and held a hand to her forehead. He pulled the curtain closed behind him. The fight forgotten, Edmond and I stared at the drawn curtain in an agony of anxiety. I know my heart was tight and hot in my chest. I don't know about his.

At last, the doctor came out from behind the curtain. He said, 'She has brain-fever. She may recover, or she may not. I will prescribe medicine to make the fever go down. If she is to recover, she will come out of her faint in a day or two, maybe more. She will be very weak. She will need to rest for weeks, maybe months.'

'I will look after her,' I said. 'That's what I came to do.'

The doctor shot a glance at Edmond and me. He said, 'Is either of you her husband?'

'No,' I said, flushing scarlet.

'No,' said Edmond casually. 'I'm her cousin.'

'Well. She could stay here, yes, but she will need a nursemaid as well as a night attendant. It will not be cheap.'

'I have money,' I said, before Edmond could answer. 'And my parents—my mother could come and look after her. My grandfather was a doctor.'

'Good,' said the doctor. 'Bring her here as soon as possible.' He scribbled something on a piece of paper. 'Have these mixtures made up by the castle herbalist. She should take them three times a day, once she's recovered. *If* she recovers.'

A dreadful shiver rippled over me, from head to foot. I said, 'What are the chances, Doctor?'

'Even, I should say,' he said, smiling grimly. 'She will need your prayers, as well as my medicines.' He paused at the door. 'I will come back in two days' time. We will know by then.'

And he was off, shutting the door firmly behind him. Edmond and I looked at each other. He said, 'You're in love with her, aren't you?'

'Yes,' I said. I added, 'Are you?'

He smiled. 'No. I'm very fond of her, but only as a cousin. Oh, I can't say I haven't thought of marrying her; it would simplify things for us in some ways.'

'What things?' Anger was mounting in me again.

He didn't answer that, or not directly. Instead, he said, 'You're not right for her, Jacques.'

'Not good enough, you mean? Isn't that strange, to hear such words from the apostle of Rousseau, the follower of Robespierre, the man who writes liberty equality fraternity or death!'

'Don't be so bitter, Jacques, it doesn't suit you,' he said wearily. 'It's got nothing to do with your birth, or your parentage. You are *not* what she needs. You're not strong enough. She needs a strong man who understands her.'

'And you are such a man?'

'I am her cousin,' he said. 'I understand her. Anyway, I've decided not to marry her.'

I snorted. '*You've* decided! What of Flora in all this? You fill her head with rubbish, you tear her from her mother, you bring her sick as a dog to a place where she might die—and you dare to talk of deciding! You dare to think you know what's best for her!'

'You are tedious,' he said and, turning on his heel, he went out of the cottage.

I turned back to the bed. Flora lay just as before, her lashes soft on her waxwork cheeks. I knelt by the bed. I said all the prayers I could think of, all the prayers that I'd ever heard, over and over and over.

I heard a sound behind me. Edmond said, rather hesitantly, 'Perhaps you can tell me where your parents are. I will go and fetch them.'

I finished my prayer. Without turning around, I told

him. 'My horse is tired,' I added. 'I do not think you can take him.'

'I will get a fresh horse. From the village . . . I'll go there now. And I'll also take that prescription to the herbalist.'

'Very well,' I said. I didn't want to look at him.

He sighed. 'I'll be back as soon as I can. Someone from the village will bring some food, later—I've ordered a chicken, a little salt, herbs, some wine, bread.'

I didn't answer. He sighed again. I heard him going out, shutting the door quietly behind him.

After a little while, I got off my knees. I looked around the cottage. There was little furniture—just the bed, two chairs, a table, a wood box and a shelf, on which stood a tallow lamp, two wooden bowls, two spoons, a rusty knife, and two earthenware mugs. It was warm enough in here—the fire had clearly been lit for some time, and was burning merrily. There was a book on the table. I picked it up. To my surprise, it wasn't the politics or philosophy I'd expected, but the beautiful sixteenth-century poetry of Pierre de Ronsard. I knew Edmond had liked Ronsard, once, but I would have thought he'd discarded the poet along with all the rest of the old world he was so dismissive of. Perhaps it was to please Flora.

I caught sight of something under the table. It was a thin bundle wrapped in wet cloth. I picked it up and unrolled it, gently. It was a bundle of rose cuttings.

They were already beginning to bud. The tears I hadn't shed yet started to my eyes now. The gravity of Flora's danger struck me with renewed force. She had brought the cuttings, even though she must know this was not the time to plant them. True, it had been a rather cool spring and early summer but roses have to be planted in winter. If she had brought them with her, it really did show how disturbed her mind was. These cuttings had no chance, no chance at all. She was doing it all for nothing.

A wild anger filled me. Edmond had known this too. Yet still he had taken her off with him. I looked at the cuttings in my hands and wanted to snap them in two or throw them on the fire. Instead, I did a ridiculous thing. I went outside. I looked around for a big, sharp stick. I dug a patch of earth, right by that cottage, in the full sun. It was hot work, for the ground was rather hard and dry. But I managed it. I planted those rose cuttings, and then went and fetched water from the stream. I watered them well, and patted the soil around them. I was weeping as I did it, knowing it was for nothing, that the cuttings would die. But somehow it seemed like the right thing—no, the *only* thing—to do.

I went back to the cottage, and looked in at Flora. Nothing had changed. Her breathing was just as harsh and rattling, her skin still hot to the touch. I had a sudden fear that she would die, right there in front of my eyes. I drew up the chair, pulled back the curtain, and sat by the bed. I picked up Pierre's cross, and put it on her breast.

'Our Lady, Mother of God, mother of us all, protect my darling. She left her home because she loves you and wants to honour your name with her rose,' I whispered, and now the tears ran down my cheeks. 'Please, sweet Mother Mary, intercede with your divine Son to save her.' I prayed over and over, offering up everything I had, my future, my sanity, my life, even, if it meant Flora would live.

Time passed. I saw to the fire, and prayed, and watched. An hour or so after Edmond had left, a ragged boy came to the door with a basket full of the food Edmond had ordered. I had no stomach for food, but I paid him and took it. I thought, maybe I would make Flora some chicken soup. Chicken soup was what my mother always ordered from the cook for us if we were ill.

I fetched more water from the stream, and filled the big iron pot that hung over the fire. I took the rather rusty iron knife that lay on the shelf, and hacked at the chicken until I had it in a few bits. I dropped it into the water with the salt, the herbs and, after a moment's reflection, a splash of the wine. I put the lid on the pot. I looked at the fire. It was going well, but I needed to make sure I had enough wood not only for the cooking, but for the whole night. Flora must not catch cold. On top of a fever, it would be fatal.

I looked in the wood box. I would need more. Stripping off my coat, I went outside in my shirt. There was a splitting-block at the side of the house, an axe lying by it, and a pile of uncut logs. I had seen Pierre chopping wood before. It didn't look difficult. I heaved a log onto the block, and swung the axe.

And recoiled in terror as the axe seemed to leap back at me. I cursed, knowing I'd had a narrow escape from chopping off a finger or a hand. I swung again, but this time only managed to make the axe rebound on the tough wood. There must be a way of doing it properly, but I didn't know what it was. I felt annoyed and helpless and stupid. I knew all about writs and briefs and the ins and outs of the law, but I had no idea how to chop wood! Yet I must have some more wood for the fire. I looked around. Then I saw there was a great deal of dead wood lying about under the trees. If I gathered enough of that, I would maybe not need the logs . . . It was late spring, after all, not the dead of winter.

It took me several hot, tiring trips to fill the wood box with scraps and twigs and twisted branches. The ragged boy came back while I was in the middle of it, with the medicines made up by the herbalist in two little dishes. He looked astonished to see me in my state of sweaty dishevelment, but I was past caring.

By the time I'd finished stacking the wood, the chicken was bubbling merrily in the pot, and the cottage was filled with a pleasant smell that, despite myself, made my stomach rumble in anticipation. I was just about to go over to the pot and lift up the lid when I heard a faint sound from the bed.

I rushed over. She was stirring. I put a finger very lightly to her cheek. It felt cool! Astonished, I touched her forehead. There was no doubt about it, the fever had abated! I said, 'Flora, Flora.'

Her eyes opened. I will never forget that moment. She looked straight at me. Her blue eyes were very clear. She smiled, very faintly. Then the lids came down over the blue, she gave a little sigh, and her head turned to one side. She was asleep.

Terrified I was making a terrible mistake, that she was, in fact, dying, I put my ear to her chest. It rose and fell, gently. I could even hear the pace of her heart. I knelt down. I picked up the little cross and kissed it. Tears rolled down my cheeks, tears of gratitude and relief and love and awe. 'Thank you, thank you, dear Mother Mary, sweet Virgin, and your dearest Son, thank you, thank you. I will never forget.'

I knew a miracle had occurred. There was no other explanation for the rapid change. I hadn't even given her the medicine yet. I felt as though a hard, heavy, bitter shell that had grown around my whole being in the last few years was cracking open and I was being reborn, light as a feather, invincible with love, into the light, into beauty, into the knowledge of God's eternal world of kindness and love and mercy.

How long I knelt there I don't know. But, in time, I got up, slowly. An immense well-being, a great peace, had settled on me. I leaned over and kissed Flora very gently on the forehead, and then drew the curtain and let her sleep. I stirred my pot of soup, and poked the fire, and then ate and drank, appreciating each mouthful. I added more water to the soup, and settled the fire down, then lay rolled in my coat in front of it. The cottage was dark, but the waning moon had risen, and through a hole in the shutter I could see its silver light. Just before I fell asleep, I thought I saw a vision: the form of a woman, in pale robes and veil, standing by Flora's bed. Then my eyelids closed, and I was fast asleep.

Twenty-one

I was woken by her voice. It was weak, but quite clear. She whispered, 'Mother?'

I got up at once. It was morning, and the sunlight was flooding in through the hole in the shutter. The fire had died down. I pulled aside the bed-curtain. 'It's me, Flora. It's Jacques.'

'Oh, Jacques!' She smiled. 'I thought I'd dreamed you were here. And Pierre.'

My heart turned over. I said, 'No. It's no dream. Well, at least *I* am here.'

'Not Pierre? I thought I saw him too.'

'No. I'm sorry. He couldn't leave his children.'

'Of course,' she said. 'I must have seen him in a dream.' Her eyes widened. 'Where am I? What am I doing, lying here?' She made as if to sit up. I rushed forward. 'You've been ill,' I said, gently easing her up. 'Very ill.'

'I don't know this place,' she said, in a puzzled voice, looking around her. 'I don't remember coming here.'

'You've been ill,' I repeated. I gestured at the herbal

mixtures. 'There's some medicine there which I have to—'

'I don't understand,' she interrupted. 'Why did I come here? Are we near home? Where's Mother?'

I looked at her. She had forgotten everything—her quarrel with her mother, her flight with Edmond across France, her desperate mission for her rose, coming here. Well, perhaps it was for the best. I said, very gently, 'Your mother is at home. She will be very happy to know you are better.'

She sank back down onto her pillow. 'I am glad,' she murmured.

I fetched the medicine, and gave her a spoonful of it. She took it meekly, but made a face as it went down.

'I know,' I said, 'it's horrid, isn't it? But it will help to make you strong.'

Now she saw the cross. Her eyes widened. She said, 'Did you bring this, Jacques?'

I was about to say yes, that I had made it for her, when something—the memory of Pierre's face—stopped me. I said. 'I brought it, but it's from Pierre. He said you should always carry it.'

She smiled, very sweetly, and held it, very gently, against her breast. 'Did he? Then I will.' Her eyelids closed. In an instant, she was asleep again. I tiptoed away, and went outside. In the bright spring sunshine, I stretched, and yawned, then went to have a quick, refreshing wash in the stream. I felt a sense of light-bodied ease, a sense of remoteness and peace, as if we two were alone in the world, in a fairytale cottage in the woods . . . I thought of Danton and his republic of chicken soup and vegetable growing. It was a cheerful dream, that one, and peaceful, and gentle. Then I caught sight of the axe, and smiled ruefully. Not everything was peaceful and gentle!

A couple of hours later, Flora woke up. I managed to give her a little broth, without meat. She drank it cheerfully, and didn't ask me any more questions, but just seemed to accept the situation. She was obviously still weak, I thought, in shock from the brain-fever. It was better to let her recover in her own time. It didn't matter if she didn't know where she was, or how she'd got here.

When she fell asleep again, I went out to the splitting-block. I eyed the axe. I was going to beat it, I thought. I wasn't going to be defeated by a mere woodcutter's tool. I looked at the log, trying to remember what I might have heard about such things. Then it came to me—something about the grain. You had to split it along the grain.

I hauled the log onto its end. Now I could see the grain, the lines that fissured the wood. Carefully aiming, I swung the axe. This time, I heard a crack as the blade swung in and split the wood. Not altogether successfully—it got caught half-way. I was struggling with it, pulling it out to begin again to finish the cut, when I heard voices.

I looked up. There was a party of people coming towards me: Mother, Father, Edmond—and Casgrain. Father's face broke into a huge smile as he saw me. 'Why, Jacques! You're turning into a woodcutter, are you!' He strode up to me. 'Let me help.' He took off his coat and rolled up his shirt-sleeves. 'I haven't done this in years, but let's see if I haven't forgotten everything.'

He took the axe, and swung it down neatly. The log split in two. He grinned. 'I can still do it!'

'You're stealing Jacques' thunder,' Mother said, smiling at the two of us. Edmond looked at us all in some astonishment. Then he said, crossly, 'You look just like a peasant, Jacques, with that dirty face and your shirt all crumpled and your shoes muddy.'

'Nothing to be ashamed of,' said Casgrain, speaking for the first time. 'Good honest work never hurt anyone, Edmond.'

Edmond snorted, and changed the subject. 'How is she?'

'Well,' I said, and I couldn't help grinning as I spoke. 'She's so very much better.'

'Don't be a fool,' snapped Edmond. 'You heard what the doctor said.'

'A change came in the night,' I said. 'It was a miracle. I prayed to the Virgin to make her well, and she did. Flora is quite well, but weak. She doesn't know where she is, or how she came here. But she knew who she was, and she knew me. And she seems to be at peace.'

Edmond repeated, 'Don't be a fool.' He strode into the cottage, followed by Casgrain and my parents. He went over to the bed, and drew aside the curtain. He laid a finger on Flora's sleeping cheek. He said, sounding stupefied, 'The fever's gone.'

'I told you,' I said.

'It can happen like that,' said Casgrain, nodding. 'A great fever, if it's going to go, often vanishes suddenly, like a thief in the night. I've seen it on the battlefield. It can seem like a miracle.' He was looking at Flora as he spoke, and I felt a sudden spurt of unease. What was he thinking? I could never read that man well.

But Mother was looking around the cottage. She said, 'You've been making chicken soup, Jacques!'

'Wonders will never cease,' said my father.

Edmond picked up the dish of herbal mixture. He said, 'She's had this?'

'Yes,' I said. I looked at his challenging expression. 'That was after she woke up—after the fever had left her. Besides, you know medicine never works like that. It's hit and miss, if it works at all. Time's usually the greatest healer. I'm sorry, Edmond. You're going to have to accept the fact it was a miracle.'

'Pah!' Edmond exploded, and he stalked outside,

slamming the door behind him. An instant later, I heard the sound of the axe hitting the wood. My parents and I looked at each other.

My mother sighed. 'That poor child has never been at ease in his own skin,' she said, 'and so he seeks to impress the world by outraging it.'

Casgrain said, softly, 'I fear you are right, Citizeness. Edmond is not the most reliable or stable of men.' His gaze was thoughtful on Flora. 'I am glad to see the young Citizeness is better. Do you have a good doctor for her?'

'A local one,' I said.

'She will need a proper place to stay till she recovers,' he said.

Father said, 'Edmond thought the Count might take Flora in. She would be more comfortable in the castle, to convalesce, perhaps.'

'The Count of Ermenonville? He is a good man. A patriot,' said Casgrain tonelessly. 'It may be for the best.'

'But you don't want that, do you, Jacques?' said Mother quickly, seeing my dismayed expression. 'You want to look after her here.' She took off her coat. 'I am happy to stay here too. We can bring in straw to make an extra bed. I will make it all cosy and comfortable. We will not need to trouble anyone else.'

'If that is your desire,' said Casgrain, and bowed. 'Now, if you do not mind, I will . . .'

He stopped. Flora's eyes had opened. She said, 'Jacques?'

'I'm here,' I said, clasping her hand. 'And so are my parents. And Monsieur Casgrain.'

'Citizen Casgrain,' he corrected, without anger. 'I am very pleased to make your acquaintance, Citizeness Bellegarde. Your cousin Edmond has told me a great deal about you.'

'Has he?' she whispered.

'Indeed. But he did not tell me how beautiful you were, Citizeness.' His blue eyes rested thoughtfully on her. 'But I see you are tired, and need to be alone with your friends. I wish you a speedy recovery, Citizeness, and I hope that our paths may cross again some day.' And with that he was off, closing the door of the cottage gently behind him.

My parents and I looked at each other, relieved by his departure. Flora said, a little fretfully, 'Who was that?'

'A friend of Edmond's,' I said. 'From Paris.'

'Ah.' She closed her eyes, briefly, then opened them again. 'My mother . . .' she began, struggling to get up again.

'You lie down, dear,' said Mother, quickly going to her side. 'Your mother is away, Flora. But she will be back soon.'

'Good,' said Flora, 'I want to see her.'

'And so you shall,' I said, making a sudden decision.

I'd wanted—oh how badly I'd wanted—to stay with her here, in a timeless woodland idyll. But that had been selfish; I could see that now. She needed her mother. I could do that for her, if I truly loved her. And Mother was there to look after her now. I knew she'd do that as if Flora had been her own daughter.

Father took me aside. 'You'll exhaust yourself, Jacques.'

'It doesn't matter,' I said. 'I'll rest a little along the way.'

'Then I'll come with you.'

'No,' I said, quickly. 'I'd rather you were here. With them. It's a safe place.'

'You are worried about Edmond's friend,' he said, correctly guessing the source of my unease. 'I don't think you need to be—he seems to be a man who keeps his own counsel and, for one of those fire-breathers, he seems a decent enough young man. But very well. I will stay. Take care, Jacques, my dear son, and return soon.'

'That I will,' I said. 'I promise.'

Twenty-two

So it was all arranged. The Count was indeed a kindly man and agreed readily to help my parents. The cottage was transformed with a little more furniture, a feather bed for my parents, and food was to be sent over every day. Strangely, Mother was happy in her new situation; she said she hadn't felt so bright in years. She was looking forward to cooking, and looking after Flora, and reading to her, and gardening.

I showed her where I'd planted the roses, and she—God bless her—looked at those dry sticks and didn't tell me that they wouldn't take, that they were already dying, but that she'd look after them. Flora herself didn't appear to remember about her rose at all; we thought it best not to mention it in front of her. Later, maybe, if the roses survived, she might remember.

Edmond accepted what we had decided without argument. He had lost a good deal of his arrogance. Perhaps it was because Casgrain had reproved him. Or perhaps the whole situation was tiresome to him now that his grand gesture in whisking Flora away from 'benighted' Bellegarde had fizzled out into an embarrassing complication. Perhaps he'd been really afraid Flora might die. Perhaps, though, it was only that his arrogance didn't intimidate me any longer. I had quite lost my awe of him. I saw him clearly now—and I saw his weakness. I thought of Casgrain's words, and Jonathan's, and Mother's, and Pierre's, and Madame de Bellegarde's. Convinced of his own superiority, judging others with peremptory ease, he never saw that others might be judging him, and finding him wanting.

My journey back to Bellegarde was uneventful, if rather tiring and slow. In my worry about Flora, I had almost forgotten about the other things that had happened, that hectic week, so it was with a small but certain shock that I saw, as I rode into the village, that there were still troops there. They seemed completely uninterested in my presence, however, and more interested in chatting to a couple of pretty girls who were drawing water from the village well.

Our housekeeper Jeannette, who had stayed in the house to protect it from intruders, told me that the Captain himself had left with most of his unit to help quell a riot somewhere else; but he had left those few soldiers there to protect our new priest, and also to force the villagers to go to his Mass.

'They're not bad sorts, the men he left here,' Jeannette said. 'They don't really want trouble. They make half-hearted attempts to round people up at ten o'clock; one of the soldiers even tried to ring the bell to call people—because they couldn't find anyone to ring the bell, you see. But he couldn't do it, the bell sounded sick, people laughed. That Father Martin, he wasn't happy, but he said he'd be patient, they'd try again next week. But at midday, you see, the bell rang, and everyone came to church, just as Father Jantot had told us to! It bamboozled the soldiers—they didn't know what to do, all that great crowd in the church, silently bobbing up and down, in time to the Mass being said so far away. A couple of the soldiers said we were bewitched, that we were crazy, but the others laughed and seemed to think it a good joke. I have a feeling they don't hold the new priest in their hearts any more than they hold any other priest. That was last week. This Sunday—yesterday—Father Martin himself came knocking on everyone's doors, and said they must come to Mass. He had the soldiers with him, and he ordered them to drag people out. So the people came, sullenly, but did not respond to the Mass at all, and he was forced to shorten it. Then at midday, the bell rang again, and the church was full again, of people listening to an invisible Mass, a Mass we could only hear in our hearts.' Her usually dour face was full of the enjoyment of it. How the villagers must have enjoyed cocking a snook!

'I can't imagine this will be allowed to go on forever,' I said.

Jeannette smiled faintly. 'I don't think they can arrest us all, Monsieur. Can they?'

'I wouldn't put it past them,' I said.

Madame de Bellegarde looked haggard and worn, as if she hadn't slept for a long time. Her face went deathly pale when she saw me. Her hand flew up to her throat. She cried, 'Jacques! She's not . . .'

She couldn't finish her sentence. 'No, Madame,' I said gently. 'She is very much alive. She has been very ill, but she is getting better. And she is asking for you.'

Such joy leaped into her eyes then! 'Then you must take me to her. At once!'

'Yes, Madame. That is what I have come for.'

'Where is she?' she said, clasping and unclasping her hands.

I told her. I told her the whole story. She said, wonderingly, 'How very wonderful, to be so blessed by Our Lady's love and protection.' Her eyes filled with tears. 'And to be blessed by the kindness of people—of Pierre, with his marvelous gift and you, Jacques. I cannot even begin to know how to thank you and your family, how I can repay you.'

'There is nothing to repay, Madame,' I said quietly.

After an instant, I said, 'I don't want to hurry you, Madame—but we will need to leave soon.'

'Yes. Of course. You're right. We must leave. I would have liked to thank Pierre personally too, but he is back in the woods. His children, who are still sickly, are being looked after by his aunt. I will arrange to have a message sent to their home, and gifts. I will speak to my people about arrangements for the house, too. Your father has advised me on the best legal ways to protect my property against seizure; and Pierre and his friends will also protect it, with their own hands and wits. I know I can trust them. I will tell them the truth of where I am going, but they will tell anyone who comes snooping that I am on an extended family visit in the North. It's known I have a nephew there. I will gather together a few things for the journey. It won't take me long.'

She was as good as her word. She reappeared a short time later, dressed in travelling clothes, clasping a rather large bundle. She said, breathlessly, 'I've brought some of Flora's favourite books, and her flute, and her Dresden china shepherdess, that she loved so as a little girl. And some fresh clothes. We'll pass by the kitchen and collect a basket of good food, a ham, wine, some cheese, sweetmeats. We'll be able to have some fine picnics, we women, in that cottage, whilst the men go and hunt game for us!' She laughed then, like an excited young girl.

'Just so long as I'm not expected to chop too much

wood,' I murmured, taken by the same excitement. How strange—how strange—that the new world of peace and unity and fraternity amongst all humans was indeed ours for the taking now, that it wasn't a public thing of kings and parliaments and mobs and speeches in the street but the painful journey of a human heart, into a happiness that was as old as the dreams of man, yet as real as the ground on which we stood.

Twenty-three

We made good progress, the first day on the road. This time, instead of dog-legging through Brittany, we went up the centre, and put in at Tours. The town was very busy and agitated, with lots of people out on the streets, the National Guard patrolling nervously, and wild rumours flying of the imminent—yet again!—invasion of the Prussians, who never seemed to lose a battle and were beating back the exhausted invaders, our own French army, mercilessly.

Some said that the Prussians weren't just pushing the French out of their territory; they were sneaking into France disguised as French men and women. Some of the more excitable 'patriots' also claimed that these enemies without had the help of the enemy within—the *aristos* and the King and Queen. After all, the war was probably a ploy on their part, it was said, dismissing the fact the revolutionaries had wanted the war much more than the King. I did not take any notice of this wild and tedious talk; we had heard such things for weeks and even months.

We set out early the next morning. Everything seemed quiet. We had left Tours some distance behind when, all of a sudden, the horses' pace slowed. I looked out of the window to see what was happening, and saw a group of National Guard on the road. They had signaled to the coachman to stop.

Seconds later, a soldier came to the window. He had the leering, heavy, flushed face of the habitual drunkard. 'Out, Citizen, Citizeness,' he slurred. 'We have orders to stop and search all coaches today.'

Madame de Bellegarde looked anxiously at me. I said, 'We are in a great hurry, Citizen. We are going to a relative who is very ill.'

'They'll wait. Come on, out.'

We had to do as we were told. The soldier's truculent glance took in the quality of Madame's clothes, and my lawyer's black suit. He barked, 'Where are you going?'

'Paris,' I said, quickly.

'Where have you come from?'

'Tours.'

He nodded. 'And before that?'

'From our village.'

His eyes narrowed. He said, 'You will address me as Citizen Sergeant!'

'Yes, Citizen Sergeant.'

He peered at me. 'You have a strange accent, Citizen.'

Not knowing what he meant, I faltered. 'It is common in my part of the country, Citizen Sergeant.'

The sergeant jerked his head at a couple of the other soldiers. 'Search the coach.'

'Please,' said Madame, 'be careful . . .'

The sergeant stared insolently at her. 'So the lady has a tongue, after all. Why don't you wear the tricolore, my friends?' he added, giving us a wolfish grin. I could see now that he was the sort of man who enjoys every tiny bit of power that is afforded to him. He was playing with us like a cat plays with a mouse.

A wild anger flooded through me. I said, quietly, 'I was not aware that it was a compulsory requirement these days. I must have missed the passage of that law, I suppose, Citizen.'

It was a mistake I was to dearly regret. The sergeant flushed brick-red. Between clenched teeth, he said, 'They will like your jokes at the guard-house, I am sure.' He gestured to his men. 'Seize this man. He will come back to Tours with us and explain his disrespect of our revolution to a higher authority.'

I was seized and pinioned, with my arms behind my back. Poor Madame de Bellegarde made a movement towards me, but I shook my head. At that moment, the soldiers who had been searching the coach came out with our belongings.

'Books, Citizen . . . a porcelain figure . . . a flute . . .'

The sergeant sneered, 'Aristos, without a doubt! Have you looked to make sure the books aren't seditious?'

'They're collections of fairytales, Citizen.'

'Ha!' Frowning a little, he picked up the figurine of the little shepherdess. He turned it over, peering into the hole in the base as if there might be some secret document concealed there. He gave a low whistle. 'Made in Dresden,' he said. He turned to us. 'Dresden, you traitors!'

We stared at him, completely uncomprehending.

The sergeant hissed, 'Spies! Spies! That's what you are! Prussian spies! They warned us! And here you are! Here you are, on your way to kill us all!'

He was spitting the words out, his eyes wild. I thought he'd gone stark staring mad. I said, because Madame de Bellegarde seemed unable to speak, 'Citizen Sergeant, I must protest. We are good French citizens.'

He caught me a terrific blow on the side of the head, so hard that I thought for a moment I must faint. I staggered. He was on me in an instant. He was shouting in my face. His breath reeked of wine.

'Do you think I am a fool? Do you think I am an ignorant fool? Dresden is in Prussia, is it not?'

'If we were Prussian spies,' I said tightly, 'we would hardly carry an advertisement of the fact, Citizen Sergeant. Besides, what do you think the figurine could possibly mean, if I'm a spy? There are no hidden papers in there, you checked yourself!'

'Shut up, you spy!' he yelled, hitting me again. My head swam. I saw black stars exploding in my mind. 'Take them immediately to Tours—the two of them—yes, the coachman too—they're probably all spies.'

'No,' I said, thinking rapidly. 'They're not spies. I came across them on the road . . . I made them take me in the coach. I said I'd kill them if they didn't. That was why she said to be careful . . . she was warning you about me, that I'm dangerous.' Madame de Bellegarde looked desperately at me, but I ignored her, looking away, willing her to understand. She must get to Flora, if I couldn't. 'That figurine . . . it's mine. Let them go, Citizen Sergeant.'

The sergeant glared at me. 'You're a nice one for fairy-tales.' But his drunkard's mind wasn't working very clearly. I could see the idea didn't seem as ridiculous to him as it would have done to a sober man, or one less haunted by paranoid conspiracies. He said, 'They're all to go. But he's obviously the dangerous one. The others may well be his victims. We can sort it out at the guard-house. But we'll all get a medal, boys, for unmasking a Prussian spy!' He grasped the figurine in his hand, a cunning look in his eyes. 'And as to this—we'll get it out of you soon enough. It's a signal no doubt, a code of some sort.'

I could see that some of the other soldiers were looking a bit dubious. I clung onto that perception. I said, coldly,

'You're wasting time, Citizen Sergeant. At any moment, I may try to escape.'

That did it. He bundled us back into the coach, with two soldiers guarding us, and took his seat next to the coachman. With a look of triumph on his stupid, florid face, he thumped hard on the side of the coach, and we were on our way back to Tours.

The guard-house was full of prisoners, not very well-guarded, as they waited for a magistrate or some such thing to hear the charges against them. Soldiers sprawled amongst them, playing cards and gossiping. It appeared that lots of 'Prussian spies' had been caught that day. The 'spies' huddled close together, looking as unlike a bunch of clever, devious Germans as you were likely to get. But the atmosphere in there was like a circus; it was as if the catching of these 'spies' had been enough to put everyone else into high good humour. My spirits rose. I whispered to Madame, 'They can't all be stupid drunks. We'll be released. I'm just chafing at the delay.'

She whispered back, 'You don't know what you're saying, Jacques. You should never have said those things. You must deny these ridiculous accusations. I will not have you put in danger for my sake.'

'Please, Madame. It is *you* Flora has asked for. She needs you by her side. I think they'll release us, once they know the full story. But even if I'm held for a few days, it won't matter. I'll make my way there somehow. But you must go, Madame.'

I broke off as a soldier approached us. 'You are to come with me,' he said tonelessly, gesturing to Madame and I and the coachman.

'He is innocent,' Madame began, shooting me a defiant glance, but the soldier shrugged wearily.

'Tell that to the Captain,' he said. 'I'm not interested. We have been up to our necks in so-called spies today. It's very tiresome.'

My eyes met Madame's. This was promising!

The Captain, a thin, tall man in his early thirties or so, looked exhausted. He listened to Madame's explanation of our trip, he listened to the Sergeant's excitable story, then held out a languid hand for the figurine. He looked at it, and at the manufacturer's mark. He looked at me, at Madame, the coachman. He said to the Sergeant, 'Is this all you found?'

'Yes. Isn't it enough?' the Sergeant barked.

'For God's sake, man!' The Captain thumped the table. The tricolore cockade in his hat almost flew out, in his agitation. 'Do you know how busy I am? There are real traitors and liars and brigands and spies in our midst, Sergeant, and you bring me as proof of these people's identity a figurine from Dresden! Why, my own lady has one just like it on her shelf! Are we to arrest her as a spy, too?'

The Sergeant had gone pale. He stammered, 'No, Citizen Captain, of course not.'

'You should control your drinking,' said the Captain, coldly. 'We expect our National Guard to be sober and beyond reproach. I may recommend you are demoted.'

The Sergeant was sweating now. 'Sir . . . Citizen . . . I meant only to . . .'

'Release these people,' said the captain, turning back to his papers. 'And stop wasting my time.'

I couldn't help the huge smile that crept over my face then, at the sight of the Sergeant's discomfiture. But it was too early to celebrate. For just as I was about to follow the others out of the door, the Sergeant said, in a strangled voice, 'Citizen, maybe I was wrong about the woman, and the coachman but what of the young man? He said he was a spy. Why would he do that? What possible cause could he have to do so?'

The Captain raised his head. He looked searchingly at me, in silence. After a moment, he said, 'Perhaps you are right, Citizen Sergeant. It is a strange reaction, I grant you. People usually protest their innocence. It could bear some looking into. Very well, then. We'll hold him in prison till we check him out fully. The others are to be left alone. Do it, Sergeant.'

I didn't miss the look of triumphant hate that flashed

across the Sergeant's face then. I had made an enemy. There was nothing for it but to do as I was told. I wasn't really worried; I still felt invincible, protected, in the very lap even of Our Lady, who had intervened directly to save Flora's life and who surely blessed our future together.

Passing an anguished Madame de Bellegarde outside, I managed to whisper to her, 'Don't worry, Madame. Everything will be fine. Please get to Flora . . . stay with her and my parents—and take them to England as soon as you can. I'm sure I'll be joining you all very shortly. I have nothing to reproach myself with. They will have to let me go, eventually.'

My last sight of her took in the anxiety on her face, just before the coachman hustled her away before the Captain should change his mind.

Twenty-four

I was flung into a dim, cramped, straw-strewn cell already occupied by several men. I was just settling myself into a corner when a voice whispered in my ear. 'Psst, Jacques!'

I knew that voice! I said, 'Jona—'

'*Chut*,' said my English friend, his familiar grin flashing at me from the dirty face of a vagabond, 'you remember me. I'm Thomas Tuvier,' he said, in a slightly louder voice, in fluent French. 'From Nantes.'

'Thomas,' I said, 'how wonderful to see you again.'

'Not so wonderful, friend,' said Jonathan, drawing me aside to the darkest corner of the cell, where no one wanted to linger, because of the stench from the waste bucket. 'I thought you were in the north. I heard that from our mutual friend Casgrain.'

'Ah,' I said carefully, 'you've been in Paris?'

'Yes,' he said, shooting me a quick look, 'earlier, that is. How did you come to be here?'

'I was a fool—I made a swaggering sort of joke. It wasn't taken well,' I said.

He smiled. 'No—not with Prussian fever infecting everyone.'

'How did you get taken?'

'Oh, I was caught up in a demonstration, yesterday, and I was pounced on by a Guard—I shouted *Vive Tom Paine* so he'd know I was on the right side—but unfortunately he didn't know our hero's name and thought I'd sworn at him in German!'

We looked at each other and burst out laughing. The others in the cell looked reproachfully at us. But I didn't care. The feeling of lightness that had buoyed me up ever since the miracle of Flora's cure made me look even at my present predicament with a certain hilarity. I just could not take anything else seriously.

After a little while, Jonathan said quietly, 'We're going to have to get out of here together, don't you agree?'

I nodded. 'I don't think the Captain really believes I'm a Prussian spy,' I said. 'I doubt that he'll hold me for very long. And I'll tell him you're a friend of mine.'

He looked at me and shook his head. 'I don't think we'll wait around to be questioned,' he whispered. 'Have you any idea how long that could be? The Captain has better things to do than waste his time personally questioning us. They're holding prisoners in every cell. He'll be waiting for the arrival of some dedicated magistrate. We could be here for weeks.'

I looked at him in dismay. 'I can't possibly . . .'

'Neither can I,' he said. 'That's why I'm not waiting. Agreed?'

'Agreed,' I said, trying to sound cool, though my heart was beating fast with an excitement I didn't want to show.

He grinned. 'Good man. Don't ask questions. Tonight. I'll wake you. Meanwhile, best get some rest, my friend. There's gruel at midday, but no other food. Nothing else to do but sleep.' And with a little nod at me, he stepped back a few paces, found a space in a corner near the door, curled up, his hat over his eyes, and appeared to go to sleep.

I was seething with impatience. I couldn't work out how he could go to sleep, just like that. I couldn't possibly.

For a while, I covertly examined my fellow prisoners. They were a motley crew—all ages, all walks of life, most looking uneasy, even anxious, a few resigned, and even fewer utterly indifferent, like Jonathan. Several of them looked like the inside of a cell wasn't exactly foreign territory to them. Nobody seemed to be getting ready to make a dash for it but then, what did I know? This was all very new territory to *me*. I looked around the cell, too, trying to work out how Jonathan thought we'd escape. Short of making a run for the door, I couldn't see how we could do it. The window was too narrow and small and barred too of course; but could there be, perhaps, a grating in the floor, under all the straw? Perhaps Jonathan knew where it was. I was sure, anyway, that he was used to getting out of tight spots; and I was only glad he hadn't already done so, before I was flung in there with him. What a piece of luck that had been!

Midday came, and with it the promised gruel. This was disgusting stuff, thin and watery, with an unpleasant smell. I let a skinny, sallow youth with huge, hungry eyes have mine. He gobbled it down, glaring suspiciously at me, as if I might change my mind. But I was far too excited and nervous to even think about eating, let alone touch that vile mess. I went to sit near Jonathan and, drawing my knees up to my chin, fell into a romantic dream of an imagined future with Flora.

Time passed. My heartbeat slowed, my limbs grew heavier. Around me, other men talked softly or sat or lay in a trance. Jonathan hadn't woken up. The cell, which was lit only by the tiny window, grew progressively darker. The stench grew heavier. More time passed. My head lolled onto my shoulder. I woke up with a jerk; but I couldn't keep my head upright, all my thoughts sliding into vagueness, my limbs as heavy as lead. Darkness fell; the cell was silent now, except for the sound of sighs and snores. I fell in and out of a light doze, waking now and then with a start.

It must have been at least midnight when a voice spoke in my ear. 'Ready?'

My head was full of dark fog, my limbs like stone. But

I managed to prise open my eyes. Jonathan was bending over me. 'Time to go, *mon ami*,' he whispered. 'Stay crouched down . . . you understand . . . follow me.'

Still half-asleep, half-thinking I was in a dream, I followed him—not to the window, or a grating in the floor, but to the door, which was ever so slightly open. Not understanding at all what was going on, I followed Jonathan as he slipped out. The door closed softly behind us, and was carefully locked. A young soldier whispered, 'Come on, then.'

Obviously, nobody was worried about prisoners escaping. The guard-house was as quiet as the cell had been, soldiers sprawled in corners, snoring. It was strange, passing amongst all these sleeping people, as if we were in Sleeping Beauty's castle. I was beginning to wake up, and to wonder what was happening. Why had the soldier let us out? Who was he? Had Jonathan bribed him?

We reached the street door. The soldier opened it. He spoke in a low voice to Jonathan, shook hands briefly with him, shot me a quick look, nodded, and vanished back into the guard-house, closing the door behind him.

It was pitch-black in the street, except for the lantern over the guard-house door. We left that light well behind as, not speaking, we hurried into the next street and down an alleyway. At one point, Jonathan stopped, listened, and pushed me into a dark doorway. 'The Watch,' he murmured in my ear. I could hear the tramp, tramp of feet only paces away. It was as well to keep completely quiet. There was a curfew: the Watch policed the city streets at night, and anyone out at this hour would be sure to be thought a malefactor and arrested on the spot.

The tramp of feet passed. I took a deep breath. Jonathan whispered, 'Don't relax yet. We have to make it across town, to the home of a friend. Are you fit?'

'Am I *fit*?' I retorted, indignantly.

He grinned. 'Good. Follow me, then. We must be quick.'

By the time we reached our destination, I could understand why he'd asked me if I was fit. It was a journey undertaken at a gallop, through alleys, over walls, keeping out of sight and sound of the Watch. At last, we came to a house set back behind a fairly high garden wall, only a block from the city gates, which were of course locked and patrolled. We scrambled over the wall, dropping down into a large, well-tended vegetable garden. Jonathan said, 'Wait here' and vanished silently up the path that led to the back of the house. I sat down on the edge of a garden bed and recovered my breath.

He was back in moments, with a tall, silver-haired old man clad in night clothes. 'This is my friend Jacques, Monsieur Perrin,' Jonathan said.

The old man nodded and smiled in a friendly fashion. 'You are welcome. Now you'll be hungry and tired no doubt. I'll get some bread, some cheese, some wine. You can sleep in the tool-shed. It's warm and dry and no one will disturb you there. The gardener has a couple of days off and is visiting his family in the country. We'll leave tomorrow morning. I can take you to Blois or nearby.'

He took us to the tool-shed, a snug little mud-brick building with a bare earth floor. Gardening tools were lined up against the wall, hessian sacks were stacked along a shelf, and these Monsieur Perrin spread out on the floor. 'I'll be back soon,' he promised, and left us.

I was bursting with curiosity by now. 'Who is he?'

'A kind old gentleman,' said Jonathan, vaguely, settling down on a sack. 'Ho! It smells strongly of garlic in here, don't you think? I suppose they must keep their crop here when it's ready.'

'Jonathan, please, tell me. How did you manage to get the soldier to let us out?'

'Oh, he's a kind *young* gentleman,' said Jonathan lightly, then, catching my exasperated expression, he added, 'Look, Jacques, you have to understand that I have friends in quite a few places in this country. The radicals—the Jacobins *and* the Girondins—may think they've got everything going their way, and that they have no real opposition, but they're wrong. There's no opposition to speak of in parliament, because politicians are too ambitious or too cowardly; but in the villages, and towns, resistance is growing, men are organising, already.

They know for certain that they can't rely on this weak and useless government to save France from disaster. They understand Burke's words that for evil to succeed, it is only necessary for good men to do nothing. *They do not intend to do nothing.*'

I said, sharply, 'Do they know you're English, your friends?'

'I doubt it. It doesn't matter. I am truly their friend,' he said.

I let that pass for the moment. I could hardly appear ungrateful for our escape. I said, 'So you've been in France a while, making these links?'

'Oh yes.'

'What do you think's going to happen, then?'

He looked at me in some surprise. 'Why, the King will be overthrown, of course. The radicals will take over. I'll wager that by the end of the year France will be in their hands. And against that day, we have to have links everywhere in this country because nothing is surer also than that, once they're successful here, the radicals will declare war on England, and everywhere else, too. Including everyone in their own country who doesn't agree with them.'

His matter-of-fact tone chilled me. 'Don't be absurd,' I stammered. 'Only madmen could think they could declare war on the whole of Europe and win. Why, we can't even win against the Austrians and Prussians! And the people hate the war. What you say is crazy—quite beyond the borders of sense.'

He smiled faintly. 'You know our radical friends, surely, Jacques. Do you think they are what the respectable would call *sensible men*?'

'No, but . . .'

'They are men of faith, Jacques. *Their* faith, to which they hold as true and as fanatically as any Inquisitor. They *know* they are right. They will *show* the world they're right. I've got to know them well, our radical friends, Jacques. They are fired with a pure self-righteous zeal to create a new and sinless and just world. They will do *anything*— use *any* method—to create this world.'

'Danton—' I began.

'Pah! Don't put your trust in men like him! I grant you he is less unpleasant than that cold fanatic Robespierre, or Saint-Just, or Marat, or Hébert—but he is nonetheless dangerous, because he is ambitious, and he wants his will to prevail. They think they know what is best for everyone. All of them are like that. No power on earth will change their minds. And they do not fear Heaven's judgment either, because either they do not believe there is anything greater than Man, or else they are convinced Heaven is on their side, anyway.'

I shivered. 'I cannot believe in their success.'

He shrugged. 'Can't you? It seems to me that even if your mind refuses to believe, your heart is telling you otherwise—or else why would you be planning to leave France with all your loved ones?'

I was saved from answering this unquestionably just observation by the re-entry of Monsieur Perrin, with the food. He left us with it, promising to wake us at first light. We were to leave in his market cart, he said. It was unlikely our disappearance would have been noticed: there had been so many people arrested that it was doubtful the paperwork had kept up, and the guards wouldn't know who was in the cell. Only the Sergeant who had singled me out might realise my absence, but he wouldn't be back on duty till the morning, and it was unlikely he'd take the trouble to go and see me, anyway.

Jonathan didn't talk any more about the political situation after that, for which I was thankful. Truth to tell, I felt that the politicians could all go to the Devil, as long as my loved ones were safe and well out of this nightmare. So instead, as we ate and drank, we spoke lightly about Jonathan's family, and he said how glad they would all be to see us, and how there was a comfortable house to rent only a few miles from Willesdene, which he was sure would suit us and so on—peaceful and happy talk of a future that I knew now was within my grasp. After a while, we grew silent, and rested, and it seemed like no time had passed when Monsieur Perrin shook us awake.

Outside was the grey light just before dawn. We

followed Monsieur Perrin to the stables, where a covered market cart, harnessed to four huge draught-horses, stood waiting. The cart was filled with barrels and sacks and piles of vegetables; we hid under the sacks, and he covered us with vegetables. Then the cart rumbled off over the cobblestones, stopping very soon at the gates. We heard some murmured conversation as Monsieur Perrin spoke to the guards, then the gates opened and we were through.

He'd told us to keep quiet and stay hidden until we were well out of the city. It wasn't a very pleasant experience; we could feel every bump, every jolt, the sacks were suffocating and dusty, and I desperately wanted to sneeze. I was very glad when after what seemed like hours of agony, the cart stopped and Monsieur Perrin's voice said, 'You can come out now, lads.'

I didn't wait to be told twice. The old man restrained a smile when he saw my dirty face and dusty clothes. 'Now look, boys, if we're stopped, you're my workers, helping me with my market load. You look the part well enough.'

Nobody stopped us. We saw National Guardsmen once or twice along the way, but they were less zealous than the ones on the road to Tours, and seemed to have no interest in us whatsoever. The cart finally rumbled into a market town some distance from Blois, and there we said goodbye to kind Monsieur Perrin and continued on our way. It is not important to describe how I got to Ermenonville—what is important is all those things that came beforehand, and that gave me my first experience both of prison and of the clandestine world of the agent. Suffice it to say that Jonathan and I parted on the outskirts of Paris—he said he had business to attend to, but would come and see us at Ermenonville in a few days' time. After that, avoiding the city, I made my way north, arriving at the cottage in the woods a few days after leaving Tours.

When I came up the path, the very first thing I saw was Flora, sitting on a chair in the sun, a wrap around her shoulders and on her knees. She still looked frail, but her colour was better, her eyes brighter. Her mother and mine were sitting by her, embroidering. Mother saw me first, and jumped up, a hand to her mouth. Flora looked up to see what the matter was. Her eyes met mine. She smiled. Her mouth formed my name, so sweetly.

I forgot about seemliness. I ran to her side, and knelt by her chair. I took her hands, and kissed them fervently.

'Jacques,' she said. 'Oh, I'm so glad you're back . . . I knew you'd be here soon. I told Mother. I told your mother.'

Now I looked at Mother's face properly. I said, 'What's wrong?'

'It's your father,' she said. 'He became worried about you, when he heard what had happened. He's gone looking for you.'

'Oh, no!'

'Don't worry. I'm sure he'll be all right. He's a careful

man. He'll learn what happened soon enough, and he'll be back.' Her lip trembled a bit, but her eyes were bright. 'But how did you get away, Jacques?'

'Through the grace of God and the kindness of friends,' I said cheerfully, and sitting down beside the three women, I explained what had happened, embroidering it a little to make it even more exciting. I was rewarded by the brightness of their eyes, and the gaiety of their laughter and, especially, by Flora's gentle touch on my hair.

Twenty-five

Days passed. We got a letter from Father. He knew I was safe, and had decided to go back to Bellegarde to wind up all our affairs before returning to us and setting sail for England. He would be gone three or four weeks at the most, he wrote. We tried not to let that worry us. And indeed, those were warm, pleasant, happy days, in our remote little hide-away.

Because the cottage was already full, I slept outside, under a tree and the glorious stars. Flora was improving visibly; the doctor visited a couple of times and said she would soon be well enough to travel. Yet the memory of what had brought her here still eluded her, and none of us spoke of it. She sat in the sun with me for hours, and I read to her, and we talked. Days passed. Weeks. As her legs got stronger, we began to take short walks. Sometimes our mothers joined us; sometimes they sat in the cottage and embroidered, talked or cooked. It was a time of perfect, peaceful domesticity—and I even learned to master the axe a little better!

Once or twice the Count of Ermenonville came walking through the woods to pay a visit to us—or rather, I suspected, to our mothers—and once he sent his carriage round to invite us all to partake of cakes and tea, and showed us the island, in the middle of the lake in his gardens, where Rousseau was buried. He was a great talker, this Count, but though prone to reminisce about his famous late guest, he did not, thank God, engage us in any political discussions at all. We had decided not to tell anyone that we were planning to go to England, but had told people that we would go back to Paris once Flora was better.

Edmond did not visit us, though he sent a note saying he would come when he got the chance. Meanwhile, Casgrain sent a basket of fruit, and a letter informing us he was going away on campaign and would be gone for weeks. We were all relieved, me most of all. I remembered the look on his face as he'd looked at Flora, and had feared what it meant. Had he fallen for her? But his leaving on campaign seemed to prove he hadn't. We had nothing to fear from him.

The rose cuttings, as I'd thought, had all died—save one, which struggled desperately to survive and still showed green when you scraped at it with a fingernail. Then one day I saw, to my joy, that it had produced a bud—and a few days later, a rose. It was only small, nowhere near the size of the ones Flora had grown in

Bellegarde, but it was definitely her rose: white, streaked with pink, and with a heady smell. When Flora saw it that morning, her face changed. She asked to be brought close to it. She sniffed it. She looked questioningly at us. 'It's so beautiful.'

Her mother whispered, 'Do you recognise it, darling? Do you remember it?'

'Yes,' said Flora slowly, in a slightly puzzled tone. 'I seem to remember there were a great many of them. I remember holding them.' Her eyes sharpened with the effort of memory. 'I grew them!' she said, startled. 'I grew them.' She looked at the rose, and touched it gently. 'It is the rose of Our Lady,' she said, at last, after a silence. Tears sprang into her eyes. 'It is Our Lady's rose. She answered my prayers.' Despite the tears, her face was radiant.

'Yes,' said her mother. Her eyes were wet too. 'She answered all our prayers. She kept you safe, my darling. She kept you safe.'

'Yes,' said Flora, and she touched the hazel cross lightly with her fingers. She'd taken to wearing it around her neck, on a thin string.

Mother and I tiptoed away as Flora and her mother hugged each other. Mother said, 'I think that now she will be truly healed, body and soul.'

'Yes,' I said, moved even beyond tears, my heart full to bursting with love, and hope, and relief. It was still too early to begin planning for when I could ask Flora to marry me; I knew I could not even think of asking her while she was still in this frail state, vulnerable as a little child. But now that the balance of her mind was being slowly, gently repaired, I could look forward to the day, not very long hence, when it might become right to broach such things.

A few days later, Jonathan arrived. He silently appeared at our door while we were eating breakfast, and gave us all quite a turn. He had come to tell us that he would arrange our passage on a ship from Boulogne to England. He would send associates to help us make the trip to Boulogne in wagons and carts. It would be slow but safe. He would also arrange to have forged papers for us, and would organise to have Madame's coach and horses sold—it would be better to do that very discreetly. She and Flora should also leave behind any fine clothes or anything that might give away their status. Persecution of anyone thought to be an 'aristo' had intensified in recent weeks. He told us that there had been some very unpleasant incidents not long ago; several people had been shot and feelings were running very high.

He also said we should write to Father, telling him what we were doing and enjoining him to join us in England as soon as he possibly could. Soon, it would be the third anniversary of the Bastille riot—14th July—and there was trouble tipped to break out. To me, privately, he said that he had heard from his informants that Marat was gaining in power, and that he and other *sans-culotte* leaders in the Paris municipality had told their friends in parliament that this date would be a propitious one on which to overthrow the 'tyrant'. The radical parliamentarians had not yet agreed to this. Though they were determined to overthrow the King, they wanted a more significant excuse. They wanted to strike at exactly the right moment. If the coup was to succeed, it must appear completely justified. But it was only a matter of time. Something would be found. They knew the street fighters and mob leaders wouldn't wait forever.

Paris, he said, was a vipers' nest of intrigue. With the end game in sight but no end, either, to our army's defeat on foreign battlefields, and the menacing approach of the Prussians, the atmosphere was frantic. Spies, informants and go-betweens from all factions worked day and night; deals were struck between different leaders, only to be betrayed almost immediately. The stakes were very high for any ambitious politician, for a misstep might mean death or exile.

This unpleasant news brought an end to our idyll. Taking care not to alarm Flora, Mother, Madame and I discussed the situation, and came to the conclusion that we must do as Jonathan advised us. I was concerned about the length of time a letter would take to reach Father; we had received a letter from him a few days before, dated several days previously—informing us he was well, and had nearly finished everything. With the roads even more troubled, the letter might take more than two weeks to reach him. But we would have to go well before that. And then he wouldn't even know which ship we had sailed on.

In the end we decided, against my mother's instinct, to send him a letter only when we knew which ship we were to go on. That would have to wait till Boulogne. We would leave for the port in two or three days' time, with the people Jonathan would send for us. The forged papers would declare us to be an extended farming family, he told us. All our fine clothes would be sold, along with the horses. We must look the part.

Then, a couple of days before we were due to depart, who should turn up but Edmond—and Athénaïs Casgrain with him! I saw them first; I'd been gathering wood in the forest and heard the sound of their voices. Without greeting them, I raced silently through the woods back to the cottage, to warn the women. On no account must anyone breathe a word of our plans, I said—they, above all, must not suspect what we were going to do.

I didn't say we could not trust Edmond any more. I didn't need to. We were no longer friends, but not enemies either. It was just that any natural sympathy which we'd once had, born of our youth, and in Edmond's case, of our shared childhood, had faded quite away under the pressure of events.

Even now, sitting in this terrible place, I can only marvel at the sangfroid of Madame de Bellegarde. Even if she still had the indulgence of kin towards Edmond—though that had been sorely tested—people like Athénaïs Casgrain represented all she most loathed. She was a representative of a new world that had laid waste to her own and would soon destroy it completely.

Athénaïs spoke freely, dressed immodestly, and constantly interrupted, even when she wasn't being spoken to. And yet Edmond's aunt spoke to her courteously and coolly, as if she were an unexpected but not unwelcome guest.

Having not seen Athénaïs for some time, I was surprised by her evolution; last time I'd seen her she was a forthright but not immodest young woman. Now she laughed too loudly, hung on Edmond's arm, made outrageous comments which she must have known would offend us, and treated Flora with regal indifference. I wondered what had happened to make her eyes so hectic, her speech so frantic, her movements so jerky. Perhaps Rousselin had merely lived up to his unpleasant reputation. She certainly looked like a creature haunted by something.

Edmond did not explain her presence. But reading between the lines, it seemed clear that she had been painfully discarded by Rousselin, and had crawled back to take refuge with her less important, but kinder, former lover. I thought it spoke volumes about Edmond's feelings for her that he'd agreed to take her back. He must love her, in his own way.

But I thought it typical of Edmond's selfish arrogance that he hadn't even considered how his family might view the girl—I didn't expect him to have the slightest thought for Mother and me, of course. Athénaïs seemed immune to any scruples on that score, too. They had brought a basket of good things from the city and clearly thought we would welcome their presence with delight and gratitude.

Edmond prattled on about the excitements in his life. Things were really looking up, he said; he had several large commissions, and he'd been appointed to a committee on revolutionary arts and public festivals, run by the painter David. It was very exciting work, he said, and very important—so important that Casgrain had even given him permission to leave the National Guard. Casgrain himself was away fighting the Prussians, still. He'd distinguished himself in battle, and everyone thought he'd be rewarded with a proper political position when he came back. Athénaïs, meanwhile, had begun to make a name for herself on the stage, acting in revolutionary plays written and produced by her friends. Things were wonderful! Things were tremendous! We must come to Paris and see them! We must share in their good fortune!

For all their boasting, an unexpected pity gripped me as I listened to them. Edmond had said they'd moved house; and now he told us Casgrain had 'given him permission' to leave the National Guard to sit on a committee of paint-daubers and party-planners. It all indicated that he was being pushed to an outer circle. Casgrain and his other political friends must not trust his judgment or stability, even if they still thought enough of him not to break with him altogether.

Of course none of us breathed a word about our own plans. Madame de Bellegarde thanked Edmond for his kind invitation, but said that we were going to head back to Bellegarde very soon, that Flora must convalesce at home. Edmond wasn't really interested; it was clear he'd decided that his intervention had not brought the result he wanted and now he'd just be glad to put the question of his recalcitrant aunt and cousin well behind him. Besides, he said grandly, if ever any of us did have any trouble, we were to apply to him; we had to remember that he had the ear of all the most influential men in the country.

They left late in the afternoon. I accompanied them through the woodland paths back to their little gig which they'd left parked at the edge of our woods. When we were well out of earshot of the cottage, Athénaïs said to me, with a little shudder, 'Poor you, Jacques, having to go back to the country! Bad enough being stuck in this dull forest in the company only of women! It would drive me mad . . . We can take you back to Paris if you like, can't we, Edmond?'

'Don't be silly, dearest,' said Edmond. 'Jacques loves it like this, don't you? He loves the simple life.'

'Just like Rousseau,' said Athénaïs. She laughed. 'Well, you can keep it, Jacques. It's not for me. I need to be in the midst of action, of real happenings!'

I smiled faintly. They were obviously completely unsuspicious. I said, 'It's not that simple, our life. We're hardly peasants. Neither Rousseau nor we have ever really had to fend for our own crust. Still! It's been quite pleasant. And it's been good for Flora's health.'

'She did look better,' said her cousin. He shot me a glance. 'You haven't proposed to her yet, have you?'

'No,' I said.

He smiled to himself. I knew what he was thinking— that I had seen the error of my ways. That I had given up on my dream—that I had understood, as he put it, that I was not right for her, that I was not what she needed. I had no intention of telling him anything in my heart. I did not trust him.

Athénaïs looked at the two of us. Her smile was impish. 'Oho, a little situation, is there?'

'Nothing at all,' I snapped.

'I still don't think you're right for her,' said Edmond. 'But it is your life. And hers. You needn't worry. I'm not after Flora myself, you know.'

'No, he's after me,' said Athénaïs, roguishly. Edmond shot her a fond glance. Somehow, it touched me, that pathetic little scene; the two of them, wrapped in their own little world, their delusions of importance. It made me say goodbye to them a little more fondly than I would otherwise have done.

Yet I thought I would probably never see them again. It was not a prospect that would distress me unduly, I thought as I made my way back through the woods to the cottage. But I could not help a certain melancholy creeping into my thoughts as I walked. I had said goodbye to Pierre and now to Edmond.

The four friends were now well and truly scattered, separated, no longer bound by anything, not even that vow we'd made, so long ago. But what did that matter? Flora and I—each other's best friends, loving friends, and, I hoped, much more than that, in the not-too-distant future—were still together, and always would be.

Twenty-six

This morning, I woke up from a few hours' restless sleep to the realisation I have only two weeks left. I have tried not to sleep, to write and read day and night, because I must finish before they come for me. But it is impossible. My body cries out for sleep. It cries out for dreams.

Yesterday, they came for one of my cell neighbours, Louis Tullard. Over the weeks I've been here, I've spoken to him quite a lot. We'd become real friends, though so much separated us. He'd been a fire-breathing radical, from the very beginning; but he was now their enemy too. Like so many of those men I'd met that night of Athénaïs' salon—Brissot, the Rollands, Condorcet, Danton, Hébert, Desmoulins, all dead now, all dead—his radicalism hadn't saved him.

He had dared to question the motives of the green-eyed prig who sat at the head of the Committee of Public Safety; had dared to wonder aloud if stern Brutus had not become Caligula, glorying in blood and evil. They tell me he went to his death without tears and screams, unlike Hébert, but with no stirring speeches of defiance either, like Danton, or calls for justice, like Madame Rolland, or even gentle forgiveness, like poor King Louis; but merely with a glance bleak as a winter's night.

Poor man! He had lost everything, even his dreams, even his faith in his new world. And he feared the idea of an afterlife; he hoped he would just become insensible, a rotting corpse, that his spirit would not exist any more but he was afraid it would survive and he would have to face whatever was there beyond. Desolation, futility and despair was all he left with, and all he left behind him.

Is this why I'm writing? Because I cannot bear the notion that desolation may be the only legacy I leave behind me? I do not know.

I will not write about our last days in the cottage at Ermenonville, or our departure from it one moonlit night. I will not write about our slow journey to Boulogne, which passed without incident if not without acute discomfort, in farmers' carts and wagons, and crowded public stagecoaches. I will go straight on to the scene in Boulogne itself, where we arrived one afternoon.

The town was packed full of people, many of whom were passengers bound for England. The National Guard and municipal officials were out in force too, patrolling the streets, stopping people, asking for papers and making rude comments about deserters but otherwise not attempting to stop anyone. It was not yet a crime to emigrate, though it was already an occasion for opprobrium and suspicion. All the inns were full, so we decided to go straight to the captain of the ship Jonathan had booked for us—the *Destiny*—and ask if we could immediately take up our quarters while we waited for the next day's sailing.

No sooner said than done: Captain Eden of the *Destiny* was happy to give us permission. The women had a small, cramped cabin allocated to them, but I was to bunk down on the floor in the men's quarters, all other private accommodation having been taken by wealthier and more important passengers than me. It suited me fine; I doubted I would want much sleep at all.

I was just waiting for the ladies to emerge from a nap in their cabin—we planned to go ashore to eat—when a familiar voice hailed me. 'Jacques! Jacques Verdun!'

I turned. To my astonishment, my father's friend, Monsieur Rochas—he who had tried to get the Mayor of our town to help us—stood there. He looked as amazed as I did.

'I didn't know you were bound for England!' he said.

'Nor I you, sir.'

'It's more than time,' he said. 'I am taking my wife and myself out of harm's way.'

'Harm's way, sir?' I asked, puzzled. Monsieur Rochas was in the municipal assembly. He had supported the Revolution from the beginning, though he was a moderate. What had happened to cause him to flee?

He looked curiously at me, searching my face. 'You don't know!' he cried.

'Know what, sir?' But already my blood was running cold.

'I thought you must have heard.'

'Heard what?' I asked, suddenly struck with a deathly fear. Behind me, the cabin door opened, and my mother stood on the threshold. She had heard my last words. She'd seen Monsieur Rochas. She went deathly pale.

'What has happened?'

He bowed. 'Madame, I am most relieved to see you well.'

Mother closed the door behind her. She came towards him. 'Please, Monsieur Rochas. What's happened to my husband?'

'He's been arrested, Madame. He's been taken to a prison in Nantes.'

She interrupted. 'On what charge?'

'Obstructing an official; conspiring to hide a renegade priest; assaulting a National Guard. Oh, and assaulting the Mayor.'

'The Mayor?'

'Of our town,' said Monsieur Rochas. 'I'm afraid I was accused of having approved. Which is why I had to flee, or run the risk of being arrested myself. I'm not a brave man. I don't want to go to prison and have my family disgraced.'

Mother stared at him. 'But I don't understand. My husband is a peaceful citizen. He was in Bellegarde to wind up our affairs. He would never use violence.'

Monsieur Rochas sighed. 'Your husband, Madame, is a man with a passion for justice. He became involved in certain problems in Bellegarde. He tried to negotiate a reasonable compromise, but the authorities would not budge even a hair's breadth. They became tired of him. And he, it must be admitted, grew tired of them. He went to try and get the Mayor to intervene, but I'm afraid that jumped-up bullfrog would not listen. So he punched him on the nose. The other charges, well, they've just been added for good measure.'

My heart was swelling with pride as well as fear. I said, 'We cannot leave him in prison, Mother. I will go and get him out.'

'Don't be silly, Jacques!' Mother cried. 'How can you get him out? Just because you escaped from a prison once doesn't mean you are invincible. Besides, these charges against a respectable lawyer are ridiculous. They'll never stick. He's never been involved in politics.'

'You know we cannot leave him there, Mother. It might take a long while for his case to be heard. The prisons are already full. His health is not good. In a damp and dirty prison cell he could get ill again and even die. We cannot take that chance.'

'Then I will go with you,' said Mother.

'No, Mother. You must go on to England, with Flora and her mother. You know the Wills family, and they do not. They will need you there.'

'I think I can make my own decision,' said my mother, with a flash of temper. 'I will not have my son dictating to me.'

'Please, Mother,' I begged. 'I am sure Father would want it. He would want you to be safely away from all this.'

'He would want *you* safely away, too,' she snapped. Monsieur Rochas, who had been listening to all this with an air of discomfort, broke in to say, 'Madame, if I may say so, I do believe the boy is right. But if you are determined to go, well, I offer myself as guarantor and protector of the other ladies. I have been to England several times myself, and speak tolerable English. And if you give me the address of where they are to go, I am sure I can accompany them there.'

'Would you, Monsieur Rochas?' Her smile was warm. 'You are a good friend.'

'But Flora and her mother don't know Monsieur Rochas—' I began.

'We can introduce them right now,' said Mother firmly. 'I am sure they will understand our situation.

Besides, Jacques, if I go there is no need for you to come with me. I can likely deal with authorities better than you can.'

'I can't let you go on your own,' I cried. 'Mother, you don't know what these people can be like.'

'Don't I?' she snapped. 'Out of the egg only yesterday, it seems, and thinks he knows more than his mother!'

The cabin door opened. Madame de Bellegarde came out. She closed the door and looked at us with a little smile. 'Forgive me. I could not help overhearing.'

'Madame de Bellegarde, Monsieur Rochas,' said Mother.

He bowed over her hand. '*Enchant*é, Madame.'

'*Enchant*ée, Monsieur.' Greetings over, Flora's mother turned to my mother. 'If I may say so, Hélène, I think you should let Jacques go with you. It is important to him, I know. And Flora and I will be quite safe, especially with this gentleman's kind guidance. We will be looking forward to your arrival in England. But you must do what you must do.'

I should have been pleased, then, but I wasn't. All at once, a demon of self-doubt nagged at me. Was Flora's mother taking this attitude because secretly she was glad her daughter and I would be separated? What was she intending to do in England? Perhaps they might disappear . . .

I felt bitterly ashamed of these nasty little thoughts.

To dismiss them, I said, too heartily, 'You see, Mother, you are outnumbered. I will go with you. We will get Father out. And we will take the next ship to England.'

My mother looked at me, then at Flora's mother. She shrugged a little. 'Very well. As you will. But if you are to come with me, Jacques, you are to follow my instructions, not act according to hot-headed whim. The bravery of young men is all very well, but womanly wiles can sometimes be the much more successful policy. Isn't that so, Monsieur Rochas?'

He smiled. 'My wife does tell me so, indeed, Madame.'

'Sensible woman,' said Mother. 'Now then, what about that dinner? Monsieur Rochas, would you and your family like to join us?'

'Indeed we would, Madame,' he said.

And so that evening all of us had dinner together in a tolerable eating establishment. We laughed and talked and joked, a little overtaken by a kind of desperate hilarity that held more than a trace of unease in it. When we finally parted, it was well past midnight. Mother and I came back to the ship; we would farewell the others at dawn just before we went ashore again. I don't think any of us slept much that night. I certainly didn't. My mind kept turning things over and over, assailed by vague premonitions, unease, doubts, questions.

All night, I tortured myself. I was mad, I thought desperately. I should stick to Flora like the proverbial limpet. I should not let her out of my sight. Or else she would forget me. She liked me, yes, she liked having me around, but she hadn't said she loved me. She hadn't said she wanted to be with me always. I hadn't asked her to marry me—but surely she must know that was what I wanted. Yet she said nothing. She didn't make it easy for me to speak. Did that show she *didn't* love me? That I was her friend, yes, but could never be her lover? Did her mother know that? She knew her daughter best, after all.

Was her kindness towards me—her apparent willingness to accept the prospect of my becoming her son-in-law—was it just an expression of her honour, her feeling she owed me a debt of gratitude? Once safely in peaceful England, would her older feelings of aristocratic pride return? She wanted, above all, her daughter's safety and peace of mind. There were many gentlemen of far greater birth and breeding and wealth than me in England, after all. Of course, they were foreigners. But for Flora, an alliance with one of those English gentlemen might well bring much more safety and protection than marriage to an impecunious young Frenchman of less-than-ideal family background.

I castigated myself for these dark imaginings. Flora's mother had shown no sign of such ugly thoughts. She had been nothing less than friendly towards me, genuinely so. Yet I couldn't push the unease from me, the premonition— fool that I was, I didn't even consider it might have another source than my pathetic self-doubts. But then, I suppose I felt that Flora herself was invulnerable—she had been blessed with a miracle from Our Lady, and she carried Pierre's miraculous cross.

It was I who had bargained away everything in my prayers of entreaty as she lay ill—and I was afraid that Heaven would call on that debt. Yet I did not seriously think of changing my mind and going to England with her, leaving my mother to deal with the authorities in Nantes on her own. How could I do that and have any self-respect at all? Not to speak of the fact that it would look very bad indeed to Flora's mother—who might start to think I was, indeed, clinging like a limpet to them because I was afraid they'd abandon me, forget me, once they set foot on safe shores.

Our farewells the next morning were solemn and controlled. Flora seemed quite calm—she told me she'd offered up prayers for my safety to Jesus and the Blessed Virgin, and that I would be safe under their protection. She pressed on me a little handkerchief which contained dried petals of the rose we had grown at Ermenonville. She said she would see me soon in England. She would look forward to it. I was not to worry about her. I worried about her calm—the self-doubts nagging at me again—but at the same time I knew she meant exactly what she said. And I knew too that once we were reunited in

England, I would propose to her. I would not wait any longer.

So it was with a heart both hopeful and fearful that I disembarked with Mother and stood on the quay as the ship slowly drew away. Flora and her mother and Monsieur and Madame Rochas stood on the deck and waved to us, and we stood there and waved back till the ship was only a fast-disappearing dot on the horizon.

Twenty-seven

Mother and I reached Nantes a few days later, without incident. After having satisfied ourselves as to which prison my father was being held in, we went calling on all Father's associates, friends, colleagues and even acquaintances in the city, asking for testimonials, letters of recommendation, and so forth. I saw a completely new side to my mother during those days—to those rather self-important men, she played the part of tearful, bewildered wife, begging for their consideration, and pretending no acquaintance with the politics of the situation. She emphasised the fact that she was sure there had been a mistake, and that it might even have been a case of mistaken identity.

It was an approach that worked wonders, most of the time—it is always pleasant to some kinds of men to gratify their own image of themselves as benevolent protectors. Back in our lodgings, however, with the letters and testimonials firmly in hand, Mother read them with a brisk contempt for the smug condescension of men who took good care to be always on the right side of authority, no matter what it might be. My father, the letters implied, was a naïve, unworldly country lawyer who had blundered into a difficult situation; unlike the writers of the letters, he did not understand how the world worked.

They may have been patronising and untrue to my father's essential nature, but they were nevertheless what we wanted. Though not everyone we applied to agreed to our pleas, enough of them did to produce quite a respectable pile of character references. Next came the second step of our campaign. This was an interview with the prison governor. As we'd hoped, he was a confused man rather overcome by events and not at all sure as to what his own future held, let alone that of his prisoners. Besides, he had a native chivalry which made him feel uneasy about seeing a woman, especially a woman as respectable and yet still as handsome as my mother, in distress. He read the testimonials and letters, and gave us permission there and then to visit Father the next day. He would see what could be done about Father's case, though he couldn't promise anything. There was a backlog of cases, we had to understand. And every family considered their kin innocent, of course.

We arrived for the appointed visit, nervous and excited, and were taken by a warder to Father's cell. He was rather better off than we'd feared. He had at least been able to pay for a few modest comforts: a straw mattress, a couple of blankets, a jug of water to wash in every morning. He shared the cell with only one other prisoner, a merchant who had been sent to prison for neglecting to pay his taxes, an offence always regarded very seriously by any government, of whatever stripe. To our great relief, Father also seemed fit and well; he was even a little annoyed with us at first for having postponed our voyage to England in order to come looking for him. But I think he was also very touched, and pleased. He heard all our news about Flora's recovery and our meeting with Monsieur Rochas with great pleasure. 'They will be in safe hands,' he said.

Then he told us all about what had happened in Bellegarde. Matters between Father Martin and the people had come to a head when the priest attempted to say Mass at midday, the time specified by Father Jantot for his 'invisible Mass'.

Father Martin had intoned the words, but the congregation had acted as though they were hearing another Mass in their heads, the one said by Father Jantot in the depths of his woods, and so they did not sit or stand or kneel at the new priest's words, but at those of the 'invisible' Mass.

Father Martin had been so unnerved by it that he had not even been able to finish saying his Mass. Instead, he had stood in the pulpit and screamed at them for being heathens and heretics and superstitious, irrational savages, and told them that they were doing the Devil's

247

work, that they would be damned, that they would pay. None of it ruffled the villagers, who just dumbly kept kneeling and standing and sitting and bowing their heads in time to the Mass in their heads. 'It was a strange, even eerie sight,' said my father, repressing a small shiver, 'and yet somehow grand. Your friend Pierre—he was in the congregation that day, and he had the oddest look on his face—as if he were standing in another world.'

'I know that look,' I said, remembering.

'I felt then that Father Martin and the people were themselves in two different worlds, and that these worlds were enemies on the deepest level. I felt my impotence sharply then. How could I possibly think I could be of any use? This was not a battle for the law and the practical concerns of men, but a metaphysical battle of wills which only one side could win, resoundingly, and one side could only be crushed. And I could no longer believe one side was as good as the other, not even as a lawyer; my heart was with the people of Bellegarde, not with the new priest and his Inquisitor's dreams of perfection. I had thought I might mediate; now I was ready to admit defeat and leave. And then, to everyone's surprise, Father Martin himself left. Two days after that fiasco at Mass, he was simply gone. He had not been as strong as everyone, including myself, thought; his belief was not as strong as that of his opponents, and so he had simply lost heart and gone. And his bodyguards had gone with him. So the villagers thought they had won—that by their steadfast refusal to be intimidated, they had worn down the authorities.'

He paused, and wiped a hand over his forehead. 'They were happy too quickly, of course. Once it seemed the coast was clear, Father Jantot was fetched back from the woods, and he gave a Mass of thanksgiving which all the village attended. And so, you see, he was in Bellegarde when the soldiers came back, for Father Martin had complained bitterly of his treatment. Happily, they were seen coming down the road by one of the outlying farmers, and the tocsin bell was rung to sound the alarm. I was asked to hide Father Jantot, and so I did, in our barn under the straw.'

My mother's hand crept into his. Her eyes were bright. 'You did the right thing, Michel.'

'They were suspicious, and searched everywhere. They accused me—and others—of harbouring renegade priests. By some miracle, they didn't find him. He's a small man, as you know, and had buried very deeply into the straw but they were sure he was there, because an informant told them—everyone in the village swears no one local would ever betray them, but I think you never can tell.'

'What happened to Father Jantot then?'

'The soldiers stayed at our house, making me a virtual prisoner, unable to go to the priest, unable to speak to anyone in the village. They guarded the gardens, the orchard, they had a watch on the roads leading in and out of the village. They were sure Father Jantot was still in the vicinity of our land, and they were determined to catch him before he escaped their clutches again. But they reckoned without Pierre. I still have no idea how he did it; I only caught a glimpse of his shadowy form as I stood at the window desperately wondering what to do. But somehow he got that priest out from under the very noses of the National Guard, and spirited him away.'

'Pierre is like that,' I said, proudly. 'He has an uncanny talent for things.'

'Uncanny is right,' said my father. 'I was rather shaken by it, I can tell you, when I received a message the next day telling me the priest was safe, and far away.'

'Did he take him back to the woods?'

'I think not—there was some notion that place might not be safe any more, for the Guards would redouble their efforts to find him, and I would not be surprised if Pierre's taken him into deepest Brittany, where the soldiers aren't too keen to venture—or further, even. But the priest's escape made the Captain very annoyed, and he decided to teach me a lesson—I think he believes I had something to do with the spiriting away of Father Jantot, though they had me under surveillance. So they arrested me and marched me off to town.'

'And that's when you hit the pompous bullfrog,' I said cheerfully. 'Monsieur Rochas told us.'

Father laughed aloud. It lifted the anxiety from his

face. 'I regret to say that was most satisfactory. That swaggering jackass with his neat cockade! He came to gloat over me. I could not resist a swipe at his big red nose.'

'Michel!' said Mother. 'What a way for a respectable middle-aged man to speak!'

'Middle age be dashed,' said my father. 'But anyway that is the only charge they can really substantiate against me. The rest is just moonshine, and they know it.'

Mother told him about the testimonials. He shook his head in mock disbelief. 'Jacques,' he said, turning to me, 'did you ever realise what stuff your mother is made of?'

'Or your father?' retorted my mother tartly.

'I do now,' I said, honestly, and we smiled at each other, filled with a loving complicity and a hope that made our hearts sing.

'It will take a little time,' said my father after a while. 'We will have to be patient. But I am hopeful we will win through. Besides, that Mayor has many enemies. There are a great many people—even many other Republicans— who consider him exactly as we do, a jumped-up bullfrog with an overweening self-importance. They still have a sense of the ridiculous, and may well help us. Here's a list of people you should go and see over the next few days. Argue our case with them.'

Twenty-eight

But history was conspiring against us. It was while we were in the house of one of those important citizens who might help our cause that we heard some shocking news. The Prussian Army had massed on the frontier, ready to invade. The French Army no longer held a single village in Austrian or Prussian territory, and was in full retreat.

Then in late July the head of the Prussian Army, the Duke of Brunswick, issued an extraordinary manifesto to the people of France. If they did not want the country destroyed, they must abide by certain conditions. The Prussians, he said, did not wish to govern France, though their army would occupy it for a short while. They wanted only to put an end to anarchy and to the attacks on throne and altar. They wanted to restore to the King the security and liberty of which he'd been deprived. Any attempt by the Parisians to seize the King or continue their anarchy would mean the destruction of the city and the hanging of every single one of its inhabitants when the Prussian Army reached Paris. The city would be turned into a cemetery. Any other Frenchmen who resisted the Prussian incursion would be treated as enemies and killed, but no Frenchman would be molested by the army otherwise. The Prussians would leave as soon as peace and order had been restored. Many people in France wanted to see this happen, he said, and he was sure the rest would see sense.

At a stroke, the rash, stupid, haughty Duke had achieved the exact result the radicals must have been praying for. The justification they'd been waiting for. The King was a traitor! He had sold us out to the Germans! The nation was in mortal danger! As Mother and I hurried back to our lodgings, excited, scared crowds were already surging into the streets, as the town crier shouted the frightening news throughout the city.

And if it was like that in Nantes, imagine what it was like in Paris, threatened with imminent destruction by the Prussians! Howling mobs surrounded the Tuileries Palace, though they did not yet dare to storm it. Cannon were hauled out by excited citizen soldiers. Anyone who looked or spoke or acted like an 'aristo'—which had become an all-purpose code word rather like 'heretic' in the time of the Inquisition and bore no relation to noble blood any more—was in imminent danger of death, or at the very least a beating.

Rumours surged and ebbed: the Prussians were already in the country, they had captured Lille, they were marching swiftly on Paris, they would be there in a few days.

The Army of the North, commanded by General Lafayette, was swelled by thousands of volunteers surging from all the different parts of the country, eager to defend their homeland against the advancing Germans and Austrians. It was said that several of the émigré nobles who had taken shelter at the Austrian and Prussian courts were in the invading army, ready to wreak terrible revenge. Every day, crowds rallied around speakers in the squares who whipped the people into a frenzy with terrible descriptions of just what would happen should these barbarians take Paris, and every day thousands more volunteers swarmed north in a desperate attempt to stop the enemies of the nation. Many also came to protect Paris from Prussian attack. The capital was invaded by radical fighters and fearsome thugs from every corner of France, including the most frightening of all—the wild, raucous, brawny men from the back streets of Marseilles, armed to the broken teeth, red bandannas holding back their greasy, tangled hair.

Imagine Mother and me, trying to conduct our campaign for Father's release under these conditions! For Nantes too was shaken with patriotic fervour, and all ordinary work stopped. Thuggish bands held up citizens and demanded their papers. Woe betide if you went out without a tricolore ribbon! Their retailers must have been the only people to make money hand over fist in those days.

It was useless even trying to get an audience with any official; they were working day and night trying to shore up the city's defences, both in manpower and buildings— for it was rumoured that other attacks would come from the coast, from the perfidious English, from the Italians, the Spaniards, as well as all the spies and traitors within who would lose no time in falling on all the brave sons of the Republic. Meanwhile, in Paris, the Assembly had been thrown into utter chaos, and the radicals met with the mob leaders and street fighters and laid their final plans.

Father was remarkably philosophical about the delay in our own plans. 'It's safer to be in here than out there just now,' he said. 'I just want you two to be as careful as you can.'

Of course, in the chaos, all mail had been completely disrupted. We hadn't even been able to send a letter to England. How glad I was that Flora and her mother had got away in time!

Mother and I spent the time composing letters to local worthies, talking over what we might do, visiting Father whenever we could.

The ladies with whom we lodged, a pair of sweet elderly sisters, were quite nonplussed by the commotion, saying it would all pass over, it always did, and those cursed cheeky

Germans would be given a good beating and sent back over the border. Even they had become used to the state of anarchy in France, and had almost made their peace with it. How strange people can be!

Then one morning we were woken by shouts in the street. I flung open the shutters and called out, 'What's happened?'

'The King is finished!' a man shouted up to me. 'The day of the Republic has finally arrived!'

I flung on some clothes and hurried downstairs. A crowd was gathering. Everyone was talking at once. I listened feverishly, but didn't learn much more. I ran back inside and told Mother and our two hostesses. One of the sisters was so excited and frightened that she fainted. It took a while to bring her round.

We learned a little more as the days wore on. The radicals had finally struck. Georges Danton had seized control of the Paris municipality, known as the Commune, and of the city's National Guard. Meanwhile, Marat's mob had stormed the Tuileries Palace, armed with cannon, rifles, pistols, bayonets, pikes, scythes, anything they could lay their hands on. The National Guard unit which was supposed to protect the palace had turned tail and run away.

It was left to the King's loyal Swiss Guard to try and defend the royal family, but they were vastly outnumbered and were slaughtered, the mob hacking them to pieces.

The mob then wanted to kill the royal family but were instead persuaded by cooler heads amongst their leaders to seize them and imprison them in the fortress of the Temple, a grim medieval tower in central Paris once home to the Knights Templar. So the King, the Queen, their two children and the King's sister were all flung into the Temple. The rest of the Court was either killed on the spot or locked up in other prisons around Paris, there to await trial. In days to come, many more arrests would be made. Those of the old regime who were far enough away fled for their lives; General Lafayette, for instance, defected to the Austrians, leaving the army in disarray.

Meanwhile, Parliament had taken the vote that would turn the mob's action into law, and declared the overthrow of the King in early August. The Assembly collapsed. Panic-stricken, half of the deputies fled Paris at once. New elections were announced for September and an Executive Council, dominated by the Girondins and Jacobins took control till then. Edmond's friends were now in positions of great power. Their glorious day had arrived at last!

Twenty-nine

Just four days after the overthrow of the King, the first guillotine appeared in a Parisian public square, and the first victim—a civil servant high up in the administration of the National Guard—died on it a few days later. He was joined by dozens more, soon hundreds, soon to be thousands, as more and more guillotines were installed. Meanwhile, the Executive Council invited all men of goodwill—even foreigners—to join the great French experiment, and put themselves up for election to the new parliament, to be called the Convention. Several foreign radicals, among them our old friend Tom Paine, accepted the invitation at once. Such was the enthusiasm for these foreign friends that Paine was elected deputy of Arras, despite the fact he could not speak a word of French and his speeches to the parliament had to be translated!

But all this political excitement didn't push the Prussians back. The desperate courage of the French army and its savage new volunteers was certainly beginning to have an effect, but the enemy was still advancing, and morale, after the desertion of important officers, especially the General, was not very high. Danton made impassioned speeches in Parliament about patriotism and daring, but soon, we thought, the Republican government would have to go back to the old days of conscription; there just were not enough men willing to throw themselves on Prussian cannon. Liberty, equality, fraternity or death, indeed!

Nantes was just as turbulent as Paris. The network of radical agitators that had been introduced into every town sprang into action and seized control of the municipality. There were random searches, beatings, arrests, murders. Rival mobs battled it out in the streets; Mother dared not go out any more, and even I had to be very careful indeed. I took pains to look as much like a radical as I could, with a red woolen bonnet and a tricolore ribbon . . . and a recently acquired loaded pistol in my pocket.

Night curfew was strictly imposed, but knots of men gathered on street corners to talk excitedly all day, though sometimes the National Guard or the Jacobin militia would take it into their heads to disperse them. Food became scarce; bakers' and grocers' shops were looted and burnt by rioters who claimed the tradesmen were conspiring with wicked 'aristos' to starve the people. Those who could, fled with whatever they could take with them. Houses emptied, and shops closed.

Meanwhile, we heard sporadic news from the countryside that revolts had broken out here and there. Not far from our own town, peasants protesting at the overthrow of the King had marched on their local municipality, murdered its radical mayor and fought a fierce battle with the National Guard, which had ended in the rebels' defeat and massacre. It was reported that the victorious soldiers had marched home with the severed ears ornamenting their hats. But Bellegarde, it seemed, had not yet joined the revolt; it must be still simmering in uneasy calm.

We would have been worried about our village's fate, had it not been for the much more pressing worry about Father. I tried to visit the prison when I could, but it wasn't the safest thing to do. We knew we had to get Father out of there, but no one in authority had any time or inclination to listen to us. Father himself enjoined calm on us; so far no one had molested the prisoners. The guards were themselves rather confused by the turn of events; it might well be possible to bribe some of them to let him out. But the trouble was, you could not be sure of these people. They were at the whim of the emotions of the moment; and they could turn on you in an instant. He was cultivating one or two of them, Father said. Soon he'd be able to know for sure.

I fretted and fumed. I could not bear just to run around in circles trying to get answers that never came.

And deep down in the part of me that Pierre had called 'the sensitive', the unease about Father was growing into full-blown premonition. I hardly even thought of Flora during those days, except to be truly thankful that she and her mother were safe and well, out of reach of this snowballing nightmare. At least I didn't have to worry about that; I pictured my darling in Willesdene, walking with the family, laughing over trifles, becoming again the carefree, charming girl she'd once been.

At last I could wait no longer. I decided that despite the danger, I would leave Nantes, go hotfoot to Paris, find Casgrain and get him to intercede for us with his friends. That garrulous barrister Danton, with whom I'd discussed English poetry and the plays of Shakespeare, was Minister of Justice now. He might not remember the dull little poet-lawyer from the provinces whom he had met at his friend's lodgings two years before, but he might, too. He was a man of impulse, I knew, and he could be generous. Perhaps we might be lucky. It was better than waiting for deaf local officials to take any notice of us while anarchy reigned in the city.

Father agreed that it was worth trying, though I could tell he was reluctant, because he had grown to heartily dislike and even hate the radicals. But he also knew things must move swiftly or catastrophe might come on us swiftly too. It could be prudent to use the card of friendship or at least acquaintance, at a time when the radicals might be flushed with triumph and disposed to be generous.

So, enjoining Mother to be sure to stay indoors and Father to keep a low profile, I collected my necessary papers for travel, and on the morning of August 29th, took the public stagecoach to Paris.

It was a journey of three days that seemed to take forever. The roads were full of hurrying people, soldiers and civilians, and from the windows of the coach we glimpsed, here and there, terrible, terrible sights—bloated dead bodies in ditches, half-starved, abandoned children crouching around firesides, a head on a pike whose sightless eyes stared at me from a doorway. The stink of fear and excitement, mixed, hung over everything; people were expecting the Prussians to invade at any moment— they were already over the border.

My companions in the coach were mostly of a radical turn of mind—or at least, those who weren't were keeping mighty quiet. They spoke excitedly about events, the coming of the Republic—which would be proclaimed as soon as elections were finalised—and the dawning of a new age of revolution. I listened to them, not saying much, except when I was challenged by a particularly truculent young man about what I thought, when I feebly agreed that yes, it was all very exciting, wasn't it? He looked at me in contempt but ignored me after that, for which I was devoutly glad. I wished to attract no attention at all until I had safely arrived at my destination.

At one of our stops, we learned very bad news. The Prussians had entered France. They'd taken Longwy, and then Verdun. They were maybe ten days' march from Paris. The closer we got to the capital, the worse things seemed. There were burning carts and coaches at the sides of the road, and mobs of dangerous criminals roaming around. On the outskirts of the city, houses abandoned by fleeing owners had been looted and ransacked. Footpads, pickpockets and burglars had a grand old time; both the new administration and the National Guard had other fish to fry.

But the centre of the city was calm enough. Here, the soldiers were out in force, and the crowds were orderly. There were patriotic signs everywhere, and recruitment was going strong. The city was preparing itself for battle. The stagecoach set us down at the terminal, and I went straight off to Casgrain's house. By this time, I was dirty, dusty, unshaven and sweaty. I must have looked rather like a member of the mob. So when Casgrain's manservant opened the door to me, he told me roundly to go away, he didn't let in scum.

I managed to tell him who I was. He looked me up and down. 'Your friend Citizen Bellegarde doesn't live here any more.'

'I know. I've come to see Citizen Casgrain. Please.'

'He's far too busy. He's been made a commander, now,' said the servant, with great pride.

'Please, Citizen—will you tell him I need to see him on a matter of great urgency?'

'Everyone wants to do that,' said the servant. 'You will have to make an appointment. Send a letter.' And he shut the door in my face!

I felt like beating on that door and shouting insults and screaming but I knew full well that wouldn't help me. So, disheartened and depressed, I went to look for a cheap inn where I might spend the night. I would try again the next day.

It was after I'd found the inn that I suddenly had an idea. Why wait on the pleasure of Casgrain, who, after all, despite his promotion was still only a soldier? I needed help from a politician, and an important one at that. Time was pressing. I must get back to Nantes as quickly as I could, before the Prussians invaded the capital.

Why not go direct to Danton, or failing that, to Robespierre, or even Marat, who was now at the head of the city's feared Committee of Surveillance? I had met them, after all. So instead of writing a letter to Casgrain, I wrote a note addressed to Danton at the Ministry of Justice and gave it to a boy to deliver. I told him to say it was an important and highly personal letter, from a fellow admirer of Shakespeare. Then I settled down to wait.

I had no reply that night. But the next day, I received

a note from the Ministry. It wasn't signed by Danton, but by Camille Desmoulins, who was now his secretary, and granted me an appointment with the great man at midday.

I was thrilled! I washed and shaved and dressed with great care, brushing the dirt out of my clothes, borrowing some linen and a shabby but respectable frock coat from the hotel, and scrubbing at my shoes till they looked presentable. I knew Danton did not equate dirt with revolutionary purity, as did stinking Marat. He would not appreciate a smelly petitioner . . . I pinned the tricolore ribbon on my hat, rehearsed the radical slogans I thought I might open with, if the wind were blowing that way— though you never knew, with a man like Danton—and, hailing a *fiacre*, set off.

Alas! I sat with various other shabby petitioners in the corridors of the Ministry of Justice for hours. Midday came and went without my name being called. People clattered in and out of the building all day; Commune officials, National Guard, street fighters, respectable folk, all kinds. But neither Danton nor Desmoulins emerged. Hours passed. At length, near six o'clock, a uniformed man came out of the offices and yelled, 'All citizens are to go home! Interviews are over for today!'

There was an immediate clamour of protest, with everyone, including me, waving our appointment slips and shouting. The official shrugged and said, 'Go home,

265

citizens. The Minister is too busy to see you today. Come back tomorrow.'

'Tomorrow's Sunday!' yelled one man.

'Come back Monday then,' said the official.

I fought my way to the front of the angry group. 'Please, Citizen,' I said, to the official, 'I'm a personal friend of Citizen Danton and Citizen Desmoulins.'

The man guffawed. 'Isn't everyone, these days?'

'But I am really.'

'Shut up,' said the official, exasperated. 'Go home to your bed and come back Monday. Unless you want to see the inside of a Paris prison, of course.'

What could I do but leave?

Walking disconsolately back to my hotel, I decided I must call on Robespierre. He, too, had shown a little interest in me. I shrank from the idea of calling on Marat—the man frightened and repelled me. So I went to the Cordeliers district, and soon found my way back to Robespierre's house.

He was in, eating supper with his lanky, silent brother Augustin, the Duplays, and Jean Casgrain. After polite greetings, I was taken into Robespierre's study. Casgrain came with us. Robespierre sat at his tidy desk, his hands resting on a leather-bound notebook placed there, and he and Casgrain listened carefully to my story, which I'd suitably embroidered for their benefit. I ended by making an appeal to him as a man of great probity and integrity who understood that virtue must be fought for if it is to grow in the hearts of men. Robespierre's green eyes surveyed me thoughtfully as I spoke, and when I'd finished, he turned to Casgrain.

'It seems your friend has been converted to our philosophy, Jean.'

'It does seem like it,' said Casgrain, his wary eyes searching my face.

Robespierre said, 'What has caused this conversion, Citizen?'

Anger was mounting in me; an anger that I had to lie and cheat and misrepresent myself and my family in the eyes of these two abominable Pharisees. But I controlled it and said, meekly, 'I have thought very carefully over all the discussions we had and I do understand now that anyone who does not like virtue must of necessity be vicious; and that in order to destroy the vice which exists in the world, we must uphold virtue at all costs. We must perfect men and make them pure and sinless.'

Sheer pompous nonsense, but neither man seemed to think so, though they also did not look altogether convinced by my effusions. After a small silence, Robespierre said, 'Have you tried to see Citizen Danton?' He added, with a touch of spite, 'Of course, he is *very* busy these days.'

In that moment I understood. Robespierre was jealous! I knew that hot-blooded Danton and cold-blooded

Robespierre had never seen eye to eye, despite their supposed alliance. Danton thought Robespierre puritanical and dull; Robespierre thought Danton coarse and corrupt. All the radicals had their eye on the prize of power. Danton had moved quicker, though, with Marat, whom Robespierre despised, and Desmoulins, who'd once been Robespierre's close friend. I was glad now I hadn't mentioned my abortive mission to the Ministry.

Now I said, 'Oh, no, Citizen. My thoughts went to you first and foremost, as the virtuous heart of the Revolution.'

It seemed like shameless flattery to me, and Casgrain looked rather sceptical. But not Maximilien Robespierre. A faint smile lit up his feline face. He liked the flowery compliment, and the implied criticism of Danton. 'I may not have the powers of the Ministry of Justice, but I do have my meager resources. Where are you staying?'

I gave him the name of the hotel. He nodded. 'I will see what I can do.'

'Citizen,' I hazarded, 'may I know when?'

'No, you may not,' snapped Robespierre, and I understood I had to keep my mouth shut, and wait on his pleasure. I swallowed my bile, nodded meekly, and thanked him profusely. He smiled tightly and opened his notebook. Robespierre was a man of order and method. He liked to keep records of all his dealings. No doubt he was about to write an account of our meeting. He dipped his quill and began to write. I had time to glance at his distinctive, precise script, before Casgrain took me out of the study and escorted me to the front door.

To make conversation, I said, 'You must be very worried, Citizen Commander.'

He looked at me in some surprise. 'Worried? Oh, you mean the Prussians.' A grim smile crossed his stern face. 'This stupid war was always going to cost us dearly. It was started by those power-hungry fools of Girondins and that idiot of a King. But I know the people are brave enough to withstand these tyrannous attacks. And I know my men will resist to the last breath. They know liberty now. They will never allow any foreign tyrants or intimate enemies to take it from them.'

'Oh, no,' I said, feebly. 'That could never be.'

Casgrain looked closely at me. 'You puzzle me, Citizen. Your words are fine, but there is no fire in your eyes. You are not a hypocrite, are you, Citizen? We do not like hypocrites, you know.'

My simmering anger saved me. I yelled, 'How dare you say that to me, Citizen! My heart burns with a fire that can never be put out! And I am ready to die for it!'

'Shh,' said Casgrain, with a faint smile. 'Citizen Robespierre likes peace and quiet; he does not like vulgar brawling in his house.' He looked sideways at me. 'How is Citizeness Bellegarde?'

I swallowed. 'She is well. Very well. Quite recovered. Didn't Edmond tell you? She is back home.'

That had been a calculated gamble on my part, and it worked. He shrugged. 'Edmond and I do not see each other much these days,' he said. 'I do not approve of the way he conducts his life.' He put a hand on my shoulder. 'I am glad the Citizeness is safe,' he said. 'Pass on my best regards to her.'

'I'll do that. I certainly will.'

'Good. I will try and remind Citizen Robespierre of your petition for your father if I can.'

'Thank you, Jean,' I said, genuinely touched despite my unease at being in this place, with him.

'And good luck with the Citizeness, too,' went on Casgrain, and this time his smile was warm. 'She seems a lovely, gentle soul. And I admire your persistence and fidelity. Of such steadfast virtues will our Republic be forged, and not the empty-headed frivolity and vanity of too many who consider themselves our friends. I hope that your virtue will be rewarded, my friend.'

'Thank you,' I said, again. What a strange, complex man he was! One moment I feared and hated his fanaticism; the next, I was disarmed by his unexpected humanity, despite the tedious lectures.

'You will hear from us,' he said and, nodding his head in calm farewell, he shut the door on me.

Thirty

The next day, September the 2nd, I woke late. I went downstairs at once and asked the porter if any letters had been left for me at the desk. There was nothing—I hadn't really expected anything, not really, but nevertheless I was disappointed. I went out into the street, which in Paris was as busy on the Lord's Day as it was every other day, and found a church where I heard Mass. The congregation seemed to be composed largely of women, children and old men—the young men must either be away fighting or lining up to fight. The congregation seemed restless and uneasy, and the familiar words of the Mass did not give me the peace and patience I had hoped for.

Emerging from the shadows of the church into the bright sunshine of noon, I felt an obscure foreboding which made me agitated and anxious. Because I could not bear the thought of just sitting in my room, waiting for the message to come from Robespierre—if it ever came—I wandered aimlessly about, and finally went to have a meal in a rather dingy restaurant some distance from my hotel. I sat over my plate of watery stew and fretted, desperate to be back with my parents, desperate to be on the way to England and reunion with Flora. Casgrain's words had made my longing for her, submerged in the deepest part of my being since Father's arrest, return again to the surface. I could see her face in my mind's eye, hear her light, sweet voice, and my heart bled with longing.

After a little while, I got up, paid for my meal and left. My head filled with thoughts of Flora, I paid no notice to where my steps took me or to my surroundings.

But as I turned a corner, I suddenly heard the sound of drums, and the cries of a crowd in full-throated roar. In another instant, they were upon me and, instinctively, I fell into step with them, and was swept along in their wake. They were several hundred strong, mostly men but with a few women—people of the worst type, mainly: thugs and harridans with wild, twisted faces and raucous voices. There were also quite a few soldiers, in their blue uniforms, some of them drumming and, at their head, people who looked like Commune officials in sober grey coats and hats with tricolore ribbons, sabres at their sides and bundles of papers in their hands. Apart from these latter men, the crowd was shouting and waving a variety of weapons—pikes, bayonets, swords, knives, clubs—to my horror I saw that many of these weapons were already red with blood. The crowd surged along the street, and I was forced along with them, knowing that if I broke step or tried to run away I was lost.

We halted in front of a grim building, a prison fortress. An official stepped forward and held up a hand. 'The revolutionary tribunal, the rage of the people, shall try these traitors and make them pay for their crimes, as the others paid!' he shouted, and the crowd roared its approval, and surged forward. The guards at the gate didn't present any resistance, but simply let the crowd in. Overcome with fear, I tried to fight my way out of it, but it was impossible, and I was carried along with the howling mass into the courtyard of the prison.

What I saw then has never left me.

It still comes to me in nightmares. A table was dragged out from somewhere and installed in the courtyard, and the grey-coated officials sat at it. They were the bureaucracy of murder. They installed inkstands and papers on the table, and one of the officials calmly took out his pipe, lit it and began to smoke. They detailed others to go into the cells and begin to drag out the prisoners.

There were all kinds in there—men, women and children, priests, nobles, artisans, traders, beggars, petty criminals, all of them defenceless and most of them terrified. All of them had to stand in front of the president of this mock trial and be subjected to a barrage of unanswerable questions. The charge was always the same: these poor wretches, locked up for weeks or months or even years, in some cases, were accused of being in a grand 'aristo' conspiracy to deliver Paris to the Prussians. Once the ridiculous charge was pronounced, some would be immediately condemned to death and hacked to pieces where they stood. There were many executioners ready and willing to do the deed!

Some trembling wretches were told, on the other hand, that they were free to go—whereupon they burst into tears of gratitude, and were allowed to run through the crowd—only to be caught a few paces away, and dispatched with as much glee and savagery as those poor creatures who'd been sentenced immediately.

Ten-year-old girls and doddering old priests were put to the sword with as much enthusiasm as the strongest and most combative of young noblemen or the most fiercely defensive of beggars. For not everyone went like lambs to the slaughter; many of those poor prisoners fought with a huge, desperate courage, and managed to seize weapons from some, only to be finally cut down. In the murderous confusion, it soon became difficult for the crowd to tell victim from executioner, and there were several of the mob who died that way from cuts inflicted by their own kind.

What was I doing helpless amongst this hideous butchery, this ghastly travesty of justice? How can I explain what it's like to be faced with naked evil? How can I possibly explain the paralysis of gazing on the face of the Gorgon?

And how can I describe the hideous shock that paralysed me as I recognised the face of one of the murderers—Gros Jean, the pedlar who had murdered Mathilde Pernet, in our village! There could be no doubt it was him. I'd seen him several times in the village. The outlaw murderer of helpless women had found his true calling, and patriotic applause for his acts, on this evil day.

Then I had an appalling thought. Gros Jean had come to our house a couple of times. He might well recognise me. The numbness suddenly left me. I dashed like a terrified rat into a dark, shadowy corner. And found myself landing on top of a terrified old man and a little boy of about four or five, huddled under a pile of bloody rags and dirty straw.

For an instant, they stared at my blood-stained clothing and my tricolore cockade. For an instant, our wild heartbeats mingled, and we shared a gaze that held an eternity of fear and sorrow. Then with a great cry, not even knowing what I was doing, quite forgetting my fear of Gros Jean or any of the other killers, I surged back into the crowd, fighting my way through until I found a pike and a sword, thrown down by some patriot satiated with slaughter or else dead. Howling like the rest, I grabbed these weapons, not looking right or left at the bodies that lay broken and bloody all around me. With a desperate cunning of which I had not known myself capable, I sidled back into the corner, holding the weapons, and whispered to the two still huddled there, shivering, 'Take the pike. Rub the blood on your clothes. And come with me.'

Like puppets, they did as they were told, their eyes never leaving me. I hauled them up. 'We're patriots, remember, the three of us . . . we killed lots of those conspirators. I'm your brother, your son, you're both deaf and dumb. Understand? Let me do the talking if we have to.'

They stared and said not a word and appeared not to understand at all. But they followed me meekly enough, the old man limply holding the pike, the child trotting beside me, as, sword in hand, I sidled our way carefully back into the crowd. Horrible sights could be glimpsed all around us; bloody heads on pikes, still-palpitating hearts stuck on the ends of swords, mutilated corpses in ghastly piles. I tried to hide these things with my body from the eyes of the old man and the child, but I could not do it too obviously or I would draw attention to ourselves.

Suddenly, the president of the committee stood up and called out in a stentorian voice, 'Oh people! The traitors here are no more—let us go to the next den of conspirators and thieves, and cleanse it of impure blood!' The crowd howled and surged after him, leaving their dead and wounded alongside the corpses of the prisoners they had so foully murdered. I suddenly glimpsed Gros Jean amongst those dead assassins. The sight should have cheered me, but didn't. I was far past such thoughts.

We followed the crowd; it was much too dangerous to do anything else. But once out in the street, I waited till a dark doorway should present itself, and pushed my two into there, and myself in after them. Nobody noticed us; they were all far too intent on the next storming, the next killing. They were drunk, drugged with blood-lust, deaf and blind to all else but the raging fire surging maddeningly in their veins.

We waited in the darkness for what seemed like hours. But finally the din of the crowd grew fainter in the distance. I turned to the two prisoners. The old man was pale as wax, the child grasped onto his hand. Blood stained their clothes, their faces; their eyes were the eyes of people who have looked on hell. I said, 'You'll be safe now. I'll take you to my hotel.'

The old man stared at me. He tried to speak. The words wouldn't come. He clutched at his throat and gave a kind of groan which turned into a gurgle. He shook. His eyes rolled. I saw he was having a heart attack, or a stroke. I said, 'No, no. You'll be safe now, don't die, not now, not when I . . .' I didn't know what I was saying, I was holding him tightly, while the child just grasped his grandfather's hand and stared.

But the old man could not fight any longer. He died in my arms, the child still grasping onto his hand.

I wanted to shout and scream then, to hurl hate and rage towards the sky, but I knew I must keep quiet, in case the mob came back. So I closed the old man's eyelids, picked up the unresisting child—he was as light as a feather—and after making sure the coast was clear, slowly trudged down the street. All the way, I could feel eyes watching me from behind shutters and high windows, but nobody came out, whether to help or hinder us. The good citizens of Paris did not want to be involved either with the victims or their murderers. It was safer to stay at home, behind closed doors, and pretend none of it had happened.

How I got back, I don't know. But it was still with the child clasped in my arms that I stumbled over the threshold of my lodgings. The hotel-keeper was at the desk; he stared at me as I came in. 'What in the name of God?' he began, then broke off whatever he was going to say and went to call his wife. She took one look at us, and beckoned us into their quarters. Without asking any questions, she prised the little boy gently off me, sat him down near the fire, and wrapped him in a blanket. She stroked his hair and crooned to him till his eyelids began to flutter and close. The hotel-keeper's wife looked up at me. Her eyes were full of tears. 'Sit down, Citizen,' she said gently. 'You look all in. I'll pour you a glass of wine.'

This simple kindness did more to undo me than all the horrors I'd witnessed. I put my head in my hands and shook with sobs.

After a little time, I stopped crying. I said, bleakly, 'His grandfather's dead. They killed everyone.'

The hotel-keeper's wife said, in trembling tones, 'We heard rumours. It started over at the Abbey prison at noon . . . they've been rampaging all over Paris.'

I couldn't speak. She said, 'Do you know his name?'

I looked up at her sharply. She flinched. 'It doesn't matter to me, Citizen. Poor little mite.'

'He would have been tried as a conspirator too,' I said. 'A child of his age. Some conspirator.' And I started to laugh. Like the tears, it wouldn't stop, harsh barks of laughter that tore at me and made me feel nauseated.

She whispered, 'Shh. He's sleeping. Let him sleep.'

I gulped down the glass of wine. 'Question is,' I said, gazing fixedly at her, 'are we safe here?'

She went red as a cherry. 'Oh, Citizen! How can you say that? Those murdering scum . . . they'll be punished, and severely. The Executive Council—Citizen Danton—you mark my words, they'll punish those criminals for doing what they did. They'll stop it, you'll see!' She looked at me, and dropped unconsciously into old ways of address. 'You're exhausted, Monsieur. You should go and rest. I'll look after the child, don't you fret. When he wakes, I'll give him something to eat, I'll bathe him, I'll take care of him. I've had six children, you know. I know how to look after little ones.'

I looked at her comfortable figure, her round face, her kind eyes now made bleak with bewildered sorrow. She'd believed in the new world, like so many of us had. She couldn't conceive that it had come to this. I whispered, 'Thank you, Madame. You are very kind. You are an angel.'

She went red again. 'Don't you be silly, now, Citizen. You take yourself off to bed.' And she bustled away to her pantry, her back turned to any more embarrassing protestations of gratitude.

I slept for a couple of hours, and woke with a pounding head and aching limbs. For an instant, I didn't know where I was, or what had happened. Then I remembered. I got heavily out of bed, and put my boots back on. I went downstairs.

The child was in the hotel kitchen, ravenously eating a bowl of soup. It didn't look like he'd eaten properly for a long time. The hotel-keeper's wife sat beside him, stroking his hair from time to time. When I came in, she got up and took me aside. She said, 'I've had the maid draw him a bath. We'll cut his hair. He has lice, of course.' She added, 'He hasn't spoken a word. Perhaps he's a mute.'

'Perhaps,' I said, though I doubted it. I said, 'Madame, the body of his grandfather should be given a decent burial.'

'We can't do that,' she said, frightened.

'He wasn't killed by the mob, he died of shock, afterwards,' I whispered. 'He's not in the prison yard, but in a doorway, not a very great distance away. We can't leave him there like a bundle of rotting rags!'

She looked at me, and shook her head. 'Where are you from, Citizen?' she said, in great sorrow. 'People die all the time in doorways, here. And after this day's work, there'll be a great many more abandoned bodies in Paris. If he's lucky, someone may pick the body up, and take it to a pauper's grave.'

'No,' I said, harshly. 'I will hire a cart. I will go and get the body myself. I have a little money. I'll pay for a funeral.'

She shrugged. 'You don't even know who he is.'

'What does that matter? He doesn't need a name on his tomb, but he does need a Christian burial.'

She sighed. 'As you wish,' she observed. 'But it's Sunday. Carters don't work on a Sunday.'

'No, only murderers do,' I said.

She winced, but made no reply to that, only said, 'What are you planning to do with the child, Citizen?'

I looked over at the child's fair head, bent over his soup. I said, 'I have to go back to Nantes very soon. My father . . .'

I broke off. A sudden thought had made an abyss of fear open up beneath me. If they had gone around slaughtering prisoners here—and it had not looked like an impulsive massacre, but something planned, deliberate, or why the officials with their inkstands and papers and sober coats?—then what was to stop their kind doing the same thing in prisons all over the country? What if it were not just in Paris, but everywhere? I did not understand the political machinations that had led to these hideous events, but I feared them.

I must get back to Nantes. But I must have a note from Robespierre, or how could I get Father out? Could I depend on Robespierre's good graces? I was a creature of no account to him. Besides, how was I to know whose hand was really behind the terrible events of today? Marat of course—he controlled the mob. But who else? A great power struggle was going on between the radicals, both out in the light, and down in the shadows. I doubted fastidious Robespierre would employ assassins to massacre and mutilate prisoners; the guillotine would be much more to his liking. Besides, he wasn't powerful enough, not yet. He wasn't the one in charge of the Commune— that was Marat, and Danton. But I would be a fool to trust him or Casgrain or any of them, in any way, any more. As Jonathan had said, any method to seize power was good enough—for all of them.

At that moment, a mad idea came into my head. I remembered Robespierre making those precise little notes. I could picture the script almost perfectly. I knew the form of his words. I had heard of his tiresome virtue often enough. Why should I wait? I would write a release letter myself, in Robespierre's script, and Robespierre's convoluted sentences. No one in Nantes would know the difference!

All these thoughts flashed through my head with the rapidity of lightning. I saw the hotel-keeper's wife looking at me in a somewhat bewildered fashion. I said, 'My father is in need of me, and I think I'll have to leave first thing tomorrow morning, once I've made arrangements for the burial of the old man.'

'So you'll take the child with you.' She nodded. 'I think that's wise. Best get him into the countryside—you come from the country, don't you, sir? He'll be safe there.' She glanced at the child's delicate white hands clasped around the bowl. 'Paris isn't a place for such as he any more.'

I had intended to ask her to take care of the child, till I should return to Paris. But I saw she was right. Besides, I never wanted to set foot in Paris again. The woman had been very kind. But kindness only went so far, these days. She had her own family to consider, her business. She could not endanger it for some dead stranger's child.

Well, I would have to finish what I had started. I thought Mother might be pleased to see him, too. It had always been a grief to her that she'd only had one child. He would be taken care of. He would go to England with us. Peace and quiet and love would soon efface the things he had seen today—and who knew what else beside in that grim prison, I thought. How long had he been in there with his grandfather? Perhaps his parents had died there. Or had they been among the butchered prisoners today? I had no way of knowing. And I couldn't investigate.

'Would you be able to get the child suitable clothes? I'll pay you,' I added hurriedly.

'Of course,' she said. 'But there's no need to buy, or pay, for that matter. I have cast-offs from my youngest child. And shoes—they're none too grand, but he won't need grand. We'll cut his hair short and give him a bonnet.'

'Oh, and if you have any walnut-juice, Citizeness,' I said.

She smiled. 'That skin *is* a little too white and fine,' she agreed. 'You won't know him, Citizen, when you come back from your errand of mercy.' She meant my arrangements for the funeral. 'There's a good friend of ours, three doors down—he does a spot of undertaker's work, sometimes. He'll be willing to help, for a fee.'

I went to see the man. For a gold coin, he agreed to do as I asked, and took me in his covered hearse to the spot where the old man had died. The body was still there, propped up in the doorway. Just as we were heaving it up into the hearse, I heard the drumming in the distance. I grasped his arm. 'Quick! We must leave at once. It's them!'

'They've been busy all day,' he commented, as he jumped onto the coachman's seat and geed up the horses. 'And they'll have another busy day tomorrow. There are many prisons in Paris. They're probably dancing around their bonfires and having a fine old time, right now. I heard they took all the stock and the barrels of wine from the restaurants in that quarter over there,' he said, pointing with his whip. Night was falling, and I could see the sparks of fire flying into the air in the direction in which he had pointed, and the confused noise of a distant crowd in full-throated celebration. So it was against the background of dimly heard savage carousing that we took the body of that poor old man to his last resting-place, a small churchyard at the edge of the city. There my new friend called on the services of a gravedigger, and we buried the old man, without the benefit of a priest— the local incumbent having fled some weeks ago and not been replaced—but with all the heartfelt prayers that I could think of. And I took note of the precise place where he had been buried, so I could tell his grandchild, later, when the time was right. He deserved more, I knew that; but it was the best I could do.

As we returned to the city, neither I nor the undertaker spoke. I was grateful for his silence for there were no words for what had happened this day. I had told Casgrain that my heart burned with a fire that could never be put out. Now it was terribly true. I burnt with a consuming hatred for the evil ones who had slaughtered the innocent as if they were guilty and turned the name of Liberty and Patriotism into a thing that stunk to high heaven. This is what it had turned into, that bright new dawn: into a fearful night filled with the shouts of bloodthirsty, merciless savages dancing like gleeful demons around a fire.

And so that night I took my first decisive steps on a road that was to lead to this prison. Before, I had been at the mercy of events, uncertain, unsure, wanting to see the best in those men, who included my childhood friend, those who wanted to turn our country into a paradise that could, I saw now, only live in their heads, or the otherworld, all passions spent. If it was attempted here, on our imperfect earth, this road to paradise could only lead to hell.

That night, I lost all faith and all hope that the good amongst them would prevail. I knew that the whirlwind of evil and blood that had been unleashed that day and the days to come would sweep all of the good or even the ambiguous amongst them away. I remembered that night when I'd toured the Paris underworld with Marat and I recoiled from the fact that I'd once even entertained the idea of supporting anything that such people did or thought. I thought of Casgrain's words about virtue needing terror to support it, I remembered his glib assertion about revolutionaries needing to swallow their scruples and use murderers, and my very being rebelled with a profound disgust. The Revolution became hideous to me that night; its face became the mask of Death, its heart the heart of Hell, and all who espoused it damned in my eyes.

I was not alone in my horror. The events that were to become notorious as the September Massacres, which would take thousands of innocent victims over that terrible week, lost the Revolution a great many supporters, both in France and abroad. Even the radicals—those who weren't involved, that is—were disturbed, the Girondin faction, naïve idealists that they were, irredeemably so.

This vast slaughter of the defenceless would lead to the assassination of Marat. It would destroy Danton's reputation and fatally weaken his power. It would lead to the extermination of the Girondins, and the outbreak of savage civil war in every corner of France.

And, eventually, these events would help to usher in the pure dictatorship of Robespierre, and to unleash the Reign of Terror which we all groan under today; a Terror under which the victims of the September Massacres are multiplied a hundredfold, a thousandfold, in every corner of our beloved, bleeding country.

But that was to come. Strangely, that night, I lost my fear, too. Slowly, in me was growing the knowledge that I could not run away from France, no matter that a large part of me wanted to do so desperately, longed so to be at peace, reunited with Flora, safe with my family and the poor child

I'd rescued and whose name I didn't even know yet. A strange new steel was forging itself in me, out of the fires of that day and night, and it was changing me, tempering my natural caution and turning it into hard yet not reckless resolve. I didn't yet know what I was going to do—but I knew with all my heart that I was going to resist, to fight, to take a stand against this Revolution which was just another name for the reign of Azrael, his black wings outspread across the land. My nineteenth birthday had only just been and gone—but I knew for certain now that I was a man, and no longer a boy.

Thirty-one

We left Paris the next morning, on the dawn stagecoach. The hotel-keeper's wife had given us a basket of food for the journey; she had kissed the mute little boy, with tears in her eyes, and wished us Godspeed. He looked the part we'd chosen for him, with his very short, spiky hair, the walnut-juice staining his skin brown, and the shabby hand-me-downs he wore. I looked pretty rough myself, in dirty hat, dusty suit and scuffed shoes, and nobody took any notice of the two shabby brothers, one a mute, returning to Nantes.

Everyone in the coach spoke of the massacres. A man who knew a high-up Paris Commune official told us that Marat and his friends had put out a circular that morning saying that 'the People' had quite legitimately done to death these 'ferocious conspirators' and hoped that 'the whole Nation' would act likewise on suchlike conspirators in prisons around the country—you can imagine my agony when I heard that!

But it was heartening that not one of our fellow

passengers, even those who were ardent revolutionaries, approved of such a thing; and spoke most indignantly about it, for the days when pity was to be regarded as suspect were not yet on us. Danton's government was soon to realise its mistake, attempt to muzzle Marat, and put out the feeble line that the massacres had been the work of a few vicious hotheads, carried away by the indignation of believing Frenchmen might help Prussians. Yet no one believed it for no one was punished for these crimes. If the assassins had been put on trial, after all, what stories could they have told?

One hardy soul in our coach, though, tried to argue that such crimes could not possibly be the work of revolutionaries; that the mob must have been organised and paid by royalists, desperate to make the radicals look bad and cause civil war at a time of foreign invasion. But the others treated this stupidity with the contempt it deserved. They said many royalists had met hideous deaths in the massacres, including poor, silly Princess de Lamballe, Marie Antoinette's best friend, whose bloody head on a pike had been thrust up against the windows of the Temple prison so her poor friend could see how she met her terrible end.

Another person tried to invoke the meddling hand of England, or Austria, or whoever; this was listened to with a little more indulgence—foreigners, after all, make useful scapegoats—but it was a forlorn hope that wasn't discussed for very long. Too many people had been eyewitnesses. And too many people also expected almost anything of those in power—whoever they might be.

Fortunately, the child slept nearly all the way to Nantes, and heard none of this discussion, waking only when we stopped at inns. He was always hungry; he tore at the bread and gobbled up the watery stew with such gusto that our fellow passengers began to joke about 'your mother starving the child'.

I'd had to make up a name for him—I called him Bertrand—and I would joke back that his appetite was the only normal thing about Bertrand, who was deaf and mute and a little simple, too. The forged letter in my pocket, the fire of resolve burning in my heart, I felt almost light-headed with daring and courage. I took a vigorous part in the discussions, and was not afraid to say what I thought, though I did not yet speak to anyone about what I planned to do. In truth, I wasn't quite sure, though the shape of it was growing in my mind.

We arrived in Nantes one afternoon, and went straight to Mother's lodgings. Her face went rigid with shock when she saw me and Bertrand, and as I poured out my story to her, she looked so frightened and upset that I thought she was going to break down. I asked after Father and she said in a trembling voice that he was safe, that nothing had happened so far at the prisons in Nantes.

Her eyes fixed on Bertrand, she said, 'What is to become of us all, Jacques? Oh, what is to become of us?'

I had never seen my mother so helpless. With a pang, I said, 'Mother, I have a letter from Robespierre which will set Father free. I will go to the prison right now. I will bring him back here. Tomorrow, we leave for Saint-Malo. We will get passage on the first ship bound for England.' I had determined not to tell her that I wasn't going to sail with them. 'And that will be an end to it. Bertrand will be safe with you—with us—he is very young and will forget.'

'Yes,' she said, hardly listening. 'Yes, poor child. Poor little boy. My God! Jacques! What kinds of monsters are these people?'

'Human monsters,' I said. 'No animal would ever act this way.' And we looked at each other over the child's head, our feelings too deep and awful for tears.

The news about Paris had reached Nantes that day. But it is to the credit of the city, and indeed most other cities in France—aside from Orléans—that Marat's call for the nationwide murder of prisoners went unheeded. Extra guards had been put in the prison, just in case. I was searched and questioned thoroughly by the guards on the gate, but the mention of my letter from Robespierre had the intended effect. The Jacobin's name had not been associated with the massacres; he had kept his hands clean. And he had quite a few supporters in the city. So I was allowed to go into my father's cell, while the guard took my forged letter to the Governor.

Father looked pale and worn, but said he was well enough. I told him my story—telling him everything, for I had decided to take him completely in my confidence. When I had finished, there was a small silence. I waited for the storm to break. Then he said quietly, 'Oh, Jacques! I am so proud of you.'

'Then you don't object, sir, to my decision?'

'Object? Of course I do,' he said, with a flash of temper. 'It is crazy. It will cause your mother great fear and sorrow. Dear God, it will cause me great fear and sorrow too. And what of Flora?'

'She will understand,' I said. 'I will give you a letter to give to her. If I am to be worthy of her, I must prove I am not a coward.'

'If that is the reason why you do it,' he exclaimed, 'then you are a selfish fool. You are little better than these insurrectionist brigands, intoning their slogans and parading their virtues all over the land while dipping their hands in other people's blood. You have no right to take strangers' lives just to impress a lady, any more than they have the right to do so to write Liberty in letters of blood.'

'Father,' I said, white as a sheet, 'that is a monstrous accusation! How can you possibly think that I would fight to impress Flora? She would recoil from a warrior or an assassin; she is as gentle as the roses she grows. No. It is not for her, and not for me, either, that I wish to stay and fight. It is because of Bertrand, because of his grandfather, because of all those poor people I saw, butchered in cold blood. It is because I hate this lying Revolution now, because I hate these wolves who came to us in sheep's clothing, don't you see?'

'Dear God,' he said again, and closed his eyes briefly. When he opened them he said, 'My dearest boy—my brave Jacques—you will do, I expect, what you feel in your heart is right to do, as young men have always done. But consider this—the Revolution is no foreign war. It is here, in our own land, our own hearts. It has divided brother from brother, friend from friend, parent from child. And it won't be defeated easily. What will you do if one day the enemy you face is not a stranger—but a friend? What if, for instance, you should have to face Edmond de Bellegarde, your childhood friend, and your beloved's own cousin?'

I swallowed, but answered resolutely. This, too, I'd thought about. 'If he were to be on the side of those murderers—if he were to be prepared to act as they did or even to justify it—then how can he be my friend any longer? How can friendship mean anything, then? I did not know Bertrand till a few days ago, but if Edmond had been in that crowd of assassins, I would not have hesitated over my choice for an instant. I would have saved the child and killed Edmond.'

'I do believe you really mean it,' he said quietly, his eyes searching my face.

'I do indeed.'

He sighed heavily. 'But he was not in that crowd. I do not see him as a cold-blooded murderer.'

'No,' I said, 'neither do I. But I see him as a man who would *justify* cold-blooded murder in the name of Mankind, because in truth he does not care. After all, he has done so before.' And I told him the story of how Edmond had reacted to the story I'd related, a year or more ago, about the man who'd had his assistant murdered by the mob.

Father listened in silence, then he said, rather sadly, 'What are your plans, then, Jacques?'

'Jonathan told me there was a resistance springing up all over the country,' I said, speaking in a great rush of words, for I had been thinking of nothing else the last few hours in the coach, 'and I thought I would go and see them—those I know about—and ask what I should do to help. I thought I would go to Tours and see a man named Monsieur Perrin.'

'Why Tours?' Father broke in. 'Why not your own home? There are many there getting ready, you know. Secret links have already been made with men from our village and others round about, further south, and in Brittany too. If you are really to take part in any war—and please God, I hope that everyone will come to their senses before it's too late, and good order and justice be restored and the King freed from this illegal imprisonment—then you will need not only courage but also local knowledge. You need to be in your own territory, with your own people, not rushing hither and thither about the country trying to take part in this or that. And you will need to rid yourself of the longing for glory or revenge. These men—many of them will be hard as nails already—soldiers, militia men, hunters, poachers. You don't even know how to fire a gun.'

'I bought a pistol weeks ago,' I said, excitedly. 'I haven't fired it yet—but I do believe I know how.'

He smiled. 'Everyone must do what is in their best capabilities. You will have to take orders. Pierre is to be the leader in our village, if anything happens. He's had the military service. He's brave and clever, rock-solid in his faith and determination, a brilliant strategist, and a real leader of men. He is in fact an exceptionally gifted man. In a better time, I believe he may well have gone far, despite his circumstances—made even a great general, one day. As it is, I am glad the protection of our village lies in his hands.'

I stared at him, dumfounded. He smiled again. 'You thought I didn't know all this? That I disapproved of what is being planned? Well, I do know, and I do disapprove. I am a man of peace, not of war. But I understand, though it grieves me dearly.' He paused. 'You will find our house locked and barred and empty. I will give you a document which will prove that I have given over the house in deed to you, because your mother and I have taken all our goods and gone to retire to the countryside near Rennes. You must of course keep to that story—under no circumstances say anything about England or you may be in trouble yourself with the authorities. You should go to the Bellegardes' house and speak to Pierre—'

'Pierre?' I said.

'You know he was looking after her house. Well, we have done more. It was arranged in case I should be arrested that Pierre and his children and aunt, who is looking after the twins, should move into the manor-house permanently, make it look as though they're squatting in it. Should it emerge that the Bellegardes have emigrated, what will our fine revolutionary friends do about a representative of the people taking the law into his own hands?'

'My God,' I whispered, 'Madame de Bellegarde must trust Pierre.'

'Of course she does,' he said. 'She trusts him more than anyone in this world, Jacques.' He paused. 'I have to say it was his idea, but she took to it at once. I thought it lunatic at first. But now I see the wisdom in it.'

'But the other villagers—aren't they envious?'

'Oh, one or two are—the usual malcontents. Most understand the situation. No one talks about it. Neither should you.'

'I won't,' I said.

'I have no stomach for war,' he said sadly. 'I am too old for it, too tired. And I pray with all my heart and all my soul that this country does not take that path. I still hope, Jacques, I still think it's possible, despite your young man's certainty. But it is foolish not to prepare for the worst. And cunning may succeed where boldness may not; and vice versa, of course.' He looked earnestly at me. 'I do not think you are one of these born warriors, Jacques, unlike Pierre; I do not think you are fixed enough in your steadiness for that.'

'Father,' I cried, dismayed, 'it is not really very kind of you.'

'Wait,' he said, waving a hand at me. 'I was going to say that the story you told me, of your rescue of this poor little boy and his grandfather, to me shows the path you should take in this fight. Perhaps your task is not to destroy life, but to save it.'

At that moment, we heard the rattle of the turnkey's bunch of keys. We fell silent. The door opened. The turnkey stood to one side, letting in the Governor's aide. He nodded at us. 'His Excellency—I mean—the Citizen Governor,' he corrected himself, in some confusion, 'wishes to inform you, Citizen Verdun, that you are free to go. He regrets that he cannot come and see you personally, extends his compliments to you and hopes that you have not been too uncomfortable whilst this confusing situation was straightened out.'

My father shot me a quick glance. But all he said was, with great dignity, 'I will be glad to breathe the fresh air again.'

So we walked out of that prison, neither of us daring to say anything till we were well out of earshot of anyone in authority. It was not until we were several streets away that Father whispered, 'What on earth did you write in that letter to put the fear of God into the Governor?'

'Not fear of God or even of Robespierre,' I answered lightly, wanting to laugh my triumph aloud to the sky, 'just a modest request for your release as a victim of an error of justice, and a few prim compliments about the Republican virtue of the Governor, along with a few veiled hints as to what preferment might come his way, if things worked out for the Reign of Virtue and he kept his mouth shut. Just hints, you understand—that's Robespierre's way. The Governor probably thinks now you're one of Maximilien's associates. Or at least that I am.'

'And he may well guess that Robespierre's star is on the rise now, if he's kept in the shadows over this prison massacres business and it's well known he hates Marat! Brilliant, Jacques—better to appeal to men's greed and ambition than their fear. They're less likely to want to investigate then,' laughed my father. 'We'll make a great lawyer of you yet!' Then a shadow fell over his face as he remembered the things we'd said, in the cell. I pretended not to see. Being a great lawyer had never been an ambition of mine—and was even less of one now.

Thirty-two

So it was that the next day we left Nantes, bound for the port of Saint-Malo. It was a glorious autumn morning, and as we rattled along in the coach, our own coach, I suddenly realised that it must be nearly four years to the day since the four of us—Flora, Pierre, Edmond and I— had, on Our Lady's head, sworn eternal friendship and always to protect one another. It seemed like a very long time ago. It felt as if I had been quite another person then—except for my love for Flora, which hadn't wavered, only deepened and strengthened.

I wrote her a letter, in which I poured out all my love and all my fondest wishes. I said I would write to her again soon and that she must not worry about me. I told her I still kept the dried petals from the Bellegarde rose in a sachet close to my heart and that they would always remind me of her and make me think of the day when we would be together again. Then I sealed it and kept it close by me till the time should come for goodbyes.

I wrote to the Wills family, too, but not to Jonathan

himself—Father would tell him of my plans. He might well come and see us in Bellegarde. Perhaps he might be able to help us. Perhaps, Father said, hopefully, he might go with Mr Wills to see someone in the Foreign Office, and urge them to take a proper stand against the violence. Perhaps the English government might even be persuaded to intervene militarily to help the victims of the revolutionaries, and prevent complete catastrophe. On the other hand, he added, sadly, perhaps not. They might not want to be involved; they might want to wait and see what would ensue. Worse still, they might want to stir the pot, for reasons of their own. But anyway, Jonathan would surely help—as a friend.

I'd been thinking a lot about what Father had said, about us all needing to use our capabilities, and about how I might not be a born warrior, like Pierre, but might save others. I looked at Bertrand as he sat trustingly in Mother's lap—still without having uttered a single word—and thought bitterly of the many prisoners I *hadn't* been able to help. I thought of how I'd been turned to stone at first, how the sight of evil in action had frozen my faculties. It made me feel ashamed and hopeless, until I looked at that little face again and wondered how I could ever think that. He was here, alive; if I hadn't been there, he would have been in that pile of mutilated corpses. It was as simple as that. I had had no clear idea what to do; but in that moment I had acted instinctively, and had somehow known what to do. I thought of how Father had spoken of Pierre and his exceptional gifts of scenting danger, and of understanding strategy. A born general.

My gifts were more modest but perhaps I did have this in common with Pierre—a sixth sense which told us what must be done. Uncertainty was slipping away from me like an old skin. A sense of purpose and hope grew in me. There were many Bertrands all over the country, cowering with their helpless relatives in dank cells. There were priests to hide, and emigrants to help, and prisoners to help escape. I would have a place in this fight and it could start now, before even a single shot was fired.

I had not yet told Mother I was not going with them. But I think she suspected it. She kept looking at me, her eyes filling with tears, then dropping her eyes back down to Bertrand's head. I was glad they'd taken to each other so well. Mother had been so strong during the period of Father's imprisonment, and now it was as though she could not take the strain any longer. She said very little, and hugged Bertrand to her, and looked out with bleak eyes as though she'd lost hope. Now, sitting in this prison, I wonder if it wasn't only that she knew, somehow, that I had taken an irrevocable decision and she would never see me again. It was also that she knew she must let me go. And that she had perhaps been a little more hopeful about events in France than Father or I; and that

303

my story about the massacres and poor little Bertrand's mute face finally made her feel that our country was broken beyond repair and that evil would triumph over good.

I wish I had spoken to her then. I wish I had been more trusting of her reaction. I wish I hadn't been so afraid she would try and stop me, would cry and weep and tear me in two. I wish I'd known just how brave she was, just how much she understood. It is my greatest regret, a regret I cannot even convey to her now, for all the letters we prisoners write from here are never delivered to their recipients, but confiscated and kept in the files of the Committee of Public Safety, and the Prosecutor's office.

Robespierre's regime knows nothing of pity, but knows and loves the ways of bureaucracy, and meticulously records all its dealings, and keeps files on everything and everyone. I imagine those sober-suited men in the offices carefully making piles of papers, stacking them on shelves, numbering them; all the poor cries for mercy and messages of love and expressions of defiance that are in our letters only affecting them insofar that they are more files to be numbered and recorded. We are not human beings to them, merely figures in a ledger of death, our names to be neatly crossed out once we have been, in the sardonic parlance of my late radical friend Tullard, 'shaved by the national razor'.

*

We arrived in Rennes later that day, found a hotel, signed in, and Father and I went to sell the coach and horses and dispose of all surplus goods. We would travel in the public stagecoach to Saint-Malo, in inconspicuous clothes, under the name of Nerdon. We had obtained a family passport under our own name and it was the matter of moments to ink in an extra stroke to the 'V' and close the top of the 'u' and there it was, a new identity. (I'm proud to say this was my idea—I was getting to be quite an accomplished cheat and forger, Father said, not altogether approvingly.)

With this new identity, we went to get the requisite official stamp to travel further, which was granted without question. It was not yet the time of mass suspicion, and besides, the officials of Rennes were not yet prodded into zealotry. Our trail would end here. As far as anyone knew, the Verduns had reached Rennes, stayed at a hotel, signed out again and went to look for a rental house. Meanwhile, a different family, the Nerdons, had travelled on. Our precautions were elaborate, because so far no one had taken any untoward interest in us. But it was good practice for me, Father said as we hurried back from selling our things. It was not recklessness that won battles, but strategy, and knowing when to be prudent and when to strike.

Even then, Brittany was not friendly territory for the revolutionaries, whether 'Blues' or municipal officials. They took good care not to venture out from their strongholds in the cities. Even so, many towns and cities had little stomach for the new ways. Nantes was about the only Breton city that was firmly for the Revolution, though even there, local officials had to be persuaded that terror was the order of the day—until the dreadful days of the madman of Nantes, Carrier, the bloodthirsty deputy sent straight from the Convention to make the rebellious Bretons and Vendéans 'see sense'.

But in late 1792, the greater part of Brittany was not friendly to any notion of revolution at all. The Bretons had always been stiff-necked, proud people, who didn't take kindly to 'foreigners' dictating the terms of life to them. And they had a long warrior tradition which had seen them affront the crown of France many a time. Centuries ago, there had finally been an agreement signed between the crown of France and the duchy of Brittany. Now that agreement had been unilaterally broken by dishonourable men in Paris who had abolished the duchy and imprisoned the King, and the Bretons were getting ready to fight again, this time *for* the King! In castles and hovels all around the duchy, they had begun stockpiling weapons and planning campaigns.

Jean Chouan, that smuggler I'd heard of from Father's friend Le Braz earlier that year, would be the first of their leaders. They would not fight as our men in the Vendée did at first, in pitched battles like regular soldiers, and thus they would not suffer our terrible losses, faced with the overwhelming might of the Republican armies and their cannon and heavy weapons. They would fight as the men of Brittany have always fought, in lightning-strike small bands darting out from the undergrowth, inflicting bloody, grievous defeats, and swiftly melting away. They worked with the terror of the unpredictable, with the terror of the forest.

A nervous regiment of Blues, hearing the cry of the tawny owl on some dark Breton path, could not be sure it was a bird or the rallying cry of these fearsome warriors, who came to be known as Chouans. Most Blues did not wait to find out, but took to their heels. Only a greater terror—the Committee of Public Safety, and its tireless servant, that Infernal Machine the guillotine—might hold them in their places. But in the Breton forest, the Committee is far away—and the Chouan very near.

Pierre, who had trained in Brittany, learned from those Breton tactics, which accorded with his woodsman's instincts, anyway. Right from the start his strategies in our district were designed to use our difficult terrain as a weapon against the numerically superior Republican armies. Right at the beginning he argued with other leaders who wanted to meet the enemy in fair and glorious fight on the battlefield. It was only after the armies were defeated, and it became known what hideous tactics the Republicans were prepared to visit on a broken people that minds changed, and the small, bitter, ambush-based war took the place of the big, pitched-battle war in our region.

But I get ahead of myself. It is not yet time for the war. We are on the road from Rennes to Saint-Malo, a journey which, contrary to the fears of the coachman, who said he'd been held up several times along that road, was without incident. The National Guard didn't show their faces till Saint-Malo, and even then they weren't exactly enthusiastic about taking much notice of our papers or our purpose in being there. Saint-Malo is a fishing town with a long history of smuggling, and the forces of law and order, be they royal or Republican, have never been able to control the booming trade in smuggled goods— and people—that went back and forth across the Channel from time immemorial.

We found a ship that was going to England the next day; and for a couple of gold coins, assured the cooperation of its captain, a hard-nosed young Breton named Gwillam Ar Wern, who reminded me a little of Pierre, with his broad frame, tangled black hair held back with a grubby ribbon and steady eyes, though his were grey, not black. I fell into conversation with him when my parents had gone to inspect their quarters; he struck me as a man whose acquaintance it might be useful to make, not only for this case, but in the future, if my plans worked at all.

Like most Bretons, he showed no fear at all in expressing his contempt for the politicians in Paris, and rejection of all their doings; it soon became clear, from certain hints he dropped, that he was in touch with people whom it might be worth my while to meet if I was to be successful in trying to set up an organisation to spirit people away. But I could hardly wait in Saint-Malo for Ar Wern's return; the journey to England and back—and his business in England, too—would take at least a month. I would have to go to Sainte-Marie, and come back to Saint-Malo, and possible negotiations with Ar Wern, later.

The goodbyes were wrenching, for of course at the last minute I had to tell Mother I was not coming with them. Though she had clearly suspected it, now the time came for the reality. It was a very difficult moment. She did not scream or cry, as I had feared, but said, quite calmly, 'I fear I will never see you again in this life, my son.'

I shuddered. 'Of course you will,' I said, trying to sound cheerful. 'As soon as all this is over.'

'It won't ever be over,' she said, in such a desolate voice that it nearly sapped my resolve. But Father led her gently away, a still-mute Bertrand holding tightly to her hand. As I walked away from the quay, with hot tears in my eyes, I knew that I was doing the right thing, but that it was even more painful and difficult than I had imagined. It was not the first time I would feel that way.

Thirty-three

And now I must leapfrog over time, because time is running out for me. And there are certain things I prefer to draw a veil over, for I have no wish to endanger anyone else who worked alongside me in those days. Suffice it to say that by the winter of 1792, in those first few months that had been dragooned by our new masters into what they called Year One—as if nothing had existed before then!—I was back in the village, for a short while, I thought, just to lie low after several strings of prison escapes I'd helped to carry out.

All the servants had left our house now, and there was a good deal of work for me to do to get the place even mildly habitable again. But thank God, there were still bottles of preserves, and cabbages and root vegetables in the garden, so I would not go hungry.

Two days after I arrived, it began snowing. All that week and into the next, the snow fell heavily, keeping us all indoors. Except for Pierre, who lived now in the manor-house alone with his formidable Aunt Mathilde, for his poor little twins, who had always been sickly, had died of fever not long before I came back, and had been buried close to their mother in the churchyard.

Grieving in his stoical way, Pierre was more laconic than ever, and his aunt wasn't much more forthcoming. They used only two or three rooms in the house; the rest, though neat and tidy, were kept shut and silent. It was odd to see them there at first, but soon I got used to it.

He was out hunting a lot, and often brought pieces of meat back for me, or invited me to supper. One day, he shot a wolf, too, and skinned it, hanging its pelt ready to take to the tannery once the weather improved. I watched him do it, his big, sharp knife expertly stripping the animal, the skin and pelt coming off like a glove. As he worked, he talked, a little, about Brittany and the people he'd met there, and how they were poised, ready to go.

'Go where?' I asked, though I thought I knew pretty well.

'Not to the Devil, anyway,' said Pierre, smiling thinly. 'It's easy to avoid him, these days. He wears a blue uniform.'

I looked at him, the wolf's blood staining his big, capable hands, the black eyes intent on their work, the generous mouth smiling at his own joke. I said, 'Pierre.'

'Yes, Jacques?'

'Do you think—do you really think it'll come to actual war, civil war . . .'

'There'll be nothing civil about it,' he said, smiling grimly. 'But of course it's coming. I've known it for a long time. If that devil's spawn think they can come here and do what they did to Paris, without a fight, they'd better think again. We have sharp knives and loaded guns and we're not afraid of them or of any man.'

I swallowed. 'I hope it won't come to that,' I said, my mouth dry. And I really did. Not even after all that had happened. I fought the fanatics in Paris by helping prisoners escape—but killing people? That was another thing entirely.

Pierre nodded. 'I hope so too. But I'm ready if it does.' He finished skinning the wolf and pegged out the pelt. Then he wrapped the remains in a sack and I helped him carry it outside, to bury it right away from the house, where the dogs might not dig it up. Wolves sometimes carried the rabid disease, which could be passed on to dogs, with terrible results.

Pierre and I did not talk about Flora. My friend was a man of the finest temperament, the most perceptive human being I have ever known. I knew he understood what I felt. I thought I understood what he felt. The black gift of prophecy that was as much curse as blessing to him had also made him exquisitely attuned to other people's hearts and souls. Yet he was also strong and brave and fearlessly intelligent. Had he been born in another time, he might well have had a brilliant and extraordinary career, for he was not the sort of man for whom humble birth was a hindrance.

As a child, I'd been told about the exploits of one of the great heroes of the Hundred Years' War, the Breton knight Bertrand du Guesclin, who rose from abject poverty and obscurity to become the commander of France's army. I think he must have been just such a one as Pierre.

Even after the snow cleared, we did not bother going to town for several weeks. It was still bitterly cold. But there had been a good harvest that year, and village larders were stocked with preserves and flour. Several pigs had been killed and salted away, and there was confit of goose and duck in earthenware jars. Without any discussion on the matter, the villagers had all banded together as one, so even those who had more meagre reserves did not go hungry that winter. The village was instinctively gathering itself together, re-affirming its own strength and solidarity.

And so, isolated in our rural fastness, we did not hear of the horrible fate of our poor King straight away. We did not know that on the 21st of January 1793— Year One in those murderers' calendar—he had been publicly guillotined in front of a massive, sullen crowd in Paris. A travelling pedlar brought the news. It was like a thunderclap in the village. Everyone had feared for the King, but most people could not quite believe that the revolutionaries would dare to do this, to kill God's anointed and set themselves forever in mortal sin. For the villagers, the King *was* France. To kill him meant a dagger thrust into the very soul of the country, treason and heresy more horrible than anything imaginable. Few of the villagers had any inkling that such age-old notions were now a foreign tongue to the Paris radicals, an alien language they had long ago forgotten in their rush to power and the cleansing of the world.

The villagers had never met the King. And they didn't care how the rest of Europe would react. But their grief was intense and intimate. They wept for the King as if he had been their father, and they shuddered at the unnatural crime that had been committed. Heaven itself would stand against the Republic now.

The courage Louis had shown on the day he was murdered, the words he had uttered as he mounted the scaffold, the gentle forgiveness he had extended to all his enemies, had been widely reported, as had the attempts of the revolutionaries to drown out those words as they sensed the silent, cowardly admiration of the crowd in Revolution Square. People said the words had been Christlike, that Louis was a saint, and that somehow, from heaven, he would redeem a dishonoured, sinful France.

In the village, the tocsin, the death knell, was sounded.

The church was packed for the King's requiem mass. Not a soul was missing, from the oldest to the very youngest.

But after Mass, the village men gathered outside the church, full of grief and rage. Wild plans were mooted. People spoke of gathering a vast army and marching on Paris to free the rest of the royal family, still imprisoned in the Temple—the Crown Prince, a frail little boy of ten, was now Louis XVII. They spoke of assassinating the deputies who had voted for the King's death.

Not all of them had done so, of course. Many—like Tom Paine, like the Girondins, like Danton himself—terrified by the mounting bloodlust of their allies, had urged mercy, and exile for the King. But many others had voted for death—men like Marat, and Hébert, and most horribly, the King's own cousin, Philippe d'Orléans, now known as Philippe Egalité. But it had been the coldly threatening speech of Robespierre—the strongest champion of execution—that had won the day, and the waverers on the Convention had either to comply or flee, if they did not want to face immediate arrest.

There was a good deal of overheated talk on how we could avenge the King's death, and most of the young men of the village were all for rushing off right now to fight. 'Every true man in France will join us!' they declared. 'These devils have no friends!'

Oh, sweet Jesus, I thought, listening to them—images of the hideous events of September flooding through me—my poor friends, you have no idea, no idea of what it is you would be facing, no idea of just how strong they are, and how many of them there are and what they're capable of. How could you possibly be as ruthless as them, who have no attachment to any of the things you think normal and natural?

And yet, and yet. Like them, I could feel the anger and wild desire to do something to halt this headlong nightmare, to say, stop! No further! Now it is your turn to die! It was no longer enough just to help a few prisoners escape. I wanted to do more. Much more.

Surprisingly, it was Pierre who quelled the excitement. He'd been silently listening to all the wild propositions, the naïve and suicidal plans (including, I'm ashamed to say, mine), and now he said, 'It is no good just one village rising up on its own, and hoping to persuade others afterwards. It will take patience, and careful strategy. Not only do we have to train, and gather as many weapons as we can, but we also have to send messengers out to every village and settlement and farmhouse, and gain an understanding of just how many people would really join us, when the time comes.'

'When the time comes!' someone cried. 'But the time's here. *Now*.'

'No,' said Pierre calmly. 'Do you really think we can get the numbers we need, all over the Vendée, all over France, just because the King's been murdered? Well, the

King was in danger for a long time, and who tried to help him? Only the Austrians and Prussians, foreigners, and a deal of use that was.'

'How could we do anything?' mumbled one man, into the heavy silence that followed Pierre's words. 'We're just little people.'

Pierre smiled faintly. 'Do you mean, we grumble and complain but still see ourselves as subject to laws that are mockeries of God's truth? Little people! Are we not men with free will, whose only fear should be to displease God?'

Another silence followed, but of a different quality. Then the blacksmith, Nicolas Chauvet, spoke. 'What do you propose, then, Pierre?'

His diffident tone, and the expectant expressions of the others, made me realise that my friend had indeed become, by some process I hadn't been aware of till then, the acknowledged leader of the village.

'Just that we get ourselves ready. That we speak with as many people outside Sainte-Marie as we can. I know many feel as we do. In Brittany, they are even more ready to go. But the spark is not yet set to the powder. When it is, we must be ready. There is nothing surer than that those vile creatures will not stop at the King's murder. They hardly had enough voices to carry their vote—they will have to kill anyone, everyone who opposes them now, even their former friends. But they have one fatal flaw—

they believe only in power for themselves, they believe in nothing greater than themselves. And that, my friends, that will be their undoing!'

There was a hearty chorus of agreement. I wanted to interrupt, to say no, no, Pierre, you don't have it quite right. The revolutionaries were *not* just power-hungry. They were men of faith, too—faith not in God, but certainly in something they saw as greater than themselves. It was an ideal for which they'd been willing to kill, and for which they would be willing to die. Their cause was not darkness, but blinding light: the rewinding of history, of nature itself so that Man would no longer be half-beast, half-angel, as the ancients would have it. They wanted to turn us all into perfect creatures of light, into angelic, flawless beings, perhaps even the equal of God Himself.

But I didn't speak. What would have been the point? They would have laughed—they would not have believed it—they would not have understood such grotesque pride, such absurd, over-reaching ambition, nothing less than the remaking of humanity itself. And even if they had understood, why would it have mattered to them? Uttering the thought, I would have sounded at best equivocal. I would have sounded as if I still had some sympathy for those people. And I did not want them to think that of me. I was one of them now, wholly with them, and prepared to face whatever happened. I had chosen my side in the blood and terror of that September night in the prisons of Paris. Yes, there were many good people amongst the revolutionaries—but they had lost. They had been defeated, and now they too would either be on the roll-call of enemies, or cowed into utter, shameful submission.

Thirty-four

Time was running out for the Republic. The drums of war were beating all over Europe. The execution of the King had rallied every civilised country against France. French officials and spies were ejected from most European countries, while English agents travelled freely, cementing a grand pan-continental alliance against the regicides.

On February 21, the Convention defiantly declared war on England and Holland—whilst the war against the Austrians and Prussians was still going on. Days later, mass conscription was ordered. Three hundred thousand men were needed, and needed fast. It would be the biggest conscription effort in France's history, and the most disastrous.

Perhaps the radicals thought that Paris was the whole of France. Perhaps they assumed that the bulk of our people either supported them or were passive and fearful subjects used to doing what they were told by a central authority. Perhaps they thought that sending a few hundred reinforcements to the Republican garrisons of provincial towns would be enough to ensure that all those eligible for the draft complied with call-up and meekly did as they were told. Perhaps they thought that because there had been no royalist army storming Paris after the King's execution, there never would be. Perhaps they were too preoccupied with their own internecine warfare, for already the Girondins and Jacobins were tearing each other apart. In the old parliament, the Girondins had once been radicals; now they had become moderates, and were treated with great suspicion. Marat's mob, thousands strong, invaded the parliament building with impunity, chanting bloodthirsty slogans, demanding that deputies voted the way they wanted.

So the Convention might well have been distracted. But whatever the case, they weren't prepared for the massive storm of protest and refusal all over France.

In our region, feelings ran red-hot. Riots broke out in every town; Republicans were attacked and murdered in Machecoul, recruiters put to flight in Cholet. But it was the stunning success of the uprising in Saint-Florent-le-Vieil, a little distance up the river from us, that filled everyone with hope and courage. In the days that followed, the amazing story, added to and embellished and recounted with passion and gusto, went like wildfire up and down the Loire, and inland, into every village, every church, every tavern, every farmhouse. I am not sure how much of the details I heard were true; what is certain is that the Republicans were utterly routed that day. And because it is such an inspiring story, I will tell it to you, just as I heard it.

Saint-Florent is a market town of some importance, and had been chosen as recruiting centre for all the district around. Because popular feeling there was known to be strongly royalist, the local authorities had taken the precaution of reinforcing the garrison with several hundred troops. But a holiday atmosphere had also been promoted, as a sop to what the authorities no doubt saw as the simple minds of country folk. There were jugglers and fair booths and hot-cake stalls and musicians playing, and prizes had been offered for the first to put their names up.

Around twelve hundred men from the district were eligible for the draft. At the appointed time, the men arrived—not in dribs and drabs, as would normally be the case, but in a body twelve hundred strong, with weapons in their hands—a few old muskets and rifles amongst them, but mostly knives and scythes with the blade reversed, and flails, and sticks, and any improvised weapon you could lay your hand on, on a farm. Plainly, they had acted in concert. Later, we learned the leader had been travelling pedlar Jacques Cathelineau, who was to become one of our greatest leaders, as well as a man named Forest, and a wigmaker named Gaston—

not an aristo among them, but ordinary men, men of the people.

In a body, they advanced on the square. The soldiers, well-armed with new guns and even a cannon—a cannon to become famous amongst us—watched them in alarm. Orders were shouted to the crowd to halt. They did not; the order was given to the artillery-men to fire the cannon. And oh, miracle of miracles! The cannon would not fire! They tried again. Still it would not.

The miracle heartened the rebels, but it panicked the soldiers. Truth to tell, many of the poor devils in the regular army were reluctant, humble conscripts themselves, from other provinces or from the cities. The National Guard, meanwhile, was made up of any citizen who cared to join—some were good soldiers, others inept and better at making speeches than fighting. They had had to fight rioters before, disordered crowds, but never a determined band such as this. The miracle was just too much for them, not to speak of the fact that they read death in the enemy's eyes.

The officers shouted at them to fire; a few obeyed, and some of our men fell wounded. But most of the soldiers simply threw down their weapons and ran away. The recruiters, seeing their protection gone, fled in their turn, leaving their registers and documents. The Mayor in his tricolore cockade and his pompous councillors had already taken to their heels. The field of victory was left to the rebels, who lost no time in dealing with any resistance, overturning tables and tearing up and burning every scrap of paper, every trace of those hated registers! They gathered up all the abandoned weapons—including the cannon—for victory was theirs.

It seems to me that the story which was so widely circulated left out some salient points, such as how many of our people were killed that day—and many must have been, for they were not well-armed. But the fact remains that determination won the day there, and fired everyone in the region with courage and fierce joy. Saint-Florent's magnificent example was quickly followed in every district; within days, bonfires made of conscription registers and recruiters' tables and municipal documents of all kinds burnt fiercely in every town in the region, recruiters were sent packing, and Republican soldiers fled for their lives. Our town was no exception. Swollen by crowds coming from every village round about, including Bellegarde, the local rebels made short work of the agents of the Republic and their guards who had arrived to start the draft. By the week's end, the whole of the Vendée was ablaze with rebellion.

Patient and wary, country people do not usually respond to events in the volatile way of city people, who are easily excited by every passing novelty and alarm. In a city, man marches to man-made laws and arrangements but country life has a discipline imposed on it by the elements. Time passes slowly because it must, because the seasons will not hurry themselves or transform for anyone, regardless of what some arrogant new calendar in Paris declares.

But if country people are slow to respond, once they are roused, they are not easily stopped. And now the boiling point had been reached. The revolutionaries had torn down their Church, interfered with their worship, dabbled with their customs, arrested and imprisoned their noble families, meddled with their guilds, taxed them more heavily than any King had done, imposed a myriad of petty vexations on them, defaced their loyalties, killed their King—and now they were ordering the people to die for them in wars they'd provoked by their mad violence! Enough was enough! Time had run out for patience; now it was time for war. France had to be reclaimed from the wicked, treasonous men who ruled her.

But if they were now full of rage and determination, the villagers did not lose their canny and careful instincts. They knew they must have leaders with experience in military organisation and strategy. So in every village and every district, those leaders were sought out—local nobles who'd served in the army or navy and hadn't yet fled were hauled out of their castles, and ex-career soldiers of peasant and artisan origin were fetched from their cottages. In villages where there was no one with military knowledge, those with experience with firearms—gamekeepers, hunters, poachers, smugglers—often became the leaders. Very quickly, the villages and districts began to form into real military units, each with an elected captain, and a lieutenant, who were responsible for their own community.

Quickly, the movement became enormous, turning into a veritable popular army, assembled so swiftly it made a mockery of the Republic's pitiful efforts at conscription. Tens of thousands of volunteers joined up, without any need for force or persuasion of any kind. Without nearly enough firearms for every man at first, they seized whatever came to hand and the speed and strength and courage of their attacks took the Republicans completely by surprise.

Bellegarde was just the same as other villages. All of us men joined, under the leadership of Pierre. We joined a bigger unit formed around our local town. The very first town was taken just a few days after the anti-conscription riots. Swollen with tens of thousands of passionate volunteers wearing the emblem of our armies (an armband embroidered with the Sacred Heart), singing hymns and crying 'Vive le Roi!', our armies quickly became utterly formidable, crushing local authorities and paralysing the National Convention in Paris.

Volcanic times spew out extraordinary leaders of extraordinary gifts and energy who are forged in the fire of crisis. Such had been the case for the revolution itself; such was the case for our rebellion. The greatest of them all was Jacques Cathelineau, who from peaceful obscurity rose up in Saint-Florent to spark the rebellion. Brave and intelligent, he soon became leader of the northern forces, known as the *Grande Armée*—the Great Army. Adored by his forces, admired even by his enemies, he was eventually elected supreme commander of the united Vendéan forces—the Great Army, the Central Army, the Marsh Army, which at their combined strength were more than a hundred thousand strong. How we bitterly regret his passing!

But there's also intrepid Henri de la Rochejaquelein, a general at twenty-one, and wary gamekeeper-turned-general, Jean-Nicolas Stofflet, valiant Maurice d'Elbée and dashing Louis de Lescure and kind Charles de Bonchamps, and ferocious, independent François de Charette, in his dangerous Marsh country. These men are still fighting hard, even as I write.

Our generals don't sit on hills and watch the progress of battle through telescopes. They are in the thick of it, fighting with their men, their courage inspiring them, and no differences between them, eating the same food, sleeping in the same hedges, dying in each other's arms. Peasants, artisans, traders, aristocrats, all mingle and live and die together. Not more than a hundred of our officers were of noble blood; the vast majority were of the people.

If those murderous fools of Jacobins in Paris had seen it, if they had been capable of understanding that their abstract ideals of equality and fraternity and liberty existed as *realities* in the warmth and brotherhood and love and courage of our people—if they had seen past the smoke and mirrors of their trumpery principles—would their hearts have been touched? No, because they thought we were enthralled by superstition, that our courage was merely misguided, that because the bulk of our armies were 'simple people', they could not think for themselves, could not choose for themselves, were priest-ridden and lord-ridden, lost in the fog of the dark ages while they strode on towards the light! For this is the conundrum of the age—that the men who speak so hotly as the representatives of 'the People' actually despise real people and do not think they have free will like themselves. No, we are there to be led and lied to. We are not there to make decisions, only to mildly accept what others think is best for us.

Thirty-five

We went from victory to victory in those first three months, overwhelming the Republicans, liberating countless towns and villages. The white silk of the royal flag fluttered from town halls and town gates; the registers and papers of the municipalities were burnt; the priests came out of hiding and celebrated huge open-air Masses; the cries of 'Vive le Roi!' sounded everywhere. Many of the prisoners we took switched sides and joined us. People love to be on the winning side, after all. Republican army deserters also flocked to us. We had to be very careful with deserters, of course; until they proved their loyalty, they had to be watched fairly closely, in case they were spies planted amongst us.

We captured thousands of weapons and cannon—but the favourite of them all was the one universally dubbed 'Marie-Jeanne', which had refused to fire in Saint-Florent, and had been captured by our people after that battle. Forged more than a century ago on plans designed by Cardinal Richelieu, she was both elegant and deadly. She became our mascot, our tame dragon—and our people acclaimed and petted her wherever she went, putting garlands on her after a successful battle, and polishing and stroking her till she shone.

Things weren't always easy; battles were fierce, and the Blues fought hard and often courageously. Towns changed hands frequently. Because of the tactics of our generals, who favoured attack rather than defence (and a massive 'shock' attack, too) we lost a good deal fewer men in battle than the Blues did, at least at first. Our men simply abandoned defensive positions and melted away into the countryside before the army could attack them, moving back in under cover of night to attack again.

But reprisals could be bloody. In Bressuire, four hundred savage soldiers from Marseilles slaughtered a great many of our people trapped in the town, including the helpless souls in the prison, against, it must be said, the protests of the municipal authorities. Villages and castles were burnt to the ground by retreating Republican troops, and inhabitants put to the sword. Prisoners were sometimes executed *en masse*, too. But such horrors only increased our ardour. We felt strong, we stood tall. We had done it! We had at last taken up our destiny as free men, we had said 'No!' and the enemy we thought was so strong was folding before us like ripe wheat before the scythe.

It wasn't only in our region, either. Brittany had risen, and Normandy. In May, the cities of the South and Centre, exasperated by the growing tyranny of the Jacobins, exploded. Lyon, Marseilles, Toulouse, Toulon fell into the hands of insurgents. The Bordeaux region, the Gers, the Jura, Provence, joined the rebellion. Revolts blazed from one end of the country to the other; foreign war thundered along its frontiers. The Austrians had recaptured Flanders; the Prussians were pressing in to the east, the English swept back French warships. The National Convention suddenly found itself beset by enemies within and without; the violence they had nursed for so long had now exploded from their grasp and threatened to engulf them in a sea of flame. Panicking, they devised plans for repression and reprisal: they sent out more troops to all the regions, and they established a revolutionary tribunal with far-reaching powers to arrest and imprison and execute. They approved the establishment, too, of the Committee of Public Safety, whose twelve members soon took decisions that overrode the elected representatives of the Convention. In Paris, extraordinary measures were brought in to rout out dissenters and 'traitors' of all kinds. But it was to no avail. More and more people declared themselves against tyranny, and the bloodthirsty usurpers of Paris had a real fight on their hands.

*

How can I explain what a marvellous time it was for us? We didn't have much money, we had few good weapons at first, but we had *people*. Tens of thousands of brave hearts and willing arms. Everything was improvised: strategies, uniforms, emblems, flags, songs, orders. We rode to battle on mounts that ranged from fine chargers to broken-down old mill ponies with rope bridles. We invented salves and balms for wounds based on what was to hand, we constructed portable manufactories of gunpowder and shot which were so efficient that they could be used even on the march. We had an entire intelligence network that rarely failed us and only occasionally produced any traitors (unlike the Blues, who were constantly hampered by the betrayal of their local agents and spies). Our soldiers did not have the discipline of the regular army, but they had more than its courage, and ten times its fidelity.

Everyone was a part of the struggle. The men fought and made ammunition and did the thousand and one things that must be done for an army; the women occasionally fought, but mostly nursed and kept farms going in the men's absence, and worked as information gatherers. The children ran messages and kept lookout. The priests were side by side with us, too—ministering to us, celebrating Mass, saying the last rites, confessing us. They never fought, being forbidden by their calling to use violence—but they followed their people into the thick of things as bravely as any warrior. Father Jantot, old as he was, never missed a skirmish.

There was never any need to force anyone to fight; volunteers flooded in. Most of them came from the villages and the farms, for the country people hated the Republic most particularly: they saw it as a city imposition. But even in the towns, there were many volunteers, especially among the artisans. There were no barracks; the troops stayed in their own homes till called to battle by the ringing of the tocsin in the village church. The tocsin rang from village to village, gathering great assemblies of fighters together, and they would all swarm in great numbers at the siege of towns, and the march across country. The encampments were huge, and homely; not here the neat tents of the regular army, or the rule of petty officers. After a battle, or a 'shock', as most of our people called it, the men would return home to their fields, melting away into their communities, the army dissolving, to the consternation of Republican strategists, who never had a military target to destroy.

For the tactics of our generals had been forged in an observation of their people, and how they would fight. Farmers generally have no taste for war as a career or an adventure, and no wish to stay for glory or honour. It is a practical course above all, a course of last resort, and their leaders, whether noble or commoner, had to work with that. Orthodox army strategy could not be easily imposed; for instance, it was hard to persuade the farmers to go on patrol. They fought not as soldiers, but as faithful men. They fought not for ideas, but for homely things and feelings—for their homes, their communities, their families, their ancestors, their faith, the love they bore for the martyred King, and the loyalty they bore for his poor little son. General Charette once said that the difference between us and the revolutionaries was that whilst their country was in their head, ours was under our feet, solid as the earth. That is as good a way to describe it as any.

I do not mean to pretend that all our people were good types; there are charlatans and ambiguous sorts in every army, as well as the downright bad and wicked, who see war as an opportunity and not as a tragedy. But though there were some who fought for ugly reasons—for greedy profit, or heartless adventure, or because they enjoyed killing people—such men were few and far between.

Generally our officers sniffed out cruelty and bloodlust quickly enough. Incidents of it were severely punished, often by death. I knew of one man, for instance, who was shot dead for beating a townswoman with the flat of his sword in his attempt to steal from her. Looters were put to death or in irons; anyone who molested a woman or a child would find himself facing a firing squad very quickly. Of course, there were ugly incidents which are to be eternally regretted, such as the slaughter of Republican sympathisers in Machecoul by one of Charette's units at the beginning of the war. Of all the generals, Charette always had the most ferocious reputation. And in battle, it was sometimes difficult to restrain the ferocity of troops as they fell on the enemy soldiers. War is an ugly thing, and civil war the ugliest of all.

Yet most of us knew that if God was to be on our side, we must show mercy and humanity to our enemies, and exemplary conduct towards each other. It might sound like cant but many of our people genuinely tried to live up to those ideals. Our units all came from the same communities, the same villages, the same regions; they would have to go back to them when it was over. How could they live amongst their own if they were known to be criminals and killers? It is easier to be one such in a regular army unit, drawn from everywhere, anywhere in France, especially if said regular army is told that the rebels are not human beings at all, like them, but brigands, as they called us, sub-human vermin who deserve no quarter. The wolfish instinct in humanity is easily awoken, especially if the wolf is given absolution for murdering the lamb, told that it's his patriotic duty to save the nation from brigands and slaves.

Our village unit, with Pierre as captain, of course, had become a part of Cathelineau's army soon after it was formed. We met the already legendary general in person one morning in late March 1793. At thirty-four years old, Cathelineau was tall, solid, handsome, with dark wavy hair, steady, honest brown eyes, a mind as incisive as a knife, and a gentle manner. He was one of the kindest men I have ever met, and the bravest. Modest and devout, with a bright strand of gentle humour, he attracted both immense love from his men, and quietened the fiery personal conflicts that sometimes raged between some of the other leaders. He really *saw* people; he never forgot a name. He met me very briefly, a second's handshake, a word, and then he passed on, and yet, several months later, when I was sent to him with a message, he remembered not only my name but where I came from. The greatest of our generals, he is also the most-regretted. He alone united all our forces—even turbulent Charette respected him.

Intelligent and educated—for though he came from a poor family, he had been schooled in a church college in Saint-Florent—he also had a superb natural understanding of strategy and an intensive knowledge of local geography. That came partly from natural ability but also from his work as a pedlar crisscrossing the region, becoming familiar with every road and path and village. Under his leadership, the armies went from victory to victory. People said he was a saint, even an Angel of God sent to save us.

It was easy to understand those stories. Cathelineau

set the tone for our entire army. He had a loathing of cruelty and greed and brutality. The end did not justify the means, for him. Like most of our leaders—except for Charette—he recoiled from ruthlessness, and insisted on a code of conduct for his troops. Prisoners must be well-treated; women and children unmolested; there must be no looting or pillage of villages or farmhouses or towns. Anything we needed, we must buy.

Posterity may well ask how it was that all those thousands and thousands of men, who had led peaceful, humdrum lives in the obscure countryside, suddenly changed, suddenly became fighting men ready to face battle. It is one thing to be gifted as a natural leader of men, like Cathelineau, or my friend Pierre. It is quite another for the rest of us. But just as volcanic times forge extraordinary leaders, they may fire ordinary men with a courage they may otherwise never get a chance to display. It is not an easy thing to explain, and I can only speak for myself. Before, I was still hoping that war would be averted, somehow; after, I was glad it had not been. That is all I can say about it, the only way in which I can explain it.

Perhaps you cannot see me in the army. Well, it is true I am not a good shot, but I can defend myself with a sword as well as any man, and I am not a coward. But in war, a good leader will use the talents of his men in the most appropriate way possible. Pierre had seen something in me those years of our childhood, and those times we'd spent together in the woods, hunting, had made him understand precisely what task I should best be fitted for. And I had told him a little—a very little, for I did not want to boast—about what I'd done, in the prisons. Quite early on, after the putting to flight of the recruiters but before the army marched to its first pitched battle, he came to my house to talk to me about it.

I have said he was a man of the utmost delicacy and perception; nowhere did he show it more clearly than then. He said to me, 'Jacques, it is essential we have reliable and brave messengers, scouts, gatherers of information—and I should very much like you to be in charge of it for our district. It is not only deeds of arms we need, if we are to win, but guile and intelligence. It seems to me you understand how our enemies think, and you know how to use subterfuge. What do you say?'

I stared at him, overwhelmed. I had never considered such a thing. But strange to say, the idea took root in my mind at once, and I knew that he was right—that in this I would find my niche, where I could be truly useful, and truly valuable.

So Raoul Jantot (Father Jantot's nephew) and his formidable mother Toinette and I crisscrossed the region, posing now as peasants, now as bourgeois or artisans, depending on where we were and what our task was. It was useful having Madame Jantot with us; she not only distracted suspicion, so that we appeared to be a family; but she was handy with a rifle herself. We carried messages and despatches and letters, not only from our unit but from all the units round about; we had devised any number of ingenious methods to hide them-in false-bottomed purses, in hollow walking-sticks, in the linings of hats. Raoul, who knew the country like the back of his hand, was the one who planned the routes.

Thirty-six

One fine morning in April 1793, we arrived at a rendezvous in a remote part of the countryside. We hadn't been told exactly what to expect, only that there was something important for us to take to field headquarters, where several of the generals were assembled after the first battle of Fontenay. When we appeared at the isolated house, we were met by a suspicious farmer, musket in hand and huge guard dog by his side, who asked us in a surly voice for the password.

'I don't mind telling you I'll be glad when they're off my hands,' he growled, as he led us to the barn. We looked at each other. What did he mean?

We came into the barn. The door creaked as the farmer closed it behind us. It was rather dim in there. I could feel prickles at the back of my neck. I shot a look at Raoul, who gave a tiny nod. The three of us had often spoken of what we would do if we were caught in a trap. One of us must at all costs get away to raise the alarm. Raoul and I were both determined (though we hadn't said anything) it would be his mother. If we were caught, Raoul and I would fight hard, try to cause a diversion so she could escape and get help.

The farmer said, 'They're here.'

I thought I heard a tiny sound, quickly suppressed; then in the next instant, shouted in alarm as a voice said, very close to my ear, in English, 'By all that's wonderful, Jacques Verdun!'

I recognised it at once. It was Jonathan's voice! 'Dear God! What in the world are you . . .'

'Same as you, I rather think, my friend,' he said. 'Messages to deliver, you know.'

Another voice said, rather harshly, 'You know this messenger, Monsieur?'

'I rather think I do,' said my English friend, then, to the farmer, 'for the love of God, Monsieur, will you please open that door! It is mighty close and stuffy in here.'

The farmer did as he was told; the sunlight flooded in, illuminating the scene. There was Jonathan Wills, dressed like a pedlar, in dusty clothes and battered hat, a bag slung over his shoulder; there was his companion, dressed in the modest clothes of a ploughman, his neck a little too white for the disguise.

Predictably, Jonathan was the first to recover. Taking off the battered hat, he bowed low to Toinette, and shook hands with Raoul and me. He said, 'My friend Jacques looks too surprised to do the proper introductions,

341

so I must. My name is Jean and my companion's is Ludovic.'

'This is Raoul Jantot, and his mother, Toinette,' I said.

'Enchanted, Madame Jantot,' said Jonathan, bowing again. Toinette looked at him, then me, suspiciously, as if to say, who's this popinjay?

Raoul also looked wary. He fixed Jonathan with a glare and said, 'We were told there was something we had to take to the General. Do you have . . . ?'

'It is my friend Ludovic here you have to take to the General,' said Jonathan lightly. 'I have to go on to Brittany, to run other errands—but I'll warrant the General will be very pleased to see what you bring.'

It dawned on me then. The man was an important émigré noble, bringing news and promises—maybe even funds—from his fellow exiles. Jonathan must have accompanied him from England. It was a dangerous thing to do, for of course France was at war with England. There were garrison troops at La Rochelle and Saint-Malo and Lorient and many other points along the Vendée and Breton coasts. But there are many deserted landing-places too, and fishing boats have plied these seas for centuries, and fishermen know every unobserved beach. It was not the first time or the last that people would be landed clandestinely.

*

We had a good dinner of roast meat and cheese, provided by the farmer, and rested that night in his barn. But it was nearly midnight when the others dropped off and I finally managed to speak to Jonathan alone, and put to him the questions I'd been burning to ask but hadn't wanted to voice in front of the others.

'How are my parents?' I had not received any letters since the first one months ago informing me they had safely arrived; now France was at war with England, no letters were getting through.

'I have been away from home for several weeks now, but when I last saw them, they were both very well. They have settled into life in England, though I know they miss you. But Bertrand, the little boy you rescued, who they have adopted, grows apace and looks better by the day.'

'I am very glad,' I said, my heart lightening at the news. I hesitated, then went on, 'There are other people from my village there . . .'

'You mean Flora de Bellegarde and her mother,' he said with a sideways smile. 'As I said, I have not been at home for some time, but as far as I know, all's well. They have taken a house a few miles from us. They live quietly. Very quietly. Though not for lack of invitations.' He paused. 'I understand Flora is homesick and would very much like to return to France, but her mother will not hear of it, of course.'

'She is quite right,' I said, though my heart burned

with the sweet hope that it might not just be the village she was homesick for. Then I remembered my manners. 'And how is *your* family, Jonathan?'

He laughed. 'Very well. You should see my little girl, Amy. She is grown so big! Jenny is very well too, and big herself with our second child. And my sister Charlotte. I declare she has grown half a foot since you saw her last— you would not recognise her! As to Jane, she has grown a bosom, and is most conceited as to her figure, but she is still the same old bookworm as ever was. And I'm an uncle twice over, Jacques—yes, to Emily's sons, Robert and Giles. Father has had a spot of the gout, this year, but otherwise he is well, and Mother is the same as ever.' He grinned wolfishly. 'And what of your brothers in arms, Jacques? What of our Ancient Gaul?'

'Pierre? He is the captain in our village; he is a good campaigner, and a fine leader.'

'Ah! So I was right! And Edmond? He finds himself on the other side in this, does he not? Are you still in communication with him?'

'I haven't heard from him for a long time,' I said. 'I think he is still on the side of the Revolution but not, I think—I hope—on the side of the King's murderers. I never heard him utter any bloodthirsty sentiment towards him. I suppose only that like so many other people, he is lying low and hoping for the storm to pass. He is an artist, not a politician, after all.'

'You are an unusual man, Jacques. Even in these times, in these circumstances, you try to be fair. Edmond is still friends with Casgrain, is he not?'

'I have no idea.'

'I have heard Casgrain might be sent to your district,' he said, 'with his unit.'

'Really?' I said. Truth to say, I didn't care a fig about Casgrain, or any of his ilk, any longer. Let him come to our region! He'd soon see that our armies weren't to be lightly dealt with!

'He's in a good position,' said Jonathan lightly. 'His cousin Robespierre's star is in the ascendant, from what I hear. The Girondins are as good as dead—their day is over. The Jacobins are supreme. And it is Danton, Marat, Hébert and Robespierre who count for most these days. But from what I hear, our Maximilien may well trump even the other three, eventually.'

Remembering the green-eyed lawyer from Arras, I said, 'You really think so? He seemed to me an unlikely sort to ever get further than some officious post. He's far too prim and cold to beat those dangerous men.'

'He's very clever,' said Jonathan. 'Much cleverer than the others. He lays traps for them and spreads lies and rumours—no, he is no Macbeth, perhaps, like the others. But he would make a perfect Iago.'

I shuddered. 'How hideous it must be in Paris!'

Jonathan smiled faintly. 'Paris isn't hideous at all

for people like your Edmond. The Opéra is still going strong; the theatres are full of new plays, the restaurants are overflowing, fashions, I believe, are growing more outrageous by the day. The painter David's committee is busy beautifying the city with garlands and flowers and is planning what they say will be a marvellous festival for the 14th July.'

I looked away. 'Edmond is a frivolous fool. But the Republic doesn't have long to run. Robespierre will never reign, because we will have defeated them all long before that.'

'Yet they speak of extermination,' he said, watching me. 'They speak of destroying all rebel provinces completely. They speak of total Terror, visited on all the land, and not just Paris.'

I laughed. 'Big words! Ha! France is not Paris! They have terrorised Paris into submission—but not the rest of us. They may think they rule Paris—but they do not rule us. You'll see for yourself.'

'I'm sure I shall,' he said. 'I have to say, Jacques, there are many in England who are relieved that you French haven't entirely taken leave of your senses, haven't entirely turned into zealous inquisitors and philosophis- ing murderers! Where had the wit of France gone, they say, her old lightness of heart, her gaiety, her swaggering chivalry, her sublime mockery, her gallantry? The tur- gid and bloodthirsty ramblings of your revolutionaries are not at all a fair exchange for Monsieur Perault's fairy tales or Monsieur Ronsard's verses! Which reminds me, Jacques—what of your poetry?'

'I haven't written much, recently,' I said. 'There isn't time.'

'There's always time,' said my infuriating friend, clapping me lightly on the shoulder. 'Write a nice lilting lyric, Jacques, a sweet love song, a beautiful lightsome thing—don't turn into a solemn ass like the others, always with your eye on some higher ideal.'

'I'm not,' I said, smiling a little to mask my irritation. It was all very well for him, an outsider, to say such things. He could be detached from what was going on. For him, it was a risky game. For us, it was life or death.

Thirty-seven

We plan and we plot, we humans. We try to impose on the universe patterns we can recognise, on human nature things we can categorise. But when the world turns differently; when our fellow humans behave in ways other than we dreamed— when our best-laid plans and fondest fancies turn out to be will o' the wisps, what then?

After taking our leave from Jonathan the next morning, the rest of us set off back to camp. It took us two days. When we arrived, the camp was crowded and very busy, for several of the other Vendéan generals had arrived for a council, and many of their followers were there.

I took 'Ludovic'—whom in all that time I'd barely got to know, as he kept himself to himself—to the generals' quarters. Then I went to find Pierre and report back to him on the things we'd seen during our time away, not only the troop movements we'd glimpsed but all manner of things. It was something I always did; Pierre kept a meticulous record of everything I reported, even the seemingly trivial. He was building up an intelligence dossier which he said was as important to us as the strategic planning of battles.

He was in a tent at the far end of the encampment. As I came close, I could hear his voice—not slow and considered as usual, but sharp, choppy, raised. And then—then I heard the other person's voice, and stopped dead. For it was Flora's, and she sounded as if she was pleading with him.

Pierre spoke. 'You shouldn't have come. I'll have someone escort you back to Brittany. You will catch the next boat back.'

There was something wrong in his voice, something I didn't understand. The way Pierre was talking to her, it was so—unfriendly. More than that; it was rude. He had not called her Mademoiselle. Just 'you'. It was so unlike him it made me feel very uneasy. I wanted to rush in and greet her. But something made me hesitate.

'No, Pierre,' she said, now. 'You can't make me go. Not now. You don't really want me to go. I know you don't.' Her voice was soft. It made little shivers go up and down my spine.

'You must. I can't let you stay.' His voice was trembling a little.

Her voice strengthened. 'I am not a child living in a dream any more, Pierre. I am a woman. I know my own mind. My own heart. How do you think I've felt, sitting in England, reading the newspapers, knowing you risk your life every day while I tend my roses? You say you saw me in a dream—as I saw you in mine. I knew you needed me, Pierre. I knew I had to come.'

Pierre spoke. 'Those were dreams. Just dreams.'

'You of all people, Pierre! You know it's not so.'

'I should never have told you,' he said. 'It was the shock of seeing you that loosened my tongue. And I have had other dreams. I have thought of you tending those roses. I have imagined you in a rose-garden in England, and I was glad. If I fight, it is because I must. But you do not have to. You *should* not have to.'

In that moment, something hit me with the force of a hammer-blow. Or a dagger, thrust straight to the heart. And I understood at last what I should have realised a long, long time ago. *Pierre loved Flora.* Not in the way Edmond had described, like a faithful dog with its mistress. Not in the way I'd thought, the naïve adoration of a peasant boy for an unattainable lady. But like a man, loving a woman. Hopelessly, maybe. But truly. And deeply.

And Flora loved him too. There was no doubt in my mind of that. In the past, perhaps, that distant past before the Revolution, she might have lived her whole life and never known the truth of their mutual feelings. Too much separated them, then.

But the times had not only turned the world topsy-turvy and changed the way people thought about each other—

they had also displayed, with utmost clarity, who people actually *were*, in their inmost beings. Not peasant or noble or merchant or whatever silly label we cared to assign—but varieties of character of men and women. Courageous or cowardly. Ambitious or honourable. Ruthless or self-sacrificing. Pierre was no longer just the peasant boy with whom Flora had grown up, the childhood playmate who accepted her every whim, because of who she was. He had emerged in his own right, as his own person. And she had realised that she loved him. Everything in their lives had pointed to this. She had come all this way for him. It was not I, who had so longed for her, who was her soulmate, but *him*.

My head pounded. I could not bear my own thoughts. And I could not bear any more skulking like the spy I was, listening in to other people's conversations. I lifted the flap and strode in.

They sprang apart. They'd been standing so close together that the thought of it made bile rise in my throat.

Pierre stared at me. It was the first time I had ever seen my self-possessed friend really dismayed. It was almost like looking into the face of a stranger. As to Flora—well, she looked different, and it wasn't just the disguise she wore. She had raggedly chopped off her beautiful hair to chin-length, her face was streaked with dirt and tears, her slight body enveloped in a billowing smock and trousers

351

too large for her. But more than that, there was a change in the expression in her eyes, in the way she carried herself. She had said, 'I am no longer a child.' And it was true. You could see it straight away. She had grown up. She was a woman. I saw all these things, and understood, but I felt no pain. Not yet. I was just numb.

I said, 'I heard voices.'

Pierre recovered quickly. 'Oh, Jacques. I am glad you are back. Look who . . .'

'Flora,' I said, ignoring him. 'I would hardly have known you. Your disguise is excellent. You would make a good spy.'

She shot a look at Pierre. 'Really? You think so?' I could hear the embarrassment in her voice, could hear her wondering whether I'd heard everything. I acted utterly composed. It was easy, because of the numbness.

'Jonathan had no idea you were coming,' I said. 'You must have laid your plans of escape well.'

'He's here?' she said, faintly.

'No. But I saw him, just a few days ago.'

'But what is he doing in France?'

'Didn't you know? He's a spy. An English spy. Very useful to us.' I paused. 'In fact it's quite convenient, I suppose. We can send a message to him in Brittany and he can take you back to England when he returns. Isn't that right, Pierre?'

He didn't look at me, or at Flora. But he nodded.

'No, I will not go,' she said, her chin up, eyes blazing. 'Not with him, and not with anyone else. I don't want to go. I'm staying. Not to fight, perhaps, but there is a good deal else I could do. Help in the care of the wounded, for instance.'

'You have to go. It's not safe, for a lady in your position,' I snapped. 'Is it, Pierre?'

'No,' he said, softly, 'it is not. And what I or anyone else may want, Flora, is not important. You should go. For your own safety.'

A wave of rage filled me. For the first time, he had called her Flora. How dare he. How dare he even lift his eyes to her? I was tormented by the tender way he'd said it, by the way he looked at her, his feelings so plain on his face. I hated him. I hated them both. I said, harshly, 'I will tell you what he will not, Flora. You must go. For your safety. And for all our sakes. Can't you understand? Must you always have your own way?'

'Why are you talking to me like this, Jacques?' she said, and her eyes filled with tears. 'I thought you were my friend. My dear, kind friend.'

'I hoped I might be more than that,' I said, unable to keep the bitterness from infecting my voice.

She stared at me. 'I don't understand.'

'For God's sake, Flora. How can you be so blind and deaf and stupid?'

'Don't swear,' said Pierre, harshly, getting up. He

towered above me. 'And don't you dare speak to Flora like that.'

'How dare you lecture me—' I broke off, biting my lip so hard it bled. I wanted to say more—things which would have insulted her and made him instantly into my most bitter enemy—but something stopped me. I don't know what. I like to think it was love. But perhaps it was just cowardice. Instead, I said, 'Forgive me, Flora. I spoke out of turn.' I swallowed, and turned to Pierre. 'So, you're going to allow her to stay, are you?'

'I will not be spoken of in this way, as if I was of no account,' said Flora, her eyes blazing. 'It is my choice to stay. And stay I shall.'

'We must speak to the General,' Pierre said, helplessly. 'We will be guided by what he says.'

'Very well.' I strode to the tent opening. 'It is up to you, after all. You are the unit commander. You can do as you please, and go to the Devil if you like. But don't say I didn't warn you.'

'Please, Jacques . . .' he began, but I had walked out into the open air, my throat burning, my heart aching, my head full of unbearable thoughts.

Thirty-eight

The General said Flora might stay, as a worker in the field hospital. So she put on women's clothes again—but the rough serge of the people—and went cheerfully to nurse the wounded. I did not try to see her. And I avoided Pierre. It was easy enough in a camp the size of ours. Besides, I asked for, and got, a transfer from his unit. I thought that perhaps he or Flora might come and see me, persuade me to forgive them, or whatever they might think: but I was determined not to.

In the event, they did not seek me out. Perhaps they were ashamed. Or perhaps nothing mattered to them now that they were together. I was tormented day and night by the thought of it, imagining his big hard peasant's hands on her soft skin—imagining her fair head nestled into his brawny shoulder. I knew Pierre would not want to bring her into any form of disrepute, but we were at war, and we were often close to death, and far from home and the old life, and they were in love.

I could not bear my thoughts. So I volunteered for

every mission out of camp that I possibly could. I became known for my fearlessness—which I knew really to be reckless disregard. Then came the day I was sent to Nantes. It was an important mission, for we were planning a big attack on that city and had to gather as much information on troop movements and numbers as possible.

Nantes was still firmly in the hands of the Blues. But it was open to attack: the city was not walled, and its fortifications were weak. Open on two sides to the Loire River, it was defended by ditches, a few parapets and a few hastily built-up temporary walls. Cannon and artillery had been installed on as many sections as could be covered, but the city lay open in several directions. And just beyond it was the Breton countryside—and the Bretons were in general no friends of the Republic.

The links between us and the Chouans had been getting stronger by the week; but we still fought separately, each defending their own region, in their own way. Truth to say, there was sometimes suspicion between us, jealousy as to aims, ideas, personalities. But this attack was to unite us all—the Vendéan armies, and the Breton armies. For Nantes was in Brittany, and if Brittany was to be freed, then Nantes must be freed first.

I had to rendezvous with Henri le Goff. Jonathan's old friend was now one of the most important clandestine leaders of the Nantes rebels. On the surface, however, he seemed every bit the respectable fishmonger he had always been. His business enabled him to have a good many contacts in the fishing fleet, both on the Loire and on the coast, and so he had, of course, proved invaluable. But he was also a very clever man, able easily to bamboozle the authorities into thinking he was a good 'patriot', as our enemies called themselves. He had no scruples about wearing the tricolore cockade, and hanging the Republic's flag from his window, and shouting 'Vive la République! Vive la Convention!' with the best of them, and then calmly returning home and planning a daring sortie, a landing of émigrés or an ambush of Blues.

I knew Le Goff reasonably well by now. I'd been to Nantes several times before to see him. I had prepared my usual cover—a Republican lawyer, at a loose end. I didn't use false papers here; there was no need. No one knew the politics or background of the Verduns of Bellegarde in Nantes. And if pressed I could orate on the General Will and how repression was really liberty and how in an ideal democracy a man must always be subject to the government, for in that virtue resides.

In the past, I'd rather enjoyed those moments when I had to prove my bona fides as a comfortable little armchair radical to some municipal official or Jacobin busybody who stopped me in the street and asked for my papers. It was so funny to recount it afterwards to Henri le Goff in his house in rue Sainte-Croix; doubled up with laughter, we mimicked the officious tones of the bureaucrat or the barking jabber of the fanatic, and felt ourselves to be invincible, because we were free, and we could laugh at the foolishness of our enemies and not simply hate them.

But this time felt different. This time, as I crept into the city, I looked at the bustling crowds and thought how soon these people would be fleeing in panic when our armies fell upon them like wolves on sheep. I'd felt no pity for them, before, because images of that bloody September in the prisons kept coming to my mind.

But now I felt something almost like fear. Had I become what I most hated? Had looking at monsters turned me into one? Could I really contemplate the destruction of this city with the equanimity of one who knew he was right, beyond any possible doubt? I'd thought once I could. I'd thought I was a man strong and implacable, like the others. Now I was not so sure. Now I was back to my old, uncertain self, and I hated it, because I knew it was not to do with real pity or compassion, but because of what I'd heard in that tent.

I was a man scorned. A lover slighted. I'd loved her for years and devoted my life to her. But I'd been passed over for another. And for one like him. For a *peasant*! No matter what the times had made him, at heart that's what he was, a nasty voice in my head murmured.

I'd never have thought these things before, if it hadn't been for that. Pierre was my friend. Almost as dear to me as a brother. That's what I'd thought. Or had I, really?

Had all my praise of him, my defence of him against Edmond—had that just been because at heart I really felt he was inferior to me, and so needed defending against his superiors? I had been patronising him and all along, I thought, angrily, he'd been laughing at me.

I was so absorbed in my unpleasant thoughts that I found I'd reached le Goff's house without realising it. Then I stopped. There were National Guards outside the house! My heart thumping, my mouth dry, I drew back into the shadows before they caught sight of me. I waited. I had a horrible feeling something was very wrong.

I didn't have to wait long. Suddenly, the door was flung open and Le Goff appeared. There was a bruise on his face, a cut on his chin. His arms were gripped firmly on both sides by two great hulking soldiers. And with them was . . .

My God, it was Jean Casgrain! And he was clearly in charge . . . What was he doing here? Then I remembered what Jonathan had said. He'd heard Casgrain was being sent to the region, with his unit. They must be part of the reinforcements the city was getting. Le Goff must have been betrayed by someone in the network. What was going to happen to our poor friend?

But I didn't really need an answer to that question. I *knew* what would happen to him. My mind whirled. I had to get back to the camp, as soon as possible. I had to tell them that Le Goff had been captured. If he was tortured, then he might reveal our plans to take Nantes. He didn't know the full extent of them; but enough to lead to disaster. Of course, he might not break. But even if he didn't, the Blues would likely know soon enough that he was at the centre of the resistance in Nantes. They'd find other members, weaker links; they might make them talk. They knew less than Le Goff, but if you got a lot of scraps of information, then you might combine them all.

It was too late even to run back to camp. I had to stop them getting Henri to the torturer's chamber. I had to stop them knowing anything at all. I felt for the pommel of my sword. For an instant, I trembled. And then, without giving myself time to think, I charged across the street, yelling 'Victory to the Republic! Death to traitors!' And before the startled soldiers could intervene, I'd plunged my sword into Henri le Goff's breast.

It was a lucky hit, right in the heart. He fell without a sound. As he fell, he looked at me, once. I thought I read gratitude in his expression. I hope that's what I read. Then his eyes rolled back, and he was dead.

Around us, the street had miraculously emptied. Henri le Goff had been a respected trader here. But the good Republican citizens of Nantes had learned caution along with everyone else. Until the situation could be properly explained to them by the right authorities, they preferred not to know.

The soldiers dragged me up. One of them punched

me in the mouth. I reeled from the blow. I could feel my mouth filling with blood. I tried to say, 'Long live the Republic!' But before the first word was out, Casgrain strode to me. He stared into my face. Astonished recognition flooded his features. He said, 'Citizen Verdun. What is the meaning of this?'

I swallowed. I could taste the metallic tang of my own blood. 'Forgive me. I was taken by passion when I saw him. The dirty traitor!'

'You know he was a traitor, Citizen? How?' Casgrain's eyes held a watchful, wary expression; I could see he was puzzled by my sudden appearance, and by my behaviour. But he wasn't yet suspicious. I had to make sure he didn't become so. Not until I had a chance to escape. I had to improvise, and quickly.

I don't know why the idea came to me. I've thought about it, sitting in this prison cell, and still I don't know. But the words came to me as if they'd been there all along. 'You remember Flora? She joined our cause. We were going to be married. But her uncle, who is now the head of the family, and an enemy of the people, was, as you can imagine, furious. He's in England. But he arranged to have her kidnapped'—I pointed dramatically to Henri le Goff's body—'by this man, who is a consorter of aristos and émigrés and all sorts of scum. But I got to him— before he could get to her.'

Casgrain looked at me in silence for a moment. Then

he said, 'I remember the Citizeness in question. I can understand your feelings. But are you sure?'

'Sure of what?'

'That this man worked for *aristos*?'

'Absolutely. He was an enemy of the Republic,' I said, kicking at poor Le Goff's corpse and hoping his departed spirit would understand what I had done, and forgive me.

Casgrain gave a faint smile. 'And an enemy of Citizen Verdun too, it would appear.' He looked me right in the eye. 'Well, it would seem you were right, Citizen. We received information that this man was a traitor. Yet most of his neighbours spoke of him as an honest fishmonger.'

'They are virtuous but naïve. And he was a clever man, even if he was a black-hearted rogue,' I said unctuously. 'Don't you know, Citizen Casgrain, that the enemies of the Republic will do anything—lie, cheat, steal, kill—in order to achieve their miserable aims?'

'I do not need any convincing of that,' he said. Though he still watched me, I thought something in him had relaxed. Then he said, 'Show me your papers, Citizen.'

Thank God I wasn't here under false ones. I handed them over to him. He perused them and handed them back. He said, 'Are you living in Nantes, now, Citizen?'

'Yes,' I said at once, giving him the address of my usual lodgings, which were run by a spinster lady of irreproachable Republican ideas.

'And the Citizeness?'

'She is even now waiting for me. We are to be married this very day.'

He looked from me to Le Goff's corpse. 'You spill blood on your wedding day?'

'While he lived, we weren't safe,' I said, astonished at myself for spinning such a devious fable. 'And nor was the Republic,' I added.

Casgrain smiled. 'You do not need to convince me of your patriotism at every step, Citizen. I believe you.' He motioned to his soldiers to let me go. 'Well, you have saved us the bother of a trial. The city authorities will not be ungrateful. And you, my friend! It is strange to meet again under such circumstances, but I am glad. I would be honoured if you would let me be a witness at your wedding.'

'It is I who would be honoured,' I lied, glibly. 'It is this afternoon, at three o'clock, at the town hall. The Mayor himself is to . . .'

'Yes, yes,' he said. 'I know the sorts of arrangements that have to be made. And I can see how impatient you are to get back to them.' He put a hand on my shoulder. 'Till three, then. I will look forward to it, and to meeting the Citizeness again.' And with a gesture to his soldiers to pick up Le Goff's body, he turned on his heel and walked away up the street, his tread ringing confidently on the cobblestones. I watched him go for a moment. There went a man who slept well at night, I thought, for he knew he was right, without a doubt, without question.

But now I had to get out of Nantes, and fast. It was still two or three hours till three o'clock, but Casgrain might find out my lie well before that, if he asked the Mayor or even the clerks at the town hall, for they'd tell him there was no Verdun marriage scheduled that day. It was unlikely he *would* ask; he had believed my story, or else he'd never have let me go. It wasn't just my protestations of Republican virtue, though he liked them well enough and believed them—after all, the last time we'd met, in Robespierre's chambers, I'd convinced him of that. It was also the fact that he most likely could not think of any other reason why I might kill Le Goff. I was just an unimportant lawyer with Republican pretensions. He'd met plenty of those. Why should he think I was a rebel? Besides, he was a soldier, not a judge. He spared no tears over the fate of the man. It was one less thing to worry about, one less piece of anti-Republican scum to neutralise. And then there was his attitude to Flora. Something in him had softened at the mention of her.

I slipped out of Nantes on foot without attracting any attention, but on the outskirts I did something rather reckless, which in normal circumstances I'd have never done: I stole a horse outside an inn. Fortunately the owner was in the inn making merry and didn't hear me taking it, or there might have been real problems. As it was, the horse proved to be a bit of an old nag who had to be spurred unmercifully to make it go faster than walking pace. I was in a lather of anxiety by the time I got back to the camp—as was the poor old horse, who looked like he might keel over and die at any moment.

I went straight to the General's tent, where I found Pierre and several of the other unit commanders, poring over a map. They looked surprised to see me—I wasn't due back for a few days. I told them about the reinforcement of the garrison by the National Guard. And I poured out my story of Le Goff's capture and death. Instead of telling them what I'd said to Casgrain, however, I said I had simply persuaded him that I was a good Republican who hated rebels. I could tell none of them liked it. They mourned for Le Goff. But they also saw the necessity of what I'd done.

Only Pierre didn't join in the comments, most of them grimly approving, that came my way. He was looking at me as though he'd never seen me before, and didn't like what he saw. I didn't care. I didn't care about anything he thought. Not any more. I had killed a good man, and for the rest of my life I'd have it on my conscience, even if I knew it had been for the best. Besides that, even the private passionate feelings I'd thought so important were of very little consequence.

Thirty-nine

Time passed. The attack on Nantes was imminent. Sometimes, as preparations heated up, I wondered what Casgrain thought, now he knew my story about the marriage was a lie. Did he think I had joined the rebels? Or had he not made the connection yet? Did he think I had killed Le Goff for sordid reasons of my own? Whatever it was, he clearly had neither time nor inclination to pursue the matter. Republican spies would be aware that there was to be an attack on Nantes, even if they didn't know when. They would be nervously waiting, trying to gather information, watching for the big movement of troops that would signal the first shock.

As to us—well, when you have grown used to victory, and it seems that Heaven itself is on your side, and that ultimate success is in your grasp, you can grow careless. We had taken so many towns and villages. And Nantes was encircled. Their large garrison had been reinforced by Casgrain's men, but it wasn't enough. As I've said, Nantes is not an easily defended city. The defenders would have to rely a good deal on artillery and heavy weaponry to rebuff our attack. And as everyone knows, it is dangerous to rely on machines, for captured by the enemy, they can be easily turned against you. A good set of stout walls can be of a great deal more use to a city under attack. We expected a hard fight; but we were hopeful of victory. We had too many natural advantages. And we had a good plan. We were going to attack in the dead of night, at two in the morning, when battles are rarely fought. It is a time when the spirits of the besieged would be at their lowest ebb. A time when we could catch them by surprise.

But from the start, the campaign confounded our expectations. It had been planned that Charette's army would approach the city from the southern banks of the Loire, and the bulk of the army under Cathelineau from the north. At exactly two o'clock on the 29th of June 1793, the cannon would bombard the city, destroying the defences, and then the bulk of the men could pass through.

But though Charette was at his appointed post as planned, and began bombarding the city at the time arranged, the other cannon did not arrive till nearly six hours later. For Cathelineau's forces were held up by unexpectedly fierce resistance around the city. At last they reached Nantes, and soon overwhelmed the city's defences, driving the Blues out from every command post and every position. Soon the Republicans were retreating in disorder, escaping in every direction. An advance force, with Cathelineau at their head, entered the main city square to deal with the last rags of resistance. Victory seemed assured. Then at that very instant, disaster struck.

Pierre's unit had reached the city sometime before. But I had stayed with the bulk of the General's forces, further back. The suburb my detachment first came into had already been taken by our advance forces, the weaponry captured, and a great many men killed, injured, or put to flight. But we had been told to go cautiously, for there were still scattered defenders holding out behind cover of houses or walls and snipers were an ever-present danger. So we crept quietly along the deserted, shattered streets, avoiding the bodies, abandoned weapons, torn flags, and broken masonry which were scattered throughout them.

I'd been excited when we set out, full of expectation, of heat; now, as we crept along, I could feel a strange, clear coldness invade me. It is one thing to speak of battle; another to see its effects up close. Before I'd killed Le Goff I'd never been the cause of anyone's death. Then I thought I was inured to it. But I was wrong. Death in battle is everywhere. The dead men are no longer figures in a tally, but broken human bodies. They were of both sides. Many of them were very young, no older than me. And the enemy soldiers were not foolish people I could trick with parrotings of Republican prattle. They were hidden, determined strangers, ready to deal out sudden death, in an instant.

We came to a street corner, which gave out onto a market square. There was a lull in the fighting. Suddenly, Pierre's unit emerged from a side street, led by Pierre himself. He was wounded, I could see that at once. He carried his left arm stiffly. I could see the blood on his shirt. Over the heads of the others, he caught my eye. With a shock, I thought, he's wearing his other face— something's wrong. He's seen something!

I had an overwhelming urge then to fight my way through to him. But it was too late. The order came to advance. We flowed on, through the square, into the road beyond, which led directly into the city. Pierre led his unit out first of all. I had to fall back with mine, and lost him from sight.

We advanced cautiously through the streets, careful to look out for snipers who had already caught some of us unawares. But there were no more shots; no more resistance. The defenders of Nantes seemed to have fled. Yet I could feel hidden eyes on us as we went. The ordinary citizens of Nantes were hiding in their houses, crouching behind their shutters, waiting for the storm to pass.

A little later, near the city centre, we heard a great din up ahead. Our captain told us to hurry, we had to get to the battle in time to help our men. But before we could reach the square, a horseman came galloping towards us. I recognised him as one of Pierre's men. He waved a red handkerchief and shouted, 'Stop! The General! The General is shot! He is mortally injured!'

A great cry came up. 'No! No! It's not true!'

'It is!' shouted the man, his face twisted with grief. 'We had just come into the square; it seemed empty; we advanced—the General lifted one arm up, for victory—and all at once, a shot rang out. It should not have wounded him fatally—but it glanced off his elbow and buried itself in his chest, and he fell like a great tree! Oh, men! Those devils got him! They got our Saint, our Angel!'

His news was taken up throughout the ranks, disbelieving cries, shouts of fury and grief, as the men, ignoring the captain's orders, rushed forward in a body to the square. It could not be true! It could not! Jacques Cathelineau had been with us from the beginning. His example had inspired the whole rebellion. He was not only our General, he was our guardian angel! How could he be mortally injured? How could God have allowed this?

You must remember that a popular army like ours is not like a regular army. It is held together not by military discipline but by fidelity and hope. It is not bound to ideas, but to beloved human beings. From that moment, the battle of Nantes could go hang as far as most of the men around us were concerned. Fighting Blues could wait. But General Cathelineau must be taken back to camp. He must be taken care of. He must survive to lead another day!

If Cathelineau had been able to speak, he would no doubt have urged them to go on ahead, and to leave him there. But he was unconscious; the shot had felled him like a bolt of lightning. All the men could think about was getting him away, and no one wanted to stay there without him; a stampede had started amongst the ranks, and very soon it was unstoppable. Men surged back from the square, following those who were carrying Cathelineau's body preciously, like a holy relic. Groaning, weeping unashamedly, all taste for battle vanished, the hundreds and hundreds of mourners streamed out of the city centre, abandoning the positions they had gained.

Even then, it might not have mattered, for there were no defenders left in Nantes to speak of, if it hadn't been for an incredible blunder on the part of the Prince de Talmond, who was leading a force coming into the centre from another angle. Ignoring the old adage to 'Build a golden bridge for a fleeing enemy', he sent his men in pursuit of the Blues, forcing them back into the city and into defensive positions at the very moment when he should have tightened his grip on the abandoned city.

But we only knew that later. At the time, we were completely preoccupied by what was happening.

I will pass over the rest of the events of that disastrous day. Suffice it to say I went to join some of the few men who had not simply stampeded after Cathelineau; I fought hard and mechanically, and I was told later I did not acquit myself too badly. But it was as if I were an automaton, and I remember little of it. We were beaten back; by the evening, we were all in retreat—in rout, really—back across the Loire, and into the safety of our own territory. We were not pursued, for the enemy was just as exhausted as we were. Everybody retreated to their own camps, to lick their wounds and mourn their dead. There would be no more battle for a long time.

Forty

Like the others, I marched disconsolately back to the camp.
I had a superficial wound in the leg, and went to have it
dressed in the field hospital. I looked for Flora among the
nurses, but did not see her. I was not anxious about that,
not at first, because I was exhausted beyond real thought.
It was chaos there and she might be anywhere—most
likely tending to Pierre's wounds, somewhere private. He
hadn't died in the battle, I knew that. I had looked for his
corpse in the city, and in the makeshift morgue that was
near the hospital, but he had not been amongst the dead.

Utterly drained, I slept all that night and all the next
day. I woke, refreshed, to discover that the camp was
being packed up and people preparing to go home. On
an impulse, I went back to the field hospital, which was
being packed up with the rest, the wounded loaded onto
carts to take them home. I asked after Flora but nobody
knew anything. But one of the nuns who ran the hospital
hailed me and told me that someone had been asking
after me; it was one of the seriously wounded, she said,

he'd been unconscious but had recovered consciousness yesterday. He wouldn't last the night, his wounds were too great. He couldn't be moved.

I already knew who it would be before I got there. I have searched my heart and my memory to discover if I felt joy or sorrow at the sight of my fallen rival, who had once been my dear childhood friend. But I think I felt nothing at first. Nothing at all.

He should have been a pitiful sight, lying helpless and dying on the stretcher, all colour gone from his hard, handsome face, his big body broken like a discarded doll's. But the eyes that looked up into my face were the same as ever: black and glittering and full of something I could not explain, a spirit that was as strong as it was unusual. When he saw me, he smiled, and the smile transformed his face with sweetness, so that I suddenly felt a lump in my throat.

'You came, Jacques. I am glad.'

'Pierre.' I sat beside him. I could feel my heart thumping. 'Are you comfortable?'

'As much as they can make me, friend.' He reached out a hand to me. I looked at it, not wanting to touch him; but then, I don't know why, my own hand moved, and I was clasping his.

'I have to tell you about Flora.'

'What?'

'I arranged to have her sent out of harm's way, before

the battle. She would not agree at first, but I begged her.' A flush came over his face. 'I begged her to think of the life in her.'

I stared at him. He said, gently, 'We were going to tell you. A priest married us—quietly, some time ago now. It was wrong, I know—her family has not been told. But we couldn't bear not to be with each other. As man and wife.'

I did not want to hear more on that. Interrupting him, I said, 'Where is she? Where did you send her?'

'I sent Raoul with her, to take her across the Loire in a boat—Conan Ploedic's boat—into Brittany. A village called Donges. It is a stronghold of our cause. Conan has family there. I told her I would meet her there. But now . . .' He paused, and I could see the tears glittering in his eyes, tears he would not shed. 'I do not think I can keep that promise.'

'You want me to,' I said, and my voice sounded odd in my ears.

'Yes. Do you remember the vow we made, Jacques?' he said. 'Do you remember?'

The lump in my throat grew bigger. 'Of course.'

'I don't have much time, Jacques. I need you to promise me that you will always look after her.'

I swallowed. My stomach churned. 'Don't speak like this, Pierre. You will get well. You will go back to Flora and you will live happily with her for many years to come.

Your child will grow up with you. And you will have many more.'

He closed his eyes briefly. He said, 'I hurt you grievously, my friend, without intending to. Will you forgive me?'

My scalp burned with cold. 'Forgive what, Pierre?'

'You loved her,' he said, simply. 'I knew that.'

'She did not love me, Pierre,' I said. 'She loved you. *Loves* you. And that—that is the beginning and end of it. It is you she needs, not me. And there is nothing to forgive in that. You did not seek it. It sought you. It is the way of things. It is what is meant to be.' And as I spoke, strangely, the words seemed suddenly to ease a burden from me. Because they were *true*.

He smiled. 'You are a good man, Jacques. A man of true heart.'

'Please,' I said, rather harshly, 'do not praise me, for I am not at all what you say.'

'As you wish,' he said gently. 'Then you will promise?'

'You are not going to die,' I said. 'You will get better.'

His smile was impish now. 'I will try. But if I don't . . .'

'If you don't, I will do it. I promise. I swear on Our Lady. There. Will that satisfy you?'

'Yes,' he said. 'Thank you, Jacques. You are . . .'

'Stop,' I said, touching him awkwardly on the shoulder, and getting up. 'I need no more words of praise from you, Pierre Bardon. Save your energies for getting well.'

'. . . I was going to say a true friend,' he said gently, looking at me with his bright eyes alight in his pale face.

I had an image of him suddenly as I'd seen him before the battle, with that 'other face'; and the memory made me say, 'Did you have a vision, before the battle, Pierre?'

'It was why I sent her away,' he said, without surprise. 'She and I were together on the side of a great river, and it was sunny. Then a shadow blotted out the sun, and I saw his wings—his black wings—and I knew the Angel of Death was coming. When the black wings lifted I saw we were separated by the river; but at her side was someone else—and I think that someone else was you. So you see, Jacques. You understand.'

I could feel prickles of cold up and down my spine. 'Yes. I understand.'

'Good. And now, will you please ask the priest to come and see me?' He closed his eyes, and I crept away, my heart thumping, my hands shaking.

I prayed for him. I did, with all my heart. And if a nasty little voice inside me tried to whisper, well, once he's dead, you have a chance again, I firmly slapped it down, I closed my ears to its blandishments. I told myself that I really, really hoped he would get better; that he and Flora—his wife Flora—would have a long and happy life and many children and grow old together.

Forty-one

But it was not to be, of course. Pierre was too grievously wounded, just as the nun had said. He was given the last rites and died at dawn. I was by his side when his spirit slipped away. I still can hardly write of it now. I can scarcely believe that he's really gone—that the vital, powerful, extraordinary spirit of Pierre Bardon has gone from this earth for ever.

I knew I couldn't leave his body there, in that alien ground. I had to take him back to Bellegarde, to be buried with the rest of his family in the churchyard. There was no one left of the Bardons, except for his aunt.

After the funeral, I immediately set off back to Nantes. The roads were empty. The countryside had an exhausted and waiting air. There were one or two patrols about, but I avoided them by the simple expedient of hiding in ditches and fields till they'd passed. The Blues were just as nervous and tired as we were, and had no stomach for battle just yet. What I didn't know, of course, was that the Committee of Public Safety had ordered large reinforcements into the area, from the battle-hardened troops of the East and North frontiers. Things were about to get a lot more difficult for our people. But those troops hadn't arrived yet; for the moment, it was the calm before the storm.

I got to Nantes without trouble and went straight to the harbour. I knew that unlike some of the other inhabitants of Nantes, many of the fishermen were royalists. Yes, they said, Conan Ploedic was about. You could find him over there.

Conan Ploedic was a wiry little man with a shock of red hair, a weatherbeaten face, ropy muscles in his arms, a sudden, broken-toothed grin, and a very strong Breton accent. He listened to my story with a still face. Then he said, 'I took a lot of people across that night, Monsieur. Women, men, children. What did they look like?'

I described Flora and Raoul. He frowned. 'Could be I did see them, yes. Well, her, anyway. Him I don't remember. But not that night. I saw them the night *after* the battle. And she wasn't on my boat.'

A pulse leaped in my throat. 'What do you mean?'

'I noticed her because she was beautiful. And because she was unconscious. Sick, perhaps.' He looked at me curiously. 'But she wasn't with that man you described.'

'Who, then?' I said, utterly baffled, the unease in me mounting.

'A smallish, strong-looking man. Blue eyes. Hollow

379

sort of face.' He spat on the ground. 'He was with several National Guards. He seemed to be some sort of captain, for they deferred to him.'

I stared at him. 'What?' My mind was spinning. I couldn't think straight. I swallowed down the questions Ploedic could probably not answer, and said, 'They were going—to Donges?'

'To Donges, Monsieur? I doubt it. On the way to Paris, most likely. I mean, National Guardsman. What would they do in Brittany? They'd have their throats cut in two minutes.'

Paris, I thought numbly, as terrifying light burst in on me. Paris. Yes, that's where Jean Casgrain and his men had taken her. Because he'd believed me. He thought she'd joined our cause. He thought he'd rescued a virtuous Republican lady from the rebels!

A dozen suppositions jumped to my mind. Perhaps they'd got caught up in the fighting, she and Raoul. Maybe she'd been injured. Knocked out, anyway. Perhaps Casgrain had seen her with Raoul. He'd have recognised her, but not him. He'd have assumed Raoul was a rebel. Maybe another kidnapper. He'd killed Raoul. He'd taken her to what he thought was safety. But when she awoke, when she saw him, when she spoke to him, he would know none of it was true, what I'd said. What would he do with Flora then?

I could see Ploedic looking at me strangely. But he

didn't pry. I thanked him, rather incoherently, and left. I raced to the stagecoach booking office, and bought a ticket for Paris. There were six passengers in the stagecoach with me. Four of them—three men and a woman—were very talkative, the other two women mute as statues, and as to me, at first I kept pretty much to myself and my thoughts.

The talkative ones were all Republicans, and the men were full of boastful talk about how they had helped to completely rout the rebel forces. I glanced at their comfortable figures and cheerful pink faces—they were traders or merchants in Nantes—and thought to myself that quite likely, they had been watching the whole thing from the safety of their shutters. The woman, meanwhile, claimed she'd been on the spot when Cathelineau fell, and implied that she knew things about that incident that would not augur well for the rebels. Of course, then the others wanted to know exactly what this mystery was, and she said, in a stage whisper, that she'd heard, on good authority, that the General had actually been shot by one of his own soldiers. 'You see,' she said, as the others exclaimed, 'I heard that the *aristos* could not bear the thought that a man like that should be at the head of an army, and so they arranged for him to be disposed of, and to make it look like he fell in battle!'

I could not help it. I gave a little snort of laughter. She looked crossly at me. 'What's the matter, Citizen?' she said. 'Don't you think that those brigands are capable of anything?'

The others looked at me, offended too. I shrugged. 'Really, Citizeness,' I drawled, and I could feel the eyes of the two silent women on me as I spoke, 'what is the good of such foolish stories? We must respect our enemies, not speak of them as if they were stupid children. If we do not—they will win. Is that what you want, Citizeness?'

She shot a quick look at me, at my sober clothes, my brown hair tied plainly back. Her eyes flickered. She said, uncertainly, 'Of course not, Citizen.'

The other boasters also looked at me cautiously. Plainly, the thought had leaped into their minds that I might be a Jacobin enforcer, or an informer, or some such. In any case, it cooled their ardour a little. But the other two women had dropped their eyes, and I noticed they shrank away from me a little. I thought, they are royalists, I'm sure of it, and in fear of their lives. I determined to keep an eye on them and make sure nothing should trouble them along the way.

But nothing of event happened. It was a wearisome trip. The coach stopped in Angers the first night. The two silent ladies got off there. I got down to help them unload their luggage, which they accepted with hardly a look at me. As they picked up their bags, I whispered to them, 'Good fortune and safety attend you, ladies, and long live the King!'

The younger looked as though her eyes would start out of her head; the older had gone a little pale. She recovered quickly. She looked at me and said, in a soft, sweet voice, 'These are odious times we live in, when even true hearts must veil their very speech. Good fortune, Monsieur, and thank you.' And they walked off, frail but somehow gallant, their heads held high. I wanted to go after them and say that they should be careful with all strangers, but nevertheless her simple trust heartened me.

Forty-two

We reached Paris two days later, on the evening of July 15. It was very hot, and as I hurried from the coach terminus to Casgrain's house, I was soon in a lather of sweat. The streets were as crowded and bustling as ever, but it seemed to me as if the very air of the city had changed. It was permeated with a strange, heavy stink, the metallic smell of blood. The guillotine was doing its daily work on the Place de la Révolution, and had become a favoured entertainment for a certain kind of Parisian.

But it wasn't just the smell of executions that seemed to hang in the air. I felt as though the gutters had never been washed clean of the blood of September, and as if the wind was blowing towards the city the stench of the burning towns and villages of the provinces. I had entered the belly of the beast that was devouring all of France, and now, at the last minute, it seemed to me in a moment of sheer, numbing horror that my courage must fail.

Cursing myself for my weakness, I forced the feeling

from me. And soon, I was knocking at Casgrain's door.

Casgrain's manservant answered. He looked suspiciously at me. 'What do you want?'

'I'm a friend of Citizen Casgrain. I should like to see him.'

'The Citizen is not here,' the servant growled. 'He's gone to the North.'

'The North!'

'Who are you to ask, anyway?' he demanded.

'Don't you remember me? My name is Jacques Verdun. I am a friend of . . .'

'Ah.' His look softened. 'He said you might come, Citizen Verdun.'

I was too taken aback to respond.

He went on, 'You are to go to Citizen Bellegarde's lodgings.' He gave me the address. 'They will tell you what you need to know.'

I stared at him.

'They will tell you what you need to know,' he repeated, and shut the door firmly in my face.

There was nothing I could do but set out at once for Edmond's house. It was only a few doors from where he'd lived before. There was a swarm of ragged brats playing in the street who stared at me curiously when I knocked on the door.

The woman who opened the door wasn't Marinette,

the servant Edmond and Athénaïs had before. This was a round little woman with a dour, suspicious face under a tight cap. She said, 'Yes?'

'I wish to see Citizen Bellegarde.'

She looked me up and down. 'Your name, Citizen?'

'Verdun. Jacques Verdun.'

'Wait here,' she said, and shut the door in my face. I heard her footsteps retreating, then silence. I waited. In the distance, I could hear some kind of tumult going on, but paid no attention. The city was always full of noise.

At last, the door opened again. Athénaïs stood there, behind the servant. She looked pale and much thinner than when I'd last seen her. 'So you've come, Jacques. I'm glad. Edmond isn't here. But he'll be back later.' I saw her hands were shaking a little, and unease mounted in me. 'Are you hungry? Thirsty?'

'Athénaïs, I've come for—'

She interrupted me. 'Berthe, will you please go and prepare some soup for Citizen Verdun?'

The woman frowned. She looked from me to Athénaïs and said, 'Very well, Citizeness,' and stumped off.

'Sorry. I'd prefer not to talk in front of her,' said Athénaïs, with another of those false, bright smiles. 'You don't mind, do you?'

'No.' I suddenly felt sorry for Athénaïs. She looked hollowed-out. Anxious. Almost afraid. I wondered if the unprepossessing Berthe was a spy. 'What happened to Marinette?'

'Oh, she left us,' said Athénaïs lightly. 'Actually, I dismissed her.' All at once, dismayingly, her lip trembled, and tears came into her eyes. She said, 'Forgive me,' and dabbed a handkerchief at her eyes. 'It's still raw, I suppose.'

I stared at her.

She saw my puzzled expression and said, jerkily, 'Our darling little boy—Edmond's and mine—died, three months ago. Scarlet fever. There'd been an epidemic of it, and I'd told Marinette to be so very careful about where she took him for walks, and she took him to a fair at the Palais Royal. And I think, well maybe it was there that he . . .'

'Oh, Athénaïs,' I said, gently, and laid a hand on her arm. 'I am so very sorry.'

She looked at me, her eyes still swimming with tears. 'Thank you.' She paused. 'Jean said you might come. But I didn't think we'd ever see you again here, Jacques.'

'No,' I said. 'I didn't think I would, either.'

We looked at each other. Then she sighed and said, 'Well, come into the salon. We can talk there while we wait for Edmond. He really shouldn't be long.'

The salon was a crowded, pleasant, sunny room, with little china statuettes and bibelots on gilded tables and several pictures on the walls. Only one was Edmond's, I saw—a rather charming portrait of Athénaïs as a nymph;

the others were by other hands. Athénaïs saw me looking at them. 'A couple of fellow students of David,' she said. 'Not half as good as Edmond, I think, but he says it doesn't do to exhibit yourself too much in your own drawing-room.'

I could see she was trying to stall me, to prevent me from asking her what we both knew was in our minds. But I wasn't going to let that happen. I said, 'Athénaïs, you know why I've come, don't you?'

She nodded.

'Please, is Flora here? If she isn't, please tell me where she is.'

She rubbed fretfully at the stuff of her gown. 'I think we'd better wait till Edmond gets back. Really I do.'

Just then, the door banged. I heard footsteps coming down the hall. In the next instant, Edmond came in. He was red, as if he'd been running. He saw me and stopped dead. 'Jacques! My God!'

'Edmond—' I said, getting up.

'You've come at a fine time,' he cut in. 'Marat's just been murdered!'

We both exclaimed, 'What?'

'I've just come from there. There's a huge crowd outside his house. I ran all the way. It was a young woman by the name of Charlotte Corday – a Norman girl, I believe. She stabbed him in his bath!'

'In his bath!' I echoed.

'She got into the house by pretending to be a supporter of his from Normandy, there to give him an eyewitness report of some incident or other, for his newspaper. Well. You know his skin disease has got very bad recently and in this hot weather he spends most of his time in the bath, reading, writing, eating. He was defenceless, taking down her story. She stabbed him in cold blood!' He tugged nervously at his hair and stared at us. 'You know what this means, don't you? They think she can't have acted alone. He had many enemies. There's going to be a hell of a purge in Paris!' He shot me a frightened look. 'It's not going to be safe out there tonight, or for the next few days. The mob will go looking for the conspirators, and I doubt they'll be too fussy about evidence.'

Athénaïs had gone completely white. 'Was the woman captured?'

'Yes. It seems that Marat managed to cry out in his agony, and his wife Simone came running—she and her friends restrained the woman and someone went to get the police, though it appears she didn't really try to get away. The police had to protect her from the crowd, though. They would have torn her limb from limb.'

I said, 'She has done all of France a service.'

They both stared at me, aghast. Edmond said, 'Are you mad, to say such things?'

'Come on, Edmond. The man was a monster. And

I know you did not like him. You said yourself he was bloodthirsty.'

'Hush,' he said, going pale. He shot a look towards the closed door, as if afraid that someone might be listening. 'You don't know what you're saying.'

'Marat was responsible for the September Massacres,' I said coldly. 'He swam in blood, he gloried in it. Well! The Swiss doctor got a taste of his own medicine! I can't say I'm sorry, though it seems peculiarly horrible to me that only a young girl should have the savage courage to do what three-quarters of France dearly wished but was too scared to act on.'

Edmond said, wearily, 'You don't understand. Marat dead is twenty times more fearsome than Marat alive.'

'I doubt it,' I said. 'He didn't believe in the afterlife, not even a pagan one, did he, so he can hardly sit up there on a cloud and rain down thunderbolts on the infidels who dare not honour his name!'

'For God's sake, Jacques.'

'So you still invoke Him,' I said. I don't know why, but my fury had come back. 'I wonder you should dare.'

'Stop it,' he said, tiredly. 'You're upsetting Athénaïs.' It was true, as I saw with a pang of remorse. She was weeping, silently, her hands over her face.

I took a deep breath. 'Forgive my ill manners,' I said. 'I did not mean to hurt you.'

'Why have you come, Jacques?' said Edmond.

'You of all people don't need to ask that,' I snapped. 'Casgrain entrusted her to you, didn't he? I've come for Flora.'

The colour drained out of his face. Shock sprang into his eyes.

My heart began racing. There was something very wrong here. I said, urgently, 'Edmond, please.'

He looked at me. 'Come with me,' he said, quietly, 'there's something I must show you.'

He took me to his studio. Pictures in various stages of completion were stacked around the walls. On the easel was a half-finished portrait of what I knew at once to be Marat, in the toga and laurel wreath of a Roman Caesar. He saw me looking at it, and with a sad, sardonic look, he draped a sheet over it. He said, 'Don't judge me, Jacques. We all have to survive, somehow.'

'I'm not judging you, Edmond,' I said wearily. 'I'm beyond all that. I made a promise to a dying man, and I'm going to keep it whatever happens.'

'A promise to a dying man?' he said, then as a sudden understanding came into his eyes, he said, 'My God. Pierre?'

'Yes. He is dead. He was a braver man than either of us, Edmond. And she loved him. *She married him, Edmond.*'

His eyes flew open in shock and utter horror. 'My God, you can't really mean that she and that peasant were . . .'

'Don't you dare say anything about him,' I said fiercely.

391

'Just tell me where she is. Where did Casgrain take her?'

He swallowed. I could see his Adam's apple bobbing in his throat. He said, unhappily, 'Oh God, Jacques. I hoped I'd never have to tell you.'

Ice froze my spine. I stared at him.

'She's dead, Jacques. I'm sorry. Jean did bring her here a few days ago—she—he'd found her injured somewhere—and he—he said he'd saved her from rape or some such thing—he said he—he loved her and wanted to marry her, but . . .'

'What?'

'I know. I was surprised. I'd never realised that he . . . well, anyway he had to leave almost immediately for the North—another campaign—and he asked if I could look after her. He said you might come, if you were still alive. He made some remark about you—about you being in love with her too, and said that he hoped the best man might win.'

'He said that, did he?'

'Yes—he seemed to think you'd taken to the patriotic cause in Nantes. Is that—is that true, Jacques?'

'He and I mean different things by patriotism,' I said, through stiff lips. 'But enough of him. And of me. What happened to Flora?'

He made as if to touch me, but I drew back. 'Jacques, I'm sorry. So very sorry. Flora was on the point of death when she arrived here. We took her to the doctor but

there was nothing he could do. Nothing anyone could do.'
He paused, and there was a long silence. 'She died two
days ago. Peacefully, without pain.'

There was a roaring in my ears, the taste of blood in my
mouth. From a long way away, I heard a voice speaking,
and I didn't even know it was my own. 'Where is she?'

He stared. 'We buried her in the cemetery near . . . I'll
take you there, if you like. But not tonight. Tonight, it's
too dangerous. The mob's on the rampage.' He put a hand
timidly on my shoulder. 'Believe me, Jacques, if I could
have spared you . . .'

'Yes,' I said, dully, the roaring still in my ears. Nothing
made sense any more, nothing.

Forty-three

There's not a great deal more to tell. I cannot describe the night I had there, the agonies of sorrow and horror and guilt, the bleak numbness that came after. But the next morning, we took a cab to the humble graveyard where they had buried her, and I saw the plain wooden headstone, with the initials 'F.B.' burnt into it, and 'greatly loved'. There had not been much time to do anything else, said Edmond gently, though I hadn't asked. Later, he would have a beautiful headstone made for her, he would design it himself, and he would see to it that the grave was always kept flowered.

I nodded, dumbly, but I didn't really take any of it in. I could not believe that Flora, my beautiful Flora, lay cold and rotting there under the hard ground and that I would never, ever see her again in this life. The black wings had triumphed. She had gone to join Pierre across the river of death, and I would never see her again. The words tolled ceaselessly in my ears. Everything else had fled, everything, even the image of my living love. Everywhere,

I saw death. Everywhere. The city was a miasma of death, of blood, of suffering. It was accursed, and we were all accursed with it.

Coming back from the graveyard, the cab had to pull up to let a crowd of people stream past. They were wailing and mourning and howling, some of them tearing their hair, clawing at their cheeks, shrieking their wild love for their dead hero Marat and their savage hatred for his killer.

Marat's funeral was being held in the streets of Paris. All of the Convention would be there, every municipal official of Paris, and a gigantic crowd of citizens. It would be the most elaborate funeral ever staged, a pageantry of colour and extravagant grief. That afternoon, it seemed to mock my own despair, the pit of numbness into which I had descended. The crowd wept and shrieked for a mass murderer, the government of France paid homage to a man who gloried in the blood of others.

But I could not even weep for a beautiful, charming, loving girl who had lit up my whole life, even if she had chosen another. I could not shed even one tear for Flora. All I could think was that I would never see her again.

When we got back to Edmond's place, he said, timidly, 'I loved her too, you know, Jacques. She was my sweet cousin. I wish I could have saved her. I really do. You must believe me.'

'I do, Edmond,' I said, quietly. 'I do believe you.'

'What will you do, now, Jacques? You are welcome to stay here as long as you want of course.'

'No. Thank you. But I won't stay. I can't. She's not here.'

He stared at me, startled. 'Not here? Whatever do you mean?'

'That's only her grave, and the shell of her. She's not there. Not in this place of death.'

He swallowed. 'I see. You will go back to Bellegarde, then.'

'Maybe. I don't know.'

'Well, if you need—'

'I need nothing,' I said, then as I saw him wince, I added, mechanically, 'thank you.'

He took hold of me. 'Please. You must promise me, Jacques. While you're in Paris, you must—you *must*—keep quiet. Things have changed here, you know. You must keep your mouth shut. Those things you said yesterday, about Marat—promise me you'll never repeat them in public. Promise. You owe it to Flora's memory to take care.'

'Yes,' I said. 'I promise.' But as I spoke, somewhere deep in my soul a horrible fury warred with my terrible grief. Marat and Flora, in the same breath! Marat and Flora, joined in the one phrase! It was unbearable.

*

Just as it is only one stitch that finished an entire tapestry, or a drop that fills a glass, so those well-meaning words of poor, frightened Edmond sealed my fate. I do not wish to tell too much of what happened, the very next morning. The depositions against me are numerous, after all. Many citizens saw me standing outside the place where they brought Charlotte Corday for trial, and heard me shout those words that will be in my condemnation: *'Vive Charlotte! Vive le Roi! A bas Marat!'* 'Long live Charlotte! Long live the King! Down with Marat!'

Three times I managed to say it, before the soldiers roughly seized me and manhandled me away.

I wasn't the only fish scooped into the net that day. In fact I am a nobody beside the majority of them. For though the Corday woman had acted alone, she had been a Girondin supporter. Her act provided the perfect excuse for the arrest of all the Girondins still left in Paris after their expulsion from the Convention the month before, not to speak of all stray royalists and federalists and even those who made a joke about the last bath of Marat—for even the sardonic Gallic spirit of France is a crime these days.

Stop, you say. Tell me. Why did I do it? Why? Why? I cannot explain it, my dear friend. It was a moment of madness, but divine madness. Or perhaps diabolical. I don't know. I saw death everywhere, then, and I wanted it so. I didn't want revenge. I just didn't want to live. I wanted to cross the raging torrent back to her, do you see? Even if it meant Pierre was there too. Because in the end, we had both loved her. And so we were true friends. Brothers in arms, for ever.

And now, I come to the end of this. I know it will reach you, for I trust the kindly guard who has sworn to bring it to you. Do not weep for me. I am almost content. The fury has left me, and the numbness, and the pain. All that is left is love, and memory, and hope. My past will become my future, do you see? For, my dear friend, *I see her now*—yes, I see her—she is there, stretching out her hand.

Last night, I had a dream. She was standing beside Pierre on the banks of that stream, and she was smiling at me and beckoning me across. It was a beautiful silver river, like the stream that ran in our childhood, bordered by golden elms. They beckoned me across, and I knew that someday, the four of us would be together again, laughing by the side of the silver stream, and no black wings would ever shadow us again. For in the end, these cursed times did not wither our hearts and destroy our friendship, and for that I thank God, in His infinite mercy.

Epilogue

1 May 1854, Paris

I rubbed at my gritty, swollen eyes and pushed the manuscript away. All night, I'd been reading. Slowly, I got up from my chair. My limbs ached fiendishly, as if I had run a race; my spine felt made of molten iron. I rubbed at my neck, as if I could feel the pressure of a blade; and my nose was filled with a strange, sweet, metallic smell. The smell of blood.

I went to the window. It was early morning. Outside, the bustle of the day had begun. It promised to be a beautiful day, the sky was pale blue, and filled with fluffy little clouds. I opened the window and breathed in the air. It was fresh and springlike, on an ordinary, busy Paris morning.

I turned away from the window and went to my desk. I pulled out a little drawer on the side and took out a little box. I opened it, and looked at the thing inside for an instant, then closed it, put it in my pocket. I picked up the manuscript, put on my hat and coat and went out into the lovely spring day to find a cab.

As we went up the stairs to the Baron's bedroom, his valet told me in a whisper that Monsieur had slept peacefully last night. It was apparently unusual.

And he looked all the better for it. The eighty years that he had lived were still etched into his face, but his eyes were brighter than the previous day, when he had given me the manuscript to read. He gestured to his valet to go out and close the door, and waved me to a chair beside his bed. He looked at me, and gave a faint smile. 'You look rough this morning, my poor Dumas.'

'I haven't slept at all, Monsieur. I stayed up all night with this,' I said quietly, and laid the manuscript down on the bed beside him. He glanced at it.

'So you read it all, I take it?'

'Yes, Monsieur.'

'Ah.' He paused. 'You'll want to know what happened next. Poor Jacques! He was put on trial the day after he wrote those final words. I'm not sure if he would have written more. Perhaps. But in those days, you know, they didn't make you wait much between sentence and execution. He was accused of treasonous utterance against the Republic, and conspiracy, and sentenced to death the very same day. They didn't waste much time on him— there was much bigger game, as he said. That night, they transferred him to the Concièrgerie, and two days later he was in the tumbril on his way to the guillotine.' He paused, swallowed. 'They say he died bravely.'

'They *say*, Monsieur?'

'For Heaven's sake, man,' he said with a flash of temper, 'what do you take me for? I did not see it with my own eyes, if that's what you mean. But the guard who smuggled this manuscript out and gave it to me—he told me. He went to it, do you see, because he respected Jacques, and thought a man shouldn't go to his death alone. I could not. I could not go.' He bit his lip. 'Do you see? I wanted to save him. I really did. I tried to contact his parents, though writing to England was a treasonous offence in those days. But the letter to them never arrived. They didn't learn about it till it was too late. I even tried to find Jonathan, to no avail. Anyway, Jacques didn't *want* to be saved. He wanted to die. And besides, it was not easy, in those days, to step out of line, to perform even an ordinarily decent act. We were all afraid.'

His voice trailed away. He was looking at the small painting that hung above the mantelpiece. It was a painting I'd seen many times before, but never *seen* before, if you take my meaning. It showed three children, barefoot but dressed in the costume of last century, playing by the banks of a stream: a serious-faced boy with long brown hair in a ponytail, a tall, broad-shouldered, dark boy with piercing black eyes, and a laughing fair-haired girl in blue muslin. Behind them, stretching into the distance, was an avenue of golden elms, blazing like living torches.

The Baron sighed. 'Yes. It's them. Pierre, Flora, Jacques.' He paused. 'Do you know, my friend—I envy them. They are still themselves. They never forgot who they were, in the heart of themselves. They never turned into time-serving cowards, like me, turning like the weathercock with whatever political wind best suited my ambitions. No, don't speak. It's true. In the eyes of the world I am a success. In the eyes of the world my poor friend Jacques is a failure.' He gave a gusty sigh. 'Yes. I survived it all. All the convulsions. The Terror, Thermidor, the Directory, the Empire, which made me the Baron of Bellegarde again, the restored monarchy, the Second Republic, and now the Second Empire. I have prospered mightily. I am rich. My career has been good, if not of the first rank. I have had so-called friends in the best society. But no wife or lover who would stay with me, no real friends. Now I know. I know it is *I* who am the failure, the empty shell, the hollow man, while they were real men and women. Whole people.'

There was a silence. I said, gently, 'Monsieur—will you tell me what happened to the others?'

'The others?' he said, a little distractedly, his eyes still on the painting and its three figures. 'Well—my brother-in-law Jean Casgrain never made it back to Paris. He died in battle on the Prussian front. At least he died a soldier, not a butcher, and he was spared the shame of Robespierre's death. My poor Athénaïs never had another child—she was carried off by the cholera that raged in Paris in the summer of '94. Jacques' parents never came back to France. Jonathan survived the war—he was sent to France on two more missions, but was captured in the landing at Quiberon—he spent a year or two in prison but was released eventually and returned to England. I believe he became a lawyer like his father, and prospered. My father brought Flora's mother to Austria to live with his family, but she didn't last long, poor thing. And the village of Bellegarde . . . well, you know what happened in so many villages in the Vendée after the Committee of Public Safety decided to make an example of that wretched province, to burn every village and town and to turn the place into a cemetery where only wolves, grown fat on corpses, would thrive.' He shuddered. 'I believe they intended to exterminate all the native Vendéans, no matter who they were. Atrocious crimes were committed, as I am sure you are well aware, things that seem to come out of the very pit of Hell. Well, you understand, in January of '94, a column of Turreau's soldiers arrived in Bellegarde. They killed a great many people, and burnt the village to the ground, including Bellegarde Manor.' He looked at me, his eyes anguished, as if begging absolution. 'You understand, by then we were in the Great Terror, and Revolution was devouring all her children—

and I was afraid. I was mortally afraid. We all were if we weren't mad, and many of us were both. A tear was enough to condemn you, a tone of voice, a gesture. I could do nothing, nothing. Nothing.' He was silent an instant, then spoke again, his tone changed. 'Well, Dumas, my friend?'

'Well, what, Monsieur?'

'Dumas, you know I've had nightmares for years. You know I long to be free. What is your conclusion? Can I make reparations? Advise me, man! You are my lawyer! That's what I employ you to do! And remember the reward I promised you—half my fortune if you can propose the right solution.' The flash of renewed temper had driven out the fear, and the blue fire of his eyes suddenly seemed to make the years drop away from him, revealing the imperious young man he had once been, the bright young revolutionary who'd dreamed of changing the whole world with the fire of his passion.

I looked at the old man who had once been Edmond de Bellegarde, Jacques' friend, to whom he'd so unexpectedly entrusted his story, and I said, slowly, 'But Monsieur le Baron, you see, I still do not understand. Reparations for what? It seems to me that you have to reproach yourself only vanity and the idealistic foolishness of a young man who believed in the promises of wolves in sheep's clothing. You may have been afraid in the end, too. But many people were. And you never murdered anyone, did you? You never denounced anyone. You tried to save Jacques . . . and you held onto his manuscript, even though if it had been found, you might well have been in danger.'

He interrupted me with a curse. Breathing heavily, he shouted, 'Devil take it, man, do you have to have it spelled out to you? *I lied to my friend Jacques.* I told him a grievous, terrible lie. And by that lie, I drove him to an act of useless folly which condemned him to death.'

I stared at him. 'You mean, Monsieur . . .'

'Yes, yes, yes! Flora was *not* dead. She was very ill. I had her taken back to Ermenonville. I thought it best. I thought if Jean Casgrain loved her, then perhaps it was best if Jacques never saw her again. I thought Jean was the best man for her, the safest one.' He closed his eyes, briefly. 'When Jacques was taken to prison, I should have told him. But I couldn't bear to. I was still afraid. We needed Jean's protection, Athénaïs and I. And so I said nothing.'

I stared at him in horror. He gave a tiny, sardonic smile. 'You see, Dumas, now? You understand the terrible thing I did?' His hands clenched on the coverlet. 'I discovered pretty quickly that she was with child, at least three months gone. I realised from what Jacques had said that it must be Pierre's child. I hated him still then, despised him as a benighted peasant. God forgive me, the thought of that child repelled me.'

'What of Flora herself?' I asked, hardly trusting myself to look at him.

'You mean, why didn't she escape us? She couldn't, Dumas. She had been so ill. So ill she took months to recover. And the balance of her mind was affected. She had lost her memory. She was like a docile child.'

I said nothing.

'Flora died giving birth to her baby. Athénaïs would have liked to adopt him, but I refused. I took him to an orphanage. I have no idea what happened to him, even if he survived. Times were hard. I never told my aunt there had been a child. Never.'

He pointed to the rose on his bedside table, the fragrant white rose streaked with pink, known as the Lady of Bellegarde, for which his garden was famous throughout France. 'I took a cutting from the rose poor Flora grew in Ermenonville, so long ago. It is all I have left of her now. I have learned that the little boy Bertrand grew up to become a consolation to my poor friend's bereaved parents. But I never saw any of them again. How could I, with these sins on my conscience?' He looked at me. There was a chilling despair in his eyes. 'Well, Dumas, now you know. You know more about me than any man alive, more even than my confessor. You know I have done great evil. No. Don't try and tell me it isn't so. Tell me what I must do, in this world at least, to begin to repair what I did. You are a man of sound business sense and good intelligence. Don't respond to me like a sentimental fool. Tell me what is your advice.'

Instead of speaking, I reached into my pocket and took out the little box. He watched me, lips a little open, a certain fear in his eyes. It gave me a strange pang to see it, a twist of fierce pleasure and deep pity mixed.

I opened the box, and put it in his hands. 'What do you see there, Monsieur?'

He stared at me, then down at it, and then at me again. His voice had become an old man's again, broken, quavering. 'I don't understand.'

'Please, describe what you see.'

'A miniature. A child.' He looked at me, puzzled. 'Why are you showing me this?'

'It was my father's, Monsieur,' I said. 'My father was an orphan. He never knew his parents. But when he was five, he was taken out of the orphanage and adopted by a couple who loved him as their own. By Richard and Adeline Dumas. Kind people. My grandparents are dead now, but I remember them well from childhood. It was they who commissioned this miniature, of my father as a child.'

The Baron stared at me. But he said nothing.

'As you can see, my father had very dark eyes,' I went on. 'Black eyes, and fair hair. Very striking. It is strange, for when you first showed me your painting, I felt an odd familiarity about those children, as if I'd seen them before.' I looked up at the old man. His skin was stretched tight across the bones, his eyes were like hollow sockets. No longer did he look in any way young, but old as the hills, old as Death Himself.

He forced a ghastly smile. 'You are telling me you are the grandson of Pierre and Flora,' he said. 'Is that not so?'

I nodded.

'You do have a look of them,' he said, at last. 'Fool that I am, never to have seen it. Did you seek employment with me because of it?'

I shook my head. 'I had no idea you were in any way connected. Not until I read this manuscript.'

He laughed, without amusement. 'Well, Dumas, then God must be a joker, after all!' He was silent an instant, then went on, 'I suppose you must hate me, now. You must want revenge. I do not blame you.'

I swallowed. 'No, Monsieur le Baron. I do not hate you. Why should I? I am Dumas, your lawyer, and you asked me, I think, for my professional opinion.'

He stared at me without speaking, his hands trembling on the coverlet.

'You offered me half your fortune, Monsieur. I do not need or want it. But it is plain to me now what you must do.' I tapped the manuscript. 'This is my advice to you. You must have this published, expensively, beautifully published. Nothing must be left out. I think it is

perhaps the reason he wrote, and what he hoped for—
that maybe the story would help to heal the wounds a
little.'

He turned his head away, but not before I'd seen the
tears appear in those haughty blue eyes. After a little
while, he said, 'You will draw up a will for me, Dumas.
In it, you will say exactly what you advised—but you will
also say that you are to be the executor of this—and that
you will write an epilogue explaining why we do this. You
will write exactly what we have spoken about. You will
hide nothing. You will put half my fortune into producing
the best, most beautiful edition money can buy—and
what is left over you are to have.'

'No, Monsieur, I do not want it. Any of it.'

'It's tainted money, is that it?' he whispered.

'Perhaps.' I paused. 'But it's more than that. You have
kin, Monsieur, even if unsatisfactory—your half-sister in
Austria, and her family. You have good, faithful servants.
Remember them, generously. For myself, I should like
only one thing.' I pointed to the painting of the three
children over the mantelpiece.

He looked at me for a long moment. There were tears
glittering in his eyes. 'Very well,' he said softly. 'Very well.
It is as you wish.'

'I will go straight back to my office and draw up the
will,' I said, getting up. 'I will bring it back this afternoon for witnessing and signing.'

He nodded, but did not look at me. 'Thank you, Dumas.'

At the door, I paused. 'God is merciful, Monsieur,' I said gently. 'You must remember that.' He looked up at me, then, and the strange, sardonic smile flitted over his face again. But he said nothing, and so I left him there, and went out of that sunny, haunted room and down into the bustle of an ordinary day.

Acknowledgements

This novel developed over a long period of time, and there are several people I would like to thank for their support and encouragement over that time: my husband, David Leach, who with unfailing good grace and sharp perception read several different versions of the manuscript without complaint; Michael Thorn, who first saw the potential in the novel; Margaret Connolly who as my agent has always encouraged me; fellow authors and friends Cassandra Golds, Felicity Pulman and Wendy James, who gave me some invaluable early responses, and equally to Kate Forsyth, for her lovely quote. And of course I would like to greatly thank Mary Hoffman and Stephen Barber at The Greystones Press for their belief in this novel, as well as their thoughtful and painstaking editing and attention to detail of every aspect of production.

And to my father, Georges Masson, to whom this book is dedicated and who told us children stories of the tragedy and glory of the Vendée, special thanks are due, as well as to my very much missed late mother Gisèle

Masson, who as a perceptive and rigorous reader did so much to help hone my early skills as a writer.

It is a great joy to see *Black Wings* make its way out into the world between beautiful covers—so thank you all, so very much.

Historical note

This novel is a work of fiction, and its main characters—Edmond, Jacques, Flora, Pierre, Jonathan, Casgrain etc.—are fictional, but of course it includes real people as minor or cameo characters, including Marat, Robespierre, Danton, Desmoulins, Cathelineau, and so on. I also partly based aspects of the character of Edmond on the painter Anne-Louis Girodet de Roussy Trioson, a young aristocrat who was a pupil of the great revolutionary artist Jacques-Louis David. Girodet was an enthusiastic supporter of the Revolution in its early days but later he prudently became a supporter of Napoleon and then of the restored monarchy. However, Girodet should not be seen as a model for Edmond, only as one source of inspiration.

Against a background of real historical events, the novel recreates the atmosphere of the early years of the Revolution, leading up to the beginning of the Reign of Terror, which was ushered in by the September Massacres of 1792, the execution of the King in January

1793 and the seizure of power by the extremist Jacobin faction.

The Vendée uprising began shortly afterwards, after the attempt at forced army conscription caused widespread unrest throughout France. It's important to note that in the early times of the Revolution, its reforms had been widely welcomed, including in the Vendée, but as the new politicians in Paris became steadily more authoritarian and extreme, unease and then rebellion began building in several parts of the country, and especially in western France, in Normandy, Brittany and the Vendée, which exploded into full-blown conflict in 1793 and beyond. It was in the Vendée and Brittany that the conflict hardened into actual prolonged civil war, but as noted in the novel, this was conducted in different ways in the two provinces, with the Chouans of Brittany opting for ambush and guerilla attacks rather than open battles, as occurred more in the Vendée.

Though this is not in the main timeline of the novel, and not within its concerns, it may be useful for readers to know that by late 1793, the disparate armies of the Vendée rebels had suffered crushing military defeat at the hands of the Republican armies. But this wasn't enough to satisfy the ruling Convention in Paris which in early 1794 sent out what can only be called death squads to the Vendée to, as surviving Convention documents attest, exterminate every last man, woman and child in this 'benighted province'.

'Not one is to be left alive'.

'Women are reproductive furrows who must be ploughed under'.

'Only wolves must be left to roam that land'.

'Fire, blood, death are needed to preserve liberty'.

'Their instruments of fanaticism and superstition must be smashed'.

These were some of the words the Convention used in speaking of the people of the Vendée. And they found plenty who were happy to carry out these wishes.

The former aristocrat Louis-Marie Turreau de la Lignière took command of what are known in the Vendée as *les douze colonnes infernales* (the twelve columns of hell), which had specific orders to kill everyone and everything they saw. 'Even if there should be patriots [that is, Republicans] in the Vendée,' Turreau himself said, 'they must not spared. We can make no distinction. The entire province must become a cemetery.' And so it proved. Just in the four months Turreau operated in the Vendée, for example, it is estimated his units murdered between 20,000 and 40,000 people. There was not even any pretence of discriminating between fighters and civilians; documents of the time, still kept in army records in Vincennes, tell the chilling story, whose echoes have tolled repeatedly around the world through the centuries since then. The generals speak coolly of objectives achieved, exterminations of entire settlements systematically and rigorously done, provincial cleansing carefully carried out and wholesale slaughter accompanied by the attempted eradication of culture. Some modern historians of the Vendée, such as Reynald Secher, even go so far as to talk of a 'Franco-French genocide', but this is disputed by most scholars, though it is acknowledged that what was done there prefigured, in its fanatical brutality and cold bureaucratic cruelty, later ideologically based State crimes. There were also of course actions against the Chouans in Brittany; but not as draconian and wholesale as in the Vendée, which had specifically been made an example of. Perhaps that was because it was considered more 'French' than Brittany, which with its different language had always seemed more 'foreign'. Thus, in the eyes of the Convention, it could be seen as more shameful and inexplicable that a heartland French province should reject their 'enlightened despotism' than was the case for the Bretons, who had always been seen as perennial rebels.

Whatever the truth of it, Robespierre's execution in late 1794 brought some respite to the martyred province; but it was not until 1799 and the ascension of Napoleon

Bonaparte that the Vendée was able to attain some measure of peace. He had much respect for the Vendéans and Chouans; he called their war with the 'Bleus' or Republicans, *Le Combat des Géants*, and concluded treaties with them which partly reinstated liberties of religion, culture and provincial assembly, though it did not completely pacify the more hardened rebels.

In a historical irony, the attempted eradication of the Vendée actually created an even stronger sense of distinctive cultural identity in the province, an identity which persists to this day and which keeps the memory of both the suffering and the courage alive.

My father's family originates from the Vendée, and though our ancestor Gilles Masson left his native Longeville sur Mer in the early 17th century to emigrate to Ville-Marie in the colony of New France (now known as the city of Montréal, in the Canadian province of Québec), ties between new and old France remained strong. Most of the early French settlers of Québec were from western France, including a large proportion from the Vendée. Fortunate enough to be far away from the horrors of what happened there during the Revolution, they must have still been deeply affected by the news that reached them of the fates of their ancestral villages and town. To this day, there are still close ties between the two places, including an active Vendée–Québec Association, http://vendeequebec.fr/

My great-grandfather returned to France in the late 19th century, married there and stayed, completing the cycle begun two and a half centuries earlier, and though he settled further south on the western coast than the Vendée, near Bordeaux in fact, stories of the Vendée persisted in the family. As a child, I heard many from my father, and read about them in books in his library, some of which were contemporary accounts of the revolutionary period in both Brittany and the Vendée. As a teenager, I used some of this background to write a short story called 'Les Chouans', set around an ambush in Brittany, which in some ways prefigured a little of the themes in *Black Wings*, such as conflicting loyalties and betrayal, albeit in a much more sketchy form.

For years, I thought of writing a much longer exploration of this extraordinary historical period and how it personally affected the lives of people from different backgrounds. But it took a long time before I felt able to tackle such an enormous subject in a way that would be accessible and entertaining as fiction but also true to historical events as they unfolded in the lives of French people at the time. Without the benefit of hindsight, I wanted to plunge readers directly into the world of Jacques and his friends.

Bibliography

In the course of writing this novel, I read a great many books, and a list of the most important non-fiction resources I used follows. But as well as non-fiction, I read several novels in both French and English, including Victor Hugo's *Quatre Vingt-treize* (*Ninety-Three*, a reference to 1793) published in 1874; Honoré de Balzac's *Les Chouans* (1834); Paul Féval's *Chouans et Bleus* (1840); Anthony Trollope's *La Vendée* (1850); Leon Garfield's *The Prisoners of September* (1975) and Hilary Mantel's *A Place of Greater Safety* (1992).

Non-fiction resources include both primary and secondary sources:

Allen, Rodney, *Threshold of Terror* (1999)

Bernet, Anne, *Histoire générale de la Chouannerie* (2001)

Burke, Edmund, *Reflections on the Revolution in France* (first published 1790)

Carlyle, Thomas, *The French Revolution: A History* (first published 1837)

De la Lignière, Louis-Marie Turreau, *Mémoires Pour Servir A l'Histoire de la Guerre de la Vendée*: memoir of the infamous Republican general and leader of the 'colonnes infernales' death squads in the Vendée, an extraordinary and chilling justification written in 1795, and published subsequently in several editions—I have one from 1824.

De la Rochejaquelein, Victoire, *Mémoires de Madame la Rochejaquelein*: memoir of Vendée leader Henri de la Rochejaquelein's feisty widow, first published in 1815—remarkable first-hand account of life on the battlefields and war camps of the Vendée.

Loomis, Stanley, *Paris in the Terror* (1964)

Marambaud, Pierre, *Sur les traces des colonnes infernales* (1996)

Paine, Thomas, *Rights of Man* (first published 1791–2)

Secher, Reynald, *A French Genocide: The Vendée* (1986)

Sparrow, Elizabeth: *Secret Service: British Agents in France 1792–1815* (1999)

Tench, Watkin, *Letters from Revolutionary France* (written mainly 1794, edited by Gavin Edwards, this edition published 2001): Tench, also noted for his writings on the early days of the colony of NSW, was involved in a failed British attempt to help the Vendée and Breton rebels in 1794, which resulted in him being taken prisoner by the Republicans; the letters were written from captivity and give an interesting British view of the situation.

Tulard, Jean, *Guide historique des guerres de Vendée* (1993)